Dan Jacobson was born in Sou[...]
parents. He has worked as a [...]
journalist in South Africa and also spent some time [...]
kibbutz in Israel. He moved to England in 1955 where for many
years he pursued a career as a freelance writer of fiction and
essays. He then entered academic life and eventually became
professor of English Literature at University College London.
He also held visiting professorships and fellowships at
universities in the United States and Australia. Since his
retirement from University College he has resumed working as
a full-time writer. His novels and stories are strikingly various
in nature and set in many countries – among them South Africa,
England, ancient Palestine and the Republic of Sarmeda, a
country of his own invention.

THE BEGINNERS

A novel by Dan Jacobson

HOUSE OF
STRATUS

This edition published in 2001 by House of Stratus, an imprint of
Stratus Holdings plc, 24c Old Burlington Street, London, W1X 1RL, UK.

www.houseofstratus.com

Typeset, printed and bound by House of Stratus.

A catalogue record for this book is available from the British Library.

ISBN 1-84232-133-1

It is not thy duty to complete the task;
but neither art thou free to desist from it

THE ETHICS OF THE FATHERS

PART 1

1

In spite of his age, Avrom Glickman was still upright and slender. The hair of his head was dark and curling, that of his full, spade-shaped beard was white; and the contrast made his face seem strong and decisive. But there was no strength in his grey, short-sighted eyes: only a weak bewilderment and amiability.

His single leather bag had been stowed in the cabin that he was to share with eleven others during the journey to Southampton; now he and his sons, Meyer and Benjamin, stood on the deck of the Union Castle liner. It was a bright, clear day. From the boat Cape Town looked like a village, dwarfed by the huge bulk of Table Mountain immediately behind it. The town was no more than a scattering of iron roofs, of church steeples, of gables, of trees: then the mountain rose, at first gradual in its slope and faintly green, but soon rising sheer, precipitous and bare, slashed here and there by great gulleys which zigzagged down its flanks. Darker and lighter shades of brown yielded to the blue of distance and height, and then abruptly the ascent was cut off by the wide, flat top of the mountain. Beyond it were a few white clouds, and the sun shining.

The three men leaned in silence over the rail, staring down at the confusion of Cape Coloured porters and white passengers, occasionally glancing at the stillness and emptiness of the mountain above. The brothers looked much alike, neither taking after his father. They were both thickset, the elder more powerful in build than the younger, who was more a boy than a man; they both had heavy features and protruding lips, and wore their hair brushed directly back from their foreheads. Once, when a porter slipped and stumbled, the older brother, Meyer, laughed briefly; the father looked to see what his son was laughing at, and smiled, too, though he had seen nothing.

Finally Meyer said impatiently, in Yiddish, 'It's time to go. Come, Benny. Goodbye, father.'

Avrom Glickman's eyes filled immediately with tears, and he held out his arms to his son. Reluctantly, ungraciously, Meyer came forward; he broke from his father's arms as soon as he could. Then it was Benjamin's turn. He too submitted stiffly to an embrace.

Nodding, holding a hand of each of his sons, though they pulled away from him, Avrom said, 'I'll bring Mama back with me. I'll bring her safely.'

'Good, that's what we want.'

Still Avrom held on to them. 'I'll tell her what fine boys you are. She'll see for herself when I show her the money we've saved.'

Meyer could not restrain himself. 'We've saved?' he repeated ironically. '*We've* saved?'

A moment later, with a last, brusque word, they had left him. His hands trembling, Avrom felt in his pocket for his spectacle-case; he opened it and took out the wire-rimmed spectacles and put them on clumsily. One earpiece jumped away from behind his ear; but he let it lie where it was, in his beard, anxious to watch his sons go down the gangway. Already, it seemed, he was too late. He could not see them on the gangway, nor on the quayside. Without waving or waiting they had just left him on the boat, among so many strangers, to face the risks of the three-weeks' journey over the sea. He sniffed deeply, self-pityingly, and wiped his nose with the back of his hand. Then, with a gesture that was already like a habit, he touched the inside of his jacket, weighed down with the fifty gold sovereigns he was carrying back to Lithuania – enough to bring his wife and two youngest children back with him to South Africa.

He remained at the rail, looking about him with curiosity and interest, his glasses still hanging askew. The tears had dried in his eyes; on his lips now there was a faint, absent smile. A steward moved about the deck, announcing through a megaphone that all visitors had to leave the ship immediately; around Avrom people were kissing one another, laughing, crying. A group on the quayside began singing 'Auld Lang Syne'. A few minutes later a deep, prolonged blast from the ship's siren made the boards of the deck quiver. Below, groups of labourers slowly wheeled back the gangways; they looked like immense, ungainly, long-necked insects, squatting back on their haunches.

Almost stealthily, a space of water opened between the quay and the side of the boat; bits of wood, fruit peels and other rubbish on the surface of the water spread out more widely; the people on the quay receded, their hands still waving, or cupped around shouting mouths from which no sound could be heard. More and more of the town, then more and more of the peninsula came into view, on both sides of Table Mountain. But the edge of coastline was the first to slip below the horizon; presently even the mountain began to shrink, until all its bulk was reduced to a single brown shoulder of land, standing high out of the sea. Losing size, the mountain lost its colour. It became no more than a smudge, a tiny mark on the horizon; then it was gone.

Avrom remained on deck, until it was out of sight. His sons, he knew, would already be back at work. He was relieved to be on his own. He had his ticket, he had some pocket-money, he had fifty sovereigns to bring back home. There was no one on the boat who knew that the money for his passage and the fifty sovereigns had all been saved by his sons, and none by himself, out of the miserable wages they earned, Meyer as a grocer's assistant, Benjamin as a butcher's assistant in the Coloured area of the town. There was no one on the boat who knew of all the jobs that Avrom had failed to keep, while his sons had been saving; of the horses he had bought with borrowed money and sold at a loss, of the dairy business he had established in a backyard with a single cow that had died, of the surplus army blankets he had bought from a fellow who hadn't them to sell, of the gifts he could not afford which he had made to beggars, cripples, hard-up acquaintances. The reproach Avrom always felt in his sons' gestures, expressions and words, even in the way they simply went to work in the mornings leaving him behind in the room they all shared – these were behind him, below the horizon; his wife's asperities were many weeks ahead.

A stiff breeze was blowing on deck, and Avrom roused himself. There were surely some other Jews on board with whom he could talk. Cheerfully, humming under his breath, he set out to find them.

2

Several weeks later Avrom sat on a platform on Bremen station, waiting for his train to the East. He had arrived safely in Southampton, travelled to London, stayed in London for a few days with a *landsman* by the name of Pogrund, and then taken the steamer to Bremen. He knew that he was on the right platform, and though he knew also that he was several hours too early for his train, he was determined not to move until it came in.

While he was sitting there, with his leather bag on the bench beside him, a train pulled in and discharged its passengers. They hurried away, and in a matter of minutes Avrom was left alone on the platform once more. The train stood empty, its engine hissing and sending steam up to the glass and iron roof far above it; then slowly it clanked away. Avrom stared at the rails, and at the grey platforms that ran parallel to one another beyond, until the black roof arched down over a row of offices and kiosks clustered around the station entrance. He had been sitting for an hour already; on an impulse he began walking, simply to stretch his legs. The platform was a long one, he walked deliberately, and his eyesight was poor; so it was some time before he realized that in fact he was no longer alone on the platform. On the bench at the far end sat a woman with three children around her.

Almost as soon as he saw them Avrom saw too that they were Jewish. The woman was wearing a brown wig; the boys, under their cloth caps wore *payess* trained to go behind their ears. The boys were neatly dressed, in overcoats belted at the back. Something about the way they were standing around their mother arrested Avrom's attention; then he saw that they were trying to comfort her. She was in tears. Avrom hesitated, not wanting to intrude, but he was too curious simply to creep quietly away from them.

Cautiously, he approached: when he was a few paces away he cleared his throat and asked, 'Is there anything a Jew can do?'

The children turned startled, clean faces towards him; the mother looked up. She was a young woman, Avrom saw, and a good-looking one, too. Her eyebrows were black, under a wide, pale forehead; the tears in her eyes made them shine darkly. Her lips were turned down; they were small, precise and colourless.

7

'Can I do something to help you?' Avrom asked again. He put his bag down on the platform at his feet. 'What's the matter, woman? Why are you sitting here like this?'

The woman covered her face with her hands and burst into sobs. Her slight shoulders shook. The children stared suspiciously at Avrom; then the youngest began to cry loudly. His brothers followed his example. The noise was pitiable and embarrassing; Avrom retreated from it a few paces down the platform. The woman's luggage was scattered about the bench; and, at last, because he could think of nothing else to do, he began to gather it together. He piled it neatly in a heap, and retreated once again.

A little later Avrom sat on the bench with the woman. Her story was that she came from Latvia and was on her way to America, to join her husband who was already there and who had sent her the money to come. On the train which had just brought her to Bremen she had lost, or had had stolen from her, the handbag which contained her money, her tickets and her travel documents.

What could Avrom do? He knew no one in Bremen. He had his own train to catch. He told her to go to the police, to tell them about her loss, and to ask them for the address of a rabbi. There must be someone, some Jewish organization, which would help her. But even as he offered it, his advice seemed to him useless, of no help. He stood up and walked around the bench; he patted the children on their shoulders; he tried to avoid looking into the distracting darkness of the woman's eyes.

Rising within himself was an impulse that at first he could translate only into a heartfelt wish that his train would come soon, immediately, and carry him away from the woman; and then only into anger. 'Go!' he shouted at her harshly. 'What are you sitting here and waiting for? Go! Do what I tell you!'

His anger frightened her. She rose at once and reached for her bags. Each of the children took one, she took two. Bowed, wretched, puny, the little family group began to trail away down the platform. She did not look back at him. Avrom sat on the bench, and watched them go; the woman walked with small labouring steps. Then he turned his head, so that he wouldn't be able to see them. He waited for some minutes before looking again in the direction they had gone. He could see them no longer. Avrom gave a sigh, a groan, of relief and pain.

He struck himself on the chest. It was there that there lay the impulse he hadn't dared to confess to himself; there lay the answer to the woman's plight.

A moment later Avrom began to run after the group. He shouted as he ran, words, oaths, prayers. Now his only fear was that he would be too late; that they might have already left the station. But he did manage to catch up with them, on the station concourse. Without a word, he tore open his coat, he ripped at its inner lining, he took out the heavy purse with the fifty sovereigns in it, and held it out to the astonished woman.

She stared at him uncomprehendingly. 'Take!' Avrom shouted, in a tone even fiercer than the one in which he had told her to go. 'Take, it's gold from Africa!' He thrust the purse towards her, then actually flung it at her. It struck her on the arm and fell on the ground. His chest heaved, and with every breath he was conscious of the lightness of his coat, relieved of the weight he had carried in it for so many weeks. Rid of that burden, he felt an extraordinary sense of moral release, as though he had discharged an obligation he had been living under for far longer than the time that had passed since he had met the woman, longer than his journey; at least as long as the years he and his sons had spent in South Africa. As though someone else had made the gift, or as though he had been its beneficiary, Avrom was rewarded, while the purse still lay on the ground, by the sense he had of the world as a place where charity was available, after all, to those who were distressed and helpless. The ignorance, the innocence of his sons, toiling in squalor, not knowing that the pennies they were saving for one purpose would be diverted to another, seemed to him as noble and necessary as his own action.

Avrom himself remained ignorant, would always remain ignorant, of how much of revenge against Meyer and Benjamin there was in what he had just done. All he was conscious of was a loving-kindness that embraced the woman, his sons, and himself, indiscriminately.

3

The woman seized his hand and kissed it, her tears falling on it. She had taken his name and address and had sworn that her husband would pay back in dollars every one of the sovereigns; she had called him a righteous man, a protector of orphans, an angel of God. Then she left him, she to continue her journey, he to continue his.

The joy Avrom felt survived his separation from the woman; it sustained him throughout almost the remainder of his journey. He travelled on one train, then on another; in the cart of one carrier and the cart of another. It was only when he was a few miles from home that, without warning, his happiness and self-satisfaction deserted him, and he realized the enormity of what he had done. He had been so carried away by his own sense of benevolence that previously he had actually looked forward to telling the story to his wife and to his cronies in the village; now, more simply dejected than self-reproachful, he began to dread the moment of his arrival.

The carter let him off at the side of the road. After his years of absence in distant, dry Africa, the richness of odour, line and leaf within the woods was both strange and familiar to Avrom, as he walked the last couple of miles to the village; he knew intimately everything around him, yet that very intimacy surprised and delighted him. How happy he would have been, coming back to the village as a man who had prospered in Africa! To those who had remained behind he would have been someone to be listened to, envied, respected. Instead … Who would believe his story? What would his wife say? How could he explain to her what he had done? He had let himself be robbed, that was all – robbed by a sad story and a pair of tearful black eyes, robbed by a pack of children.

His arrival caused a sensation in the village; messengers flew ahead to his wife with the news that her husband was back. She ran out to meet him, then dragged him inside the little house and shut the door on the onlookers.

Her reaction to his news was worse than any Avrom had anticipated. He had imagined her screaming, rolling on the floor, tearing out her hair. But she did not say a word. She stared forward at the bare floor.

From their mother her sons had inherited their stocky figures, their full features and forward-thrusting lower lips. But what in their expressions was vigorous and strong, in hers had been worn into a naked heaviness of the bone, a rigid clamping of the jaw. For four years she had been waiting. Occasionally a remittance had come, more often an assurance that they were saving, that they hadn't forgotten. Now Avrom was here without the money; those years were wasted, a waste of years lay ahead.

The children, with frightened faces, peered around the door at their father, whom they did not recognize. 'They'll send the money,' Avrom said. 'I could see she was an honest woman.'

She did not seem to hear him. That night when he came into bed, she turned her back on him. 'I'm your husband,' he protested. 'I've come back after a long time.' She paid no attention. Soon she was asleep.

Avrom lay on his back and prayed that the woman's husband would send the money.

His prayer went unanswered. It took another four years before Meyer and Benjamin had saved enough money for Meyer to make the long trip home, and to escort his father, mother and younger brother to the new country. His sister, who in the meantime had grown up and was engaged to marry a man in the village, remained behind.

PART 2

1

The Rosing brothers lived in a sprawling, iron-roofed, single-storied house of a characteristic kind, with white plastered walls, a wide cement stoep running all around it, and rectangular wooden pillars holding up the roof over the stoep. Each of the wooden pillars branched out, just beneath the roof, like the arms of a candelabra; in the nooks between these arms, wasps and even birds used to build their nests.

A path ran from the front stoep to a wooden gate, on either side of which was a cypress hedge that gave off in the heat a faint resinous odour, which would become suddenly intense when you plucked a few fronds from it and crushed it between your fingers. To the side of the house there was a ragged orchard of peach, fig and pomegranate trees; among the trees were scattered various objects that looked as though they had been there almost as long as the house itself. There was a rain water tank, an unused dog kennel, a rusting plough, a chicken run inhabited by a red rooster and a few dejected hens, an iron windmill which pumped water from a well into an open, slimy-walled little dam. Behind the house, across a sandy yard, were the servants' rooms, a few lumber sheds, and two stables, one converted into a garage, the other housing an old Cape-cart, its shaft and body covered with dust. The iron-shod tip of the shaft rested on a solitary brick which the weight of the shaft had slowly driven deeper and deeper into the earthen floor.

The yard of the house adjoined the yard of the shop. When you opened the gate of the yard you looked across a bare plain towards the Dors River, which was marked only by the tops of the trees that grew along its sunken course. In front of the house, set at a distance among a grove of bluegum trees, were the few low buildings of the railway station, the house of the railway officials, and the hotel. To the south you could see the girders of the bridge that carried the railway and the main road over the curve of the river. To the north, both road and rails ran dead straight until they were lost to sight at the point where the gradual upward slope of the veld at last met the sky.

But though, outside, there was so much empty space and glaring light, indoors, both in the shop and the house, there was darkness and a lack of air. The shop was a crowded jumble of goods of all kinds – blankets and tins of food, boots and sacks of meal, patent medicines and overalls, saddles and china-ware – ranged on shelves or displayed on zinc-topped counters. The house was filled with heavy furniture, and every room was guarded from the sun by curtains, mosquito screens, and slatted wooden blinds, swinging on hinges. There were books only in Manny Rosing's empty room – school books and others, as well as the remnants of his boyhood enthusiasms for fishing, stamp-collecting and chemistry experiments. The only photograph in the house was a large, oval portrait of Jacob Rosing's late wife, hanging over the sideboard in the dining room.

Jacob Rosing had just the one son, Manny, who had studied medicine overseas, in Edinburgh, and was working now in Cape Town. Elias Rosing was a bachelor. Jacob and Elias had been living in Dors River for almost thirty years. When they had come to Dors River there had been no railway line, no telegraph, and barely even a road: now the mail train going south passed through every morning, the passenger train going north every evening, and goods trains clattered through at odd times of day. Jacob and Elias knew all the white people in the district, and most of the blacks; their houseboy and cook-girl had been with them for years. Once a year, separately, each brother went to Muizenberg for a three weeks' holiday; more often they went by train to Lyndhurst – on Jewish holidays, or for visits to the doctor or dentist, or to bank the money which, between visits, was kept in the big green safe in Jacob's room. So the years had gone by, scorching summer succeeding upon bleak, dry winter, in an alternation of heat and cold which did nothing to change the look of the landscape.

2

It was with these two brothers, cousins of her mother's, that Sarah Talmon, daughter of the late rabbi of Marniyus, in Lithuania, came to stay immediately on her arrival in South Africa. Her mother and her younger brother, Samuel, went to live with another set of cousins in Germiston, near Johannesburg. These were the best arrangements that could be made, for the family was penniless. Their fares had been paid out of a collection made among relatives and former members of the rabbi's congregation, who had presented them to South Africa.

At the time of her arrival in South Africa Sarah Talmon was in her middle twenties – just a few years older than the century itself. She was a plump, large-headed girl with shapely legs and slender hands. Her soft, curling hair was cropped short; her features were small and her forehead was wide; her brown eyes were candid, behind the horn-rimmed spectacles she wore. In the old country she had enjoyed, at her mother's insistence, and against the wishes of her father, a secular education at a gymnasium, where she had shown a particular aptitude for languages. She had learned German, French and English, as well as Russian (Yiddish she had spoken at home, and her father had taught her Hebrew); and in every one of these languages she had read as much as she had been able to. Her reading had promised her that life would be abundant in its stresses and beauties, terrors and satisfactions, surprises and reassurances. She believed her books – in fact, it dismayed her that she believed in them far more than she did in her own experiences. Only her young brother, Samuel, had roused in her a protective passion from which she never felt distant, about which she was never doubtful. In Africa, strange Africa, she had hoped, things would be different.

So Dors River came as a profound shock to her: it seemed to offer an abundance of blank spaces only; space and dust. The dust rose from every car wheel, every horse's hoof, every flock of complaining sheep driven to and from the railway paddock, every stick dragged in the sand by the piccanins who hung around the shop and whose cries had no echo in the wide spaces where they played. The triviality of the cluster of habitations around the railway lines, the baldness and emptiness of the veld that surrounded it, were revealed at a single glance: because nothing was withheld, nothing at all, it seemed to the girl, was promised her.

Jacob and Elias, both of them bent, bald, thick-bodied old men who looked so much alike they might have been twins, were kind enough to her in their way: they gave over to the running of the house, and complimented her on her cooking. In the evenings they talked to her of their boyhood in the old country, and of the changes they had seen in Dors River and Lyndhurst; they told her of the histories of the people whom Sarah saw passing the house on their way to the shop – which she seldom entered. Jacob spoke often, too, about Manny, whom he was expecting shortly for a holiday at home before he left once more for Britain, where he was going to specialize in psychoanalysis. 'A whole new science, imagine!' Jacob exclaimed. The thought of it obviously made him uneasy, in spite of the pride with which he spoke. The brothers also encouraged her to go to Lyndhurst for weekends, where she could, they said, 'meet other young people'.

But much of the time Sarah was left on her own in the dark, airless house; and she was often in tears when she woke in the mornings, roused unwillingly to consciousness by the raucous, foolish, trailing calls of the hens in the *hok*. The sense of her own loneliness and a half-pleasurable anguish at the uncertainty of her future seldom left her, as each day slowly passed. In the late afternoons, when the sun was setting and the air was cooler, she used to walk by herself along the banks of the river, among rocks, reeds and camelthorn trees; on these walks she recited aloud in her East European accent the poems of Shelley and Tennyson she was trying to learn by heart.

> *'Tis not too late to seek a newer world.*
> *Push off, and sitting well in order smite*
> *The sounding furrows; for my purpose holds*
> *To sail beyond the sunset, and the baths*
> *Of all the western stars, until I die.*

She kept a diary, and filled it with vague, grandiose plans. She might become a doctor; she might become a poetess; she might become the wife of a famous man. Or she might spend the rest of her life in Dors River – at times, even that prospect had something grandiose about it, in her own imagination; she thought of herself as a kind of female hermit of the veld, or a doer of good works in the tiny squalid Dors River location.

One evening she came back from her walk along the river to find that Manny Rosing had arrived, a few days earlier than he had been expected. From above the river she had seen the train from Cape Town halt at the station and then move off, an

19

elongated, black disturbance against the horizon, which it had taken many slow minutes to reach. But it had left behind this prematurely bald young man, sitting at his ease in a light, loose suit, in the front room of the house. Standing at the door she saw him from the side before he saw her: his face was sharp, almost wedge-shaped, thrust forward to the point of his long nose and chin, under a receding forehead. The back of his head and neck was flat. When he stood up his movements were lithe; he was shorter than he had appeared to be in his chair. He crossed the room to greet her.

'You're Sarah.'

'You're Manny.'

He held her hand in his, looking at her closely, without embarrassment, with something like amusement in his eyes, which were a pale brown in colour and set closely together. 'Father tells me you've been looking after him very carefully.'

'He managed before I came. The servants do all the work, really.'

'That isn't what I've heard. He'll miss you when you go.'

'I have no plans to go.'

'But you've got no plans to stay? Not in Dors River?'

'I have no plans.'

'Then we must think of some.' He was smiling confidently, almost scornfully. Discomfited, Sarah felt herself growing warm under his scrutiny. Her hand was still in his, and she pulled it away.

'I must go and see that a bed is made up for you.'

When she came back into the room she found Manny talking to his admiring father and uncle about the work he'd been doing at Groote Schuur hospital, about the letters of introduction to various people in London that the head of the department of psychological medicine had given him, about 'the Institute' at which he would be studying. He talked of going to Vienna 'to sit at the feet of the Master himself, if he'll have me'; of the 'incredible backwardness – the primitiveness, really', of what passed for orthodoxy 'in this benighted country'. The two old men nodded uncomprehendingly but proudly at everything he said. Manny took no notice of Sarah, yet she felt that much of what he was saying was directed to her; there was no need, after all, for him to try to impress the old men. She sat listening to him, and looking at his slightly stooped posture in his chair, the quick forward movement of his head when he wished to emphasize a point, the habit he had of running his hand back over his brow, as if feeling for the hair that was no longer there. She was relieved that nothing more was asked of her than to listen to him. At supper he still spoke almost entirely to the two old men, asking them about their affairs, about people he knew in the district and in Lyndhurst, about their speculations in the cattle and sheep which they grazed on pieces of hired land around Dors River.

After supper the two young people found themselves alone on the stoep. A small oil-lamp provided the only light; outside, from the darkness, there rose the persistent but irregular call of the crickets among the trees in the orchard. Sarah's wicker chair was a few paces from his, half-turned away, near the edge of the stoep; he sat in shirt-sleeves and a waistcoat, his back to the wall of the house. From his pocket he brought out a pipe and tobacco-pouch. When the pipe was lit he sucked absently at it and watched the smoke rising in the air. 'It's strange,' he said at last. 'I was born in Lyndhurst, and now I'm going to London. You were born in Marniyus, and now you're living in Dors River. What a world! How long have you been in South Africa?'

'Six months.'

'Only six months! Your English is very good.'

'I learned English in the old country, at school. And I go sometimes to Mrs Wheeler for conversation lessons.'

Mrs Wheeler was the stationmaster's wife. Manny smiled when he heard this. 'I shouldn't think she has much conversation.'

'It helps. And I read a lot.'

'There isn't much else to do here.'

'No.'

Sarah stood up and walked to the end of the stoep. She looked out, over the trees, to the stars scattered thickly and brightly in the sky. She said, 'Sometimes in this country – here, anyway, it's all I know – I think there's more life in the sky than there is on the ground. In the daytime there are such clouds there, shifting and piling on top of one another – they're like mountains and valleys and rocks. It's another geography up there, always changing. And at night … look at it now! Look how many stars, and how bright they are. We never had stars like that in Lithuania.'

'You're lonely,' the man said.

'Yes,' Sarah confessed gratefully, turning to face him. She spoke directly to him, her hands working together in front of her. 'I am lonely here. But I feel it's wrong for me to say so. Where would I be better off?' She smiled, but the movement of her hands went on. 'You asked me about my plans. I wish I did have plans, real plans. Instead I have nothing but daydreams. And doubts.'

'We all have doubts,' Manny said.

'You don't seem to have many.'

'You don't know me.'

Presently he said, with a restless jerk of his legs, 'Don't you understand, my job is to spread doubt. So how can I be without doubts myself?'

'I thought your job was to help people, to make them confident?'

He shook his head. 'Not in the way you imagine?'

'In what way then?'

He glanced at her, as if wondering whether it was worth his while to speak seriously to her.

'What we want them to do is to accept their lack of confidence, to know they'll never be confident again.' It seemed that he was going to go on, but he did not.

Heavily, almost obstinately, unwilling to be put off, she asked, 'What do you mean? What do you mean when you say people will never be confident again?'

'Well ...' He drew the word out, then, with a slightly mocking obedient tilt of his head, he answered her. 'Well, as we imagine people might have been confident when they believed in God, for example. Or when they believed that the world was a place which changed slowly, if it changed at all. Or when everybody thought he'd been given a self or a soul which he could learn to know and could struggle to improve.' He looked up: she was listening earnestly to him. 'We know that that old self no longer exists. It's dead. It's been killed – not by us, you understand. Or not just by us. We're simply the first, among the first, among the first, to recognize what has happened. And the first to say that if it's dead then you must throw it away as you would throw away any other old rubbish. It has to be done.'

He was crouching slightly forward, the thin, fairish, waving hair on the back of his head glinting in the lamplight, his eyes resting flatly upon her; he looked as though he were coiled under the blade of his own head. 'Modern writing, modern art, the political resolutions, the psychoanalytic movement, they're all parts of the same transformation. You see it at work everywhere. You see it inside, deep inside, everyone you meet. It's in you, in me, even in my father. It's a breaking-down, not a building-up, you understand, that's begun.'

'And after it?'

'Who can say? We don't know. We can't know. What will emerge, if it's to be truly new, must astonish us, isn't that so, or it wouldn't be new.'

'You speak like a *narodnik*, not a psychologist.'

He laughed at the comparison, leaned back, and fiddled with his pipe. 'Have you ever read any psychoanalytic literature?'

'Never.'

'It's time you began. I have some books with me. We'll read them together.'

Their glances met. Sarah was the first to look away. 'I'm very ignorant.'

'So tell me what you have read. Let me judge for myself.'

She began to tell him, glad that he had asked; in spite of what she had just said she was sure he would be impressed by the range of her reading. He listened attentively, yet Sarah was aware that his attention was directed more to her face, her gestures, her expression, than to what she was saying. The knowledge didn't embarrass her; having been silent for so long, ever since she had come to Dors River, she spoke without constraint, pausing only to search for an English word now and then, and sometimes offering in its place a Yiddish one. He nodded quickly each time she did this, to show her that he understood, that he was following her closely.

They were interrupted by Jacob and Elias, who had not let Manny's arrival disturb their habit of reading from the front page to the back – the one handing to the other each part as he finished it – the daily paper published in Lyndhurst, which arrived for them with the evening train. The two old men sat with them for a few minutes, then they shuffled off, for bed.

Manny turned in his chair and watched them go through the front door. 'You see,' he said to Sarah, as if proving some kind of point, 'what different people we are in their presence from what we are when we're alone together.'

'I feel it also,' Sarah said. 'I didn't at first, but I do now.'

He moved his head at her reply, in a curiously sharp, intimate gesture of acquiescence or satisfaction, at which something in Sarah flickered for the briefest instant, and then sank away. The strain of it, the knowledge that it had happened, left her heart beating clumsily. She rose to her feet. 'I must also go.'

'You're early birds in the country.' He got out of his chair and held out his hand to her. 'You know, I came home only because I felt I had to see father before I left – for his sake. But I wasn't looking forward to the visit. I am now.'

'So am I.'

They laughed breathlessly, each aware of the closeness of the other's face. Jerkily, she left the stoep. She was glad that her bedroom was at the side of the house, and that its window did not open on the front, where Manny was still sitting. She lay awake for a long time in bed, conscious of the peaceful still darkness outside, of the chirp and stir of the insects, of the half-hearted creak and rattle from the windmill when a faint breeze sprang up and almost immediately died away. When she closed her eyes it was as if she saw again all the stars in the sky; they wheeled slowly under the dark arch of her lids. 'I'm not so lonely,' she said aloud, savouring the denial.

3

They took their books to the river, in the mornings, and looked out for a shady place and a shelf of clear sand where they could sit. The river bed was wide, but there was little water in it, and there were many places where they were able to cross over, stepping from one rounded, veined, blue-grey boulder to the next, between the stretches of idle water, or over the streamlets that flowed here and there, each one along its own track. They looked every day for a new place, though it was not always easy to find one; many of the trees, which were all willows or camelthorns, seemed to grow from mere cracks, crevices, slivers of soil, among the boulders. And the shade they did find was cool only in comparison with what was beyond it, where the sunlight was reflected dazzlingly from the rocks, from the muddy, dark-green water, even from the stems of the reeds that grew in clusters. Usually they chose to sit under a willow, for it was a prettier tree than the camelthorn, and its drooping branches provided more shade.

They disturbed few living things – the small, pearl-grey Namaqua doves with long bills, whose cooing echoed among the stones, or the goats, sheep, and hump-necked Africander cattle that occasionally came down to the water to drink. Once they clambered around some rocks and were startled to see a *likkewaan* a few yards in front of them: a scaly, heraldic, dragon-like creature, fully three feet long, with a throbbing throat and an uplifted head, standing braced at an angle from its own heavy tail. But for the movement of its throat it might have been made of the rock amidst which it lived; then with a harsh scrape of sound and a splash it had plunged into the nearest pool and was gone. A few times, too, they were disturbed by small groups of piccanins, dressed in rags, who had come to the river to hunt for doves with their catapults or to catch fish with home-made rods and the hooks they had bought at the Rosings' store. But for hours on end there would be no stir of life around them. The only sound would be the cooing of the doves, the only movement that of the clouds overhead, which massed together in corners of the sky, making high purple and white halls of air, and then drifted away, bringing no rain.

Sometimes they simply succumbed to the heat and stillness, and to their nearness to one another. There were moments when he was conscious of nothing but the slither of her clothes when she moved, of the roundness of her arms, of the shadowed places of her neck; as if with some unbearably acute inner sense he felt the shifting weights of her, which he had not dared to touch, when she leaned back, stooped forward, folded her arms. They touched each other seldom, but she sensed his restlessness and was roused by it; she watched him when he stood up abruptly and went exploring around them; she waited for him to return and drop down by her side once more. And when he did turn to his books they found in them an excitement of another kind: it excited them both that he should be introducing her to what the books contained, to the thrust and flux of unassuaged sensualities, primitive rages, rudimentary gratifications, truncated gropings of mind, which were his and hers alike, inescapable, self-renewing, fed by and feeding every demand and fear. The presence of each provoking in the other zeal and shame, curiosity and pride, they followed the texts, pronounced the words, repeated the arguments; they smiled or laughed occasionally, and met each other's eyes less often. They were liberated and constricted by every paragraph. They never doubted the truth of what they read; or rather the truth of it seemed to them borne out by, contained within, their own excitement, and by what they felt to be the poignance and nobility of their being able to read together such books in this bare, unpeopled, unrecorded corner of the world.

One day, however, Manny did not touch the books at all: instead, almost fiercely, he questioned Sarah about herself. No, she admitted, she had never before been alone with a man as much as she had been with him. Yes, she was frightened – not frightened, she corrected herself, nervous. Yes, she had been embarrassed, very embarrassed, by some of what they had read together. No, she did not believe in God, she believed in none of the things her father had brought her up to believe: she had never believed in any of them, as far as she could remember. No, she had never told her father this; while she had been at home she had done everything (except in the matter of going to a secular school) that he had expected her to do, without argument or comment. Of course this had been a strain for her

27

sometimes, but she supposed she had taken it for granted that one day she would leave home and then would be able to live as she liked. No, she had never been away from home for any length of time until her father's death. Yes, their *shtetl* had always been a peaceful place, even during the war and the troubles after it. When the Germans had come they had behaved very well, and she had worked in an administrative office they had set up there – the Germans had asked her to, because she knew the language, and her father had agreed because he thought it would be good for the Jewish community if she obliged them. No, she had not had any affairs with any of the German officers, or with any of the young men who had come to study under her father; she laughed at Manny's notion that she might have. No, her father had not seemed anxious that she might remain an old maid. Yes, sometimes she was anxious about it herself. But she was anxious about everything in her future.

'And in your present? Now?'

'I told you – I'm nervous.'

'Why? Because you're alone with a young man?'

'Not just a young man. With you.' Yet, behind her glasses, her eyes were soft, open, hopeful.

'What do you think I might do to you?'

'I don't know. That's why I'm nervous.' Her voice shook. When he leaned forward and kissed her on the lips she trembled. It was the first time they had kissed. She was conscious only of the strangeness of it. What next? She tried to draw him closer. 'Come,' she said, not knowing what she was saying. Her lips found his again. This time his kiss seemed to run through her, too quickly, it was gone before she had learned to know it. Yet she had been touched, he had summoned all of her together for that instant.

Unwillingly, she opened her eyes and saw that he was sitting back; on his lips was the faint sardonic smile she had seen the first time she had met him. The sky behind him was blue; a few green, tapering leaves hung across it. A dove called. The fullness within her rose in answer to the sound, and she burst uncontrollably into tears.

He took her home very soon afterwards, and from then on he kept his distance from her; he stayed in the house, saying that he had letters to write, he spent more time with his father and uncle, he went to Lyndhurst for a day, he even jokingly served behind the counter in the shop. Tormented, the girl went about the house, wondering what she had done wrong, how she had offended him, what she could do to set matters right. Should she not have let him kiss her? Had it been her tears that had changed his attitude towards her? Should she have shown herself less eager for his company? Should she have refused to listen to his reading? But what else could she have done, at any stage? In her mind she went over every conversation, every exchange, they had had together since the evening of his arrival, and nowhere could she find a point at which she could have acted other than as she had. When she thought of their mornings by the river they seemed to her – in their tense freedom, excitement, and boldness – already so distant she could not believe they had taken place only a few days previously; she could not believe they had happened in these surroundings she knew so well, where space imprisoned her, emptiness confined her, vacuity exhausted her.

She sought Manny out, then avoided him, then sought him out again, waiting for a word of explanation or tenderness from him. He spoke to her kindly, distantly, politely. But at any agitated movement of her hands, any rise in her voice, he turned away. The days of his visit passed inexorably. She burst into tears at the dinner table, startling Jacob and Elias, who looked expectantly at Manny when she fled from the room, confident that their psychologist son and nephew would be

29

able to explain this phenomenon to them. But he merely raised his eyebrows, shrugged, and muttered something inaudible.

Then it was Manny's last day in Dors River: he would be leaving on the next morning's train. Sarah had been dreading the day, but she was surprised on waking to feel more at peace with herself than on any morning that had preceded it. It was too late now to mend whatever had been done or undone. And for the first time it occurred to her that perhaps she had done nothing at all wrong, that she had nothing to be ashamed of or to reproach herself about. She made no effort to meet Manny, none to avoid him. The morning passed, the afternoon passed. In the evening she set out for her usual walk along the river. Manny met her at the gate of the backyard.

It was sunset. Simple, flat reds and yellow filled the western half of the sky; there was nothing between that immense brightness and the level earth.

'You're going for your walk,' Manny said, embarrassed. 'Can I join you?'

'Why do you want to?'

'It's my last chance.'

'You didn't use the other chances you had.'

'I'd like to use this one.'

He fell in beside her. But instead of going across the bare plain that led to the river, she turned and began walking towards the railway lines, leaving the shop and the station behind them. He followed. There were no sounds but those of their footsteps, dull on the sand, harsh on the dry grass that grew in meagre clumps, here and there. They came to the fence which shut off the railway line, and walked along a path that went with the fence. Path, fence, rails, ran straight. The blazing, still sunset was on their left, the distant river to the right, the diminishing cluster of low buildings behind them.

'You're angry with me,' Manny said.

She shook her head. 'No.'

'What then?'

Still walking, she turned to look at him. He looked small, sharp, ill-at-ease, against the spaces around him. 'Disappointed,' she said.

'Why?' he asked brutally. 'Because I didn't seduce you?' She made no answer, but walked on. 'Is that what you wanted?' she heard him say from a little behind her.

'No!' she cried, halting so suddenly that her body remained slightly bent forward while she spoke. 'I just … I wanted –' She breathed out, a long shaken breath. 'I had what I wanted,' she said simply. 'For a moment you gave it to me. Then you took it away.' He was about to speak, but she would not let him. 'I don't believe you've ever thought about me, except as someone to impress and excite and then to disappoint. Well, you did it. You can be satisfied. I hope you are. I don't want you to walk with me any more. Please leave me. Go away from me now.'

'No.'

She did not say another word until they returned to the house. But Manny talked. He cajoled, explained, argued, accused, pleaded, raged. He had been thinking of her, he had restrained himself for her sake. He was leaving, he could not become involved with her, he had acted out of consideration for her. It had been wrong for him to disturb her with his books: she was an innocent, a rabbi's daughter, a green girl from Europe. Couldn't she understand why he had held himself back, wasn't she grateful to him for doing so? He had kept silent before only because he had been sure she did understand. What was the matter with her, anyway? Why was she living in Dors River? What kind of cowardice kept her there? She could go to Johannesburg or Cape Town, she could find work, she could teach Hebrew, she didn't have to bury herself in the veld, keeping house for two old men whom she herself had said did not need her. She was like a child, not like a grown woman; she was fixated on her father; she should think seriously of undergoing treatment; she was wasting her life.

31

His head jerked, he opened his lips, the words came out. Now he was talking about himself. He supposed to her he seemed a lucky man – educated, free, someone who could do as he liked. What did she know about it? He was the doctor-son of a Jewish storekeeper in Dors River. There was nothing very grand about that, whatever she might think. This desert was the place where he came from. Who was he to take up a subject like his, to think about London and Vienna, to talk about the transformation of the modern consciousness? Beyond shame now, in a frenzy of self-scorn, he mouthed out his own phrases derisively. Then he shook his fist at her, as though she were the one who had jeered at them. He had his ambitions and he was going to carry them out, he was going to be in front, he was going to go where others were afraid to go, he was going to make people listen to him. In London. In Vienna. Right in the middle of the world. He would show her, he'd show everyone what he was capable of doing. He would make his mark, make his name, he'd win through, right through.

But this time they were back at the house, standing at the front gate. The light in the sky had shrunk to a single red flare in the west; the earth without colour or form. 'I understand,' Sarah said sadly. 'What use would I be to you – the daughter of the rabbi of Marniyus? No wonder you let me love you for just such a short time. But I didn't think – I never imagined that you could have been so frightened of me.'

He reached out for her, but she slipped away from his grasp; he heard her footsteps going up the path, but did not follow her.

4

The next morning, she, Jacob and Elias saw Manny off at the station; then they returned to the house, Jacob wiping his eyes; he was sure he would never see his son again. Her eyes were dry. She and Manny had done no more than shake hands, like strangers, when he had left. But she had told him that she had decided to follow his advice and to leave Dors River, at which he had nodded in approval, before turning away – a spare, quick, bald young man who she, like Jacob, was sure she would never see again.

Six months later, when she was living in Johannesburg and working as a Hebrew teacher, she had a letter from Manny, in which he told that though he had tried hard to do so, he had been unable to forget her. He had found he could not put out of mind her candour, her gentleness, her intellectual eagerness, the sweetness of her face, the beauty of her figure. He loved her, he said, and was ready to save money to pay for her fare to England, or to ask his father for the money, if she wanted to join him. He could never forgive himself, he said, for not having seized the chance that had been given to him on his last visit home.

The letter came some weeks after Sarah had become engaged to Benjamin Glickman, whom she had met at a Zionist function at which the children from her Hebrew school had sung some songs. The letter did not move or disturb her; in a curious way it did not even surprise her. She did not reply to it, and told her husband-to-be nothing about it. When they went on their honeymoon, it was at her suggestion that they went to stay with Jacob and Elias. Jacob had written inviting them to come, and they had been glad to find a place where they would not have to pay anything for the fortnight's holiday they were taking, for Benjamin had only just made a fresh start in a business of his own – he had taken over the assets of a bankrupt butter factory – and they had no money to spare.

So Sarah saw once again the veld and the sky, the Karroo shrubs and the rock-littered river, the railway line and the white-plastered house which had been all she had known of South Africa for so many months. Once again she heard the hens squawking and grumbling in their pen, and the dogs barking at Dors River Station, and the sounds of trains approaching or receding. But the emptiness and blankness of the place, the loneliness of the lives the Rosing brothers lived no longer threatened her. She was no longer frightened of them. Instead, she felt a deep compassion for the country itself, as if it were a sentient being that knew and grieved over its own barrenness and pallor, that felt the ugliness and weight of the rocks that lay on it, the harshness of the scar the Dors River cut across it, the fierceness of the stroke of the sun each day. Of Manny she hardly thought at all.

At night, in their room, she let her husband do what he wished with her; and he, a man in his mid-thirties who had always been awkward and shy with her before, was roused to an intensity of desire that only her passive yet total compliance could have provoked in him. His touch never made her tremble; yet she was glad she was able to satisfy him so easily. Her attention was directed elsewhere; where she did not know. But she thought much of the children they might have.

PART 3

1

In November 1945, the war in Europe having been over for several months, the family of Mr and Mrs Benjamin Glickman in Johannesburg received a telegram from the Directorate of Military Transport, giving them the date of their son's return to South Africa, on a direct flight from Cairo. The telegram had been expected for many weeks, and the news it brought had been keenly awaited. Just for this reason it seemed to surprise the entire family. Sarah Glickman read the telegram over and over again, as if afraid of missing some meaning the words contained. Benjamin Glickman took the telegram to business that morning, and showed it to the girls in his office, to the white workmen in the factory, and to a commercial traveller who happened to call on him. And the two younger children, Rachel and David, rehearsed how they would behave and what they would say when they saw their soldier-brother. David imagined his brother as being tall, soldierly, and brusque, and yet impressed with his, David's manliness: Rachel made up her mind that she would not rush at Joel when she saw him, but would wait for him to come to her. 'Who is this young lady?' she imagined her brother saying, and she smiled calmly in anticipation, as she had decided she would smile at him when he asked the question.

The family was expecting that Joel would telephone from whatever civil or military airport he landed at, and that they would then go out in the car to meet him. As it happened, Joel's plane came in at four in the morning, and he took a lift with a military truck to the centre of town. From there he took a taxi to the house. When he arrived all the members of the family were asleep, the doors of the house were locked, the windows were barred. Joel peered through the glass panel in the front door, and saw the hall still dark with shadow, though outside the first rays of the sun were lying on the rooftops on the other side of the street. He left his kitbag and suitcase on the front stoep, and walked around the side of the house. In the yard he saw Annie, the African maid, as she was going from the servants' quarters to the kitchen. She was wearing a white overall and a *doek* on her head; her feet were bare. She gasped with fright on seeing the stranger in a soldier's uniform; then she recognized Joel, and the grimace of fear on her face changed immediately into a delighted smile.

'Baas Joel,' she cried loudly. 'Ach, my young master.' She crouched, almost as if she were bowing to him; with one hand she clutched her overall at its open neck, hiding the sight of her breasts, swelling apart and paler in colour than the rest of her brown skin. Joel had his hand out, and she took it, still clutching with her other hand at the neck of her dress. 'I'm so happy to see you, Master Joel.' She was upright now and moved from side to side at the end of her extended arm, as if to view him the better. 'We been waiting for you so long. And the madam will be happy, and the *oubaas* too.' Then she ran to the kitchen, clapping her hands. 'I must make coffee, the whole house will want coffee now.'

Joel smiled, watching her go, touched by the warmth of her greeting. He followed her into the kitchen. There was an African houseboy there, who stood in the middle of the room with a broom and dustpan in his hand, listening to Annie's excited talk from the sink. She was filling the coffeepot with water. Joel had never seen the houseboy before, and merely nodded at him, before going through the kitchen into the passage that ran the width of the house, with rooms sprawling from it on both sides. He closed the kitchen door behind him and walked down the passage, until he came to the bottom of the hall; he looked towards the front door, through which he had been peering a few minutes before. Then he broke the peace of the place. 'Is anybody at home?' he shouted.

'Joel!' There was a shriek from Rachel's room; she was the first one out, in her pyjamas. 'Joel's here!' They ran towards one another; they embraced, Joel picking her up and carrying her a few paces; by the time he put her down all the other members of the family were around him. His mother kissed him, his father hugged him, his brother shook him by the hand; they plucked at his clothing, uttered cries and murmurs of greeting. In the confusion of the scene, Benjamin tried to assert his authority. 'Come into the breakfast room,' he said. 'Sit down, you must be tired.' But the others all spoke at once: Sarah asked about his luggage, Rachel told him they'd been expecting to go to the airport, David was asking what sort of a flight he'd had. And Benjamin himself made no move to go.

When they broke apart Joel looked at the faces around him. 'It's wonderful to be back,' he said, and sighed with relief and pleasure. 'It's what I've been waiting for.'

For a moment the rush of their emotions was stilled. Then Joel said, 'Don't cry, mom. This isn't the time to cry.'

Rachel too began crying. She and her mother clung together, and the three men in the family, smiling slightly, looked at the women and at each other – moved by their tears, even proud of them, yet proud too that they themselves felt no impulse to weep.

'Come through,' Joel said, putting his arm around his mother's shoulder. 'What's that you said about coffee?' he asked his father.

'I said nothing about coffee,' Benjamin answered, leading the way into the breakfast room. 'But I'll see that it comes. Annie!' he shouted.

'Coming, master,' was the reply from beyond the kitchen door.

When Annie brought the tray in, the family was seated around the table. 'What do you think, Annie?' Rachel demanded of her. 'Didn't I tell you that Master Joel was coming today? Did you recognize him?'

'Recognize me! Annie was the first to see me. Weren't you, Annie?'

'Ah, master,' Annie said shyly, as she put the cups and the milk jug and the coffeepot on the table. 'Master looks fine.'

'You look well too, Annie.'

'Thank you, master.' Shyly, yet gracefully, Annie withdrew from the room closing the door behind her.

'She's just the same,' Joel said. He looked round the table. 'You're all just the same. None of you looks any older.'

'You'll find big changes,' Benjamin said sententiously, but his younger son interrupted him.

'He won't. Nothing's changed. Everything's the same.'

'I don't believe that,' Joel said gently, seeing that the interruption had irritated his father.

'Everything's the same and everything's changed,' Rachel said.

Joel looked steadily at her for a moment. 'You've grown a little taller. But you're still the same.'

'There, you see!' Rachel exclaimed, and she smiled, not gravely, as she had intended to smile, but simply with pleasure that her brother should be back from the war and that she should have grown while he had been away.

2

'Good morning!' Benjamin said, as he came into the front office, and the women there were quick to guess why he stood smiling at the door.

'Has Mr Joel come already? How is he? Did he come this morning?'

Benjamin began moving through the office, nodding at every phrase he said. 'He came back, he's fine, he looks no older, like a boy in uniform, it's wonderful to have him back.'

'It must be a great day for you,' said Mrs du Plooy, the oldest of the women, and the most soberly dressed, in a shiny black dress tight across her broad body.

Benjamin had reached the door of his own office. 'It's his mother that feels it most,' he said. 'And Joel himself, of course. It's their great day.' He shrugged, as though surrendering the day to them. But he added, 'You'll have a chance to see him soon. I expect he'll be coming in one of these days.'

He spoke so happily that the women in the office could not help feeling that it would be a special pleasure for them to see the young man. However, once their employer had disappeared behind his door, they smiled knowingly and patronizingly at one another.

Later in the morning there was a long-distance call for Benjamin from Cape Town. It was his brother, Meyer.

'Hullo, Benny, I got your letter this morning. You're expecting Joel today?'

'He's back already, he came in this morning.'

'Is that so? How is he?'

'He's fine.'

'Wonderful! I remember what a great day it was for us when Morry came back.'

'Yes, thank God, both boys came back all right. It's something to be grateful for.'

Meyer laughed; the sound was like a crackle over the line. 'Grateful to who?'

'I don't know. But I'm still grateful.'

There was a pause, a hum on the line; the sound seemed to trip over some obstruction, then hummed steadily again. 'Listen, Benny,' Meyer said, 'I've been thinking over what you wrote in your letter. We must meet and talk it over.'

'Yes, we can't talk now.' But Benjamin could not restrain his curiosity. His hand moved across the table, touched at the cord of the telephone, then held on to it. 'But what do you think? Can you say anything?'

'I think you want to take into your hands more than you can carry.'

'That's for me to judge.'

'We'll see. Look, I have to come up at the end of next week anyway. Then we can have it out.'

'Good, the sooner the better. Will you stay with us?'

'No, I'll stay at the Langham. Can you book me in? The last weekend of the month, from Friday.'

'Of course, I'll do it now.'

'All right, Benny. My love to the family, and to Joel especially.'

'Thank you. Remember me to Roise.'

'Ja, I will. Goodbye.'

Benjamin replaced the receiver, and sat for some time with his hand on it, as though about to make another call. But eventually he just raised his voice and called, 'Miss Curtis'. When the girl came in he said, 'Pamela, will you phone the Langham and make a booking for my brother for the weekend after next – from Friday on. If they're full try the Carlton.'

The girl acknowledged the request by writing it down on her pad; she was about to go when he called her back. 'You've never met Joel, have you?'

'No, Mr Glickman. He's been Up North all the time I've been in the office.'

'Of course, you've only been here … how long have you been here?'

'Nine months, Mr Glickman.'

'Always precise – hey?'

Miss Curtis smiled, lowering her head. She was small and dark-haired, with high-coloured cheeks; her head of hair, drawn over her temples and tied simply at the back, was thick and heavy, too heavy for the size of her face. It made her seem burdened, more frail then she really was. Her features were regular, and her brown eyes were full of light. She spoke softly, and with an accent that was more 'English' than South African, though she had been born in the country; her manner combined timidity and alertness. From the first day Benjamin had been pleased with her. She was, he had said at home, 'a find'; she was neat and sensible and could use her head.

He said to her now, 'Well, you'll get to know him when he comes to the office. I'm sure he'll be coming. Occasionally,' he added, precisely because he hoped that Joel might be coming in more than occasionally, once he was discharged from the army; he hoped that Joel might want to join him in the business. But he did not say anything of this to Miss Curtis. He merely smiled and nodded, to dismiss her.

But she did not go. Instead, as if from a distance, she said, 'My father was killed in the war.'

Benjamin's heart contracted with pain and surprise. The girl, too, was taken aback at what she had said. When their eyes met, he saw in hers an appeal, or a fear of reproof; she leaned against the door-frame, to support herself. Benjamin lost sight of her, his eyes filling with moisture – for the day, for the war, for the safe return of his son, for the death of Miss Curtis' father, a stranger, a *goy*, who had been killed fighting Hitler. 'You didn't tell me this before,' he said softly. 'Why not?'

The girl spoke immediately, but it was not in answer to his question. 'He was killed at Sidi Rezegh. I was only fourteen when it happened. My mother said he was too old to go, but he volunteered, he went all the same. He was in the armoured cars.'

He nodded his head slowly. 'I remember Sidi Rezegh, in the newspapers,' he said.

'I don't. I just remember –' But she did not say what she remembered. She stood with her hands in front of her, at the waist of her navy-blue skirt; one hand held the dictation pad, the other hand was open, with the tips of her small fingers curved inwards. She was wearing a blue and white checked blouse, buttoned up to the neck, and just above its little collar a nerve pulsed in her throat, as if at the strain of bearing her head upright. She swallowed, to still the pulsation, but the nerve fluttered again.

'I'm terribly sorry, Miss Curtis – Pamela. I'm very sorry. If I'd known I wouldn't have spoken to you about my son ...' She was silent. There was no reproach in her silence; but he went on, like a man explaining or excusing himself. 'I had a sister in Lithuania. We've heard nothing from her since the war began. And you know what Hitler has been doing to the Jews in Europe. Do you know?' he asked, looking up.

'I've read about it.'

Her reply told him little, but he spoke as if she had made the bitter answer he had wanted. 'Then you know how much hope we have.' He went on angrily, after a pause, 'I begged her to come out. But her husband was happy where he was; he thought he was a rich man, doing well, on what me and my brother used to send him. She had a married daughter with children, also – and a son, a few years older than Joel. Where are they now?'

Again the room was silent. From the other office, an adding machine chattered, chattered, paused, chattered again. The sound seemed to rouse the girl. 'I'm very sorry,' she said, using the words her employer had used to her a moment before.

'No, I didn't mean to –' Benjamin began, but he could not explain why he had told her about his sister. Guiltily, he felt that after boasting to her of his happiness, he had attempted to cap her bereavement. He wanted to say something to the girl that would make sense out of their loss and his present happiness. 'At least –' he began, wanting to say something about Hitler or freedom or democracy, to tell the girl that her father had not died in vain. But he could not bring the words out, they embarrassed him. He stumbled, repeating, 'At least …' Then he said quietly, 'I don't know what it's all about, Pamela. I've lived – what? Three times as long as you have? More? And I just don't know why things must happen as they do.'

Unexpectedly, Miss Curtis smiled. Her teeth were white, large and even. She said, 'You always think older people should know.'

'They don't, believe me. That's just one of the great disappointments waiting for you.'

Smiling still, she looked down at her pad, and left the room. Her employer was ashamed that he should have worried for a moment whether or not he had allowed himself to be too familiar with her. How could he begrudge her that familiarity, after what she had told him about her father? Thinking of the dead man, Benjamin remembered the living; he wondered what Joel was doing at home. Talking perhaps, unpacking perhaps, showing some more of the souvenirs he had started to show them after breakfast. There had been badges, propaganda leaflets, folders of photographs of the Italian cities he had been in, a German bayonet.

On an impulse he called Miss Curtis back into the room. 'Pamela,' he said awkwardly, 'my daughter, Rachel, is giving a party at the end of next week. There'll be lots of young people there. I don't know if you'll know any of them – but perhaps you'd like to come?'

3

David had gone off to school. Rachel, who was in the middle of her first-year exams at the university, was in her room, having promised her mother that she would put in two hours of unbroken work, in spite of it being the morning of Joel's return. Sarah and Joel were in his room. The room was exactly as it had been when he had left: his books were still on his bookshelf, the photographs of the school rugby teams he had played in still hung on the walls, his little radio still stood on the bedside table. The room had hardly been used while he had been away; only occasionally it had been given to friends of David's or Rachel's who had stayed overnight, or to visiting relatives. Now, looking clean and refreshed in a white shirt and a pair of grey flannel trousers, Joel lay on the bed. He had shaved and bathed. Sarah was sorting out the clothing she had unpacked from his bags. Most of it was in a heap on the floor, to go into the wash: harsh military shirts and underwear, khaki shorts, a filthy fatigue overall.

She threw the last item on the heap; then sat at the bottom of the bed, Joel pulling back his feet and lifting his knees to let her do so. 'Well,' she asked, 'how does it feel to be back?'

Joel smiled at his mother. 'No,' he said. 'You tell me what I've come back to. How have you been? What's been happening here?'

'Oh – everything's just gone on.'

'Dad? David? Rachel?'

'All of them.'

'And you?'

'Me most of all. Just the same, nothing new.'

While he had been away Joel had thought he wanted nothing at home to change. Now, hearing his mother's words, he felt a slight, unidentifiable disappointment. 'No happier?' he asked.

His mother looked at him in surprise. Her hands had been idle in her lap, but when she spoke she clasped them together, moving her fingers within one another. She said, shrugging, slightly, 'You know how it is, Joel, as long as you were all right, and the children, and your father ... Why do you ask me? What do you expect?'

'I don't know,' he answered, lying back on his bed. 'I don't know. It doesn't matter. I've got enough, being here.'

Sarah sat in silence, her hands still working together. Her arms and wrists were full, but her fingers looked old, their joints stood out, as though their flesh had been worn away by the habitual movements of her hands. As if making a confession, she said, 'All the time you were away, Joel, I just tried to think about you, without ... without thinking about what you were doing. There was no other way I could do it. You understand what I mean?'

'Of course,' Joel replied. Along the length of his own body he looked at his mother, through half-closed eyes. 'Actually, I suppose I tried to do the same kind of thing. I mean I tried just not to think about what I was doing, or might be doing. At any rate, while the war was on. Afterwards it was just like a boring holiday. But during the war ...'

He paused, then admitted, 'I was never in much danger, really. They kept the whole lot of us back in the reserves, right through the winter, because we were so young, everybody said. When they moved us forward it was right at the end – there wasn't any front any more. All we did was to chase after the Jerries in our trucks. And we'd find them waiting in the villages, in the squares, with their hands up. I hardly fired a shot, and I'm damn sure I didn't hit anything. We'd jump out

47

of the trucks, when they'd say there's some resistance – up there in a farmhouse, or in a church, or something and we'd creep along behind some walls, and somebody would start firing, and I'd fire too, God knows at what. And I'd have to tell myself that that's what I was *supposed* to be doing. It was all so unreal. I'm sure it would have been different if I'd had to be at it longer. But I was lucky. The Jerries strafed us a couple of times when I was at Santa Barbara, in the reserves, but they never did much. They had no air force left. One plane, two perhaps they'd come out, low, and we'd run like hell to get under cover. Usually they'd be gone by the time we got to the trenches. Only once I saw some chaps hit.'

He stopped abruptly, knowing that what he had said had upset his mother. Yet, guiltily at having seen so little action he could not help feeling soothed and flattered by her distress; he had, at least, seen more action than anyone who had stayed at home.

> *'Soldier from the war returning,*
> *Spoiler of the taken town ...'*

Rachel was at the door; she stood there in an attitude of declamation, one hand extended. Then she came into the room. 'I've done a whole hour's work, I can't do any more. I want to join in the talk. What have I missed?'

'Nothing at all,' Joel said. 'Come in, Rachie. Roachie. Cockroach.'

Rachel pointedly ignored his teasing. She took his battledress blouse from the back of a chair and slipped it over her shoulders, the sleeves hanging loose. It was absurdly bulky over her small body; the triangular green and gold Sixth Armoured Division shoulder-flashes hung halfway down her arms. She went to the mirror and saluted herself in it. She thought she looked very attractive in the tunic, in a waif-like, refugee-like way. She shook her hair free at the back of the collar. In the mirror she could see that the others were watching her, so she scowled at them and showed her teeth. 'Say fellas, I'm gonna get me a coupla Jerries before breakfast. Just hand me that howitzer and I'll mow 'em down.' When she spoke again the Hollywood accent was gone; she addressed her own image in what she hoped was a clipped British manner. 'Private Rachel Glickman reporting for duty, sah. What? A general? Make me a general?' She simpered, curtseying to herself in the mirror. 'Thank you, Your Majesty, but I'm devoted to the arts of peace. I'm writing my exams at the moment, and that takes up all my time. But I can recommend my brother to you. He's very brave, very fierce, and even bigger than I am.' She saluted, scowled once more, and turned her back on the mirror. 'The war's over!' she cried. 'We're all going to live happily ever after.'

'That's my plan,' Joel said.

'You won't find it so easy to carry out,' Sarah put in.

'Well it should be,' Rachel answered. 'What's the point of it, if we can't be happy?'

'Ask your grandmother,' Joel said. 'She's the one with the direct line to God.'

'That line's disconnected.'

'Not for Bobbe?'

'Of course not for Bobbe. But it is for us.' Rachel brought one clenched fist to her ear, the other to her mouth. 'Hullo, God, are you there? Look, I didn't ride on a bus last *shabbes*. Isn't that good? And you should see my milk plates and my meat plates, so separate you'd be delighted. Sure, God. Of course, God. As you say, God. Whatever you want, God. See you next *Yom Kippur*. Can you imagine us on that line?'

Both Sarah and Joel were laughing. 'What do you think of her?' Sarah asked proudly.

Rachel answered the question. 'He loves me.' But no sooner had she spoken than she looked at Joel, afraid that he might deny it.

Joel nodded. 'I suppose he does.' He rose from the bed and touched his mother's lined, prominent forehead with his fingertips; he ran his hand over her soft, short, silvering curls. 'And you too, Mom.'

'Then everybody's happy!' Rachel exclaimed, throwing the army tunic from her shoulders on to the floor. Sarah picked it up, taking it into her hands, turning it over and feeling it between her fingers.

'Happy enough,' she said calmly.

'And sleepy enough,' Joel added. 'I had no sleep on the plane last night.'

They left him to sleep, after drawing the curtains. For Joel the relief and surprise of his arrival, the firmness and solidity of the rooms and furniture he had for so long carried in his memory, the vivacity and quickness of people whose images he had had to fix in stillness in his mind – all these impressions, and a hundred others, from the motion of the plane which still seemed to rock his bed, to the cry of a hawker in the sunlit street outside – all were lost in the warmth which was about him and within him, spreading wider, spreading deeper. And the warmth was sleep.

4

'Vile,' David said aloud to himself. 'Vile.' Even as he said the word he liked its literary, almost archaic sound; and his enjoyment of it seemed to him in itself vile. He had sworn that from the day of Joel's return he would not do it again; and yet here he was, on the very day he had named, washing the evidence of his vileness from his hands. And in the school lavatory too, of all crazy places, where anyone might have come bursting in, and overheard him or seen him. From the basin David looked over his shoulder, though now he was doing nothing more guilty than holding his hands under a running tap. So Joel's arrival had helped him as little as any of the previous occasions for reform that he had set himself; he was still what he had always been. And what was that? Vile.

The school was empty. From the cricket field David heard the resonant, desultory knock of bat against ball. Even further off was the noise from the school swimming bath. At once high-pitched and distant, it sounded barely human, it might have been a noise coming from a poultry-yard. Standing in the entrance to the lavatories David saw a part of the Senior Quad, all its rooms and windows deserted; to the left were the bicycle sheds, with not a single bike parked in them. As always when he saw the school empty and defenceless, David's thoughts ran immediately to violence, arson and defacement. Yet, even as he walked across the Senior Quad, his mood changed, and he felt a kind of nostalgia for the school, though he stood within it. Looking at its whitewashed walls, its elaborate Cape Dutch gables cocked up against the sky, he thought how much like a venerable and decent seat of learning it seemed, devoted to the increase of wisdom in the world.

The notion of wisdom reminded David of what he had been doing in the lavatory. 'Vile,' he said aloud; but with even less conviction than before. He did not believe that there was anything really wicked or sinful in what he had done – he felt, rather, that had he been a truly strong man he would simply never have done it. He would either have stuck to his resolution, once he had made it; or he would have no need to make such a resolution at all, having succeeded in doing better, much better, with his lust. He would have had a woman by now; not one woman, but many women.

The side-entrance to the school grounds led to a lane; the lane led to a main street. Carrying his school-case, David made his way to the bus stop. He knew that his mother had been expecting him back early; he himself had wanted to see Joel again, to listen to his stories, to look at his things. But just because that treat had been awaiting him, he had volunteered to stay behind to do an hour's cataloguing in the school library. And from the library, knowing his weakness and deliberately indulging himself in it, even indulging beforehand in the remorse he would feel afterwards, he had gone into the lavatory. So Joel had come back – so? Did the whole world have to be turned upside down?

How David wished that it would be turned upside down! Instead, he stood waiting for the bus where he always stood, and, the bus was as long in coming as it always was. But while watching out for the bus David saw a familiar figure approaching, and his impatience disappeared. From a distance he had recognized Bertie Preiss, by his walk. One arm hung down Bertie's side, carrying his case; the other arm was behind the small of his back, and his hand gripped the arm with the case. Preiss walked as if he were holding himself upright – and so, in a way, he was; as a child he had suffered from a spinal disease, which had left its mark in this strained, upright carriage. Because of his illness, Preiss had been held back at school; he was three years older than David, though only a year ahead of him, in the matric class.

'Why're you so late?' David called out, as Bertie approached.

'I ask the same of you.'

'I've been cataloguing in the library.'

'Sucking up to odd Skilly? I've been watching the cricket.'

'What's it like?'

'Boring. That's why I'm here.'

For some minutes the boys talked together idly. Occasionally a car or a cyclist passed along the road; pedestrians were even more infrequent. The road was wide, and sloped steeply downhill, with the railings of the school grounds to one side and large suburban houses on the other, each with its garden and trees in front of it. A pale, tenuous, almost watery green light was reflected from the trees in leaf, and the clumps of grass that rose knee-high from cracks in the pavement. Above the roofs, the sun hung calmly in a sky that did not have a single cloud within it.

'My brother came back this morning,' David said.

'Really? Joel?'

'Ja.'

'How is he?'

'Big-stuff soldier-boy. Ribbons, souvenirs, the lot.' Though he spoke scoffingly, David was proud of his news, and Preiss knew it.

'So now the world's safe for democracy.'

'Democracy!' David made a loud, lewd noise. 'Pigmentocracy!'

'Hey, you unfortunately pigmented fellow,' Bertie said, addressing an African on the other side of the street, 'do you know that the war's over and you've been liberated?' The African did not hear the words – Bertie had not intended him to – and he padded steadily on, his bare feet slapping on the pavement. He walked with a swagger, each haunch rising and falling under his khaki shorts and his black arms swinging. The two boys, in their blazers, caps and flannels, their cases at their feet, watched him go. 'Alas, he doesn't know it. The helot is sunk into his helotry. You should go and agitate him.'

'Not today, thanks. You're the agitator around here, anyway. How's the night-school?'

'It's all right. When are you coming to teach in it? You promised you would.'

'One of these days,' David answered guiltily. But he knew how he could discomfit Bertie in turn. Appraisingly, David studied his friend's scrawny figure, his face that seemed to go back directly from a wide, flat mouth to large spectacles that looked as though they were supported more by the bones of his cheeks than by the bridge of his nose. 'Rachel's giving a party when her exams are finished,' David announced. 'It'll be for Joel, too.'

'Is that so?' Bertie asked, but David added nothing to what he had said. 'How is she?'

'She's in the middle of her exams, so she's in a bit of a state. And she's pretty excited about Joel coming back.'

'I can imagine.'

'Ja, it's hard to get a coherent word out of her,' David said, lording it over Bertie by speaking so patronizingly and familiarly about Rachel.

Mutely, miserably, Bertie waited to hear whether he would be invited to her party. In his mind he peopled it with Joel's friends, servicemen with ribbons on their chests, and with Rachel's classmates, their best dresses rustling and hissing. They laughed, danced, gossiped about the university he would have been attending with them, had it not been for his illness.

It would be best if he weren't invited, Bertie decided; he wouldn't enjoy it at all.

Then David relented. 'You're invited. I've seen the list.'

'Hell thanks, Dave. That's terrific.'

'Don't thank me. Thank Rachel.'

The two boys exchanged a glance, then both looked away, down the street.

Yet they stood peacefully, happily now – Bertie happy because he had been invited to the party, David happy because he had been the bearer of good news. He felt very fond of Bertie, and punched him gently to show how fond of him he was. Bertie merely smiled, recognizing the gesture.

Just then David saw the bus approaching up the hill. 'Thar she blows,' he cried, suddenly eager again to get home. One day he, too, would come home a hero, to be touched and wept over. 'Bestir yourself, Preiss. They're waiting for me.'

54

5

The *shul* looked exactly as it had when Joel had last seen it. Everything was the same. The dais in the middle was approached by the two little steps Joel had last ascended on the occasion of his *barmitzvah*; in front of it were the padded leather seats for the synagogue dignitaries. Ranged in a shallow incline on both sides of the dais were the rows of wooden seats, each with the name of an occupant on a brass plate affixed to it. Facing the dais, and at some distance from it, was the Ark of the Law, where the scrolls were kept, with a heavy gilt-embroidered curtain drawn across it; above the Ark was a marble architectural fantasy of domes, pillars and minaret-like towers, representing Jerusalem, perhaps. Above, running almost entirely around the circumference of the building, was the gallery for women. And above that, again, receding from the gallery, was the interior of the dome which surmounted the building – white, plain and lofty, with a great chandelier of brass and cut-glass suspended from its midpoint. The cantor and his assistant were in their white robes; the members of the congregation were scattered about thinly on the benches, their suits and hats dark against the pale yellow woodwork; there were two or three women up in the gallery, one of them Joel's grandmother, in a black dress and a black straw hat with a tiny veil.

All, all was the same, not least the feeling of boredom and estrangement which came over Joel immediately the service began, and which he could vividly remember feeling as a child – so vividly that for him what piety he had towards the religion of the people to whom he belonged was to be found in that very sense of estrangement. The prayers were still meaningless, uttered in a language foreign to him; the singing was still tuneless to his ear; the movements of the men at prayer still appeared to him to have no dignity; still the God to whom they raised their plaintive, discordant voices and bowed their workaday bodies – still that God did not exist. Yet Joel could not help being moved by the thought of the number of times he had sat with his father as a small child, just as he was sitting now. He remembered how he had then looked with awe at the chandelier hung from the dome, and had been enchanted by the marble city above the Ark, and had stared with curiosity at the faces of the members of the congregation. And even had he not had those memories, Joel believed that he would have been moved by the history which was embodied in the service; by the very supplication to that God in whom he did not believe.

Benjamin showed Joel the place in the prayer book. With difficulty Joel read a few Hebrew words and heard the congregation murmuring them too, then he could follow them no longer. He shrugged exaggeratedly at his father, who winked broadly back at him. For Benjamin, too, there was no truth or enlightenment in the services, though he attended them regularly. He came out of nostalgia for his boyhood, a wish to identify himself with the community, and a sense of propriety and decorum. He came also as a challenge to his wife, who never entered the *shul* from one year's end to the next, though her frail elderly mother attended zealously.

When the service ended there was a loud hollow banging as the congregants let down the little lecterns in front of each seat; that sound, too, echoed and re-echoed in Joel's ears from his boyhood. Then, a dozen times his hand was shaken by people familiar and unfamiliar to him, all of them glad to welcome back another soldier. In the foyer the congregation gathered in groups of handshaking and gesticulating men. Benjamin stood in the middle of one arguing group.

'There's no other way,' he said heatedly. 'What isn't given to you you have to take.' He was talking of the terrorists in Palestine, who were fighting against the British occupation of the country. 'Those men are fighting for us, too,' he said passionately, poking the man nearest to him in the hollow of his shoulder. 'Can't you realize what they're trying to do for you – yes, you, you –'

The man he was attacking, who was much larger than Benjamin, retreated and rubbed his shoulder, complaining that he wasn't arguing, was he now? He wore his hat right on the back of his bald head.

'Come, Dad,' Joel said. 'Bobbe is waiting.'

'Right away,' Benjamin replied. He touched the brim of his hat with his hand, in a general salutation to the congregation, and followed Joel out of the building.

Then, through the rapidly darkening streets, the three of them walked towards Mrs Talmon's flat, which she kept in the house of a pious woman who had come from the same *shtetl* in Lithuania as herself. With his mother-in-law Benjamin was jocular and deferential. They walked very slowly, suiting their pace to the old lady's. Joel talked to her, in English, of the aftermath of the war in Italy, the ruins, the hungry children in the streets, the political slogans chalked up on the walls, the gangs of *partigiani* he had helped to disarm. Mrs Talmon asked her questions in Yiddish. She was tiny, fragile and bent. Her mind was alert, but she seemed to speak as if from the edge of a curious, intensely guarded stillness, which she permitted no emotion, no word, ever to touch. Even when she had greeted him it had remained inviolate.

At the gate of the house in which she lived, they said good night and good *shabbes* to her, and she went alone up the garden path, watched by the two men. Then they walked on. The houses about them were black; individual rooms, and the streetlamps were yellow among the trees. Further off the noise of traffic was a continuous vague disturbance of the air; and the blocks of flats that were beginning to encroach upon the suburb showed themselves as immensely tall ladders of light, poised against nothing.

6

At home there was talk, food, a white tablecloth, candles burning in polished brass holders, sweet wine. But the melancholy that Joel had felt settle upon himself during the service and while walking home with his grandmother was not dissipated. After supper his cousin Jonathan Talmon arrived. Jonathan was the only son of Sarah's brother: he was a strikingly handsome, tall young man, with bright blue eyes, black hair hanging tousled over his forehead, a sharp profile, a cleft in his chin, and a resonant, cultivated voice. He was a second-hand car salesman; his ambition was to become an actor. So far he had had one or two small professional parts, and numerous amateur ones, in local productions.

To entertain them, he was soon imitating, at Rachel's request, the people who came to buy cars from him. In succession he was a Boer from the backveld, an African parson 'of de Met'odist perswashon', a bartender with his eye on a Cadillac, a spoiled Jewish boy looking for an MG, and, as well, he was himself, responding to the customers' queries, listening to their complaints, telling lies about the cars, and trying to stop his over-eager boss from wrecking the sale. He did it very well, Joel had to admit; but unlike Rachel and David, he had soon had enough of it.

Benjamin read the paper in the living room. Sarah came and joined the children on the stoep, listening with pride to her nephew. Joel got up, walked to the garden gate, and looked back at the group under the light, their wickerwork chairs ranged in a semicircle. They were set out before him as if on a stage. Watching them from the darkness, he felt his love for his family to be indistinguishable from the frustration and dejection that were like a weight on his chest. He breathed in deeply, as if to shift the weight; he pulled a face at Jonathan, blaming him for what he was feeling. But it wasn't just

Jonathan who had roused and blocked him: it was them all, it was the house, the street, himself, everything.

Throughout his time in the army – he had gone into it straight from school, shortly after his seventeenth birthday, and had served in it for two years – Joel had been hoping to come upon a strength and certitude in himself which would be inalienable. Always it had seemed to him that he would find it just one stage ahead from where he was. Before enlistment he had thought he would put on strength with his uniform; during his training he had expected to find it when he was posted abroad; in the reserves, when he had seen action; after the war, when he would come home. Now he was home; and where was the confidence, the certainty, the inward security he had been promising himself? What was he to be? Where was he to live? How was he to live? Who was there to guide him?

Standing there at the gate, he heard someone coming along the quiet pavement, and turned to see who it was. A moment later he had opened the gate and was walking with an outstretched hand towards the newcomer.

'Leon!'

'Joel!'

The two young men greeted each other enthusiastically, in the half-light of the streetlamps, and walked together up the garden path.

'God, the last time I saw you was – where? In Florence? Rapallo? Where the hell was it?'

'Florence, Florence,' the other replied as they stepped on to the stoep. He spoke with a strong *platteland* accent, in a voice which came out with a surprisingly high pitch from someone so heavy, thick-necked and tall. His hands, with which he gestured when he spoke, were small, and so were his feet; altogether, his bulk seemed a burden placed arbitrarily on him. But he carried it with his shoulders and head well back. His face was large, full and flushed, and under his nose he wore a small black moustache. Everyone on the stoep greeted him cheerfully, and Benjamin came out, newspaper in one hand and his glasses in the other, to see who had just arrived.

When they were all seated Sarah said to Leon, 'It's really like old times, having you and Joel together here again.'

'Yes, isn't it? I heard that Joel's been back a few days so I thought I'd take a chance on finding him in. He's looking all right, don't you think?'

'He's looking wonderful,' Sarah replied, so wholeheartedly that everyone laughed.

'*Nu*, Leon, what's been happening to you, since you're out of the army?' Mr Glickman asked.

'Nothing very much. I'm just getting started, now.'

'Started on what?' Joel asked.

'Work. Work in the movement.'

'What movement?'

Jonathan sang out in a thin, piping, nasal voice, '*Kol od belevav pni-i-i-i-ma*,' and Rachel laughed loudly.

'How did you know?' she asked him.

'Intuition. The infallible Talmon intuition. As soon as he came on to the stoep I said to myself, "You know – old Leon's become a Zionist." Just look at his gleaming eyes, his clenched jaw, his square shoulders, his gesticulating hands. A Zionist is born.'

'Very funny,' Joel said.

'It is too,' Rachel answered him sharply. She and Jonathan were sitting side-by-side. Jonathan reached over, took her hand in his, and began to raise it elaborately to his lips. But she jerked it away from him. A moment later, when everyone's attention was diverted to Leon, she let her hand swing loose over the arm of her chair. It brushed against Jonathan's, then clasped his fiercely before letting it go.

Leon Friedberg, who had been at school with Joel, sat at ease in his chair, sure of his welcome in the family, and proud to be able to tell them what he was doing now. He divided his time, he said, between living on *hachsharah*, a Zionist training farm near Potchefstroom, and working in the Johannesburg office of the movement he belonged to. There were twelve of them on the farm, eight boys and four girls; they would soon be expanding to twenty. His movement was Hatzofim; the youth movements had farms of their own. They had no idea when they would be able to go to Palestine – it was impossible to get entry permits, and the people who were running illegal immigrants through the British blockade weren't interested in comfortable, well-nourished South Africans who could afford to wait.

'But we'll go. Things will change soon, and then we'll go together.'

'But when did you become a Zionist?' Joel asked. 'The last time I saw you, all you talked about was getting home and lying in bed.'

Leon had listened with lifted black brows to Joel. He lowered them before he spoke. 'Since then I've been to Eretz. I had three weeks' Palestine leave when I was in Egypt, waiting to get home. I was on a kibbutz, just about the whole time I was there.' Joel waited for him to go on. He said, quietly, 'That's all.'

'You mean you saw the light?'

'I just saw the way I wanted to live.'

Benjamin sat back in his chair, gratified by Leon's words. But Joel could not help feeling that the simplicity and firmness of what Leon had said explained too little.

'We'll have to talk about it,' he said. 'I got Palestine leave for ten days, and spent it all in hospital in Cairo, with a horrible attack of Gyppo tummy. Lovely leave that was.' The flippancy of his remark seemed cheap to him, a moment later. 'You must tell me everything, I do want to know.'

'You think you might want to join us?'

'Perhaps,' Joel answered. 'Who can tell?' Half-mockingly, turning to his parents, he said, 'I've got to do something with my life.'

'You can come into the business, you know that,' Benjamin said quickly.

Joel shook his head. 'Don't rush me, dad.'

'Who's rushing?'

'Anyway, as a Zionist you should be pleased if I wanted to join Leon.'

'I wouldn't mind. Don't make any mistake about it. If that's what you wanted to do I'd be perfectly happy. It'll be a wonderful day for me when you or Leon or anyone else can go to Eretz Israel and live there if he wants to.'

'I've got to do something,' Joel repeated. He stood up restlessly. 'At least Leon is trying, he isn't pretending that things can just go on.'

Suddenly he found words for some of the frustration that had held him mute, minutes before, on his own at the gate. 'Look how we live! There's been a bloody great war, they killed six million Jews like flies, they dropped atomic bombs on Japan. And look at South Africa! Look at this country, with the kaffirs living like pigs, and the white men kicking them around. And what do we do about it all? Nothing! I come back and find that we just go on and on, in the same house, doing the same things, thinking the same thoughts, as if nothing at all had happened. How can we do it? How can we go on like this? I don't understand it, I really don't. Either we're mad or everyone else is mad. Either what I've seen and what we've all read about never happened, or all this is unreal, just unreal – all of us sitting here on the stoep with the light on, making pleasant conversation.'

'Is that what you think you're doing?' Rachel said. 'Anyway, why shouldn't we? We're entitled to live our own lives. Nothing that happens anywhere else can change that.'

'I feel that it does.'

'Perhaps it's your fault, not ours,' Rachel said, growing fiercer.

'Perhaps it is,' Joel admitted. 'But don't other people feel the same way?'

'Not me.'

'Ach,' Benjamin said angrily, 'everything has changed. No one can ever feel about things the way he used to. You think it isn't in my mind too how we live – what we should do – what's happened to us – why my sister ended up like one of those things we've seen in the newsreels and I'm here in Johannesburg with a house and a garden and a business. You think it doesn't work inside me, worry me, take my satisfactions away from me?'

Joel looked at his father. 'I know it does. Otherwise I couldn't talk to you at all.'

'So tell me what you propose to do about it,' Benjamin said. 'I'd be glad to hear.' He spoke ironically, without hope.

Pitying him, because he was so much older and had so much less to look forward to, Joel said, 'You're entitled to your satisfactions. I don't want to seem to be saying that you aren't. I wish you had more, from all of us, from everything.'

Sarah spoke unexpectedly. 'It's the little dissatisfactions that worry us far more than the big ones.'

Benjamin gave her a quick suspicious glance, ready to be offended. But he took up what she had said. 'That in itself is a big dissatisfaction, can't you see? What worse can you say about us than that? I knew, I knew, Europe was a mad house, a butcher-shop; my sister and her family was there, my son was there, nothing could ever be the same again. But if I went into the office and found that a girl there hadn't written some rubbishy letter, then I was in a rage.'

They were all silent. A little later, in a calmer voice, Benjamin said, 'Talking of the girls in the office reminds me – the other day I invited Pamela Curtis to your party, Rachel. I hope you don't mind. I felt sorry for the girl and I thought it would be an outing for her.'

'Do you think she'll fit in?' Rachel asked.

Her father shrugged. 'You must do your best. I can't take back the invitation now.'

Rachel said to Jonathan, 'You are coming, aren't you?'

'I'll try.'

'You mustn't try, you must come.'

'Orders is orders.'

For another hour they sat there, a roof over their heads but no walls around them, the evening air warm on their bare arms. It was a still, windless evening, and the light above them attracted insects of all kinds, which buzzed and blundered about, occasionally falling heavily to the ground and then struggling across the wide, smooth, polished cement floor of the stoep, or laboriously climbing up the leg of a chair before taking flight again. Once Rachel swore that a moth had fallen into her hair, and went inside to comb it out. Jonathan followed her, and they were gone for some time, but no one remarked on it. When they returned Rachel was carrying a tray with a jug of orange juice and some glasses on it, as if to explain, or at least extenuate, their absence.

Benjamin questioned Leon at length about the financial support his training-farm was getting from the Zionist Federation, and was dissatisfied with the answers. 'It's not enough,' he said. As vice-chairman of his suburban Zionist society, he was not shy to speak authoritatively on such matters. 'I'll raise the whole question at the congress next month.'

When Leon left, Joel walked with him for a few blocks, through streets that were already deserted – too deserted to be calm. 'Thanks for coming round,' Joel said, when they parted. 'You cheered me up a lot.'

'You shouldn't have needed cheering up, your first week home.'

'I did, though. That's how funny it is.'

'I know.'

And Leon did know: that was why Joel reached up and took him affectionately by the shoulder. 'Well, shall I follow you to Palestine?' he asked.

'How can I tell you what to do?' Leon was embarrassed; Joel saw the glint of a smile on his face, and the tiny uneasy movement he made with his large body.

'You're quite certain in your own mind?'

'Quite certain. I'm finished with all this,' Leon said, gesturing around him at the empty street, its darkness stretched taut between the locked, barred, burglar-proofed houses on both sides. 'There's no life here, in this country, there's nothing decent or straightforward about it. You can't find your way through it. Jews, Afrikaners, Englishmen, blacks, money-making, anti-semitism – it's all a madness, a mistake, an accident. You know the feeling. You said it yourself. But there, in Eretz – there it's different.'

'It must be,' Joel said.

'It's different even on *hachsharah*. You must come out to our place and have a look at it. You'll see what we're trying to do.'

'I will, Leon.'

'OK, Good night, boy. Keep cheerful.'

'And you.'

7

The two brothers shook hands on the railway platform, then slowly they climbed the marble steps leading from the concourse to the street. Meyer paused at every step, leaning on his heavy walking-stick, and at every pause asking another question of Benjamin. His eyes were dark grey in colour and sharp in their movement. Occasionally he nodded, inclining his bald wide head, with a few bristles of close-cropped grey hair growing from it. His brow, his cheeks, his nose and chin were all heavy, and there were many fine purplish veins just beneath his skin. He was dressed with care, in expensive well-tailored clothes; his collar was impeccably white and his shoes were highly polished. 'So, so,' he said, breathing deeply, when they reached the top of the steps. 'Where's the car?'

'Just here, the boy is waiting,' Benjamin said, leading the way out of the station.

The two elderly men looked so much like – though Meyer was much the heavier man – that passers-by smiled and glanced again at them, while they stood waiting together on the pavement. Benjamin waved his hand and the driver came up with the car. Meyer looked at him behind the wheel. 'Johannes,' he said.

The driver grinned broadly, under his black peaked cap, pleased that his name had been remembered. 'Yes, boss.'

Meyer nodded, pleased too that he had got the name right. With interest he looked out of the window of the car, as they drove through the streets, commenting on this new building or the disappearance of that old one. As always, Benjamin felt in his brother's presence both admiration and constriction. How shrewd Meyer was, how little he missed in the scene around him.

They drove straight to the factory. In the office Meyer stopped to exchange a few words with each of the women; then he and Benjamin walked across the main yard. The place was old, rambling, and yet substantially built of brick; the office-block, the factory, the paved yard and outbuildings covered entirely a small triangular block of ground, with a private railway siding on one side. Tucked in a corner of the block there was a boiler plant; in the yard, with a constant hissing of steam and clanging of metal, overalled African workmen were washing the empty cream-cans that came clattering down a chute that ran through the wall of the factory itself; across the yard the cans were ranged in order for return by rail to their owners. Two lorries were pulled up alongside the platform in front of the main building; one was being loaded with sixty-pound blocks of ice, from the other full cans of cream were being off-loaded. Each time a can hit the concrete platform a shudder ran through it from end to end. To all the noise outside there was added the continual rumble and groan of the machinery within the building, which the two owners had not yet entered. They stood in front, two thickset, bald, sallow-skinned men, at ease in the midst of all the activity, gratified by it.

When they crossed out of the bright sunlight, through the wide doors at the entrance to the building, they were momentarily dazzled, and saw little more inside the factory than the gleam of metal in strips and the white patches of overalls. Strangely, the first impression indoors was not only of darkness, but also of a kind of silence, for the noise here was continuous, at one level of uproar. Here the cans were slid on long rails, embedded in the concrete floor, towards the scales; from the scales they were pushed towards the pasteurizing plant. The pasteurizers were simply great horizontal tanks, inside which tubular aluminium worms revolved, seeming to make their way across the tanks yet never emerging from them. The cream within the tanks was whipped into constant motion; the screws dipped in, came out white, dripping sleekly, sank in again. Overhead, cream ran down the cooling towers, which were like giant-size, corrugated wash-boards; and beyond, on another level, the brown wooden churns, each one ten or twelve feet in depth and as much in height, turned with their distinctive roar.

It seemed impossible that in the tumult anyone could work or think. But, calmly, white men and Africans went about their duties, all of them clad alike in white overalls and gumboots. The factory-clerk worked in his glass and beaverboard cubicle, the tester walked down the rows of cans, taking his samples; the butter-maker looked through the glass panel in the revolving doors of the churns, signalled for one of them to be halted, and the scrubbed, gleaming butter-carrier to be thrust into it. Then, slowly, the churn revolved a few degrees, and the butter, which had been forced to the sides of the churn's inner walls, began to tip over and fall into the carrier. It fell in long, moist swathes, that looked almost like bolts of cloth. When the carrier was full it was trundled across to the moulding machine, from which the butter was extruded in long rectangular loaves. Wire guillotines descended upon these loaves, cutting them into the shape of the one pound blocks, which were check-weighed, wrapped and packed into cardboard cartons by hand. The butter itself was not touched, each pound being placed into position between tiny wooden paddles which the African workmen seemed to use as deftly as their own fingertips.

Had it not been for the war, the factory would have had an automatic wrapping and packing plant; to have one installed was one of Benjamin's immediate ambitions. As they walked about, occasionally he leaned over and shouted in his brother's ear some fragment of explanation, a snatch of figures or a complaint about a particular machine. Much of the time the two of them were accompanied by the chief tester and butter-maker, Mr Pratley. Under his nose Pratley had a wide moustache; under his moustache a set of crooked, discoloured teeth, which he showed almost continually when he talked to his employers, and which he showed, too, though with an entirely different expression, when he spoke to the Africans under him.

In his zeal to impress the visitor, Pratley could not help shouting snatches of his own complaints into Meyer Glickman's ear. 'No cooperation,' he shouted. 'Cheek! Laziness! Do my best …' Eventually, when he darted off on some errand, as he had been doing at intervals ever since he had joined them, Meyer turned to Benjamin and shouted, 'He seems to be getting worse, that fellow. You better watch him.'

'I watch them all.'

Pratley returned, shouting. Benjamin caught only the last words of what he was trying to communicate – 'Cold storage?'

Benjamin nodded, yes, they would go into the cold storage. Pratley waved his hands and shouted, and a door sunk into the wall on one side was swung open. It revealed, as if magically, a world of snow and ice – there was room after room down there, glistening with the thick columns of frost that clung around coils of pipes against the walls. The floors shone more darkly, where water had been splashed and had then frozen into sheets of ice. In the rooms the stock was kept, in cartons piled from floor to ceiling. One box had burst open, and the cubes of butter spilt out of it were as hard as blocks of wood. The men spent only a few minutes in the cold storage; but when they came out of it, the air of the churning room felt to them like a great waft or breath of heat.

8

'See that?' Pratley hissed, pointing, his tone a mixture of alarm and vindication.

'What – ?' Benjamin exclaimed. A white workman and a black were grappling fiercely with one another. The sight was shocking in its violence and unexpectedness, amidst the purposeful uproar of the machinery.

Then Benjamin saw that the men were merely playing at fighting, and that the others, who had turned from their work to watch, were smiling. He smiled also – but too late, for in that same instant the fight had become a real one. The black man was no longer giving ground; he held the white firmly in a grip around his waist, pinioning his arms to his side. The white man heaved and lunged, and managed to get an arm free; he clenched his fist and struck hard at his opponent's neck.

Benjamin had reached them. He was much shorter than each of them, but at the touch of his hand, the sound of his voice, they broke apart, with heaving chest, staring at one another.

Verster, the white man, the assistant butter-maker, was the first to speak. 'You can't play with a kaffir, they don't know what a game is,' he muttered angrily.

'Baas Verster took me from behind,' the African said.

Benjamin was ashamed that the workmen should have been brawling in his brother's presence, and the sudden display of violence had roused his own blood. 'Go on! Go on! Both of you, get on with your work.'

They stood where they were, aggrieved and angry. Both of them were young, tall and powerfully built. The African, Jacobus, was a Basuto, and had the smooth brown skin of his tribe, and its characteristic boldness and delicacy of featuring, with lips that were defined by a faint ridge running all the way around them, and nostrils flared back at the end of an almost aquiline nose. Verster's hair was blond and straight, his face was tanned, his eyes were a light, direct blue. He was Pratley's chief tormentor, according to Pratley; for his own part Benjamin had often felt there was something insolent about Verster, particularly in his gaze, which seemed to linger on one even after he had looked away. It was with just such a glance that Verster turned away now, and clumped off in his rubber boots across the cement floor. He took only a few paces, however, before shouting at Jacobus, 'I'll catch you another time. And then you better look out!'

Benjamin beckoned him back with an outstretched finger. Verster came back slowly; Benjamin levelled his finger at him. 'You watch out,' he said. 'When I tell you to go back to work, you do what I say, you don't stop in the middle to shout at others. You hear me?' Verster stared forward. Benjamin left him staring; he turned to Jacobus and shouted, '*Hamba*! What the hell are you waiting for?' Jacobus lowered his head and shuffled off hastily.

'You don't talk to me like that in front of a kaffir –' Verster broke out.

'I talk to you how I like. Go on, Verster. You were looking for trouble. So you got it. Now go back to your work.'

This time Verster turned his back squarely on his employer, and walked off without looking back. Benjamin watched him go, before rejoining Meyer. Having lost his own temper, he no longer felt ashamed or apologetic about the scene, and dismissed Pratley almost cordially.

'One damn thing after another,' Benjamin said, and Meyer heard the satisfaction in his voice.

'Wild animals,' Meyer said automatically, in Yiddish. The incident left his mind almost immediately. He had other things to think about. He was reluctant to let out of his grasp his share of the ownership of these buildings, these machines, these men, this noise and industry. Yet Benjamin was pressing him to sell, and they would have to come to a decision before he left Johannesburg. 'Come,' he said, 'let's go to the house. We must talk.'

9

Pratley was a man with many troubles. He suffered severely from dyspepsia; he couldn't meet his bills at the end of the month; his wife was many years older than he was; and his grown-up stepson frequently threatened to bugger him up. Furthermore, his relations with the other white workers in the factory were not good. Pratley was the only English-speaking white in the factory, the others being Afrikaners, and Pratley was convinced that they ganged up against him for racial reasons. They were all Nationalists, Pratley claimed, Nazis, Briton-haters, German-lovers. They hid his sandwich-box; they pinched his antacid tablets; they incited the black workers to give him 'cheek'.

Spasms of malice were Pratley's only courage. He knew that it would be best for him to say nothing about what had happened earlier in the churning room; but he could not restrain himself. He, Verster and young van Niekerk, the clerk, were sitting in the little beaverboard cubicle, with its centrifuge and testing cups ranged neatly to one side. It was the noon break; the machines were idle, and the silence within the factory seemed almost uncanny. Each man had with him his vacuum flask and *skof* tin; the African workers were having their lunch outside in the sun, on the loading platform. Pratley looked up from the mug he held in both hands and said, 'You looked bloody funny, after the old man gave you hell. As if you'd seen a spook.'

There was no response. Verster went on drinking his tea and eating his sandwiches. Precisely because of his relief at Verster's silence, Pratley felt his courage come again: it pricked him, made him stir restlessly. He said, 'Playing with kaffirs like that – what else do you expect?'

Unable to bear the danger of his own malice a moment longer he added placatingly, 'Still, he had no business to speak to you like that in front of a kaffir. I heard him. Yes, I heard him,' Pratley repeated with satisfaction, striking out once more, in spite of himself.

Still Verster made no reply. He sat heavily on his little wooden chair; the sleeves of his boilersuit were rolled up, and his bare, blond-haired arms rested on the table. Only when Pratley began unwrapping his packet of sandwiches did Verster turn to him and enquire mildly, 'You hungry?' There was a glint of light off his cheekbones, under his pale blue eyes; but his face was expressionless.

Pratley was startled by the other's friendliness.

'Yes, I am hungry. Why not?'

'You shouldn't be hungry.'

Pratley laughed nervously, waiting for the blow which he knew to be coming. Van Niekerk, who was tall, sallow and slightly pimpled, and a great admirer of Verster, laughed too. Verster had gone back to his food and was chewing silently.

Pratley had no strength. He could not keep silent, though he knew that his question would do him no good. 'Why shouldn't I be hungry? I've done a hard morning's work.'

'You call that work? Sticking your tongue up the old man's arse? A whole morning you eat his shit – and then you settle down to your lunch!' Verster turned to van Niekerk who was shaking with silent laughter and applause. 'There's an appetite for you!'

'That's no way to talk!' Pratley had half-risen from his chair; he showed his teeth and shook his fist at Verster. But the gesture was frantic, flapping, without force. 'That's how he always talks to me,' Pratley complained to van Niekerk, as though he were a sympathetic stranger who had never witnessed such a scene before. 'What kind of way is that to talk?'

'The right way,' van Niekerk said boldly, looking for support from Verster.

But Verster did not see the appeal. He had picked up a news-paper and was glancing at its headlines, and van Niekerk, who was not really a hard-hearted youth, regretted what he had said. 'Sit down, man,' he said. 'It's not the right way to talk to anyone. But you asked for it. You shouldn't have worried old Piet like that.'

Van Niekerk spoke earnestly. He always enjoyed playing the role of peacemaker. And Pratley, once the immediate crisis was over, was an easy man to make peace with. His fears so far outran his humiliations that he invariably felt he had escaped lightly, no matter what had happened to him. He sat down, lowered his head, and peevishly opened a sandwich to see what was inside it.

'Cheese!' he exclaimed. 'That's my wife for you. I've told her a thousand times my stomach can't take cheese.'

'Only shit.'

Pratley pretended he had not heard, and the men finished their meal in silence. A bell rang. One o'clock. Wearily, a little stiffly, they rose to go back to work. Verster folded the paper and put it on a shelf above the table. 'It's a funny thing,' he said. 'If Hitler had won that war, that old Jew-boy would have been finished. He'd have been cleaning my shoes. Eating my shit.' He threw back his head and laughed soundlessly. His cheekbones seemed to rise towards his eyes, concealing them. 'Well, it's a big world. There's room for all of us, isn't there?' Firmly, contemptuously, earning another laugh from van Niekerk, he pushed Pratley out of his way. 'You see what I mean? Plenty of room.'

10

When he came in Meyer looked around the living room, and saw with satisfaction that there were no changes: the Chesterfield suite, the biscuit-coloured carpet, the knick-knacks on the mantelpiece above the empty, tiled fireplace, the disregarded pictures of vague veld-scenes on the walls, were all as they had been before. Meyer sank into an armchair, and remained there, his walking-stick by his side, while a cup of tea was brought to him. He drank it eagerly, holding the cup away from the saucer. Only when the cup had been taken away from him, did he begin to talk about the business that had brought him to Johannesburg. There was a building here in Johannesburg – a block of shops and offices – that a 'certain party' was stuck with; his builders had gone bankrupt in the middle of the job, and as a result of the delay he wasn't getting in the rent that he'd by now planned to be drawing. But he needed the rent in order to pay off a short-term loan he'd taken out to finance the building, in addition to the bond that he'd got from an insurance company. So his proposition was that Meyer should come in and save the situation by becoming his partner. But Meyer's proposition was that the other fellow should get out altogether, if the insurance company was agreeable. Who needed him for a partner?

Benjamin stirred restlessly, as if Meyer's remark were a tactless one. But Meyer seemed to notice neither Benjamin's restiveness nor the possible tactlessness of what he had said. That was the one reason why he had come up, Meyer went on vigorously, but of course, as Benjamin knew, there was another reason as well. Then he fell silent unexpectedly, with a gesture of one plump, freckled hand. It was Benjamin's turn to talk.

Later the room was full of cigarette smoke from Meyer's Turkish cigarettes. Benjamin was standing impatiently at the window, Meyer was still sitting placidly in his chair. So many of their conversations had resulted in this same impatience and irritation on Benjamin's side, and on Meyer's a more obscure but resentful calm.

Finally, from the window, Benjamin lunged out, 'So – if you don't want to sell, will you buy from me?'

The idea had occurred to him before only as a fantasy, not to be spoken of. Yet it was the very risk, the attraction of his own fear, that made him go on, above an interruption from Meyer, 'Yes, I mean it. Let me go, if you don't want to go. I can find something else to do. I'm not afraid of starting again. Do you think I couldn't start again?' He struck one clenched fist against the open palm of his other hand. 'No wonder we die!' he exclaimed. 'From exhaustion alone we would die, without the wars, or the germs, or the motor cars in the street.'

'Benny, please,' his wife said. She had been sitting on the couch, throughout the conversation, and had hardly spoken before. Yet both men had been glad to have her there. They were afraid of what they might have said to one another had she not been present.

Meyer turned to her. 'And you too, want me to go?'

She shook her head, dismissing the question. 'I must want what Benjamin wants.'

'For once!' Benjamin said bitterly, turning his back to the room.

Meyer ignored the remark; it was none of his business. 'I came in,' he said to Benjamin, 'when your bank manager looked sideways at you if you wrote out a cheque for ten pounds. You remember that? I helped you, we became partners. Can you say that I've been a bad partner? Did I question your drawings, did I interfere with the way you ran things? Didn't I put up my own private guarantee for the business, that's lying there in the bank to this day? What would you do tomorrow if I withdrew the guarantee? What would the bank say to that?'

'There'd be no need for you to do it. That guarantee's never been called on, has it?'

'But why should I leave it there?'

'To help me.'

'When you send me away, I must still help you? Why?'

Benjamin leaned towards the window, closer to his own reflection. 'Because you're richer than I am,' he said, his voice hoarse with resentment. 'Because you're my brother.'

'I see. You can be business-like with me, but I must be sentimental with you?'

'There's nothing sentimental about my offer. Twelve years ago you came into the business, and you've drawn dividends ever since that first terrible year. And now I'm offering you five times what you brought in. It's a fair price. If we put the business on the market you couldn't get any better for your share.'

'Perhaps that is what we should do,' Meyer said, looking up to see the effect of his words.

Benjamin nodded, several times, swallowing with each nod. 'I've said I'm not frightened. You're a big man in Cape Town with your business and your buildings and your propositions here and your propositions there, and – as well – you have your brother under your thumb. Fine, fine for you! But not so fine for me. So let's finish it off. I've had enough.'

'Ach,' Meyer said. 'Why do you talk like this? What's got in to you, all of a sudden? For twelve years we've been managing; and suddenly you're burning, you're insulting me, looking for a fight, offering to sell up. Why? What has changed so much?'

Benjamin answered simply, 'Joel has come back.'

'And does he want to come into the business?'

'I want him to be able to.'

'I'm preventing that?'

'No, you're not preventing it,' Benjamin said impatiently. 'But I want the business to be attractive to him. I want it to be without complications, for him to take if he wants. I want to be able to show him something and say, "Here it is, if you want to come into it you can." I've got nothing else.'

Then Sarah said: 'And if he doesn't want it – and I'm sure he won't – then all the more, just for that reason, you want what you've got to look as big as possible, to be as impressive as you can make it. For the sake of your own pride.'

'So? Is there anything criminal in that? Must I be ashamed of what I've done? My father didn't have factories to offer when I was Joel's age. Or any other time. Joel can do what he likes. But let him have respect for the work I've done, the place I've made.'

'Have you spoke to Joel yet?' Meyer asked.

'No. There's lots of time. He still doesn't know where he is.'

Rachel came into the room as her mother said these words. She was followed by Adela Klein, a friend of hers, who had come to help her make arrangements for the party that evening. 'There's no time at all,' Rachel said. 'We're late already.' She crossed the room and kissed her uncle on the cheek. 'Hullo, Uncle Meyer, how are you?'

'Mustn't grumble, you know.'

Standing at the side of his chair, Rachel said, 'Adela, this is my Uncle Meyer.'

Meyer nodded amiably. But Benjamin's smile from the window was so much a grimace that Adela said, 'Rachel, we can do one of the other rooms.'

'No, this one,' Rachel insisted. She was used to getting her own way.

Adela smiled apologetically, with an embarrassed duck of her head. Her features were too large, her fair hair was too long, her legs were too plump, her stockinged legs clung together too closely under a too-tight skirt. But to the older people the soft crowdedness of her flesh was attractive, a mark of youth and good health.

'You know,' Benjamin said, explaining her to Meyer, 'Ezreal Klein, of Kosiwear.'

'Ah.' Meyer was satisfied with the explanation. 'Like her mother,' he added, with another look at the smiling, awkward girl.

'Come,' Benjamin said, 'we can go and sit outside. I know Rachel won't give us any peace until we do.'

'That's my old Dad!'

Benjamin was both proud and ashamed that his daughter should speak so disrespectfully to him. Heavily, Meyer got to his feet. 'You give us no choice. We must make way for the youngsters.'

'It's the law of life,' Rachel agreed cheerfully.

The two brothers went on to the stoep of the house, Sarah went into the kitchen. Benjamin and Meyer did not continue speaking about the subject they had been busy with before; instead, they talked of Ezreal Klein and other common acquaintances, of business in general, of what was happening in Palestine. Then they listened to the news and the stock exchange prices on the little radio Benjamin brought from his bedroom. Between the two of them there was often hostility; but there was never any sense of distance.

11

All the way from the main road to the mine-dump and the grove of bluegum trees at the bottom of the street, there were identical single-storied, detached little houses, each with its stoep and garden in front, its iron roof above, and a narrow passageway on both sides leading to the backyard. Even in the half-light, when Pamela came home from work, the street looked shabby: there were too many children and animals about, too much dust in the air, too few flowers and trees in the gardens. On one corner light blazed out of the door of a Greek shop which Pamela entered to buy a loaf of bread. It was a cheerless, cement-floored place, smelling of apples, mangoes, and the sweet drip of a cool drink machine; the one bulb overhead was without a shade, and in its glare the elderly, white-haired man behind the counter looked almost like a cadaver, with the shadow of his brow lying heavily on his cheeks, his eye-sockets quite without light. But his lips moved in a smile when he saw Pamela, and he leaned over the counter to greet her, looking above the round black head and little clenched fist of a piccanin who, on Pamela's side of the counter, was straining upwards on the toes of his bare feet.

'So, Pamela,' the shopkeeper said, 'another day finished for you?'

'Thank goodness for that. A small wholemeal, please, Mr Stavros.'

Mr Stavros bent slowly, and brought out of a bin a loaf of bread. He wrapped it in a piece of newspaper from a pile of ready-torn sheets on the counter. He was reluctant to let Pamela go, and held on to the loaf of bread instead of handing it to her. 'How's your mother?' he asked.

'Same us usual, you know.'

'I feel sorry for your mother,' Mr Stavros said, without tact but with great feeling. 'I know what it's like when your health starts to go. Doctors, pills, pains, one thing after another. But at least she hasn't got a business to look after.'

'Perhaps she'd be better off if she did have one. It would take her mind off things a little,' Pamela said wistfully.

'You mean she's alone too much? Too much time to think? That can also be a bad thing. It's the one bad thing I've never suffered from.' Mr Stavros smiled at his own self-pity, and Pamela stretched out her hand and took the bread from him.

'I must go,' she said. 'Besides, you've got another customer.'

'That rubbish?' Mr Stavros looked at the piccanin. 'Penny-lines, penny-lines, how can I make a living out of penny-lines?'

'Joybar,' the piccanin said, jumping up in an attempt to meet Mr Stavros's eye.

'See, joybars, two for a penny. How can I make a living?'

'One joybar, baas. Please baas, only one.' A halfpenny rolled across the counter, and Mr Stavros slapped it down angrily, as though it were an insect.

'You see what I mean!' he exclaimed.

Pamela fumbled in her purse and produced another halfpenny. 'Make it two joybars, Mr Stavros.'

The piccanin did not understand why he was given two joybars instead of the one he had asked for. He just clutched at them both with a dirty hand, looked from Pamela to Mr Stavros, and fled out of the shop.

'Not even a thank you,' Mr Stavros grumbled as Pamela left the shop.

With the loaf of bread tucked under her arm she went on down the street. She did not have far to go. Soon she turned through a metal gate, and walked up the little path to the stoep, where a light burned to welcome her. She opened the door and stepped into a narrow hall; through an arch, the hall led directly into the living room. The furniture of the room was cheap, pale and so heavily varnished that the grain of the wood seemed to lie well beneath each surface, as if under a depth of water. On the large radio cabinet there was a group of leather-framed pictures: a wedding photo of Mr and Mrs Curtis; one of Pamela as a baby: and one of her as a girl of thirteen, her head in profile and her chin tucked shyly into her thin shoulder. The only other decoration in the room was a frieze of sailing ships and seagulls, coloured in the lurid reds and blues of the 'twenties, running right round the walls, where the beige wallpaper gave way to whitewashed plaster. Net curtains hung across the window; and a cloth lightshade, frilled and flounced like a petticoat, was suspended from the middle of the ceiling.

Mrs Curtis had been sitting in the armchair next to the radio; she got up to greet Pamela, but did not turn down the volume of noise coming from the machine. Pamela kissed her on the cheek, lightly, dutifully. The two women were of a height; in comparison with her mother's faded complexion Pamela's was so full of colour that she might almost have been blushing, under her thick dark hair. Their voices were alike, the mother's a little higher and sweeter than her daughter's. Mrs Curtis wore no make-up at all; on her upper lip were a number of small, deep lines which came together when she was not speaking, and which gave her face an expression of fatigue and discontent.

'Is Miss Baker back?' Pamela asked. Miss Baker was a spinster schoolteacher, their lodger.

'She's been back and she's gone out again. There's something on at the school tonight, for the parents.'

'She must be cross about that.'

'I didn't ask her.'

Pamela crossed the room to the radio and turned it down, then she went into the kitchen and put the loaf of bread on the table there. A slatternly African girl stood over the stove, waiting for a pot to boil.

'What's for supper, Maggie?'

'Only eggs, madam.'

'Well, I've brought the bread.'

'Yes, madam.'

Pamela and her mother ate their meal of boiled eggs and brown bread and butter in the kitchen. They took their coffee with them into the living room. While they were drinking it Mrs Curtis said, 'I've made up my mind what we should do tonight.' For the first time since Pamela had come in her manner was really animated. 'They're showing a good film at the Gaiety; I looked it up in the paper.' She smiled at Pamela, guilelessly. 'I haven't been out all day.'

'Mom –'

'I know you're tired now, but you have a little rest, and then we'll go. You'll be glad when we're there. I thought of it as soon as I saw what was showing: I said, "Well, Pammie and me will make the effort tonight." '

'Mom, I can't, you know that. I'm going out to the Glickman's party tonight. It's all arranged, I told you about it.'

The brightness and expectancy faded from Mrs Curtis's face, the lines about her lips deepened as they drew together. 'Pamela, is it tonight you're going there?'

'Of course it's tonight. I told you it was.'

'I thought it was tomorrow, Pamela.'

Had she really? It was difficult for Pamela to believe. This was not the first time that Mrs Curtis had planned an outing for the two of them on an evening when Pamela had already arranged to go out.

'Oh, mom,' Pamela said, going over to her mother. She went down on her knees and put her head on Mrs Curtis's lap. 'We'll go out tomorrow night. The same film will be showing. I promise you.' She closed her eyes; in an instant she seemed to doze off. The darkness was barred with faint stripes of silver, comforting in their meaninglessness. She was curiously aware of her own cheekbones, under her closed eyelids; their weight, their insensience, the way they seemed to be thrust forward, pushing through the skin. She yawned widely, and her yawn woke her up, with streaming eyes, to the light of the room, and her uncomfortable position on the floor. 'I must go and change,' she said; but she remained where she was, feeling too lazy to get up.

When she went to her room, Mrs Curtis moved to the chair next to the radio. She could sit there for hours, listening to anything – talks, music of all kinds, plays, documentary programmes. Pamela heard the noise of the radio in her room. It followed her there like a reproach. She was conscious of it in the excitement of dressing, in the curiosity with which she thought of spending the evening in her employer's house. She knew that no one else from the office had been invited to the party, and was flattered at having been singled out especially. Drawing on her stockings, brushing her hair, putting lipstick on her mouth, she wished vaguely that she was taller and less shy; that she had more of a natural wave in her hair; that Miss Baker hadn't gone out and could have kept her mother company; that her father was still alive.

His photograph was on her dressing table, but Pamela seldom really looked at it: the days when she had indulged herself by kissing it and speaking to it, or by imagining it speaking to her, were long since over. Now she thought of her father for the most part as nothing but an absence; as the reason why the emptiness and loneliness of her mother's life rested so heavily upon herself.

12

Jacobus sat squashed in his desk, a battered copy of one of the Beacon Readers in his hand, and stared at the picture of Rover the Dog. There was one unshaded light in the room, and the blackboard was pitted with holes; the corrugated iron walls were decorated with dance-band announcements, Wayside pulpit posters, and a few political slogans. The thin, energetic Jewish girl who was taking the class wrote on the board, 'See me, mother. I can see you,' and elocuted the words with great care. Jacobus painfully transcribed them into his tickey exercise book. The class was all male, and every round black head was lowered to its work – but for one which wore an inane *dagga*-smoker's smile directed at the ceiling of buckled plasterboard, and another which was slumped forward in heavy sleep. There was the unmistakable rich smell of sweat in the room, and, more faintly, the smell of the mealies that some members of the class had eaten on their way to the school. The girl lit a cigarette and wrote, 'I see Rover. Rover sees me.'

Then, next door, the Merry Blackbirds struck up; they were rehearsing for the 'All-Star Jitterbug Nite', about which Jacobus and the others had been given leaflets as they came in for class. There was a saxophonist, a pianist, a drummer and a guitarist. The iron walls magnified the noise intolerably. Each chord seemed to crash down and then vibrate lingeringly. 'Oh God, those people!' the girl exclaimed, and went outside to plead with them to be silent. There she was joined by three other teachers of the three other classes, Bertie Preiss among them.

The leader of the Merry Blackbirds, a plump, very black, almost parsonical gentleman, treated them with a ceremonious, contemptuous politeness. 'I have reserved this room for my own purposes,' he explained, making a gesture of regret with one hand and bringing his cigarette to his lips with the other. Smoke seemed to envelop him for a moment; he emerged from it, talking strongly – 'If my purposes and your purposes are at cross-purposes, I regret it very much, but I can't help you.' The teachers retired and consulted together. The leader of the Merry Blackbirds called out to them, 'Silent reading is possible. But silent playing …' He shook his head at his own joke, then roared suddenly at it. The other members of his band nursed their instruments apprehensively, having greater respect than their leader for the complaining whites. But the leader knew that his position was a strong one. There were only four of these whites among a sea of Africans, within and around the Bantu Athletic Grounds; and in any case these whites were liberals, radicals, leftists, sentimentalist; of some kind – or they wouldn't have been there at all – and thus easy to bully.

Eventually, magnanimously, the leader of the Merry Blackbirds removed his band to the veranda of the pavilion, where the night school was held, and the classes were able to continue for the few minutes that remained. The teachers left together, in the car owned by the girl who taught Jacobus.

Though none of the four in the car was able to admit it, they all felt anxious, when they emerged from the safety of the classrooms into the dark, wide haphazard confusion of the Athletic Grounds and the waste spaces of sand around it, where, every evening, many hundreds of workers from the factories and 'bachelor hostels' nearby, having nothing else to do, gathered to mill about in a cloud of noise and dust.

Jacobus spent a few minutes wandering around the area that his teachers had crossed so anxiously in their car. He bought some food at a stall; he listened to a pedlar selling various kinds of *muti* and patent medicines, and to a hoarse-voiced religious enthusiast who called on him to join the forthcoming march of all true black Christians to Abyssinia; he bought a drink from a runner of illicit booze. He knew he had to be watchful all the time: there were bands of thugs who battled for the control of the area; there were *dagga-* or *skokiaan*-crazed individuals who were always ready to start a fight; there were the armed police raids that took place without warning, when scores of men were dragged away each time for not having their papers in order. But the flares of light from the stalls, the urgent voices he heard, the blasts of music from the pavilion, the trampled sand underfoot, the random encounters with bodies as cheaply dressed as his own, the distant view of the neon signs on the tall buildings away to the north – Jacobus was still new enough to the city to hunger for it all, to wonder at it, to feel himself enriched by it.

Then he ran to the centre of town, and caught one of the 'non-white' trams to Observatory. He too had to be at the Glickman's for the party that evening. When Benjamin had brought him from the factory to do some work in the garden, earlier in the week, he had heard about the party from Annie, and had offered to help her in the kitchen. She had agreed with an alacrity that Jacobus, whose wife and children were in distant Basutoland, flattered himself was not just due to her conviction that the houseboy was lazy and incompetent.

13

In the living room the chairs and tables were already pushed aside to make space for dancing; in the dining room a table was laden with chicken and slices of cold beef, with salads, rolls, pickles, and bowls of fruit salad; the sideboard was burdened with bottles of beer, wine and soft drinks. But the family ate hurriedly, in the breakfast room, off scraps. 'Cold!' Benjamin complained, stirring the food on his plate. 'And nobody sitting down. Sit down, we can't eat like wild animals.'

Meyer Glickman, who was already seated, ate steadily; Sarah and David sat down; Rachel said she couldn't eat a thing; Joel stood against the wall with a plate in his hand, as though the party had already begun. 'Sit!' Benjamin commanded him.

'Take it easy, dad.'

Sarah said to him, 'You're more excited than anyone else.'

'Excited? Me? Is the King of England coming tonight? General Smuts? You think all I have to worry about is a children's party?' But it was true that he was shy of his children's friends, and that he was unable to admit his shyness, even to himself. So in response to Sarah's remark he insulted her about the dress she had chosen to wear and the inadequacy of the arrangements she had made. Rachel cried, and then Benjamin felt penitent; though not towards his wife.

By the time the party began he was in a more cheerful mood, partly because he, Joel and Meyer had had a couple of whiskies apiece beforehand. Benjamin and Sarah welcomed the young guests formally, and these guests, who were not nearly as easy in their manners as they appeared to be to Benjamin, shook hands and then went into the next room. There were some friends and relatives of the parents too, who came; and the party split immediately into two groups. The old people sat together in the breakfast room, and the younger guests filled the front of the house, dancing in the living room and on the stoep, and eating in the dining room. The two house servants were in attendance, and so was Jacobus, who had arrived in good time; all three of them were dressed in starched whites, and they were kept busy passing around the trays of drink and food. Not much hard liquor had been provided for the young people, but several of them managed to get satisfactorily drunk on beer or wine. The girls, generally, stuck to orange squash or Coca Cola.

Emboldened by the beer he had drunk, Bertie Preiss danced with Rachel; he drew her as close to him as he dared to, feeling the warmth of her body against his. Under his fingers was the stiffness of the row of hidden hooks that held her dress together. He felt he had never before touched anything that hinted at so much. He stared solemnly at her, with immense meaning. Rachel was embarrassed by his stare, yet moved by it, too; she was in a mood to be easily moved that evening, and the sight of Joel in his uniform (he was wearing it at her insistence) had already once brought tears to her eyes. But after dancing with him for some minutes, she told Bertie that she had to leave him; she had so much to look after, she said, being the hostess.

'I'll wait for you.'

'You might have to wait for a long time. Dance with someone else.'

'I don't want to dance with anyone else.'

'But I do.'

The words were out of her mouth before she knew what she was saying. Immediately, she felt she had been cruel, and was ashamed of herself; she caught at his arm as he turned away. 'Bertie, I just meant that I have to dance with lots of people, just as I have to serve them with drinks and food and everything.'

He stood with his head turned to one side, his hands on his hip. Seeing how hurt he was, Rachel felt her power, within her guilt. She wanted to say, 'I'll dance with you later, as soon as I can,' but because she had the power to say them, the words did not come out. She said merely, 'Bertie, don't look like that.'

'I can't help the way I look.'

Rachel laughed, 'None of us can.'

'No.'

He walked away; Rachel watched him go, before running through into the kitchen to see how things were going there. Her taffeta dress was stiff around her, girdling her, making her feel impregnable.

In the next room Adela Klein came forward eagerly, as soon as Bertie entered it; she met him just a pace or two from the door. 'Bertie, how are you?' she asked in a rush, smiling, leaning towards him.

'Hullo, Adela,' Bertie answered sombrely.

The smile left Adela's lips and was replaced by an expression of concern; her body slowly straightened. 'It's terrible, isn't it?' she said in a tone as doleful as his own.

'What?' Preiss asked, surprised,

'The way Smuts answered the NRC ultimatum. He really doesn't believe the Africans are human at all! And he's the great liberal world statesman!'

'Yes,' Preiss agreed, still much surprised, but flattered that his political interests should be so well known to this girl, whom he had spoken to only a few times before. 'He's a kind of walking embodiment of the bankruptcy of liberalism.'

He was momentarily anxious lest his phrase should seem as high-falutin to the girl as it had sounded in his own ears. But she shook her head in delight at what he had said, so that her hair flew about her cheeks. 'Exactly!' she said. 'That describes it perfectly.' And she waited for him to ask her to dance.

When Rachel came back into the hall, she saw, among some guests she had already greeted, a girl whom she did not recognize. The girl was standing by herself, with her coat on; she obviously had just come in and did not know what to do. Then Rachel recognized her as Pamela Curtis. Remembering what her father had said, Rachel welcomed her with a special effusiveness, and took her into one of the bedrooms to put her coat down. Pamela was wearing a white sleeveless cotton dress, with a pattern of violet irises printed over it. Her lipstick was dark, to go with the dress. When they came out of the bedroom Rachel brought her a cool drink, and stood talking busily to her in the middle of the room. Pamela, flushing slightly, wore an uncertain smile and crumpled her handkerchief between her fingers. 'I must go and say hullo to your father and mother,' she said; but Rachel did not respond, being reluctant to take Pamela, one of the very few Gentiles at the party, into the breakfast room, where so many Yiddish-speaking, sharp-eyed, cigarette-smoking elderly and middle-aged Jews were gathered. Yet Rachel made no effort to introduce Pamela to any of the other guests either: resenting having to save Pamela from one discomfort, she was forcing another upon her.

Eventually, when Joel passed by, Rachel called him. 'Joel, come here, come and meet Pamela.'

'We have met,' Joel said, as he came up. 'We met at the office the other day. How are you?'

'Fine,' Pamela said.

'Have you just come?'

'About five minutes ago.'

'Are you having a nice time?'

'Very,' Pamela said eagerly. This was so plainly not true that Joel felt sorry for her.

'From now on you're going to have an even nicer time. Come and meet some people. Come and dance.'

14

Gratefully, Pamela smiled at Joel, and they went together into the living room, the most crowded of the rooms. Several couples in it were jiving industriously, to the loud music of the gramophone, a few others were dancing conventionally, and others again were merely watching. As they went in Pamela glanced sideways at Joel: she saw him as a swarthy, thickset young man, with features too heavy and eyes too small to be handsome. But his eyes were clear and gentle, and his face expressed frankly what he was feeling – which at the moment was shyness mixed with anxiety to be a good host. His hair was close-cropped, straight and black; he had had it cut just the day before, and a distinct, pale line ran along his temple, above his ear, and down the side of his neck, where the hair that had been cut off had protected his skin from the sun. The nakedness of this line made him look like a schoolboy; and the bulk and clumsiness of his uniform added nothing to his age. He looked even younger than she did, Pamela felt.

'I can't do that kind of stuff,' Joel said pointing at the jiving couples, and looking doubtfully at her.

Pamela confidently stretched out her arms towards him. 'Nor can I. It doesn't matter.'

'No,' he said, 'it doesn't matter,' and they laughed in surprise at their agreement, as though a great difficulty between them had been removed. While they fox-trotted sedately around the room, they made conversation about the weather and her work; when they were silent her tongue came out and moistened her lower lip with a quick, nervous gesture. Each time, her lip gleamed again. With a gentle pressure, Joel tried to bring her body closer to his. He did not know whether or not she noticed what he was trying to do; she did not respond to it, anyway, and held herself upright, away from him. She looked about her at the other couples, and Joel said, 'Who do you want to meet? I'll introduce you to everyone, if you like.'

'No – I'm sorry –' she laughed, catching her breath, apologizing for not giving him all her attention.

'Oh yes!' Joel insisted, partly for the sake of amusing himself, partly to punish her for not dancing more closely to him. When the record ended, he announced loudly, before the next one could drop, 'Pay attention everyone. I want you to meet Miss Pamela Curtis. There she is,' he cried, retreating from Pamela and pointing to her; she stood alone in the middle of the room, shrinking, bowing her head, laughing with embarrassment. 'Pamela Curtis!' He shouted the name out, like a showman introducing a vaudeville turn, and the others in the room responded by clapping and smiling, though they wondered what had provoked him to tease the girl in this way. He did not know himself. He went back to her, when the music came on again, and took her in his arms to begin dancing. They danced only a few paces when he saw that there were tears in her eyes, brought on by her embarrassment and confusion.

'I'm sorry,' he said. 'That was a stupid thing to do.'

'Yes,' she replied, more calmly than he had expected. 'It was.'

Joel had no reply to make. But when he tried to draw her closer to him, her body responded this time to the pressure. The strangeness of what they were doing occurred to Joel, as though he had never danced with anyone before in his life: that they should be moving, her soft breast against his, her legs against his, two fully-clothed conversing strangers. He looked down at her, and saw with a tenderness that surprised him, how her lips curved, and how the fullness of her cheeks overhung them slightly.

'Don't look so serious,' Pamela said, breaking into his thoughts.

'Why not?' Joel asked, a little taken aback. 'Why shouldn't I look serious? I was thinking of you,' he said, letting the half-truth go.

'Am I such a serious matter?'

'You're going to be, for somebody.'

Her eyes shone with pleasure at his answer. 'So will you.'

They had stopped dancing abruptly. Joel felt himself forced to the brink of a declaration it was absurd for him to make, so soon, out of nothing. 'But not for each other?' he asked, stumbling slightly over the words.

She shook her head lightly. 'No, not for each other.'

It was the answer he had wanted her to make: any other would have been impossible. But now it had been made he wanted to deny it. 'You think there's anyone here I could become involved with? Well, you're wrong.' Joel looked around the room, filled with Rachel's friends; embryo doctors and fledgling lawyers and their future wives. 'You know what all these girls think about all the time?' he said maliciously. 'Just one thing – their own sex. Every one of them carries it about with her like a full glass of water –' he cupped his hands, curving his shoulders inwards – 'trying not to spill a drop, not one single drop, it's so precious, such a treasure they're guarding.'

The moment he had finished it struck him that the self-conscious, self-admiring, carefully protected sexuality he had spoken of was associated in his mind with the fact that all the girls in the rooms were Jewish. And it seemed to him disloyal, unchivalrous, to have described them like that to the only non-Jewish girl in the room. 'I must find you another partner,' he said suddenly. 'You must be getting bored with me.'

Pamela frowned at his tone, puzzled to know why he had changed it so roughly. They both felt he had said too much or too little to her. They went on dancing, but the amity between them was broken; now they were simply strangers, their closeness to each other was a mere physical constriction. Joel caught sight of a man standing alone whom he knew better than some of the others in the room, and steered Pamela in his direction. 'Pamela – Michael,' he said quickly, and asked them both if they wanted anything to drink; then retreated, leaving the two of them together. They were in a group with two or three others when he returned, carrying a glass of beer and an orange squash. The man, Ginsberg, a former bomber pilot, and at present a first-year medical student, was big, plump, heavily moustached, and suspicious of Joel's reasons for having introduced him off-handedly to the girl. He accepted the glass from Joel with a murmur of thanks, as Pamela did; he went on speaking, to the others in the group rather than to Pamela or Joel, about his 'Zoo paper' and his 'Bot paper'. Joel didn't know what he was talking about until a sinuous girl with long brown hair curling and cascading down to her bare shoulders, leaned forward and said, 'Please, please, please don't talk to me about exams.' But a moment later she asked Pamela 'How did yours go?'

Pamela was put out by the question. 'I didn't have exams,' she said awkwardly.

'Lucky girl! Lucky girl!' the others in the group said. But the girl with the long hair sensed that Pamela did not feel herself to be so lucky in her reply. She asked, with a twist of her neck that swung her locket into the exposed hollow between her little, silk-swathed breasts, 'Aren't you at Wits? What do you do?'

'I type. That's all,' Pamela said. 'I type for Mr Glickman.'

'Oh,' they all said, placing her at last. They turned to one another and continued talking about their exams; the long-haired girl was soon in the middle of a description of how her mind had gone 'absolutely blank, like a wall', when she had been confronted by her Psycho One paper. Joel and Pamela found themselves standing together again.

'I didn't write any exams either,' Joel said.

Pamela nodded and smiled gratefully, sipping at her drink. While he had been out of the room Joel had been unable to remember what she looked like, he stared at her now, as if to memorize her features. She was looking a little fatigued, he thought; again he found the slight downward droop of her lips disturbing.

The long-haired girl turned with a laugh, bringing up her hand to sweep back some of her curls. Pamela started, flinching, and the movement brought the glass in her hand against the girl's elbow. The contents of the glass poured over the front of Joel's tunic, staining the dark green khaki, splashing his shoes and trouser-legs. Everybody sprang back with a cry and a laugh, except for Pamela who remained rigid, her eyes wide open, the glass in her hand still steeply tilted.

The others began brushing themselves down, and a girl went off to get a cloth; but Joel came forward and took the glass out of Pamela's hand. He was smiling strangely. She did not seem to see him, though she stared straight ahead, at the stain on his tunic. 'It's all right,' Joel said, groping back with one hand, to find a place for the glass on the table. He did not look at what he was doing. He let the glass go, too close to the edge, and it fell from the table on to the carpet; he kicked it away with one foot. It slithered, then rolled, but did not break. 'All right,' he said once more, not knowing what he was saying. Yet he felt his words and actions to be filled with meaning and reassurance.

'I didn't want –' Pamela said, her mouth opening, her lips still stiff.

'You've spilt the lot – it doesn't matter,' Joel said, taking her hand in his. A grimace crossed her features, and he realized that he was hurting her, he was holding her hand so tightly. Their eyes met. Pamela's expression relaxed, became calm, almost sleepy. She smiled, as if in recognition; and then Joel found himself pulled away from her, and someone brushing down the front of his tunic.

Pamela left the room. Joel watched her until the door closed behind her.

15

Later in the evening, while some guests still jived in one room, others played 'Oranges and Lemons', and 'Musical Bumps', they danced 'Looby-loo'. Whose idea it had been to start these nursery games, no one could remember, but those who were playing threw themselves energetically, half-drunkenly, into them, laughing at what they were doing, arguing fiercely when anyone was disqualified, clapping their hands to the rhythm of the songs they were singing.

'Prizes!' someone shouted; and Rachel ran out of the room. She reappeared a few minutes later with a big sheet of paper on which had been drawn in ink a crude picture of a donkey; she also had some strips of material and a box of drawing pins. 'Pin the tail on,' Rachel cried, waving the strips in the air. Soon blindfolded boys and girls were staggering around, shrieking, sticking pins into one another, collapsing into one another's arms. 'Arthur wins!' Rachel shouted, when she thought the game had gone on for long enough.

'He peeped! He cheated! I saw him looking!'

'Nonsense.' Rachel was quite firm. A fair long-nosed youth stood blinking his blue eyes foolishly in the light, the handkerchief with which he had been blindfolded around his neck like a scarf.

'Prize-giving now,' Rachel announced. 'Come on everybody, stand around, give Arthur a big hand.' She produced, from behind her back, a small roll of cloth, which Arthur held up so that the others could see what it was. It was a scarlet armband, with a white circle in the middle of it; in the middle of the white circle was a black swastika. 'The genuine horrible thing,' Rachel cried. 'From the battlefields of Italy.'

Joel, who had just come into the room, was not the only one to be taken aback to see what Rachel was displaying. The others crowded around to have a closer look at it. To show it off better Arthur slipped it on his arm. 'Heil Hitler!' he yelled.

Joel tore it roughly off his arm. 'Are you crazy?' he said to Rachel, crumpling the cloth in his fist.

'Hey,' Arthur called out, 'throw das mann into Camp Seventy-five B. *Raus, donner und blitzen, danke schön!*'

Rachel's face burned with anger. Joel's was pale under the brown of his skin. 'I thought you'd have more sense,' he muttered, and walked out of the room, stuffing the armband into the pocket of his trousers. He left an embarrassed silence behind him. Rachel was the first to recover.

'On with the dance!' She ran into the next room and turned the radiogram to full volume. Soon people were dancing and talking again in both rooms. Rachel among them. But she imagined, while she danced, that everyone was gossiping about the scene.

When she judged that her absence wouldn't be noticed, she went quietly out of the room and made her way down the passage, into the bathroom. There she sat on the edge of the bath and cried. Why couldn't Joel have understood that she'd wanted to show people one of his souvenirs because she was so proud of him? That was the only reason. Why was he so stupid, so unfair to her? And why hadn't Jonathan come? He knew how much she had wanted him to be there.

She had told herself that he would come at nine, at ten, at eleven. It was now a quarter to twelve, and there was still no sign of him.

16

Joel had gone out through the front door, after his altercation with Rachel. He stood on the stoep, with the open door behind him. Pamela hesitated at the door, and then came forward.

'Did you see what happened inside?'

'Yes.'

'Do you think I was right?'

'I don't know.' Then she answered him directly. 'Yes, if it's what you wanted to do.'

'It seems priggish now. Ach, I suppose I was just fed up with the whole party, and wanted to let Rachel know it.'

They stood side by side under the light, looking across the dark garden and the lamps in the street.

'Let's go away,' Joel said suddenly. 'I've had enough of this. I'll take my father's car and we'll go somewhere else.'

'No, I couldn't. It wouldn't be right.'

'Why not?'

'It would look so bad.'

'So bad? Why?' Then Joel understood. 'Well –' he said. He wondered if she would have the courage to give her reason explicitly. In the glance they exchanged, he saw that she was wondering if he had the same courage. He smiled, and she smiled too. They had the courage, both of them, for what it was worth.

'Because I'm the boss's son?'

'And I'm the boss's typist. And this is the first time I've ever been in the boss's house. And it wouldn't do for me to go off into the darkness with the boss's son.'

'It makes me look bad, too,' Joel said. 'For suggesting it to you. As if I was trying to take advantage of your position.'

Pamela laughed; Joel saw her white teeth, dark lips, the strained frail tendons of her neck. 'Victim of a rich man's game,' she sang softly.

Amused by his own imaginings, Joel tried to picture to himself the reaction his parents would have if he were to have an affair with this girl. He saw his father's round-eyed, incredulous anger, his mother's discreet, devious encouragement. He said aloud, 'You're going much too fast. All I suggested was that we get away from this party and go somewhere else – harmlessly, innocently. Besides,' he added, 'I'm not rich.'

'By my standards you are.'

'What are your standards?' He was genuinely curious.

'Booysens,' Pamela answered dryly, naming the suburb in which she lived. Then, because she saw Joel did not treat her answer as a joke, she went on, 'My mother's on a pension from the War Fund, and I work as a typist. The house is ours, at least. We paid off the last bit of the mortage with my father's insurance. Those, sir, are my standards,' she ended with a duck of her head.

'Are you satisfied with them?'

'No. Are you with yours?'

'At the moment – after Helwan Transit Camp, in Egypt – thanks very much, I certainly am.' They were silent for a moment. Joel said, 'God, I hate the thought of going back to camp, even if it is just for a few weeks, to wait around for my demob papers. You know, when I think about it now – now that it's just about over – I don't know how I ever put up with any of it. I suppose it's always like that: you just go on from day to day, and because you're just going on you don't realize what you're doing, or what's being done to you. But when you're finished, when you see it behind you –' He shook his head. 'Never again.'

'You hope.'

'What? The army – ?'

'No, I mean, maybe it isn't just the army that's like that.'

'You're a cheerful girl!'

She ignored his heavy irony. 'What are you going to do when you've been demobbed?'

'I'm going to university,' Joel said, speaking firmly only because he wanted to appear firm to her. He was all the more surprised, therefore, to find that his decision seemed to have been made, now that he had announced it.

'What are you going to do there?'

'Probably a B.A. And then I'll see. Law, perhaps.'

Presently he asked her, 'How are you going to get home?'

'I don't know. I suppose someone will give me a lift.'

'I'm going to give you a lift. And you're going home right now. That solves all our problems. It's a perfectly respectable reason for going off with me. I promise you, I won't lead you astray.'

'Perhaps I'll lead you astray.'

'I'll take the risk.'

She hesitated still. 'If you're sure it would be all right –'

'Of course.'

'Then I'll go and say goodbye to your sister.'

Joel watched her go. Her shoulders were slender and she held them straight. He imagined himself putting his hands on the small of her back, just above the movement and width of her hips. When she turned and came back to him he felt guilty, as though she had guessed what he had been thinking of.

'What must I say if they ask me who's taking me home?'

'Tell them I'm taking you home.'

Again Pamela left him, and this time Joel did not turn to look after her. But she did not come back as soon as he had expected; so eventually he followed her into the noisy, lit-up house. He found her standing by herself in the living room, watching some of the dancing couples.

'What's happened? I thought you were coming.'

'I can't find your sister.'

Just then Joel caught sight of his mother. 'She'll do,' he said, pointing at her. 'Mom,' he called out, above the noise in the room.

Sarah came over, with a plate in her hand. 'What is it?'

'Pamela's got to go. She wanted to say goodbye to Rachel, so I said that it would be all right if she said goodbye to you instead.'

'Of course. I'll give Rachel the message. Have you got someone to take you home?'

Joel said, 'Yes, me.'

'Oh, good,' Sarah said, as if it were the most natural thing in the world that Joel should take her home. 'I'm glad you came, Pamela, and I hope you enjoyed yourself.'

'I did. Thank you very much. And please say thank you to Rachel, and to Mr Glickman too.'

'There's nothing to thank us for, my dear.' On an impulse Sarah thrust forward the plate she was carrying. There was one sardine roll on it. 'Won't you have this?'

'Yes, I will.'

Joel had expected her to refuse the sudden, silly offer of food; he found he was glad she hadn't. Sarah wandered off in the direction of the door, still carrying the empty plate.

'Your mother's very nice,' Pamela said, as she bit into the sardine roll.

'So are you,' Joel replied, without flirtatiousness, almost off-handedly, his eyes still following his mother's vague course across the room. A minute later Pamela had collected her coat, and she and Joel were walking down the garden path, towards the car parked outside.

17

In the breakfast room, Sarah's brother, Samuel, was talking loudly; most of the people in the room had their heads turned towards him. Benjamin, however, sat apart, making conversation with a large, black-haired, bejewelled, bespectacled woman, and her inconspicuous husband. Benjamin spoke slowly, for it was difficult to talk to Mr and Mrs Ritstein (in order to show everyone that he wasn't interested in what Samuel Talmon was saying), and at the same time to listen to what Samuel was saying.

Samuel was as slight and as dry as a twig; the sleeves of his cream-coloured, soiled linen jacket hung loose on his arms, his wrinkled neck seemed to fit with inches to spare inside his collar. The lines around his mouth were so deeply etched into his hard red skin, his cheeks were so drawn, his nose was so prominent, his forehead was so high, bare and exposed, that his face seemed to have become what it was as a result of attrition rather than growth. One might have thought him an outdoor man – a farmer, a sportsman, a mountaineer – whom the sun and wind had weathered; but he was too tense, too quick, too eager to talk to be anything but urban, Jewish and unsuccessful. His voice was loud; his gestures were emphatic; his eyes shone brightly under the small black tufts of his eyebrows. He laughed often, with an open mouth, showing tobacco-stained teeth, and when he laughed he brought his hands together in his lap, as though catching some thing that had just been thrown to him. He called his audience 'My good people' and 'My dears' and 'Jews, Jews', and to almost everything they said he replied, 'Of course, you're quite correct, a hundred per cent, but that isn't the point.'

What was the point? As always with Samuel, there were many points, and most of them were disagreeable to the people to whom he was presenting them. His audience might have been offended by his points, had Samuel not laughed so often and so loudly, and called them 'My good people'; and if they had not known him to be not just a great talker anyway, but also, most mollifying of all, a failure. He was an unsuccessful lawyer, an unsuccessful business man, he had been an unsuccessful soldier in the first year of the war, so long ago now, when as a foolish volunteer of forty he had had a nervous breakdown in his first training camp and had been hastily invalided out of the service. He was a failure as a husband (his wife had run away with an RAF man during the war); he was a failure, it was agreed, as a father (his daughter was training to be a hairdresser, his son sold second-hand cars and talked of being an actor). No wonder, his audience felt, he saw everything upside-down, and tried so hard to persuade others to do the same.

'In Palestine the Jews are putting their feet in a trap, their heads in a lion's mouth. The settlement of the Jews in Palestine is a disaster, an unmitigated disaster' – that was an example of the kind of point he offered to the people listening to him. Or, 'There'll be peace in South Africa only when the Afrikaners get right on top and stay on top – on top of the Jews, on top of the English, on top of the blacks. Then the country will settle down and make progress.' Perennially hard up, living in a poky flat on top of a Greek shop in Jeppe, he told the gathering of middle-class well-to-do Jews in the Glickman's breakfast room, 'My dears, you are bankrupt, finished, there's no life left in you. You have no future at all.'

They had no future, he explained, because they were nationalists, reasonable people, who calculated profits and losses and tried to maximize profits and minimize losses as much as possible, in every sphere of activity – in their businesses and their families, their politics and their personal relationships.

'In other words, my good people, I'll surprise you all,' Samuel said, with an excited smile on his face and a kind of strangled laugh in his voice, 'by telling you that you are nothing but a collection of Jews, through and through, every one of you. And because you're Jews, you want to make everything systematic, logical, sensible, subject to law. When you believed in God, he was a God of laws. Not a God of love or a God of mercy, but a God of laws. What is Judaism, if not a system of laws, of rules how to live, from one day to the next – even from one meal to the next, if you please? And what do you call Moses, why was he the greatest Jew who ever lived? Because he was Moses the Lawgiver. And you try to carry on in the same spirit now, even though you're modern people, and don't believe in God any more. So you try to live by other laws: you still look for reasonable arrangements, orderly developments, clear understandings, settled, sensible ways of living. And as you are, so you believe everyone else must become, or should try to become. If only, you think, you could explain to people that if they do this or that or something else then they will live longer, in nicer houses, and eat more butter on their bread, and have finer clothes to wear – if only you could explain this to them, show it to them, then you think they will agree with you, they must agree, they'll want what you want. That's your politics, that's your philosophy of life, that's how you try to bring up your children, and what you want the future to look like.'

'I hope so, I hope so,' someone interjected, and Benjamin abandoned Mr and Mrs Ritstein to ask, 'What do you want the future to look like?'

'It isn't the point, what I want. It's what the future *is* going to look like that matters. And what that is, I can tell you. It's what the past had just brought us, only more and more of it. Can't you see how right, how appropriate, it was for the Nazis to kill the Jews? They were people without laws, without minds, hating anything rational, anything moderate – so of course they had to kill the Jews, they had to try to kill everything the Jews stood for. And the Nazis won! That's why you are nothing but survivors, why there's no hope for you in the future. You think people will ever forget how much more exciting losses can be than profits? That's the great lesson they've learned. So do you think they'll ever listen to your explanations again?'

Meyer asked slowly, 'Even if what you say is true –' he paused and leaned forward, 'why are you so pleased about it?'

Samuel did not answer immediately, and Benjamin said loudly and ironically. 'Can't you imagine!'

104

However, Samuel made his recovery. 'Always it's the same thing. When I tell people the truth, they ask me: Who am I to tell them the truth? But that isn't the point. What matters is whether or not the truth is the truth – that's all.'

Sarah had come into the room while her brother had been saying this. At once, though she could not have known what he was talking about, she nodded her head.

Her automatic, subservient nod was seen by Benjamin, and it enraged him. 'If you hadn't been a Jew,' he said furiously to Samuel, 'you would have found a way to talk yourself into being a Nazi.'

'Benjamin!' Sarah exclaimed.

'A Nazi! A Nazi!' he repeated above her protest. 'I know your kind, with your long view and your big sweep and your talk about things being not what you want them to be, but what they are. There's a whole tribe of people like you in the world today, you run like jackals behind disaster, looking for what you can get out of it. Not materially – I mean psychologically, in your minds. You'll make a treat for yourselves out of anything.'

'And that shows I'm wrong in what I'm saying?' Samuel asked, with the same half-laugh in his voice, the same tension on his face.

'It shows me that I don't need to pay any attention to you.' And to prove that he meant what he said, Benjamin turned to Mr and Mrs Ritstein and said loudly. 'So, as I was telling you …' But he couldn't remember what he had been telling them and fell silent, with one hand pressed against his brow.

For a moment everyone waited for him to continue; then people turned to one another and the conversation became general. The display of family ill-will between Samuel and Benjamin had been watched with interest and satisfaction, but it was now felt that it would be better if Samuel were not given the floor again. Meyer began to talk to his neighbour, Ezreal

Klein, about business. Dr Aarons, a man with large, innocent, light-blue eyes, and a pleasantly smooth, full voice, who was several years younger than anyone else in the room, moved across to sit next to Samuel. 'What you've said is very interesting,' he began mildly, 'and I think there's a lot in what you said about the Jews – about what the Jews have always been. After all, they developed a whole way of life around the attempt simply to avoid trouble at any cost. But they're certainly going about things in a different way in Palestine. And you're wrong about the rest of the world too. People in Europe don't want any more blood to flow; they've had enough of it. I was there in Italy with the Sixth Div. and in Austria, afterwards. They're dazed, that's all, and they're going to want to live quietly, for a long, long time.'

'Impossible! I don't believe it. How can people live quietly when they have bombs that can blow up half the world? Just the knowledge of it, don't you see, must do something to their minds – something we can't begin to guess at, yet. But it won't make them peaceful, you can be sure of that.'

Some minutes later Meyer stood up and reached for his stick. 'Could you ask one of the children to phone for a taxi?'

It was the signal for everyone in the room, but for Samuel, to stand up. There was no need, several people insisted, for a taxi to be called: Meyer could have his choice of lifts back to his hotel in town. But it took a little while before the group had finally dispersed. On the way to the front door they had to stop and look in all the rooms where the young people were dancing and talking; they had to nod at them and smile; parents had to tell their children not to be too late and children had to reply good-humouredly or irritatedly; Mr and Mrs Ritstein had to surprise and embarrass everyone, not least Mr Ritstein, by suddenly dancing, at Mrs Ritstein's insistence, a little rumba.

Before he left, Meyer said to Benjamin, 'We'll settle the business tomorrow morning. I'll go straight to the office.' From the way he said it Benjamin knew that Meyer had already come to his decision, and that he would sell.

There had never been any doubt, Benjamin felt immediately afterwards, but that he would sell. But it was Meyer's policy never to let any other party in a transaction with him have his way easily, or even seem to do so. Benjamin respected him for this, and envied it in him. In comparison, he felt himself to be too impulsive, too quick to anger and generosity. It did not occur to him that Meyer might envy him these qualities as much as he envied Meyer's.

18

So, though he was pleased with what he had just deduced, the effect of it was to make Benjamin feel he should be harder, less yielding, more like Meyer. When he returned to the breakfast room and found Samuel still sitting there, he said harshly, 'You're waiting for something?'

'Yes, for your wife.'

'What do you want with her?'

'I want to ask her about mother.'

The vitality seemed to have gone out of Samuel, now that his audience had left him. Yet he remained unrelaxed. He sat sideways to the table, with one thin elbow on it, in an awkward, half-hunched position.

'Your mother's well, we see her regularly. You could try doing it, too.'

Samuel ignored the reproach. 'Yes,' he said absently.

Benjamin was still at the door. He hesitated, and took a pace into the room. 'I've told Sarah not to give you any more money.' He tried to speak calmly, as Meyer might have spoken, making such an announcement. 'If you want anything you must come to me and then I'll see what to do.'

'Thank you,' Samuel answered, without moving. 'You're very kind.'

'Are you trying to be funny?'

'As much as you're trying to be kind.'

'I mean what I said,' Benjamin said warningly. 'You go to Sarah once more, and that's the end.' Samuel stood up, and the two men faced each other. Sarah came into the room.

'Your brother wants to speak to you,' Benjamin said, turning aside.

'What about?'

'Money. What else?' Benjamin answered.

'Benjamin!'

'Benjamin!' He mimicked her. 'Why don't you say, "Samuel!" like that?' But he was suddenly weary, weary of them all, of everything. The children were dancing, his wife was already cringing in front of her rubbishy brother. Was this what he worked for? Who cared whether or not he owned all the shares in the Central Creamery (Pty) Ltd? Did he care himself? His anger, fatigue and self-pity dried out his throat. He felt if he tried to speak he wouldn't be able to do more than whisper. He crossed the room to the sideboard, squirted some soda from a siphon into a glass and drank from it. 'How much do you want?' he asked Samuel, with his back to the room.

When Samuel left the house shortly afterwards there was a cheque for twenty-five pounds in his pocket.

'Let's not talk about it,' Benjamin said to his wife. 'Let's go to sleep, if the children will let us.'

19

Outside, the garden creaked and stirred with the noises of insects, rustled with the whispers of couples who had gone out into it. From the house there came snatches of talk and laughter, the clatter of dishes, the music of the radiogram, the hissing, scraping sound of feet moving in time to the music. David and Bertie Preiss were sitting to the side of the house, on the low parapet that ran around the edge of the stoep. It was dark there, and the summer sky, dusted with stars, was warm and close, tangled with the branches of the trees. Bertie had a bottle of beer and so did David; both boys felt drunker and much wiser than they were.

'What's the trouble?' David asked.

'Trouble? There's no trouble.' Then wretchedly, Bertie confessed the slight he had suffered hours before. 'Rachel says she doesn't want to dance with me.'

What could be more manly than for the two of them to sit over their bottles, discussing women? David's reply was suitably embittered, without illusions or tenderness. 'Don't you bother about her. You're well out of it. I'll tell you something about my sister – she's a bitch. Nobody knows this except me. Or nobody will admit it. That's the worst thing about this family of mine. Nobody ever admits for a minute what they really feel about each other. Perhaps all families are like that.'

'No,' Bertie said, paying no attention to David's generalizations, 'I know I'm unattractive.'

'Christ, what makes you say a thing like that?' David spoke vehemently, to smother not only the pity he felt for his friend, but also his suspicion that Bertie had spoken the truth.

'What do you think makes me say it?'

In the darkness David saw the round frames of Bertie's spectacles turned towards him. 'You should have another drink,' he said.

'Or I should have had one less.'

'Well, it's too late now, so you might as well go on.'

Bertie did go on, too eagerly. Later, he was sick in a corner of the garden. Even while he retched and gasped, he was hoping desperately that no one would overhear him; that every one else by now was inside the house.

But he was overheard, by Jacobus.

'Baas?'

'Nothing. Go away.' Bertie's eyes were running, and he pushed his glasses on to his forehead, to wipe the moisture away. But he felt better than he had before he had vomited: the garden, with its burden of trees and bushes, had stopped wheeling and plunging around him, and seemed to rest where it had last fallen. And he was standing firmly on it, under a tree, with a kindly, inquiring black face leaning towards him.

'Baas was drinking too much?'

'That's right.'

'Just a little is enough for the young baas,' Jacobus said matter-of-factly, without censoriousness or scorn.

'That's right too. What's your name?' Bertie asked, after a pause, to show that he had recovered.

'Jacobus, baas.'

'My name is Albert.'

'Yes, baas.'

'My name's not baas. It's just Albert, do you hear?'

Jacobus laughed. 'I often see the young baas,' he said.

'Where? What do you mean?'

'There by the night school, baas. By the Bantu Sports Ground. I'm a beginner, in the beginner class.' Jacobus spoke proudly, as though the name of the class conferred a status on him.

'You go to the school?'

'Always, baas. Monday and Friday.'

The earth seemed to lurch away again from Bertie, as it had more violently earlier. He stretched out his hand for support, and touched the stiff, starched sleeve of the man's arm; then, beneath it, with a pleasant shock, he felt the hardness of Jacobus' swelling muscle. Bertie found the man's hand, and grasped it unsteadily with his own. Jacobus smiled, his teeth showing up vividly in the circular darkness of his face. 'I'll look out for you,' Bertie said, sobered by the encounter. 'Thank you for helping me.' His words seemed to him more meaningful than Jacobus would ever know. Pampered, fed, wined, miserable, the teacher got drunk; to his aid came the outcast, despised, cheerful pupil.

Bertie went to the front of the house, Jacobus to the back. In the hall Rachel seized on him. 'Bertie! I've been looking all over for you. What have you been doing? Where have you been?'

He shrank away from her, not out of the scorn he had felt for her and her party a moment before, but because he was afraid he might smell of vomit. 'I've been around,' he said vaguely. 'Why do you want me?'

Rachel's eyes were large and dark, in the pallor of her face. 'A whole lot of us are going to the Doll's House for a cup of coffee. I wondered if you wanted to come along.'

'Do you want me to come?'

She put her hands on her hips and her head to one side. 'What does it sound like, Bertie?'

'I must go to the bathroom, then I'll be ready. The party's over?'

'It looks like it.'

The rooms were suddenly empty. A few young people were hanging around, some of the girls already wearing their coats. The only couple still dancing were David Glickman and a thin, rather plain freckled girl, much shorter than he was, who squirmed against him. The servants were clearing things away from the dining room.

In the bathroom Bertie avoided looking at himself in the mirror, but he did scan the toothbrushes in plastic mugs and the face-cloths hanging on hooks, wondering which of them were Rachel's. He washed his face, then he took a tube of toothpaste, squeezed some of the stuff onto his finger, rubbed his teeth with it, rinsed his mouth, and came out, looking around for Rachel. When he passed Jacobus, who was carrying a tray of dirty dishes towards the kitchen, he paused guiltily, smiling and not knowing what to say, before hurrying on. In the living room David lifted his hand from around the neck of the girl he was dancing with and waved to him, but Bertie did not respond. He regretted what he had said about himself to David earlier in the evening, and he positively disliked David for having heard it.

His own weakness suddenly disgusted him. When Rachel came up to him he said abruptly to her, 'I'm sorry, Rachel, but I've changed my mind. I won't go with you. I think I'll go straight home.'

'Bertie! Why?'

'It's best, for everybody's sake. My own especially.'

His answer exasperated her. 'We're just talking about going to have a cup of coffee at the Doll's House. What's the matter with you? Why're you making such a fuss about it?'

'You're just talking about having a cup of coffee at the Doll's House. I'm not.'

'So what are you talking about?'

Bertie looked steadily at her, his expression growing both graver and softer. Then he said, 'You know.'

His gaze frightened her; then she felt proud of having provoked it. 'All right, Bertie,' she answered him quietly, when she saw he would say no more. 'Just as you wish.'

She came closer to him, she brought up her arms and put her hands on his shoulders. 'Thank you for coming to my party.'

'Ach, Rachel –' It was all he could manage to say. They kissed, someone whistled, and Bertie walked away blindly.

He found himself out on the pavement. There were cars parked alongside it, trees planted at intervals on it. He lived near the Glickmans and set off briskly to walk home where his widowed mother was still awake, waiting anxiously for him. But he did not think of her. He was waving his arms, talking to himself. 'The people must be free,' he declaimed, in a fierce whisper. 'There is a new spirit abroad among the people of

South Africa. They are no longer content to be exploited, abused, cheated, deprived of what is rightfully theirs.' He clenched his fist and shook it in the air. He imagined himself addressing a mass meeting, with Rachel at his side, and many eminent, shadowy figures beside her on the platform. 'You think I'm joking?' he demanded of the piebald trunk of a plane tree, which came suddenly into his vision. 'You'll see,' he told it, staring at its patches of green and white, lit vividly by a street-lamp. He began declaiming once more, still in a whisper, leaving the tree behind him. 'It can be done. We have history on our side, justice, and our own strength. Opposing us there is only greed, obscurantism, prejudice and inertia. Away with them! Away with them!'

The world could be a place of justice, Bertie was sure; he could win fame, applause and power within such a world. Rachel could love him and he love her; every darkened house he passed could be filled with the peace and brotherhood he had felt when he had grasped Jacobus's hand in the garden, the pride and delight he had felt when Rachel had kissed him.

20

David knew about the girl he was dancing with only what she had told him. She was a cousin of one of Rachel's friends, Milly. She was from Cape Town and she was staying with Milly for a couple of weeks' holiday. Milly had said that she must come to the party, but she had thought it a cheek to come to a party to which she hadn't been invited. But she was glad she'd come, though she'd felt a bit 'spare' at first because she was younger than most of the other girls there. But Rachel had been jolly nice to her, all the same.

'And me?' David asked.

'You too,' the girl said, and squirmed more closely against him. Her name was Mavis.

David found out that Mavis and Milly were planning to go home in Jack's car. Jack was a thin, retiring, blinking medical student who said, when David suggested it to him, that he didn't mind going to the Casablanca roadhouse. So they went to the Casablanca: Jack and Milly in the front seat, Mavis and David in the back. Before the car had travelled a block, David and Mavis had sunk into one another's arms, low on the seat.

By the time they had had coffee and a fried-egg sandwich at the Casablanca, and had driven to Prospect Drive, and had parked there, on a ridge high above the soft distant swarms of lights far below to the south, David had undone Mavis' brassiere and had got his hand well between her knees; what his tongue had done inside her mouth had made it ache at its root. The couple in the front seat talked, and Jack smoked; but they were patient, and, observing the etiquette of such occasions, did not comment on or interfere with the two in the back.

At last David managed to touch, to stroke Mavis on the moist, secret place he had been seeking throughout. She gave a single, stifled little cry, and arched her body towards him and away from him, in hunger and shame. It was the first time David had wrung such a cry out of anyone, and he was shaken by it, impressed with what he had done.

He did not object when Mavis, a little later, whispered to the couple in the front, 'I think we should go.' Jack started the car promptly. After he had dropped the two girls – David and Mavis parting with many lingering kisses, and Milly and Jack with just one obligatory peck – Jack still had to take David home. To placate and flatter him, David asked him questions about medical school; but listened to none of the answers. In his ears there was another sound. He wondered when he would hear it again; the time that would have to pass before he did seemed to him utterly dreary, without interest of any kind.

21

Pamela slept badly and woke early. As soon as she opened her eyes she was convinced, without knowing why, that something pleasant and important had happened to her: the conviction was as indubitable and soothing as the touch on her skin of the cool morning air. Years later she was to remember that moment of waking, and the peace and reassurance it brought, after so many obscure, excited dreams, in which, aware intermittently that she was lying and turning on her bed, she had nevertheless found herself in rooms full of people she did not recognize, had obsessively repeated in her mind meaningless words that became shapes and textures as she uttered them, had made exhausting journeys across rooms, across roads, across waste grounds, to retrieve what she could not remember having lost, and was unable ever to find.

Now she was awake. Everything around her was quite still. The sheets, which had been so much a part of the night's torment and unease, like living things, lay innocently on the bed; the curtains drawn across the window hung down in straight folds with a blur of light showing through the weave of the cloth. From outside she heard someone hammering, a bird singing, a car passing. That she should be lying placidly in bed, hearing, feeling, seeing, seemed to her somehow even more strange than the wild distortions of sense and image she had suffered during the night; yet in this strangeness there was no alarm, no pressure, no fear. Only one phrase was in her mind now: 'So that's how it is' – as though the strangeness of things was their only explanation, and one with which her mind and heart were altogether content. Soon she fell asleep again, and slept undisturbed, dreamlessly.

She was wakened by her mother, who brought her a cup of tea.

'Well, what sort of a time did you have last night?'

'Super. It really was, mom.'

'Tell me about it.'

Sitting up in bed, drinking from her cup, Pamela told her mother all about it, leaving out only the kisses Joel had given her when he had said good night at her front door.

22

Pamela's father had enlisted largely because he had wanted to get away from his family; and though Pamela had been only twelve at the time of his enlistment, and fourteen at the time of his death, this was something she had understood very well. So too had Mrs Curtis, whose bitterness against her husband for leaving her had become, as it were, permanent upon hearing the news of his death. 'I *told* him,' she said to Pamela, many times, 'I told him not to go. But anything was better than staying at home and taking care of us. You remember what he looked like in his uniform, so pleased with himself? Now we're the ones who're still suffering – not him, not him!'

Pamela, an only daughter, attempted to console her mother without being disloyal to the memory of her father. Pamela had always been loyal to her mother instinctively, feeling that it was her duty to stand by the other woman in the family, and, while he had been with them, to resist the charm and attraction of her father. Charming and attractive he had been, clever and sweet-voiced, but foolish too. He had been nothing grand, just a primary school teacher, whose education had ended – much to his regret – after two years in a training-college in the Cape. It had been during his very first spell of teaching in Kraankuil, a small town in the northern Free State, that he had met Pamela's mother.

He had just celebrated his twenty-first birthday, at the time; Kathy Stonier, the daughter of a wealthy dairy farmer in the town, was then approaching her thirtieth. She was still quite handsome, having thick dark hair which she wore severely compressed into place, dark eyes, and small neat bones. But her skin was altogether without lustre, her slight figure was without sap, and her father was quite without scruple in his attempts to get her married off to someone respectable and English speaking; he wouldn't consider having a Boer for a son-in-law. Young Curtis was poor, handsome and talked wistfully of the university education he had missed; so Mr Stonier shook his head sympathetically and said that he wished, how he wished, he could do something to help Curtis to get to the university. 'But a man's family must come first,' he told him. 'I must think of Kathy. Everything I've got must go to her.'

Curtis was desperately eager to go to university and take up an academic career; he was also full of romantic notions about women and love. Kathy was fragile, her manners and her voice were refined (she had been educated at an expensive girls' school in Natal), and there was a hungry curiosity in her dark eyes that frightened and attracted him. The fact that she was so much older than himself worried him a great deal, but in the end his romanticism managed to overcome the misgivings he felt. He would rescue her, he told himself – he did not say from what; he did not think that he would be rescuing her merely from spinisterhood – he would save her, he would restore her girlhood to her. At the same time, with a cynicism that was quite as unreal as his chivalry, he told himself he wasn't just being foolish or sentimental, he wasn't just carried off his feet. Far from it. He knew, he had calculated, just how well he would be doing out of the marriage. As a result of it he would be able to go to university and take up his studies seriously; he would take a degree or two in South Africa and then go to Oxford or Cambridge or some walled, cobbled, timbered German university town; he would be a man with backing and resources behind him. Picturing all this to himself, Curtis would feel sure that he was a great man of the world, a fellow who knew very well on which side his bread was buttered.

And Kathy was in love with him; there was no doubt about that. She adored him, as his daughter was to adore him later, for his flat, handsome, suntanned face, with its very white teeth, for his mellow voice, for his tall figure and slightly stooped, scholarly shoulders. She spoke in awed tones of his books and his studies; she told him how proud she would be of him when he became a professor. But just a few weeks after their marriage Kathy's father died; and it was discovered that he had been all but bankrupt, having taken to gambling unsuccessfully on the stock exchange in the last few years of his life. So poor Curtis was still nothing but a primary school teacher, married to a woman he thought of as middle-aged, with no hope of ever going to the university and becoming any kind of professor.

He never forgave his wife for having trapped him into the marriage, though in fact she had been quite ignorant of the truth about her father's financial position. Nor did he ever forgive himself his own intellectual ambitions, for the sake of which he had let himself be hurried into marriage: he developed something of a hatred of his own inclination towards books. Yet that inclination had been serious enough. Quite on his own, without much encouragement from any one he had ever met, he had chosen to study the languages and customs of the tribes of Southern Africa, he had learned to speak and to read Zulu and Tswana, he had read books on anthropology and translated African Folk-tales and verses for his own amusement. He had dreamt of holding a chair in social anthropology or ethnology; he never forgave himself for having indulged in such dreams.

So – though he kept up with his reading when all his hopes of 'doing something' with it were gone – he never spoke of books among the little boys he taught. Instead he tried to pass himself off among them as a man's man, a hearty, an athlete, a despiser of women. He joined in with the little boys when they mocked the 'swots' in the class; he told them stories of hunting expeditions he had never been on, of games of rugby he had never played in. Once he was in the army he always made a point of going to the school during his leaves, where he showed off in his uniform, and told the boys fictitious stories about the traditions of the regiment in which he held his commission.

By that time he and his family had made their home in Johannesburg. He had enlisted on the very day South Africa had entered the war, joining a ragged, spontaneous recruiting parade that made its way through the city centre to the Drill Hall, while people cheered hesitantly from the pavements and waved from the windows of halted trams. Gladly, he marched off to the war, leaving behind his wife and child in the shabby little house in Booysens, with a white mine-dump at the end of the street. He came back on his leaves, thinner, more handsome than before in his uniform. Sometimes, sentimentally, he would tell Pamela that she must look after her mother when he was Up North, because she was all she would have then: he kissed her and told her he wanted her to grow up straight and true, proud of her father. He might never come back, he said to the little girl, but at least she would remember him as a man, as a soldier, a fighter.

Pamela did remember him, but she preferred not to think of him as the soldier whom her mother fiercely, repeatedly, accused of selfishness, treachery, irresponsibility. Pamela preferred – out of loyalty to them both – to think of her father as the gentle, scholarly, kindly man he might have become, had his means been greater, his folly and misfortune less. She remembered him reading at night, in the years before the war, in the room he had grandly called his 'study'; she remembered him speaking and listening to Africans with a curiosity and respect she had seen no other white man show towards blacks; she remembered him telling her African legends and fairy-tales, acting out all the parts and revelling in each one. His gaiety and wistfulness, his wry admissions of failure, his sad confessions to her that he sometimes told the boys in his class things about himself which were not true, his frustrated curiosities and ambitions were the memories of him which Pamela cherished.

23

Of Pamela's grandfather's estate there had remained in the possession of her mother only one small piece of ground outside Kraankuil. This piece of ground, about a hundred morgen in size, had been leased for many years to a neighbouring farmer, who used it to graze his cattle on, and who had repeatedly made offers to buy it. But, though she could have used the cash, and though the return on the ground was nominal, Mrs Curtis had refused these offers. 'If I sell it, then there'll be nothing left,' she said, invariably. Her husband had jeered at her irrational attachment to those 'ancestral acres', as he had mockingly called that barren, brown, unbuilt-upon stretch of veld; and Pamela, too, had urged her mother to sell, when the two of them had been faced with the prospect of living together on Mrs Curtis's pension and Pamela's earnings. But Mrs Curtis had remained obdurate.

In 1946 a series of the richest gold strikes in South African history were made in the northern Free State. Kraankuil was among the places where gold was found.

When Pamela came home from work that day, bringing with her a newspaper that carried immense headlines about the Kraankuil strike, she found that her mother had already heard the news on the radio. She found also that Mrs Curtis already believed firmly that she had refused to sell her land precisely because she had always had an intuition of the value it might one day have. Under the circumstances it would have taken a stronger woman than Mrs Curtis to believe otherwise.

'I knew it – I knew it – I knew there must be something there' – these were her first words to Pamela, as they stood staring incredulously at each other, Pamela still clutching the newspaper in her hand. 'They've been drilling in the Free State for years. I knew they'd have to find something there.'

Mrs Curtis managed to bring these sentences out almost calmly; then she laughed, she cried, she clapped her hands and waved them in the air; she poured out glasses of brandy for herself and Pamela and Miss Baker; she even called the servant from the kitchen and poured some brandy into her enamel mug.

Though no one (least of all Mrs Curtis herself) knew exactly how the news of the strike would affect the value of her land, rumours that the Curtis's had become suddenly rich had already gone up and down the street. Soon neighbours were coming in to congratulate Pamela and her mother on their good fortune, to console themselves for their own unchanged circumstances with Mrs Curtis's brandy, and jokingly to offer their sons in marriage to Pamela. There were the van Reenens from next door, Pamela's special friend, Maisie, among them: a boisterous, blonde, fat girl, with her hair in a bedraggled permanent wave and the rings of all her boyfriends on different fingers. There were the Colemans from across the road; Mr Coleman was a hard-faced, embittered man, a panel-beater by trade, who had been feuding with the van Reenens for years. But on this festive occasion he took Maisie on his lap and fed her brandy from his glass, while his freckled fleshless wife shrieked loudly and proudly in protest. Mr Stavros came from his shop, bringing a tray of peaches as a present; he kissed

Pamela and shook hands with her mother. Pamela was also kissed by Maisie, by Mrs Coleman, by Mr van Reenen, and by Mr van Reenen's son, Jimmy, who had kissed her many times before, and much more earnestly, in cinemas and on his back stoep and hers. Old Mr Parker came in, with his yellow, trembling hands and his heavy smell of pipe tobacco, and prophesied that one day, there in Kraankuil, you'd see a city as big as Johannesburg. 'Curtisville, they'll call it,' someone said; and Mrs Curtis, who was drunk, dazed and triumphant, answered, 'Stoniersville, not Curtisville. It's what my father deserves. It's all his doing.' Then she broke down completely, and was escorted with exaggerated solicitude, by most of the women present, to her bedroom.

It was dark by the time the last of the guests left the house. Mrs Curtis lay in her bedroom with the lights off. Pamela walked with the van Reenens to the gate. Maisie was lachrymose. 'I suppose you'll be moving soon. I suppose you'll forget all about Maisie.'

'I won't, Maisie, I'll never forget any of you. Besides, it's probably all a fuss about nothing.'

But as she said the words Pamela shivered. She prayed that it wasn't a fuss about nothing; that her life would be altogether changed by the fortune that everyone was sure had been tossed overnight into her lap.

24

On her way to work the next morning, Pamela looked out of the bus window at the immense, glittering mine-dumps that reared their bulk here and there along her route to town, each one covering tens of acres of ground, separating road from road, suburb from suburb. Previously she had taken them for granted; they were to be seen all over the southern suburbs and beyond, along the entire Rand; they were as much a part of the city's scenery as its houses, blocks of flats or railway lines. Now she marvelled at the effort that had gone into the raising of these life-less, naked demi-mountains; she examined their wrinkled surfaces, from which nothing grew and off which the light sparked in a hundred sharp glints of white, brown, cream, yellow, green.

What had been done here would be done in the fields of the northern Free State: the dumps would rise out of the ground, streets and buildings would grow around them, people would walk and drive through the streets. And all for gold! Gold which no one could eat, or make clothes of, or shelter under, which could only be extracted from the earth, sent overseas, and then be buried again in vaults. There was something brutal about the irrationality of it: strangely, for this very reason, the processes seemed to Pamela almost to have the appearance of being natural or inevitable, like birth or death.

Pamela said nothing at work about her own interest in the latest strike, though it was the topic of conversation of everyone in the office, from Benjamin Glickman down to the African youth who made the tea.

25

At Pamela's insistence, she and her mother went down to Kraankuil one weekend, some months later. Pamela had never seen the place, and wanted to do so before the ground was finally sold to a firm of speculators who had offered Mrs Curtis forty thousand pounds for it – it was their intention to cut the ground up and sell it in half-acre plots to potential house-owners. They went down by train, on a bitingly chill late-winter night in August.

As it made its way through the darkness, the train momentarily illumined bristling rocks and spikes of grass alongside the track; in the morning, peering from her bunk, Pamela saw the sun rising over a brown, treeless country, where dry grass alternated with the great squares of the stubble of mealie fields, paler in colour than the grass. Dusty double-tracks ran off at intervals from the railway, to isolated farmhouses around which no one stirred. Tracks, wire fences, iron windmills all pointed away into the blue distances of the horizon which averted itself slightly with the motion of the train, but drew no nearer.

Kraankuil was a *dorp* of small, iron-roofed buildings and disproportionately wide earth roads. Every road ran straight towards the veld; the place was sunk into a pouch of the ground, and beyond it the veld lifted and sank in great shallow surges, with a momentum which it was impossible to believe had been stilled for ever. Of Kraankuil's new-found wealth there was as yet little sign, other than a rash of notices announcing 'future developments on this site', and the tall derricks of the drilling-teams at varying distances around the village. The derricks lifted themselves towards the sky, but failed to touch its hard, high, wintry surface, a single blue from horizon to horizon.

No one in the *dorp* appeared to remember Mrs Curtis. She and Pamela had lunch in the little hotel, which was Afrikaans-owned, like almost everything else in the place, but which served the dreariest kind of English food: mulligatawny soup and watery steak and kidney pie. Then a taxi took them out to the ground, which was hardly more than a mile from the outskirts of the *dorp*.

When the taxi stopped Pamela jumped out of it and began to run. Her mother stood by the fence to the side of the road, with the taxi-driver, and shouted after her 'Pam-e-la!' but the girl ran on through the veld, feeling on her cheeks and hands the coolness of the air, hearing the dry grass breaking under her feet, seeing the lemon-coloured sun jump and swing in the sky as her feet stumbled on stones and tussocks. Spikes of grass thrust themselves between her shoe and her instep, they tore at her stockings. She startled a bird from a bush, a few insects whirred away from her feet. She sang and shouted scraps of words, her mother's name, her father's; she called out 'Who wants my gold?' and 'Forty thousand pounds!' like a madwoman. By the time she reached the top of the first slow rise away from the road she was quite out of breath; when she glanced back the car and the two figures standing by it looked tiny and forlorn. Behind them, at a distance, were a few of the low rooftops of Kraankuil, like abandoned shells on a shore; in front of her the veld sloped and rose, sloped and rose to the remote, gleaming horizon. The one or two isolated farmhouses that were visible appeared as small, as haphazard, as insecure, as ships at sea. A wire fence ran into the distance, its strands and droppers dark in the sun.

Then she saw an African herdsman's hut, a few hundred yards away: a low building of mud walls with a patched iron roof. Cautiously, she began to walk towards it. She hadn't gone far when a yellow, bony, long-tailed dog rose out of the grass near the hut and began barking at her. She halted, afraid to come closer to it, afraid to turn her back on it. In the end, the dog turned its back on her; she saw the tip of its tail moving above the grass, back to the hut. She followed it, and when she was a little distance from the hut she called out, 'Hullo, is anybody there?'

The dog barked again; it was sitting on its haunches in the cleared space of reddish earth in front of the hut. A piece of sacking nailed to a cross-beam served as a door to the hut; this was pushed aside and an African woman came out, carrying a child slung on her back by a blanket.

Pamela was relieved to see that it was a woman who had come out, and drew closer. The woman was very old: her cheeks were deeply sunken, her body was bowed and frail, her ankle-length dress was filthy and torn. There were no shoes on her broad, hardened feet. She was moving her head in a strange way, from side to side, with an almost animal-like wariness, as if sniffing the air, looking at Pamela and then past her, scanning a wide arc of the void. Pamela came to a stop abruptly. The woman was blind.

Pamela simply wanted to run away, to flee back to the road and the car. But the woman called out in a frightened, penetrating voice, '*Wie's daar?*'

'*Môre,*' Pamela answered, as she approached. Her Afrikaans was poor, but she went on haltingly, 'Don't be afraid.'

'*Môre,* missus,' the woman answered, recognizing Pamela as a white woman from her voice. 'What does the missus look for?'

'Nothing. I'm just walking past.'

They stood together in front of the hut. The baby was fast asleep, its head lolling back over the edge of the blanket that supported it.

'Is that your baby?'

'No, missus, it's my daughter's. I'm just looking after it while she's in the *dorp*.'

'Are you alone?'

'Yes, missus, they've all gone to the *dorp*.'

The woman's eyes were a pale, clouded blue; iris and pupil were indistinguishable. At intervals she still moved her head from side to side in the uncertain, searching movement that Pamela had noticed from a distance. Pamela stepped forward and took the woman's hand in her own.

'Here I am,' she said.

The surprise of her touch ran through the woman's body; her fingers struggled for a moment in Pamela's grasp, before they relaxed. 'Ja, missus,' she said calmly, reassured. She made no move to disengage her hand.

Pamela asked, 'Who does your family work for?'

'Baas Eriksen, missus. He's the baas of this ground.' The name was familiar to Pamela; it was that of the farmer who had rented the land from her mother. 'His house is there, over the *bult*.'

'Have you lived here long?'

'Many years, missus. I was living here in Baas Stonier's time.'

Pamela withdrew her hand from the blind woman's. She said quietly, 'He was my grandfather.'

The woman did not seem to find this remarkable. Shaking her head ruefully, she told Pamela, 'He was a very cross baas.'

The simplicity and directness of the recollection brought her grandfather closer to Pamela than anything else in the trip had done. 'I never knew him. He died before I was born.'

'It is a long time, missus. I was young, like the missus. I can hear the missus is young.'

Pamela was intensely aware of the stillness of the air, of the strength of the sunlight and its lack of warmth; with an inexplicable vividness she saw the pale sticks of grass lying loose on the cleared patch of earth in front of the hut. It seemed to her that minutes passed before she spoke again.

'You've heard about the gold in Kraankuil?'

'Ja, missus, I have heard about it. They say there's a lot of gold under the ground here.'

'They want to build houses here. You'll have to trek if they do.'

The woman shook her head. 'I won't mind, missus.' She laughed, showing two yellow teeth set in pink and blue gums. 'All places look the same to me.'

Pamela laughed too, surprised by the joke and amused at it, admiring the woman for being able to make it. 'I'm sorry my grandfather was so cross,' she said. Then, 'I must go now.' She began to walk away, paused, and called out, 'Goodbye.'

'Goodbye, missus.'

When Pamela began running the dog barked, but it did not follow her. At the top of the rise she saw that her mother and the taxi-driver had come through the wire fence and were looking for her. She turned and stared at the hut for the last time. There was no sign of the old woman.

That night, as the train rattled and jogged back to Johannesburg, Pamela, crying and laughing at the same time, talking wildly, striking dramatic attitudes and abandoning them to sit in a heap in the corner of the compartment, told her mother that she wanted to go to university and take the degree in anthropology that her father had never been able to take; she wanted to go and live in Cape Town, which was so much more beautiful than awful, stark Johannesburg; when she had taken her degree she wanted to travel abroad – to go to England, to America, to Spain, everywhere; she wanted to buy dresses and jewels and horses and books; she wanted – she didn't know what she wanted, she was too stupid to know what she wanted. She was stupid, she was afraid, she hoped everything would be all right, she wished they'd never found gold at Kraankuil, she was glad she would never see the place again. And why did that poor blind old woman have to move? They should give all their money to a charity – to a fund to help the Africans, or to stop all wars and injustice.

Mrs Curtis listened to her patiently at first, nodding her head at some of Pamela's schemes and shaking it at others. But eventually she told the girl to pull herself together, that really she was just being childish and hysterical. There was nothing for her to worry about; everything was being looked after. Mrs Curtis spoke confidently, feeling sorry for Pamela and yet finding something gratifying in her hysteria; it compared so unfavourably, she felt, with her own firmness and commonsense, her own strong grasp of their situation.

Since the news of the strike she had become much younger and brighter in appearance, and much more sure of herself, than she had been for many years. She had dealt competently and authoritatively with the lawyers, real estate men and investment advisers she had had to consult; she had even put on weight. Pamela had seen the change and was grateful for it; sometimes she felt that that was by far the best thing their good fortune had yet done for them.

When they were both lying in the beds that had been made up on their bunks, Mrs Curtis said decisively, 'I think it's a good idea for us to live in Cape Town. I've always loved the Cape. And you can go to the university.' Then she switched off the light.

The next week Pamela handed in her notice to Mr Glickman. She still had not told him or anyone else in the office of the change in her position, and she did not do so now.

26

Even before he recognized her, Joel's attention had been drawn by the quickness of the girl's stride and the eagerness of her expression; her brow was open, her eyes were bright, her lips were set in a faint, abstract curve of contentment. He called out, 'Pamela'. When she turned to see who had called her, he stood back on the thronged pavement, looking at her, before coming forward.

The puzzlement left her face as soon as she saw him. 'I thought I might have made a mistake,' she said. 'Sometimes you think you hear people calling you, and it's just your imagination.' Only then did she say, 'Hullo, how are you?'

'I'm very well. And I can see that you're very well too. You're looking –' Joel made a little gesture with his hands, and shook his head in admiration. He leaned forward and kissed her on the lips.

Pamela did not move her head; she was still smiling abstractedly. Despite her smile, Joel apologized for what he had just done. 'I'm sorry. It's just because you looked so happy and pretty.'

Then, because Joel had kissed her, and because she was leaving Johannesburg in a few weeks' time and so had nothing to lose, Pamela asked him, 'Why haven't you phoned me all this time? Or come to see me? I was sure you would. I wanted you to, I was waiting for you to do it. I really was. And instead – nothing! Even when you came to the office those times you just said hullo and goodbye to me, and that was all. Why? Didn't you care about me at all? I was sure you did.'

Once she had spoken, it seemed natural and inevitable that they should be talking so directly to one another.

'I have thought about you – often,' he answered.

'But not enough to make you do anything?'

'The more I think, the less I do.'

'What do you mean? Because I'm not Jewish? Because I worked for your father? That's what I decided, in the end. I didn't think much of them as reasons, I must say. I don't mind because you're Jewish, why should you mind if I'm not? And I didn't have to keep on working for your father, there are plenty of other jobs.'

'And you'd have changed your job for my sake?'

'If you'd – if we'd decided that I should.' It was the first time she had hesitated. But she looked steadily at him, more steadily than he at her.

He said, his voice jerking in mid-sentence, 'It's difficult for me to explain.'

'It must be,' she answered wryly.

Neither of them spoke. People were passing continually, with a slap and click of feet on the pavement, a murmur of voices, a thrusting of bodies. Joel and Pamela felt themselves to be pushed, driven apart from one another, an obstruction to others. But they did not move.

'I'm ashamed of myself,' Joel said.

'Why?'

'Because of the state I've been in. Because everything seems to me petty and useless and up to shit, and I never give it a chance to become anything else. Do you know what I mean? Even you: I mean the prospect of having anything to do with you. I thought to myself, what's the use of it? Leave the girl alone, don't drag her into the mess you're in. Especially as there'd be so much additional mess and complication, anyway, what with you being a *shiksa*, and my father's typist, and all that. You have to have conviction to deal with that kind of thing, and conviction's just what I haven't got. And not only about you; about everything.'

Joel had raised his voice at first, so much so that one or two passers-by had turned to look at him. But by the end he was muttering; when he had finished he looked at Pamela with such an unhappy, self-absorbed, fixed stare that she felt almost alarmed for him. Yet she was angered, too, by his words. She had spoken boldly to him now about his refusal to have anything to do with her after Rachel's party, but there had been nothing bold about her feelings at the time. She had felt hurt, rebuffed, snubbed, even betrayed. She had not forgiven him for it; and nothing he had just said had made her feel she should do so now.

27

'I don't know what it is,' Joel said to her later. 'I don't even know the words to describe it. It's as though I can't do anything, I can't give myself to anything, identify myself with anything. Anything at all. I don't know what's the matter with me. Half the time I walk around thinking I must be sick up here.' He tapped himself on the forehead, mockingly. Yet he went on, 'Honestly, I'm not being funny. I'm not even trying to be interesting. Interesting! I can't think of anything more bloody boring.'

'Look, everywhere you go you see people committed to something or other. Look at my family. My father, he's committed to making a living, and being a respectable member of the community, and a big-shot on his Zionist committees. Rachel, she's committed to all kinds of contradictory things – to marrying someone and settling down in a nice bourgeois way, and to being keen on my cousin Jonathan, and to making everyone think that she's really very perceptive and sensitive underneath. My mother, she's committed to seeing her children happy, or pretending that they're happy, and to helping her hopeless brother along. So that's my family. And at the university there are hundreds of people who're committed to having a gay time, or to getting installed into their careers, and there are a couple of dozen who're committed to big radical politics. And me? Nothing. Nothing! Just to making a nuisance of myself.' He unclasped his hands and sat back from the table, on which stood a teapot, a plate of cakes, and their empty cups. 'What about you? What are you committed to? Typing?'

Pamela thought for a moment before answering. Then, apologetically, she said, 'I suppose I'm just committed to whatever happens to me.'

'But you make things happen to you, don't you? Everyone does.'

'Not everyone,' she answered, thinking of what had recently happened to her. 'Not everything. I just want to take advantage of what does happen.'

'And when it's unpleasant?'

'That too. I'd hate to miss anything because I was afraid it might be unpleasant.'

'And when it's trivial?'

Pamela shrugged, smiling at the question. 'I'd hate more to miss anything because I was afraid it might be trivial. How can you tell? How do you know what a whole lot of trivialities put on top of each other might amount to?'

'They might amount to a life,' Joel answered. 'That's what I'm afraid of. Look at the careers people want to take up. Law – all right, law – so they work, work, work, and one day they'll be able to put KC behind their names, or even be judges. And the academic ones – they work, work, work, so that one day they'll be professors. And the Dram Soc ones work, work, work, so that one day they might be actors with their names in lights. And the others, work, work, work, so that one day they'll be heads of waterworks departments, or engineers on the goldmines, or doctors in Lister Buildings charging five guineas a time. And that's all. That's it. That's the best you can hope for, until finally you drop dead. And these are the lucky ones, the rich ones, the ones at university, with opportunities and privileges. And all the others? It all seems so mean and pointless, it's all on such a petty, trivial scale, it drives me mad.'

Pamela listened attentively. His words did not seem so unreasonable to her – though she thought he was leaving out more than she could begin to explain – but his manner did. It was both frantic and lifeless; it was absorbed and yet restless, almost shifty. He took a cake from the plate in front of him and went on talking, through a mouthful of crumbs. Pamela watched that too.

'And that's not the worst of it,' he said. 'The worst is that I simply can't imagine anything being on any other scale. Do you know what I mean? And this is where I fall out with the politicals, the radicals and Communists at any rate – I mean, quite apart from what Stalin is actually doing in Russia, which I just start swearing about whenever I argue with them. No, I mean when they talk generally, when they start coming with their ideas as such, when they talk about moulding the future, changing the world, making history. Then I ask myself what I will be, what will *my* life be like when they're finished with their moulding and making. And the answer is that I'll still be me; I can't become anyone else; I may be richer or poorer, or I may be in a concentration camp, or I may be dead. But if I'm alive I'll still be bound by the things that bind me now, because they're not just out there in society or the economic system; they're right in me, they're part of me.

'When I say this people tell me to stop thinking about myself for a minute or two, if I can. But *everybody* is a self to himself, if you get what I mean. And the radicals hate that, really; they can't stand it; they want everybody to be agglomerated with every one else in one big thing which they can call history or the future. That's their way out. But I had enough of being agglomerated in the army, thank you very much. And any other kind is just a delusion – there isn't any other kind – there are only doctors and lawyers and chairmen of waterworks commissions and the poor devils minding the machines in my old man's factory.

'No,' Joel said, 'the only way we can be enlarged – if that's the word – is through religion. Not through politics or careers. And I've got no religion, I've never had one, and I don't believe I ever will. I'm even more incapable of believing in God than I am of walking on my hands across the Kalahari. So what do I do? How do I get out? How do I escape?'

Pamela waited until it was clear that he had at last finished; then she said, as off-handedly and insultingly as she could, 'Don't ask me.'

Joel looked angrily at her; they stared at each other like two people who had just had a quarrel. 'Who do you think you are, anyway?' Pamela demanded fiercely. 'Why should you escape? Why should you complain and hide away from everything because it isn't big enough or good enough for you? Perhaps you're the one who isn't big enough or good enough to find anything worthwhile. Has that ever occurred to you? I don't suppose you've ever thought that some people do what they do – whatever it is – for the sake of what they're doing, and do it as well as they can because that's exactly the way to make it worthwhile. You're just afraid of being ordinary, that's the trouble with you – and because you're afraid, you're less than ordinary, you're nothing at all. I haven't got any sympathy with you, really I haven't.'

She had spoken so violently that a heavy tress of hair had sagged halfway down her forehead. Joel watched her fingers pushing back the curve of it. It was only when she lowered her hand that he answered her. 'I don't know why you're shouting at me. I told you I was ashamed of myself. I've always thought – what I've been saying – is my failure, not just –' he gestured ironically – 'the world's.'

'I'm not shouting. And I do feel sorry for you,' Pamela admitted. 'But I'm sure I'm right – to be afraid of being ordinary is worse than being ordinary.'

'Aren't you afraid of it? Of being ordinary?'

'I know I'm not.' She blushed at the boast, then, in extenuation of it, she said, 'To myself I'm not, I can't be.'

'Actually, I don't think you are. At all.' Deflatingly, he added, 'My father's not going to find another typist like you again.'

Pamela took no offence at the remark. 'Who has he got?' she asked.

Joel smiled at her immediate quick curiosity about her successor in the office. 'Some Afrikaans girl. Married. Moustached.'

'She sounds attractive.'

'Oh, she is. I'm phoning her this evening.' He picked up his spoon, stirred it in his empty cup, and let it lie against the side of the cup. 'Tell me, Pamela, is it too late to phone you now?'

She did not answer. He looked up at her, met her eyes for a moment, then looked despondently away.

'Have you got someone else?'

'No.'

'But you don't fancy me.'

'Not any more. It doesn't matter anyway.' She paused, wondering whether or not to tell him about what had happened to her, of the money that had come to her mother, and how it had come, and of their impending move to Cape Town. Her impulse to remain silent was vindictive: after the way he had treated her and just spoken to her, she wanted him to think of her as simply living in Johannesburg, poor, available, and yet determined to have nothing to do with him, for sufficient reasons. But her impulse to speak was vindictive, too: she wanted him to know, before she finally left him, left his town, that she was no longer just a typist. Neither impulse distressed her at all; she smiled, thinking of choosing between them.

'What's the joke?'

Still she hesitated. Then she chose.

He listened with great curiosity to her story, and when she had finished he said wholeheartedly, 'What a wonderful thing to have happened! Only in South Africa – as they always say. When my father told me you were leaving I thought that it was just because you were bored, or had been offered more money elsewhere, or something. But this is special, a bit of fortune, it really is.'

'Thank you,' Pamela said, gratified by his response. 'I want to make it really fortunate. I don't know how – yet.'

'Perhaps someone will show you. I've certainly missed my chance.'

'Don't miss any more, Joel. I've hated seeing you like this, and hearing you complain and look so miserable. It seems such a waste. You can do as much with yourself as anyone else can;

you can be as happy as anyone else. And it doesn't matter if that isn't very much, or isn't very happy.' She stood up; before he had managed to get to his feet she leaned over the table and kissed him quickly. 'Goodbye, Joel.'

He was standing now. Very slightly, as if warning him not to follow her, she shook her head. She made her way between the glass-topped tables and the wicker chairs around them, past the counter and display shelves of sweets and cigarettes, and into the bright strip of sunlight that lay at the door of the café. The sunlight diminished her in an instant, turned her into a shadow. Then she was gone.

28

Joel did not move from the place for almost another hour. He ordered some more tea and let it grow cold; he sipped at it and put it aside with disgust; ten minutes later he absent-mindedly drank it down.

What he had said to Pamela of his state of mind was true; the recoil or paralysis of will he was suffering from had affected in greater or lesser degree everything he had done, or tried to do, or failed to do, since he had last seen her. He had enrolled at the Witwatersrand University to do a B.A., ostensibly as a preparation for taking law. Flush with government money he had left home and rented a single-roomed flat on Hospital Hill; he had bought a second-hand car from Jonathan, as well as a record-player, some clothing, some prints to hang on his wall, and many books. His work – he was majoring in politics and philosophy – was interesting enough and never arduous; there were films and occasionally plays to watch, there were parties to go to, plenty of opportunities for drinking, swimming, picnicking, tennis-playing. When he put himself out he was as successful with girls as he could reasonably expect to be, and he had made a few friends among his fellow-students and some of the younger members of the university staff.

Every day should have been restless with possibilities; every evening should have gleamed with chance. Instead, his days were tedious, his evenings anxious; he slept too heavily at night and woke with difficulty in the mornings. He did not know what to do with himself.

Sometimes he worked hard, driving himself through his books, attending lectures and tutorials regularly, winning alphas for his essays. At other times, for weeks, he did no work at all; he let whole mornings go by while he idled in the sunshine on the steps of the university's Central Block, or played penny-penny, like a child, with other loafers, on the flat concrete roof of the changing rooms of the university swimming bath. He got violently drunk at the parties he went to; he sat for hours in the Plaza cinema, where there were continuous performances from ten in the morning, and where they showed old pictures like *King Kong* and *Roman Scandals*; he read the local newspapers and the journals from England with a minute obsessive attention and many fierce useless opinions – following especially, as if condemned to do so, the bloody course of events in Palestine, and the development of the opening stages of the cold war; he went home and had short loud arguments with his brother and sister, or with his father, on any topic that presented itself; he drove endlessly in his car, on his own, among the hills around the city, usually at speeds which he knew neither the brakes nor the steering of the car could contend with.

All the time he was chafed by a barren exasperated self-doubt, an inflamed sense of his own puniness and isolation which his way of life could only exacerbate, and which yet made him feel totally incapable of adopting with conviction any other. Nor was it just his family or the people at the university from whom he felt himself sundered, among whom he felt himself estranged and powerless. If, in the course of his reading, he came across a reconstruction of the wanderings of the Bushmen and Bantu tribes of Southern Africa, hundreds of years before; if he happened to look up at the sky and see there the dark blue and white vistas of the summer storm clouds calmly forming and dissolving; if he remembered vividly scenes from Egypt and Italy, and thought of the armies of men and machines he had seen assembled there, all now dispersed; if he studied a leaf he had casually plucked from a tree or an insect that jumped out of the grass on to his hand; if he passed the noisy queues of Africans waiting for their buses in Noord Street every morning – then he felt himself to be a mere disconnected, irritated pinpoint of consciousness; nothing but a speck, a dot, a superfluity.

29

For some days, some weeks even, after meeting Pamela, Joel expected, irrationally but confidently, to see her again. The expectation was so strong that there were times when, in some arbitrarily chosen, nondescript street, he would linger in the hope of seeing her come out of a shop or getting off a bus; when he bought a ticket for the cinema he turned and looked back along the queue, with a greeting for her ready on his lips. He imagined clearly what she would look like, with her high colour, black hair and slender neck, how she would smile, showing her large, white teeth. He even told himself that in the future, because they had met there, that street, this park bench, the foyer of that cinema, would always be associated for him with her presence.

Invariably, he was disappointed. Pamela did not appear in front of him; afterwards those arbitrarily chosen places reminded him only of the faint sweet image of her in his mind, and of his own desire to see her again, growing fainter with every week that passed.

PART 4

1

Professor Viljoen was a small, bald, lined, ill-shaven man, with a few wisps of brown hair trailing untidily over the crown of his head and over the shafts of his metal-rimmed glasses. He walked with a slight limp; he dressed invariably in a faded sports coat and a pair of creased flannels. He was so dim a figure that in the afternoons, when the curtains of the lecture room were drawn against the brightness of the sun, his outline seemed almost blurred against the wall behind him. He spoke in a high hesitant voice with a strong Afrikaans accent, and he sneezed often. There was nothing in the least impressive in his outward manner and appearance; but Joel, having gone more or less by chance at the beginning of his second year to one of Viljoen's tutorials, went by choice to those that followed.

Viljoen was giving a seminar on the 'scramble for Africa'. Painstakingly, implacably, he explained and analyzed the effects of the ancient national enmities of Europe, of the power of new methods of production, communication and warfare, of fantasies of wealth greater than any which Kimberley and the Witwatersrand had already revealed, of debased Darwinian notions of race and blood, of missionary zeal, of wild dreams of personal and imperial aggrandizement. Joel, Peter Dewes, who was his special friend in the group and whose admiration for Viljoen had first drawn Joel into it, and several other young men and women sat and listened, made notes, leaned back in their creaking chairs, asked questions, glanced out of the windows at the blue sky and at pigeons strutting and mating on the ledges of adjoining buildings, and looked again with curiosity at the grey, hesitating Afrikaner who spoke with an intensity that seemed always to demand from the class a response to the subject as passionate and as precise as his own.

Most of the story was new to Joel, and he listened to it with a kind of disgust that was directed not only against the story itself, but also against the man who was telling it. Whatever its consequences might have been or would continue to be, the 'scramble' itself, as Viljoen presented it, was never anything but a convulsive thrust and counter-thrust of power, adorned by a rhetoric whose hollowness and irrelevance the mere passage of time had exposed, redeemed only by the rarest examples of self-sacrifice on the part of some of the individuals involved in it. But the same would have been true, Viljoen seemed to imply, of any other story he might have told the class of the movement of power from one country or continent to another: this one was merely shown up all the more completely by the poverty, inhospitability and uselessness to the victors of so many of the territories fought and solemnly argued over. Everything about Viljoen seemed to underline this conclusion; even the plainness of his appearance, the high sardonic quality of his voice, his habit of blinking his eyes a little wearily before he spoke, the small smile which twisted his lips when he compared the words of the politicians in Europe with the deeds of their henchmen in the Congo or German West Africa. There were times when Joel hated the man, thought of him as a mouse, a rat, gnawing his way into the sack of the past and finding with every quick turn of his head another morsel of fact to crunch and devour. Joel sat clenched in opposition, unable to move away, jeering inwardly, saying that it was because Viljoen was ugly that he chose to study this particular ugliness of the past. But Viljoen had a fascination for Joel which no other teacher of any other subject had come near to rousing; and he knew that it wasn't just the fascination of ugliness.

It was as much out of a kind of defiance of him as out of a desire to please him that Joel worked hard at the essays he had to do if he was to remain a member of the class. He wanted to prove Viljoen wrong on particular points, to dispute his conclusions, to wrest from the facts improving lessons and generalizations which Viljoen had either failed to see or appeared to regard as inadmissible, but which to Joel seemed the only justification the study could have. What else was there to justify it? To believe that history provided no such conclusions, was a mere endless going on, a continuation, a repetition in every generation of the same wretched, wearying, meaningless struggles for public power and private gain, was surely, Joel felt, to be led straight back into the state he had been in a few months previously, and which he remembered with a kind of shame, as if it had been a period of illness he had passed through.

As it was, he spent many peaceful, industrious hours in the university library, finding enjoyment and satisfaction in the arguments he was following, interest in the books and documents he read; the more engrossed he became in the ideas and actions of men who were dead and remote from him, the more his attempts to find hope or justification for himself in their lives could seem at times illicit, unfair to them, something gratuitously imposed on them. They had lived for themselves, after all, not to resolve his problems. He enjoyed, also, his surroundings while he worked, so vivid at some moments and so distant at others: the shuffle, whisper and occasional clatter of the other students at their work; the smell of books and oiled shelving; the light that slanted in rays through the tall windows, making precise areas of brightness where they fell and an obscurity everywhere else; even the sound of his pencil moving across the pad of white paper on his table. Ambitions, vague enough, yet more precise than any he had known previously, stirred within him: he dreamed of possessing profound scholarship, of reputation and position in the academic world, honours descending thickly upon him, of admiring students and respectful peers. He spent much time with Viljoen's own study, *The Background to Imperial Expansion in Africa, 1875-1903*, proud that he should have known the author of two such imposing volumes, bearing the imprint of the Oxford University Press. It was a new experience for him to handle the books of someone he knew, and he tried to catch in the prose the cadences of Viljoen's voice, with its precise choice of words, its parenthetical inflexions, its air of allowing for and answering the unspoken objections of the listener. One thing that disappointed Joel was that his essays did not win him higher marks. The amount of work he did for Viljoen would have won him better grades, he knew, in the other subjects he was still taking in a desultory, high school fashion.

In class, Joel was usually silent and often puzzled – puzzled especially that the zeal Viljoen brought to his subject should have had so little that was in any obvious way reformist or hortatory about it. How was it possible, Joel wondered, to have so little faith in the capacity of men to order their lives rationally, and yet to care so much that what they did should be understood as fully as possible? One Friday afternoon, however, it seemed to Joel that he at last came close to grasping the kind of demand Viljoen made of his subject, and the demand he let it make of him. It was an afternoon which changed his life, Joel used to say wryly, later – though in a way he had never anticipated and of which Viljoen would probably have disapproved, had he known of it.

The lecture itself was not a particularly interesting one. Viljoen was distracted and irritable; he cut questioners short; several times he referred the class to his own books, as if to indicate to them that he found what he was saying boring and repetitive. In turn, the class was listless and querulous: Joel felt irritated with himself for having looked forward so eagerly to this dry, unengaging period of time. He sat and scratched with his pen at the blank open page in front of him, drawing squares and faces. For the third or fourth time he heard Viljoen say, 'I've dealt fully with that point in the second volume of my *Background*. I beg those of you who haven't read the book yet please to do so. It will save me a great deal of time.' Of course everyone in the class claimed to have read the study, and Viljoen knew this; so the remark was intended to be insulting, and everyone knew that, too.

Joel put down his pen, looked up, and found himself staring into Viljoen's eyes. The professor blinked. 'Have you read the book, Mr Glickman?'

The question startled Joel. What had his expression betrayed? He felt himself flushing, and settling into a ponderous, inert obstinacy, 'No,' he said like a child, spiting himself in order to spite the others.

Viljoen looked away. 'No? You've mentioned it often enough in your essays.'

'I mean, I haven't read all of it,' Joel mumbled, like a child caught out.

'I'm sorry that I failed to hold your attention to the end.' Viljoen's voice seemed to curve elaborately around its own unnecessary ironies. 'But I suppose I should be grateful if you've taken the trouble to read the parts you've referred to.'

The class tittered; Joel grinned stupidly at his desk. Viljoen went on with what he had been speaking about before; he spoke with a little more vigour. Joel hardly attended to what he was saying. But he was aware that the personal quality of the exchange between them had affected the temper of the class: it was roused now, but irresponsible. He heard Viljoen saying, in response to some interruption, 'Yes, it is awful – if that's the word you want to use – that the past is irrevocable. It would be even more awful if it weren't.' Again Joel's attention lapsed. Then one of the students at the back said grumblingly, 'The trouble with history is that there's just too much of it.'

Viljoen answered, 'Not in your head, there isn't, Mr Powell.'

This time the class shouted with laughter, like so many school children. Powell was the sullen clown of the class: a moustached, balding, long-legged ex-soldier, who always sat slumped and impatient at the back of the room, never taking a note; instead he passed his time slowly revolving his green trilby hat upside down on his desk in front of him, as if it were some kind of steering wheel.

Viljoen waited until the laughter had subsided, then went on, as if in apology for his retort, 'Actually there's something you should never forget about the subject you're supposed to be studying, Mr Powell. It is this: If the past really does oppress you because there's so much of it, if – if,' he repeated, with ironic emphasis, 'you feel yourself crushed and insignificant in comparison with it, it's there to crush you, after all, only because you have the power to remember it. And what's true of the human past,' he went on, after a pause, 'is also true of the natural world, in a way. There's a sense in which we can say that we actually call it into being by our consciousness of it, even though it exists beyond us.'

He was speaking earnestly, though he had begun as if he were doing no more than continue the joking, informal exchange with the students into which the lesson had lapsed. 'You'll have realized, of course, that I've merely been paraphrasing Pascal on the subject of the thinking reed. How does the passage go?' He looked up hopefully. If it was one pedagogic trick of his to speak at times as if his class were composed entirely of dunces, it was another on other occasions to pretend that his listeners had read and could recall fully as much as himself.

No one in the class offered to help him with the quotation, so, with a duck of his head, he gave it to them. ' "If the universe were to crush him, man would still be nobler than his killer. For he knows that he is dying, and that the universe has the advantage over him; the universe knows nothing of this." '

The class was silent. Slightly embarrassed by his interpolation, and yet pleased with the effect of it, Viljoen went back to the subject of the lesson. Joel sat with his face lifted, wondering and grateful. The words he had just heard seemed to have been spoken straight to him. He, too, was just such another point of consciousness: that was what he had fretted and complained against. But he was a centre, a source of power, a focus of understanding; his was the force that drew the world into a constellation around him, now, even as he sat there. Buildings and voices, pigeons and blue sky, the creaking of chairs and the sight of Viljoen's tense, frail face, the dead Germans and Hereros in South West Africa of whom Viljoen was speaking – as if the movement of his mind were a physical one, Joel felt it darting and swerving, picking up words and images, letting them drop, diverted, then returning again. All, everything was his; everything that was thrust against him he could make his own.

Yet everything existed beyond him, indifferent to him, unalterable and irreversible. How were the two truths, the two visions, to be reconciled?

With Viljoen before him it seemed to Joel that the professor himself provided a living answer to the question. Surely in his work Viljoen used to the utmost his awareness and understanding not just because they belonged to him, because they reflected credit upon him, because they gave him power and position, but because at some level they, too, simply belonged to the world; were a part of it, like the pigeons and the buildings and the blue sky over them. It was at that level that the inner and outer worlds could meet and coalesce; at that level only, that private effort could become part of a shared, public truth.

Joel waited impatiently for the session to end, as if immediately it were over he would be able to rush out and begin a new, extraordinary life: one filled with a personal involvement so total as to be dispassionate and disinterested; so unregarding of self as to be fully expressive of everything within him. At last, the class came to its end. Viljoen made for the door, with his quick limping stride. In the corridor outside Joel overtook him. He did not know what he was going to say until he had said it. 'I'll try to do better.'

Viljoen did not seem surprised at this sudden absurd avowal. 'I've always thought you could do better. I haven't been satisfied with your written work. Not in the least.' He limped away, leaving Joel staring after him.

2

In spite of Viljoen's schoolmasterly rebuke, Joel was still vaguely exalted as he walked with Dewes towards the tearoom, after the lecture. Peter Dewes was short, plump, fairhaired and heavily freckled; even the backs of his hands were blotched with rust-coloured freckles. His eyebrows were hardly visible on his forehead, his eyes were pale blue, his mouth was pink and moist. When he spoke he fluttered his hands; when he listened he cocked his head to one side. He looked effete, schoolboyish and sly; but Joel, who had met him for the first time in Helwan Transit Camp, in Egypt, respected and even envied him in many ways. One of the things for which Joel envied him was that he had established himself, without much apparent difficulty, as Viljoen's best student of the year.

Joel was silent, trying to preserve his uplifted spirit from contamination by the ordinariness of the afternoon; Peter was grumbling about the weekend he would be spending with his mother, who was up from Port Elizabeth on a visit.

He went on grumbling almost all the way to the tearoom. 'One damn uncle and aunt after another. Lots of talk about the stock exchange. Endless complaints about how cheeky the kaffirs are getting nowadays. Reminiscences of great booze-ups during the war, when my Uncle Arthur was a major in the Sappers and my Aunt Mattie did great work in the SAWAS. Small cousins dancing and reciting and asking for lucky-packets. Respectful reference to my "studies", and remarks on how I get it from my father, who, being the headmaster of Lady Cranbourne Junior School, must clearly be a man of profound intellect. Oh God!' Peter wailed comically, 'I suppose all middle-classes are awful. But the South African bourgeoisie!' He turned his beseeching, mischievous blue eyes on Joel. 'Do you think they have such small vocabularies because there are so few things for them to talk about, or do they have so few things to talk about because their vocabularies are so small?'

Joel laughed. 'Ask for a grant to do some research on it.'

'I wish I could – it's a real subject. You should hear my Aunt Mattie!'

He led the way into the tearoom, a long, low prefabricated wooden hut, with large windows through which the sun came in on one side. The place was almost empty. Only a few of the tables were occupied by groups of students talking quietly, though many of the other tables, ranged in rows, were littered with used cups, Coca Cola bottles, dirty plates. The warm still air was laden with the smell of the lunches that had been served a couple of hours earlier. At one end of the self-service counter a silver tea-urn hissed somnolently to itself; at the other, behind the cash register, an elderly woman sat as immobile as the Pekinese puppy asleep on the counter beside her.

Dewes grimaced as they stepped into the room. 'Let's take our stuff outside, for heaven's sake.'

But Joel said, 'Hey, there's Leon Friedberg. Do you know him? And look who he's talking to.'

'I don't like that man, Preiss,' Peter muttered. 'And as for his little Rosa Luxembourg!' His hands wriggled at the ends of his cuffs, but he restrained the gesture, in case the others might guess he was talking of them.

'I must go and talk to Leon,' Joel said. 'I haven't seen him for months.'

He and Peter went to the counter, helped themselves to Coca Cola and sandwiches, and paid the woman, who blinked resentfully at them for disturbing her. Then they carried their trays to the table, at which were sitting Bertie Preiss, Adela Klein, Leon Friedberg, and a slight, bare-armed, black-haired girl with a strikingly smooth, tanned complexion, whom Joel had never seen before. She glanced up as he approached – her eyes were a light, sharp brown in colour, like a stone seen through sunlit water – and in the glint of that glance Joel's exaltation and confidence suddenly fused in his breast, almost painfully, around a hard bead of attention.

He and Peter sat down. 'What you doing here?' Joel asked Leon. Blusteringly, boisterously, he turned to Bertie. 'And what are you doing – talking to a bourgeois nationalist like Leon? Leave the Zionists alone, they're no good to you. Go and nag the Africans!'

'You're in a bloody good humour,' Adela said, offended, shifting with a display of much effort her chair, her books and her files to make room for the newcomers. But Bertie was merely amused by the jeer: he took it as a tribute to the reputation he had already managed to establish for himself on the campus, though he had been there for only a few months.

'Leon, you don't know Peter Dewes?' Joel said. 'Peter, this is Leon Friedberg, an old school chum of mine, now a Zionist.'

Leon and Peter nodded at one another. Leon pointed to the girl at his side. 'Her name's Natalie. She works in our office in town.'

'Natalie,' Joel repeated.

He and the girl exchanged another glance; slowly, her full lips parted in a smile, revealing a gleam of gold in one of her front teeth. She sat with her elbows on the table and her chin propped on her clasped hands; a posture that was half-indolent, half-aggressive. Her head was small and round; her hair neatly followed the curve of her skull, the ends coming forward a little, to touch her neck just below her ears. The grain of her skin showed up most clearly there, Joel saw; then he was afraid to look longer at her. 'So what are you doing here?' he asked Leon, again.

'I was talking to the SZA, at their lunch-hour meeting.'

'Oh, I'm sorry I didn't know about it – I'd have come to hear you. Was it a success?'

'It was all right.'

'Leon spoke very well,' the girl put in. Her voice was high. She sat back, laying her small, brown hands flat on the table. Their nails were bitten close; when she became aware that Joel was looking at them she quickly drew her fingers in, half clenching her fists. Again their eyes met. She looked mutinously at him, her jaw set firmly. He saw the disconcerting lightness of her eyes, her clenched fingers on the table, the swell of her breast in her white short-sleeved blouse. He wanted to tell her that he didn't mind if she bit her nails: why shouldn't she? Instead he turned to Leon.

'Did you make any recruits?'

'I don't know yet,' Leon laughed.

'I hope not,' Adela said shortly.

Natalie transferred her gaze to Adela, looking at her with an intent, silent hostility. Meaning to take the girl aback by the deliberate simplicity of his question, Joel asked her, 'Why do you look so cross?'

He felt angered and exposed, having made a fool of himself, when she ignored him. Fortunately, Adela immediately assumed that his question had been directed to her.

'Why do you think?' she demanded. 'It's incredible that intelligent people could associate themselves with a movement like Zionism. Tribalism, that's all it is, barbarism!'

'Rubbish!' Leon answered.

Both Adela and Bertie began talking at once; in the hubbub Natalie leaned forward. 'I'm not cross,' she said to Joel, in her high, small voice. 'I'm shy.' Peter Dewes was the only one, other than Joel, to hear her. He looked at the girl, then at Joel, a frown on his freckled brow.

3

In the squalid, familiar disorder of the tearoom, the afternoon seemed to lean, to yawn, to lie recumbent around them. The sun sank lower, its rays coming in more directly through the windows on the west, where, in the distance, they could see the white houses and green trees of the suburb of Parktown. They gossiped, smoked, made jokes, argued. Years later, when they used phrases like 'When I was at Wits', or 'When I was a student', as often as not the image that came into their minds was of just such afternoons of idleness and talk, confused together and yet vivid in recollection, as if all the afternoons had been one, and it had been a single, changing group which had gathered over tables laden with empty cups, bottles and open packets of cigarettes, books and papers pushed to one side. And with that image they remembered, too, an undirected sense of hope, expectancy and self-importance, which had been indistinguishable, in a curious way, from anxiety and discontent.

The argument between Leon on one side and Adela and Bertie on the other renewed itself intermittently – Leon accusing the others of deceiving themselves about the revolutionary potentialities of the situation in South Africa, and about the role which they, as Jews, could play in it; the others accusing Leon of narrowness, cowardice and reaction. Surreptitiously, Joel studied Natalie; he knew that she knew he was looking at her, though she pretended to be indifferent. Dewes listened to the argument; he, too, glanced curiously at Natalie from time to time.

'It isn't a question of me denying my Jewishness,' Bertie summed up his position at one point, firmly, dogmatically, turning his spectacled face to look challengingly at each of them in turn. 'There's nothing there for me to deny. This Jewishness you people keep talking about isn't a religion, it isn't a real nationalism because the nation doesn't exist, it's not a social force or class. What is it then? A habit? A burrow you hide inside? Or is it a prison that you've let other people drive you into, and that you're now afraid to leave? I live here and I'm going to stay here and I'm going to do as I please: I'm not going to let anyone tell me what my social role must be. I've chosen it. My job is to understand the way the class struggle is developing here, and to help the progressive forces emerge –'

'That you hope will emerge,' Leon interrupted him.

Bertie shook his head. 'No, that I know are emerging, that have to emerge because we've reached a particular stage of industrial and social development. All sorts of exciting things are going to happen in the next few years – and you expect me to get worked up about some fantastic, archaic, imperialist, racialist scheme in the Middle East! Not on your life!'

'Never!' Adela echoed fervently.

Bertie leaned over and patted her hand in mocking approval and placation. The others laughed at the gesture, and Adela coloured. But she took his hand and held it, and he let it lie in hers, on the table.

'Don't I deserve a pat?' Leon asked Natalie. Reluctantly, as if drawn from a distance, the girl patted him on the back. Leon smiled with pleasure, showing his teeth under his moustache. Joel thought he looked fatuous; then he realized that he found the sight of Leon's plump, smiling face objectionable because he was jealous.

So he vented his irritation on Bertie and Adela. 'You realize that forty years ago in Poland and Russia the Jewish intellectuals were having exactly the same argument with one another as you and Leon. Exactly. It takes a long time for some things to reach us, doesn't it? Only then it wasn't the Africans but those wonderful Russian peasants and workers whose great seizure of power was going to dispose of the Jewish problem, settle it happily for everybody – according to the people who spoke as you do. And where are they today? The ones Hitler didn't kill, Stalin killed. He's still killing them, now, while we're sitting here. You people never learn, do you?'

'Ach, Joel,' Bertie exclaimed, 'I've told you twenty times why things went wrong in Russia –'

Joel pushed his chair away from the table. 'When can I come to the *hachsharah*?' he asked Leon, across the distance he had just put between them.

'Whenever you like,' Leon replied. 'I was going to ask you why you haven't been to see us. You said you would.'

'I've been meaning to and meaning to. I never do the things I mean to do.'

'The Hamlet of Hospital Hill,' Peter said, laughing.

'It's more than a year you've been back,' Leon said reproachfully.

'Don't remind me,' Joel pulled a face. 'It's gone, and I've got absolutely nothing to show for it. The Oblomov of Observatory – that's me.'

'Who's Oblomov?' Natalie asked.

Joel was glad she did not know. 'A fellow in a Russian novel who slept his life away.'

'It sounds like heaven,' Peter said.

'Don't you believe it!' Joel exclaimed. He added, 'Anyway, I know you don't. You! Viljoen's blue-eyed boy! You can go straight ahead – you'll get a first, and then do honours, and then go to England and get more firsts, and then be a professor somewhere –'

Joel felt a pressure on his foot as if someone were nudging him to stop talking. The thought that it might be Natalie came an instant later. Then, glancing down discreetly, he saw that it was just the Pekinese from the counter, snuffling about under the table. He bent down and picked it up, holding it over the table, smiling into its tiny, receding, black-nosed face, its alarmed, protuberant eyes, in which blue glints shone. It wriggled in his hands; through its fur he could feel its frail bones sliding, slithering, as it struggled to escape. 'Hey, Chiang Kai-shek,' he said, 'What's your social role?'

'Come to mommy! Come to mommy!' the woman at the counter called indignantly. She was standing in the open space in front of the counter, clapping her hands, the flesh of her plump arms and cheeks quivering with exertion and anxiety. Joel bent over and put the puppy on the floor. 'Go to your mommy,' he said, pushing it on the rump. The dog ran off on its bent legs, its tuft of a tail waggling behind it.

The others watched it go; but they were soon back in their argument. Later Joel turned to Peter and challenged him: 'Well, what would you be if you were a Jew?'

'Me? I'd be a *nudnik* – like you.'

They all laughed at the Yiddish word Peter had so carefully timed and placed. Under his freckles he blushed with pleasure at the success of his retort. Joel, too, felt his skin growing warm; but not with pleasure. 'I've always been a Zionist,' he said awkwardly. 'I've always wanted a Jewish state in Palestine.'

He did not add to the remark, though the others looked at him, as if waiting for him to do so.

Then Peter said, 'Sure, I suppose I'd be some kind of Zionist, too. But I think that Jews are going to go on being Jews all over the world for much longer than either Leon or Preiss would like.'

This prophecy depressed them all. But Peter went on energetically, with a flourish of his hands, 'So if I were a Jew I'd try to get a first, and then do honours, and then go to England, and get more firsts, and be a professor somewhere – like you said.'

Joel shook his head. 'It's not so simple. Not if you want to take your work seriously. You know, even when I do my lousy essays for Viljoen I feel –' he shrugged, looking for a word '– constricted, somehow, by this feeling that it's not my history I'm dealing with, that I've got no authority inside it, no natural right to it, if you see what I mean. Simply because I'm not an Englishman or a German or a Frenchman. And because I don't know what kind of South African I am.'

'Hell,' Peter said, 'you're asking for a lot. Do you think I know what kind of South African I am?'

'Perhaps you don't. But it's still easier for you to find some kind of a context for yourself here. Or in England, if you go there.'

'I wonder. The grass always looks greener on the other side of the fence. As far as modern history goes, I think the Jews may be the people with most authority to tell us what's been happening in the world. So much more of it seems to have happened to them than to any other people.'

'And what do they do about it? They buy and sell and boast about their doctor sons,' Bertie said scornfully.

'That's a privilege we can do without,' Leon said, ignoring him, and speaking to Peter. 'Once is enough.'

'I'll say it is,' Joel agreed. 'Two thousand years is enough. Especially now, for people like ourselves. To be punished by God, or for the sake of God, is one thing; to be punished because there were six million unemployed in Germany, and because the Germans lost the First World War, and because they and a hell of a lot of others in Europe were poisoned with race madness, and because you'd been punished for two thousand years anyway, so that everybody had got into the habit of punishing you – no, no, that's got to end, it's just got to end.'

'It has ended,' Peter said simply. 'Hitler's dead.'

'But there are still hundreds of thousands of Jews in camps.'

'They'll get out of them.'

'Only when there's a Jewish state in Palestine.'

Later Natalie said, 'Leon, if we're going to get to the farm by supper we better be going.'

Leon looked at his watch and raised his eyebrows. 'Yes, we had.'

'Can I come too?' Joel asked, leaning back and speaking with much more casualness than he felt.

'Do you mean that?'

'Of course I do. I've got nothing on this weekend. And you've just invited me, haven't you?'

'I'm agreeable,' Leon protested. 'We're hitch-hiking, you know.'

'But I've got my car. I'll drive, if you just give me a chance to go up to my place and to get some pyjamas and so on. Have you got your stuff here?'

'Sure.' Leon pointed to a couple of canvas bags lying on the chairs at the next table.

Natalie said nothing. Joel did not look at her, or ask her what she thought of the arrangement.

4

When they came out of the tearoom they were surprised by the freshness and coolness of the air, the height of the sky, the yellowness of the late afternoon sunlight. Sprinklers whirled above the lawns in front of the library building, sending their spray wide, filling the air with a soothing, rustling sound.

Behind the Central Block, Joel, Leon and Natalie stood for a moment to look at the view of the city that opened before them. Immediately below were the Braamfontein shunting yards, a flat width of rails, like shining comb-marks on the ground; beyond were the angular, almost crystalline structures of the city-centre. White, grey, reddish-brown, reflecting light here and there, they descended in a series of irregular steps to the vague spread of the suburbs. The mine-dumps in the far south, bigger by far than everything around them, looked like huge, moored ships, with narrow prows and swelling, terraced bodies. In the clear air the city was laid out as if it were a model, which they could touch, grasp, rearrange. Yet its size was manifest, too; its weight, its permanence.

Down in the road, outside the garage where Joel had left his car for a minor repair, there was only a tumult of traffic, a confusion of silver-painted poles carrying wires, of neon signs and shop windows filled with goods. The newspapers carried headlines about the progress of the debate at the United Nations in New York on the future of Palestine. Leon remained on the pavement, reading the paper; Natalie, with a single, jerky gesture of hesitation, followed Joel into the dark, grease-smelling cavern of the garage.

The noise of the road receded suddenly. Everyone had knocked off work, and the place was deserted, but for an African attendant who was sitting in a cubicle reading a paperback novel. He led the way to Joel's car, between cars parked at angles to one another. Some had their hoods raised in suspended grins or snarls, one had a block and tackle over it, another stood high above the concrete, raised on a hydraulic jack. Chromium shone in stripes, in bars, out of the gloom; there were blurs of colour from the carbodies and patches of faintly shining grease on the floor.

With a snap of his fingers and a flash of his teeth the attendant pocketed the sixpence Joel gave him, then went off whistling loudly. Joel got into the driver's seat; Natalie began to climb in through the door on the other side. Her hair swung forward over the side of her face, and Joel leaned across and brushed it back. Nothing existed for him except the warmth of her cheek in the palm of his hand, and her small laugh or exclamation of surprise. Then he was busy starting the car, putting it in gear, inching forward, turning the wheel, reversing, going forward again, as little able to look at her as she at him.

5

John Begbie was a soft, fat, bald man, on whom, despite his bulk, his clothes always hung or lay too loosely. His trousers were too wide at the ankles, his jacket too long in the sleeves; whenever he could he unbuttoned his collar and pulled down his tie so that the knot hung several inches below his neck. Then he blew out his cheeks with relief. He looked, lolling back, like an ill-wrapped parcel which someone had dumped unceremoniously in a chair and was unlikely to call for again. Protruding from these wrappings was a round face with a pair of blue eyes, surprised and injured in expression, and a small, pouting mouth.

He and Samuel Talmon made a striking contrast, sitting together in the shade on the lawn of a house in Houghton, one

Sunday afternoon: Samuel thin, quick, restless and tense; Begbie slothful and obese, moving only to bring his glass to his lips. Sometimes he urged Samuel to drink up, man; at other moments he complacently eyed the flowers, trees, garden furniture and mown grass around him – none of which belonged to him. But most of the time he was engrossed in the discussion between them.

The house itself, which was large, new and white, was behind the two men, and they were deep in their talk, so they did not see a young man, together with a woman almost as tall as himself, come out of the front door and approach them across the lawn. The woman had her hand on the young man's arm; he had his hands in his pockets.

When he did see his wife and son approaching, Begbie looked thoroughly displeased. 'Here she comes,' he warned Samuel in a hoarse whisper. 'Not a word to her, you hear?'

'Not a word about what?' his wife asked, from a few yards away.

'You've got sharp ears,' Begbie responded, without any note of congratulation in his voice.

Samuel had risen to his feet. 'This is Mr Talmon,' the woman said to her son. 'He and your father have become very friendly, just lately. My son, Malcolm.'

Samuel thrust out his hand. 'I'm glad to meet you.'

'How do you do?'

They shook hands – with enthusiasm on Samuel's side, suspicion on the other's.

'Not a word about what?' the woman repeated.

Begbie wallowed with his shoulders in his canvas chair, as a way of showing discontent. 'We're talking business,' he said. 'It's not something you'd understand.'

'You're probably right,' she said, with a slightly theatrical sigh. Then she said, 'I told Malcolm he should come out and say hullo to you.'

'Hullo,' his father said, without looking up.

'Hullo.'

There was a silence. Then Begbie did look up. 'What are you doing here?'

'Waiting for tea.'

Begbie seemed to turn this statement over to see if some insult might lie beneath it, and, failing to find one, said, 'Goodbye,' with another wallow of his shoulders.

The two turned away without another word.

'Sit down, sit down,' Samuel was told, before they were out of earshot. 'You don't want to take any notice of them. That's how they always are. That's how they always speak to me. She's against me. The whole family's against me, they've always been against me. Look how her brother lets me into this house – only when they're away in Europe, as if I'm some kind of caretaker! They've got no respect for me, I know it. But all we have to do is pull this thing off, and then you'll hear them sing a different tune. Then they'll be boasting about their brother-in-law, John Begbie – you know, remarkable man, bit of a rough diamond, but he knows a good thing when he sees one, a real pioneer – that's how they'll talk. I know them. Roger Cartwright, Stratford Cartwright, Chamber of Mines, Probity Building Society, their children at Michaelhouse and St Andrews, trips to Europe, paintings on the walls – so, what does that make them? Nothing! Nothing in my eyes! Just you wait and see!'

With this threat, Begbie's throat dried out completely. He helped himself to more lager from the bottle to the side of his chair, and then laughed – or grunted – with a blink of his eyes. 'And how have you been getting on with your brother-in-law? I'm not the only one with in-law problems, hey? What's he say?'

'Oh, he was very impressed, very excited,' Samuel replied promptly.

Begbie was so pleased to hear this that he almost managed to sit up in his chair. However, after another glance at Samuel's drawn, woebegone face, he abandoned the attempt. 'He was? How much is he prepared to put in?'

'Well, we haven't got down to figures yet.'

'You haven't? What have you got down to?'

Samuel's head bobbed, his hands flew in the air. 'He's heavily committed elsewhere just at the moment. He's got property deals on, all sorts of things. He said he'd like to hear more about our proposition when he feels a little freer. It should only be another couple of months.'

'Another few months, another few years. If old man Plaistowe doesn't show that he's able to work the concession they'll take it away from him, he's only got it for so long. And then you know what we'll see: the big boys, the smooth boys, like my brothers-in-law moving in –'

'But we want them to move in!' Samuel cried. 'What can we do without them? I haven't got any capital, you haven't got any capital, how the hell can we work the concession unless we get some backing? All right,' Samuel added hastily, 'I've been asking around, I've spoken to my brother-in-law, and I'm very hopeful – I told you he's excited, he's impressed. But I thought you were working on your family, I thought they knew all about it and were going to help us. And now you tell me that I mustn't even say a word when your wife comes up! Haven't you spoken to them about it at all?'

'I've dropped some hints,' Begbie answered, with an air of craft.

'Those!' Samuel said, and the despair in his voice showed just how many of them he had dropped on his own behalf in the past. 'Those!'

Then each of them reflected in silence on the position they had reached: which was very much the position they had always been in.

'We could advertise,' Begbie suggested, and at the same moment Samuel spoke.

'It's grotesque, when you think of it, that people like us should be forced to sit here and – sit here,' he said, having failed to think of any other way to describe what they were doing, 'when there are all kinds of natural resources waiting to be developed all over the country, and we've got the vision to do it. And we're helpless for lack of capital. What's capital? What is it?' he demanded, clasping his hands in the empty air. 'A piece of paper, a promise, a word, an order: that's all it is, nothing else. But just because you can't issue the piece of paper, you can't give the order, then you must despise yourself, let people walk all over you, run from corner to corner, live like a dog. You say your in-laws care for nothing but money? Who cares for anything else? How can we care for anything else, when money is success, money is respect, money is power. To him who hath is given – you've heard them say that? But that's only half the story. Because from him who hasn't got is taken. They take, the whole world takes, they know how they can take, they know it's safe to take. They make you pay with your life for being poor. You walk into a room and they think to themselves: see, he's poor, he's powerless, so pluck him, tear the hair from his head, the skin from his flesh, the flesh from his bones. Isn't that the truth?'

'It is, it is,' Begbie cried, moved by this description of his fate. 'Hell, but you can talk – *wragties!* You should go into politics, man.'

Samuel's excitement had left him as suddenly as it had come. 'There's no money in politics,' he said morosely.

Begbie felt rebuffed. 'There's no money for you outside politics, either.'

A dejected silence followed.

'Yes, we could advertise for help,' Samuel said, as if the other had made this suggestion just a moment before. 'A big advert in the *Sunday Times* might do the trick.'

'It'll cost a lot of money.'

'It doesn't have to be so big.'

'It could be quite small.'

'Yes, in the classified columns.'

The afternoon was close and sultry: the sunlight had a curiously stagnant, thickened appearance or weight: there were thunder-clouds high in the sky, and between the clouds the colour of the sky was more bronze than blue. Doves called from the trees below the tennis-court, and fell silent, and called again.

Irascibly, Begbie shouted for a servant to take away the empty bottles and to bring out a new supply.

'Straight from the fridge, hey, you hear? I don't want any of your lukewarm piss.'

'Ja, baas,' the white-coated African replied, his face expressionless, stooping to clear away the litter of bottles at Begbie's feet.

6

'You're finished with him, he means nothing to you, he can't touch you any more,' Malcolm Begbie had told himself many times; but he merely had to exchange a few words with his father and all the repugnance, contempt and feeling of impotence which he had known as a child filled him again. So too did memories he still found it difficult to confess to himself – of words he had heard his father and mother exchanging, of particular smells in the lavatory which his father left lingering behind him after he had sat in it, of his father weeping and complaining that no one understood him and everyone was against him, or, in other moods, presenting to him a moist mouth to kiss. Always he had shrunk with a disgusted contraction of the nerves from the man, shrinking as much when he had been ingratiating, cheerful and free with his money as when he had been sulky, foul-mouthed and free only with his fists.

Well, it was many years since he had had to put up with either blows or kisses; but, as he walked away with his mother, Malcolm's adulthood was overwhelmed momentarily by the childish, familiar rage that made him clench his fists in his pockets, and, after a few more paces, close his eyes, as if in an attempt to contain his anger entirely within himself. But it broke out, nevertheless. 'What a creature!' He jerked his head back. 'Look at him! Look at the pair of them! Guzzling and lolling about and sponging and boasting – it's enough to make you vomit.'

They had reached the house. His mother put her finger on his lips. 'Sh-sh, Malcolm, he'll hear you.'

The light dry touch of her fingers was too much for him to bear; it was like a lover's. 'Let him hear me! I don't care. He knows what I think of him, anyway.'

Mrs Begbie stood at Malcolm's side, looking across the lawn, to the mingled patch of shadow and oozing light in which Begbie and Samuel Talmon sat together on their chairs. Of Begbie nothing could be seen but his short, fat legs, crossed at the ankles, and the top of his bald head. Samuel sat to one side, turned towards Begbie, his thin body encased in a pale linen suit, his head craned forward, his hands flying.

'Who is that man?' Malcolm asked.

Mrs Begbie shook her head and closed her eyes, with an expression which indicated not only ignorance, but also a profound desire not to learn. Malcolm couldn't help smiling to see it, and he took his hand out of his pocket to put it around his mother's waist.

Her grey hair was pulled close and flat over her head, and tied back in a bun; her complexion was faded and colourless. Yet the fine soft down on her cheeks gave her face an almost powdery sheen of lustre; the waist he was holding was slender: there was something irresistibly youthful, it seemed to Malcolm, in the half-comical deliberateness with which her delicate features could express helplessness, ignorance, scepticism, surprise.

They went indoors and sat in a large, stone-floored room that projected from the house like a verandah, and that was furnished with a deliberate cool, sparseness. With its high, hipped ceiling, its bare white walls, and its windows open on three sides, the room had an almost lantern-like look; it seemed to let out as much light as it took in. In one green corner indoor plants stood upright or trailed elaborately on the floor around the earthenware pots in which they grew; in another a collection of old copper utensils reflected grotesquely bulging fragments of the room. Tea was already waiting for them at a table, and while Mrs Begbie poured it out Malcolm listened to her speaking about the people she had seen recently, the letters she had had from her brother and sister-in-law in Europe, the plans she was making to take a flat near Joubert Park when they had to move out of the house. Malcolm listened; he enjoyed watching her movements, the sound of her voice, the taste of the tea; at an ironic distance he admired and pitied all her forlorn, indomitable gentilities. Though he sat relaxed, his legs stretched out in front of him, his bare, tight-skinned bony face was attentive, his blue eyes were alert. The contracted hardness and irregularity of his features, even the tight trimness of his neat, curling, light brown hair, offset curiously the looseness and length of his body. He looked older than twenty-two; he might only have been ten or fifteen years younger than his mother. And she spoke to him as if he were a contemporary.

'Now,' she said at last, 'what's your news?'

In return Malcolm told her about the work he'd been doing at the university, about a film he'd seen during the week. Then he said: 'All that's nothing. What I'm really pleased about is the way my own work is going.'

'Oh,' she asked eagerly, 'what's happened?'

Malcolm settled back in his chair.

It was going well, he said, that was all. But that was everything. For the very first time since he'd begun work on this long story he'd felt it beginning to respond to him, like some living thing; it was showing its own motives, which he had to elicit, its own shape, which he had to follow. It was extraordinary, he said, the change that had taken place in his feeling about the work. A fortnight ago he'd felt like a man with a flat tyre and a pump in his hand; he had simply been pumping away, almost mechanically. But now there was nothing mechanical about what he was doing; he had to be alert, cautious, obedient to the demands that he could feel the work wanted to make of him. For the first time he'd realized that this was the escape which his work offered, and which people talked about without knowing what they meant by it. One escaped from oneself, one submitted oneself to an impersonal will. And it didn't matter that the will had originated in oneself. Once it had reached a certain degree of detachment its existence was as objective as any other – at least as objective as all the other wills whose reality people never questioned, but which were also projections of themselves: the will of the state, or the will of industry, or the will of God.

'In their will is our peace,' Malcolm said, smiling.

Mrs Begbie listened to him with pleasure, almost with greed, leaning forward and nodding frequently, to show how much confidence she had in the truth of what he was saying, how deep was her faith in his judgements. As a boy Malcolm had always spoken of making a political career for himself; but ever since he had come out of the army he had talked only of becoming a writer. She accepted this ambition without misgiving, when he was with her. When he was with her she was sure he would succeed in whatever he wanted to do.

Yet, though she tried not to, Mrs Begbie could not prevent herself from frowning slightly, reproachfully, when Malcolm said, 'I showed some chapters to Swannie, and he liked it a lot. He wasn't just saying so either, I know.'

'I wish you'd show some of it to me.'

'No.'

She gave in graciously, with a droop of her shoulders. 'Sometimes I think Swannie must be an imaginary person, from the way you talk about him. Like Mrs Gamp's Sarah Harris.' She smiled at the comparison, and Malcolm laughed silently, inwardly.

'Swannie's real enough. It's just that I like to keep the parts of my life private from one another, if you don't mind.'

'You know I do mind.'

For the first time she had spoken quickly and petulantly. Malcolm looked at her, his face still contracted in its harsh lines and swellings of amusement.

The tears came into her eyes, quivered there, and were wiped away before they fell. It took no time at all: almost immediately she was looking brightly at him once more.

'That's better,' he said. 'Don't be anxious – the biggest part of my life still belongs to you.'

There was little affection in his voice: it was precisely the resentment and irritation in it which she was reassured and convinced by.

7

Samuel greeted Annie loudly in the hall; then he came into the living room, his mouth open in a grin, his hand stretched out, the tufts of hair on his head bristling upwards and sideways. '*Hoe gaan dit, ou swaer*?' he asked Benjamin, shaking his hand; it was one of Samuel's affectations to speak Afrikaans at times, like some backveld Boer. '*Wat gaan aan hierso*?' He kissed his sister with a great smack of the lips.

'You seem very pleased with yourself,' she said.

'I am, I am.'

'Has someone lent you some money?' Benjamin asked.

Samuel shook his head – not so much in answer to the question as in pitying regret at the spirit in which it had been asked. 'No,' he said, 'no one's lent me any money. I've got a better reason to be pleased with myself.'

'What is it?' Sarah asked eagerly.

She had to plead for several minutes before Samuel spoke. He enjoyed the feeling of power her questions gave him, and they helped to assure him that what he was going to say was really of value. In spite of what he had told John Begbie earlier that afternoon, Samuel had not previously approached Benjamin about the proposition he and Begbie were brooding over; he had been sure that Benjamin would send him away empty-handed. But both the optimism and the despair he always felt after an afternoon in Begbie's company had persuaded him to go straight from Houghton to the house in Observatory.

So, finally, sitting on the very edge of his armchair, he told them, 'I've been let into something that could be big, tremendous – if it's handled properly. Have you ever heard of sillimanite?'

'Sillimanite? No,' Sarah said, as if on cue.

'Well, you'll soon be hearing a great deal about it.'

'From you?' Benjamin asked.

'From me, from my partners, from the Department of Mines, from everybody who follows the economic development of the country. The demand for it is terrific in Europe, terrific, it's only just beginning. And I know that there's a mountain of the stuff in Namaqualand that's never been touched. Now the fellow who's got the concession from the government – it's all government property, but they haven't developed it – this fellow, he's looking around for others to form a syndicate with. And a fellow who knows him and who knows me says he's ready to let me into it.'

'And what are you bringing to the syndicate? Capital? Know-how? Or just enthusiasm?'

Samuel laughed delightedly. 'Your husband's on form this evening,' he said to Sarah. 'All right, Benny, actions speak louder than words. You'll see for yourself.'

'I'm sure I will,' Benjamin answered dryly. He had not moved from his place in front of the mantelpiece.

Samuel leaned back in his armchair. He spoke at length about the industrial uses of sillimanite, and the immense profits that could be made by those who 'got in on the ground floor'. A man like Benjamin, for example ...

'No thank you,' Benjamin said, without hesitation.

Samuel closed his eyes, 'I'm exhausted,' he announced, after some time had passed. Then he sat up with a jerk. 'And Jonathan has had some good news too. He was auditioned the other day at Broadcasting House and they've more or less promised him a big part in a new serial they're going to run, for a whole year. How do you like that?'

'Very much,' Sarah answered.

With an odd, strained irony in his voice, Benjamin added, 'I hope it will keep him busy. Out of mischief.' His eyes met his wife's; earnestly she shook her head at him. He looked away, up at the ceiling.

Samuel did not seem to have noticed the exchange. However, he asked presently. 'How's my little niece? What's she up to these days?'

'She's all right.' But to be in any way off-hand with her brother was more than Sarah could manage. So she went on a moment later, rubbing her hands nervously together, 'She's working hard. She's busy with some social survey her class is doing. They go to Alexandra Township every day. She says it's very interesting. But the stories she brings back about the conditions there – the poverty and the gangsters and the confusion – terrible!'

'Either them or us,' Samuel said casually.

Benjamin frowned at the remark, but he did not let it provoke him. Instead, he shifted his weight from one foot to the other, and clasped his hands behind his back. He looked severely down at Samuel. 'Sarah and I have been talking about your mother. The position is really serious: she hasn't got much time left.'

'It's definite she can't stay where she is?'

'Settled, finished. Old Mrs Greenstein has sold the house. They're going to put a big block of flats there.'

Samuel nodded his head despondently. 'Property development – that's the thing to go in for. *The* thing. If I'd had connections in that world I could have made a fortune by now. Look at the people who've done it! They're no cleverer than I am.'

'Stop thinking about yourself for a minute – just for one minute, please! I've advertised in the paper, and I've asked people at *shul*, and the members of my committee. But it's no good, I can't find anything. And Sarah won't agree that she should come here, that we should try to keep the house kosher for her sake. I said I was ready to try.'

'Sarah's quite right. What an idea – in this day and age! Mama's just perverse. It's a family trait. In the old country she

173

and my father were at each other's throats all the time – for a rabbi's wife she was a disgrace, he always used to say, she was a freethinker, a dangerous woman. But she comes to South Africa and you'd think it was the Holy Land, the way she carries on. Nobody, not Rabbi Senderowitz himself, is kosher enough for her nowadays. So let her go into a home, it's what I've thought all along. They keep plenty kosher in some of those places.'

'We went to see this new place,' Sarah said. 'Beth Basevah Tovah, they call it. It's got lovely buildings and grounds. And they're very strict about the *kashruth*.'

'Then let her go there. She'll be happy.'

'When my father couldn't look after himself any more, we didn't send him to an old-age home,' Benjamin said.

Sarah dismissed what he had said with a gesture of her hand. 'I know, Meyer kept him. And didn't Meyer use the chance it gave him! The way he used to tease and torment the poor old man, I haven't forgotten it. That's no argument to use.'

Samuel was pleased to see that Benjamin had no answer to make. 'No, man, a home's the best for her, for everybody. Take my advice.'

'And you'll pay for her? It's a very expensive place.'

'If I could, I would,' Samuel laughed guiltily, with a helpless shrug of his shoulders.

'So I must?'

'It won't be a novelty.' Samuel laughed guiltily again. 'You've been paying her rent at Mrs Greenstein's all these years. But if this sillimanite thing comes off, I'll be glad to meet my share – that goes without saying.'

'You mean saying is as far as it goes.'

Samuel lay back like thread in his chair. 'You should be glad you're in a position to pay,' he suggested.

'Don't you teach me moral lessons!' Benjamin shouted, 'What do you know about payment? It's when you want to do right in this world that you pay: it's when you don't care that no payment's ever asked. Isn't that so? I'll pay, all right. I'm used to it. But just don't you tell me what to be grateful for.'

His anger and self-righteousness silenced both the others in the room. When he went out to get drinks from the dining room, Samuel asked her, 'What's with him? He couldn't really put up with Mama and all her *kashruth*, could he?'

Sarah did not like to speak about her husband behind his back. She answered hesitantly, 'No – he's – he knows that the last thing I want to do is to run a kosher home, and that provokes him. And he thinks, maybe, if she comes, if he begins with that, then he might – find something, get something out of it for himself.'

'Pathetic! Pathetic!'

Sarah did not contradict him. The fingers of her right hand picked busily at the covering of the arm of her chair.

8

David was the only one of the children home for the meal that evening, which Samuel ate with the Glickmans. After dinner he renewed his attempts to talk Benjamin into putting some money into the syndicate. He offered to drive to Namaqualand with Benjamin the very next morning to have a look at the deposit; he referred knowledgeably to the 'alumina content' of the material and the tiny proportion of 'undesirable ferrous oxides' to be found in it; he invited Benjamin to phone up this firm of metallurgists and that firm of mining consultants to find out if there was a word of exaggeration in what he was saying. He asked Benjamin if he wanted to be like those people who had refused to believe that there were diamonds in Kimberley, gold in the Witwatersrand and the northern Free State, coal in

Natal; he reminded Benjamin of how, in 1939, he had begged him to take an interest in a manganese option in the north-western Cape that was now being worked by one of the biggest firms in the country. And hadn't he spoken about the copper in South West Africa, near Tsumeb and all those parts, long before the Americans had moved in?

Benjamin listened, but remained unmoved.

He believed a great deal of what Samuel was telling him: he was sure, though he had never heard of the mineral before, that someone, some day, would make a great deal of money out of sillimanite – just as so many others had done, out of so many other minerals, in the last seventy or eighty years of the country's history. South Africa was such a country: on top it looked dry and empty, underneath it was packed full with every kind of stone and metal that the world wanted. He knew it, he knew it well, and he had often wondered, finding pleasure in the thought, at the strangeness, the freakishness of it.

But the man who would make a fortune out of sillimanite would never be Samuel Talmon; of that, also, he was convinced.

Samuel left, bravely assuring Benjamin that he would be sorry one day. No sooner had he gone than Sarah attacked her husband. Why did he condemn all Samuel's plans out of hand – Why wasn't he prepared to look at them rationally, to try to find out more about them, before saying no, no, no? Wasn't the truth that he really wanted Samuel to be a failure; that he wanted it because it made him feel all that much more of a success?

Benjamin had listened quietly to Samuel; but he shouted back at Sarah. The noise of their argument brought David out of his room, where he had been doing his homework.

'It's so *boring*!' he protested, thrusting his head around the door of the living room. He caught them in mid-sentence, in mid-gesture; to him they looked equally exposed, angry, old, undignified. He had seen them like that many times before. 'Why don't you find something new to quarrel about, for God's sake? It's Samuel – or it's the way the house is run – or it's Zionism – or it's why the children have got so little *yiddish-keit*. I just don't know how you can go at it with so much energy, after all this time, honestly I don't.'

'You think you're smart! Get out! Nobody wants your opinions!'

'All right, so have a good time, enjoy yourselves.' David slammed the door behind him. He opened it again. 'If you knew just how sordid you sound –'

'Get out'

This time, to annoy them, he closed the door as slowly and silently as he could, and waited for a full minute before letting the knob turn with a final restrained click. He was on his way to his room when he saw Rachel in the hall. She had just come in.

'What's going on?' she asked.

'Ach, they're arguing again – this, that, your fault, my fault, his fault. The usual stuff.'

Rachel shook her head despairingly. 'In that case I'm going straight to bed.'

'Where were you this evening?'

'Mind your own business.'

'I know what that means. You want to watch it, my girl. Next thing you know you'll be married and shouting at your husband.'

'Don't worry, I'll manage better than they have.'

Rachel walked past him, going to her bedroom. From the living room came the voices of Sarah and Benjamin. His was loud, doing most of the talking; but her soft, brief replies were unmistakably defiant.

177

David listened, then drew in a deep breath. 'Boring! Boring! Boring!' he yelled out at the top of his voice, and fled into his room.

9

The storm that had been building up all day broke with two peals of thunder and a sudden, cool, penetrating wind, charged with the scent of what it was bringing. The smell of the rain was everywhere at once, minutes before the downpour began; then the noise of the storm could be heard from a distance, advancing in a rush. It fell with a single, continuing roar. Sheet lightning flared in vague blue spasms; plane trees lost their leaves, which floated together in streaming gutters; the headlamps of slowly moving cars showed the rain as a cascade of sparks or scratches against the darkness. The drops were big and bounced high where they fell, so that every surface looked as if it were pitted with a multitude of tiny, fleeting craters; just above their wild agitation was a smoother skirt-like movement, as each gust of wind blew across the fall. Now there was no thunder: only the roar of the rain, the breathing of the wind, the softer, higher-pitched sound – like an inane, rapid, unperturbed conversation – of the water in the gutters.

Sarah, in her pyjamas and a gown, her feet bare, watched the storm from the bedroom, her fingers grasping the burglar-proofing across the open window. A fine spray was occasionally blown against her, but she did not move away; she felt refreshed by it, gratefully she breathed in the new, changed air. The leaves of the trees in the garden waved and bent; the lamps out in the street appeared to be drowning, despite their height, always receding into the water which they lit up.

She gazed at the downpour, reluctant to go back to her bed. She often had sleepless nights; only within the last few years had she been able to say to herself that the suffering she endured in the course of them had no greater moral significance than that of any other kind of pain which people had to live through. The conviction of total failure and incompetence which overwhelmed her, the frenzied imaginings of disaster to which she succumbed, the envies she felt, the guilts that harried her, the resentments that stung her, the sense of her own worthlessness and lovelessness which possessed her: these were not the direct result of evil choices she had made, actions she had failed in, lies she had told, selfishnesses she had indulged herself in – though it was in such moral terms that they invariably presented themselves to her. They were simply the type of pain which she had been chosen to know. To know again and again.

10

Because he was 'English' (and, what was more, private-school English, ex-army English) Malcolm was both esteemed and suspected by the small group which gathered around Jan Swanepoel. For his part, Malcolm found it gratifying that though he knew many Afrikaners who tried to make Englishmen of themselves, he was the only Englishman he knew of who chose to make his friends among Afrikaners – though he had no intention of becoming one of them, of losing his language and what it meant to him.

Together with the people he met at Swannie's house Malcolm went to bars in Braamfontein and Mayfair, to hideous funfairs in Melville and Booysens, where they brawled with the local gangs of white roughs, to the rooms and flats of others in the group, where there was always Cape brandy to be drunk, bacon and eggs to be eaten, arguments to take part in. Once they had visited a brothel in Doornfontein where all the girls were Coloured and all the clients white, and where Swannie had vomited in the passage – he said proudly, later, that it had been at the thought of getting into bed with a *Hotnot* woman; more than once they went to help break up the meetings that the Communists held on the City Hall steps. Altogether, in their poverty, violence and insecurity, and in the sheer unexpectedness of coming across and being admitted to such a group of young Afrikaans Bohemians, Malcolm found Swannie's friend far more to his taste than the predictable, largely Jewish, well-to-do, left wing, recognized Bohemia at the university. And for Swannie himself he had a special regard.

Swannie, the son of a miner, was attending Wits on a bursary; he was majoring in English, Afrikaans and Dutch. He was a passionate reader, especially of the nineteenth-century Russian classics, and a writer of long critical essays in English and Afrikaans which he never showed to any one; he was an habitual drinker and a loud excited talker; he was a spendthrift when he had money, but would walk uncomplainingly for miles to save his bus-fare when he had none. He lived with his father, in a small, corrugated iron place, little more than a shack, once a farmhouse, in a piece of veld south of Langlaagte Mine. The house was now forlornly awaiting demolition, for the veld around it was being divided into 'desirable quarter-acre plots' and being sold off, more slowly than the developers had hoped. But, in the meantime, it was there that Swannie's friends met, and from there that they set off on their outings and expeditions. Swannie was one of the youngest in the group, but Malcolm had never seen anyone dispute his position in it.

11

Plump, round-faced and staring-eyed, Swannie sat in the biggest armchair. His hair was black and tightly curled, his skin was oily, his mouth was loose. He was dressed, as always, in a dark, shiny, faintly-striped, poverty-stricken suit much too tight for him, and was the only one there wearing a collar and tie. The dirty cuffs on his shirt were buttoned at his wrists. His short legs were stretched out in front of him, and in his hand he held a book of Yeats's verse, from which he was reciting at the top of his voice, with many large gestures and explicatory asides. The others in the room, apart from Malcolm, included Leonie Bester, a large middle-aged actress who had much black hair drawn sleekly over her head and arresting green eyes; her boyfriend, who was fully fifteen years younger than herself, and who also nurtured dramatic ambitions; a bearded painter from Cape Town who was asleep on the floor with his mouth open; and a young man whom Malcolm thought of simply as 'the stormtrooper', the bearer of a name much honoured in Afrikaner Nationalist circles, with a thin cruel face, blond hair falling over his forehead, and a scar on his cheek that looked like a duelling scar but was merely the result of his having put his head through a window when he was drunk one night.

Everyone, as usual, was drinking brandy and water. It was hot, and no air came through the small windows cut into the iron walls; the room was filled with heavy black furniture which had once been Swannie's mother's pride, but was now burned and scratched everywhere. On the walls hung many pious, illuminated mottoes in High Dutch, and a picture of Swannie's grandfather, who had been a member of Kruger's last Volksraad; or so Swannie sometimes claimed.

Swannie shouted:

'A sudden blast of dusty wind, and after
Thunder of feet, tumult of images.'

No one listened to him. The stormtrooper whispered in Leonie's ear; they drew back their heads, laughed, and leaned together once more. Her boyfriend was telling Malcolm at length about a row he had had with a producer at Broadcasting House.

'All turn with amorous cries, or angry cries,
According to the wind, for all are blind.
But now wind drops, dust settles …'

Swannie broke off. 'Hell, this wind is even more sinister when it settles than when it blows. Listen, man –'
He was interrupted by the entry into the room of a group of three newcomers. One of them was Pieter de Wet, a pimply, stammering young man who was a friend of Swannie's from his schooldays, and who now worked as a clerk in the Johannesburg Municipality. The two who were with him, a man and a woman, were introduced as Barry and Jackie, and were soon settled in chairs, with glasses in their hands; de Wet sat on the floor, next to the painter's feet. Swannie tried to go back to his poetry reading, but the man who had come in with de Wet began to ask, in a deep, slow, measured voice, as if he were some kind of census-taker, what the name was of everyone there, what each of them did, where each of them lived.
This man, Barry, was very tall and swarthy, with a furrowed brow and a head of black hair that went back from his brow in a series of waves or corrugations that were like a continuation of the wrinkles of his brow. The questions he was asking, and his ponderous way of asking them, amused the others, who began to offer him facetious replies: Leonie said that she was

Betty Grable, man, that she lived in Hollywood, man, and made bioscope pictures for a living – what did he think? He did not answer; he went on asking his questions. He stared in puzzlement at the insensible painter, then passed over him to Malcolm. Malcolm answered him straightforwardly, in English; thereafter the man spoke English only, and directed almost all his remarks to Malcolm. His English accent was 'better', more English, than that of any one else in the room, except for Malcolm, and he obviously took pride in it, enunciating his words with care. His dark brown eyes moved restlessly when he was listening to anyone else; but when he spoke his gaze became arrested, fixed downwards unseeingly at a point a few inches in front of him. There was the faintest tremor to his large hands, which had bluish, dirty fingernails, and were adorned with two rings, both of them heavy gold affairs, one bearing a monogram on its flat face, the other a red stone.

Having asked the others who they were and what they did, the stranger proceeded to tell them about himself. His name was Barry van Tonder; he had been a student at the university in Pretoria, but had chucked it up, it was a waste of time. So what did he do? He wrote – that's what he did. Mostly poetry, but plays and novels also. But he had had nothing published yet. He wasn't ready to publish. He was in no hurry. He'd publish in his own sweet time. He wasn't going to dissipate the effect of his work by publishing it in dribs and drabs.

'How're you going to concentrate it then?' Swannie asked, amused. 'In one huge fat volume?'

'Perhaps,' van Tonder answered solemnly. 'That's what I'm thinking of doing.'

Everyone, except for van Tonder himself and the girl, laughed at this answer. She hadn't said a word since she'd come in; she had merely sat in her chair, drunk from her glass, and looked around her with a shallow, idle, grey stare.

'You laugh?' van Tonder said. 'I'm not joking. I want to make a real impact. I want to make an effect. I want to feel that I've got power over my readers, man, power.'

It was a word to which he kept returning. 'Pow-er,' he said, with a drawn-out, unexpected emphasis each time, on the second syllable. Not political pow-er, not physical pow-er. He wanted something deeper, he said, more subtle, more intimate: moral pow-er, psychological pow-er.

'Oh, it's too marvellous,' Leonie put in, 'when you have your audience in your power. That's why I don't like all this work I'm doing on the wireless. There's no real audience.'

Van Tonder went on as though he had not been interrupted. 'I want to make people feel as I feel about the world. When I get each reader alone, then I can tell him what to think, how to react –'

Swannie hooted, '*Jy praat kak, man!* What sort of power is that – what's it worth, when you never see the reader, when you can't tell who he is or how he'll react to your work? He might throw your big, fat, concentrated volume into the rubbish bin, and where's your power then? You're at his mercy, chum, he's not at yours. You want power? Go and drive a ten-ton truck.'

Van Tonder was not offended. 'So why do you write?' he asked Swannie, with his air of a simple-minded, portentous census-taker seeking information.

'I don't write,' Swannie answered shortly. 'Ask Malcolm.'

Van Tonder fixed his gaze a little way in front of Malcolm. 'Why do you write?'

'Because I want to be rich and famous and have nice things said about me.'

'You think those are good motives?' van Tonder asked ploddingly.

'Motives don't matter. All that matters is the quality of the work that's done.'

'Don't come with that stuff,' Swannie said disgustedly. 'You think the quality of your motives won't affect the quality of the work you do?' He reflected for a moment, but only for a moment. 'Not that there's anything wrong with wanting to be rich and famous. You can want what you like. It depends on the way you want it, how much else you want, the strength you have to get what you want, the depth from which you want. That's what I mean by the quality of your motives. It's got nothing to do with morality, you understand. It's the charge,' Swannie said clenching his fist and pushing it slowly forward through the air, his voice seeming to grind on the word, with a heavy Afrikaans 'r' in the middle of it, 'the charge you bring that I'm talking about. In his stupid way this bloke's right when he talks about power. What he doesn't understand is that we don't read someone's work because of the power he has to make us think or feel differently, but because of the power he expresses, the power he *is*. We want to touch it, to feel it going through us: this – this – accumulation of power that some people have, that some people are. Afterwards we can moralize about the effect of having it go through us, if we like. But we mustn't confuse our moralizing, or the writer's moralizing, with what's actually been done to us. That's the only sense in which you say that motives don't matter. Don't think your work's going to express for you any power you haven't got.'

Swannie bent and groped about on the floor for his glass and drank from it. As if she had been waiting for a signal that he had finished, the girl with van Tonder yawned in utter boredom, opening her mouth wide, showing white teeth and a red tongue which contracted and thickened the more widely her mouth opened. The skin of her cheeks was stretched tight; her eyes were closed. When she came to the end of her yawn and opened her eyes, they were swimming with tears.

Until then Malcolm had taken little notice of her. Van Tonder and Swannie between them had drawn all his attention. But now, while van Tonder began repeating, at length and with great solemnity, what he had originally put forward, and some part of Malcolm's mind worried over what Swannie had said and then put it aside, he stared at the girl. She was sitting back, her head turned away from him, her glass dangling from her fingertips over the arm of her chair. She was small and young; her hair was fair and was cropped as short as a boy's; her face was round and guileless, though there was something curiously finicky, cold and yet childlike, about the set of her brightly lipsticked mouth. She was wearing a pair of grey trousers and a blouse; a thin red scarf, the same shade as her lipstick, was tied around her neck, with the knot to one side. Malcolm saw the seam that ran straight down the middle of the trousers, over her flat little stomach, and disappeared under her.

First her yawn; then that seam: he thought the emotion they aroused in him was contempt. Some minutes passed before he realized that whatever it might have been at first it was now desire. Once he had come to the realization, his desire became direct, immediate, almost vindictive in its intensity. He could not take his eyes off her.

Swannie and van Tonder wrangled, neither of them really talking to the other, or to anyone else; the painter got to his feet suddenly, snorting and smacking his lips, and staggered out of the room without saying a word, his hand groping towards his fly. The stormtrooper and Leonie were whispering together again. 'Art for art's sake,' de Wet stammered out, at something Swannie had said; because of his stammer he seemed to say in a gabble just 'Art – art – art', the other words lost. Malcolm stared at the girl, making no attempt to disguise what he was feeling. He had nothing to lose.

When at last she looked at him, and continued to look at him, it seemed surprising to him that the others in the room were unaware of what had happened between them; he would have thought it to be as audible as a word, as visible as a gesture. Again and again her small grey eyes rested on him; still neither of them spoke.

At last he said quietly to her, 'My name's Malcolm.'

'*Ja*, I heard your name when I came in.'

When she got up, saying that she was going to make some coffee in the kitchen, Swannie just shouted after her, 'Go ahead, it's a good idea.' She left the room, and Malcolm followed her a minute later, muttering some excuse about washing out his glass.

The kitchen was a dark, smelly little place, containing little but a sink, an old coal-burning stove, and a wooden icebox with a gauze door. The girl was standing at the sink, running water into a coffee pot. Malcolm put down his glass on top of the icebox. She did not speak or move, having turned her head once to see who it was that had come in. Malcolm's heart beat fiercely to see how still she stood. She was waiting for him.

He took her around the waist from behind. She was thin, a scrap of cloth and warm flesh beneath it, nothing more. He pressed his lips against her neck, above the scarf, and smelled the dry odour of her hair. He did not know what he could do with her there, or what she would do, and did not care.

Still she did not move; the tap ran on, the coffee-pot was full and the water ran over her fingers. She seemed to be abstracted, hardly aware of him. Then in her slow, rather harsh voice, she said, 'You're a fast worker, Mister Malcolm.'

He held her more tightly, unwilling to speak, lest his voice should shake, and betray his uncertainty.

She switched off the tap, and stood for a moment with her hand on it. 'Come,' she said, 'Let's see if we can find somewhere.'

Malcolm closed his eyes, leaning against her. He could not move for the moment, he was so weakened by desire, and by relief and incredulity at what she had said. 'You mean it?' he said. His voice did shake. 'You mean it?'

With a brisk movement she disengaged herself from him and opened the back door of the kitchen. He followed her.

12

Outside, from a clear blue sky, the sun poured down with a dazzling prodigality upon a small sandy yard, three pepper trees, a fowl *hok* of netting-wire and iron, and a large, tattered, rusting iron shed leaning at an angle, as if it had been blown aslant by the wind. They went first to the shed and peered into it through a glassless hole cut into one of its sides. It was too dark to see anything inside; but the girl sniffed with her head inside the aperture and said, 'It smells like kaffir to me. No thank you.'

'Where?' Malcolm said, looking vaguely around him, oppressed by the glare. He felt the effect of the brandy he had been drinking more strongly than he had indoors; the waves of light that passed over the ground, one after the other, seemed to be tugging at him, making him unsteady on his feet. 'We must be quick.' He heard his own voice as if from a distance.

Behind the pepper trees was a sagging wire fence; then a wide, flat expanse of grass, knee-high, pale brown. A few hundred yards off were two isolated roofless houses, with piles of bricks and builders' sand around them. Much further off, filling the horizon, was the white, flat-topped pyramid of a mine-dump. 'There,' the girl said, pointing at the houses.

'There may be a watchman.'

'That'll be bad luck, won't it?'

But there was no watchman. They fled, almost running now, into the first house they came to. Scraps of hardened cement were everywhere, fallen from the rough brickwork on to the earth which the walls enclosed; no floors were down, and the sun came in from above. He wanted to take her in his arms, but she pushed him away. She unzipped her slacks and kicked off her sandals; she stood in front of him in her blouse, a pair of white panties and short white socks. He reached out and touched the shadow of the hairs of her groin, visible through the cloth. Her smallness made him feel guilty and pitying; then all the more desperate to get at her. He stumbled, struggling to take off his trousers. Just before he grasped her he asked, 'What about precautions? I haven't got anything.'

'It's all right. It's the end of my month. This is your lucky day, man.'

They were in the shadow cast across the unfinished room by one of the walls, and the sand was surprisingly cool and soft under his knees. Then it packed hard, irritating him. But by that time he had finished. Jackie lay with her head on his jacket, her face turned to one side, as he had seen it before in the house. Her skin was sallow and shiny with sweat.

When she began to move, in an attempt to get up, he held her pinioned down. 'Don't go, there's no hurry,' he said, puzzled by her sudden anxiety to be free of him. But she struggled fiercely against him, whispering in Afrikaans and English that she had to go, it was so late, they'd been there so long already. He was horrible, he was a pig, who did he think he was, she was sorry she'd come, she'd never let him touch her again.

'Don't be stupid,' he told her, smiling, pinning her by the arms, watching her throw her head helplessly from side to side. 'You should have done this before, not now. It's too late now.' Eventually she laughed and opened her eyes, which had been closed while she had been fighting against him; she seemed to surrender again. But no sooner had he relaxed and begun to caress her, under the blouse she was still wearing, than she twisted free and was on her feet. She took Malcolm's trousers and chucked them through the doorway, into the open space in front of the house.

'You bitch!'

'That's what I am. That's what you must learn about me.'

The ponderousness of her English mollified Malcolm; it amused him. 'All right. I'm learning fast.' He went to the doorway and peered cautiously through it. There was no one about, only the sun shining on the grass, glinting off the roof of Swannie's house in the distance. He retrieved his trousers and came back inside.

They were both covered in red sand, filthy with it, like two urchins. They dusted each other's clothes and bodies, and wiped their faces on Malcolm's handkerchief.

'And now I suppose I'll have to go and fight your friend.'

'If he was the fighting sort, you think he'd have let us go off like this?'

'No, I suppose not,' Malcolm said, reassured.

They walked back to the house arm-in-arm. In spite of the chafing of the sand inside his trousers Malcolm felt smooth and languid within himself, weightless, easy. Even the dry grass seemed suave, in its stillness, colour and light. He tightened his grasp on her waist.

'What's your second name?'

'Verster.' She added, proudly and defensively, 'My mother's French. I'm half-French.'

'That accounts for you then,' Malcolm said, touched by the way she had given him this information, and knowing that what he said would please her.

She nodded, satisfied.

13

Still, Malcolm was apprehensive as they approached the house. But they found when they came into the front room that every one, with the exception of Swannie himself, had left. He was still sitting in his armchair, with his glass in his hand; he was now plainly very drunk. His mouth hung open, his arms were flung over each side of his chair; everything about him looked collapsed, except for his eyes, which started even further forward out of his head, and were fixed in one direction only.

'Where's everybody?' Malcolm asked, as casually as he could.

Swannie made no reply.

'*Is hulle weg*?' Jacqueline asked.

'Yes, they've gone, I told them to bugger off.'

'Why you do that?'

'Because they're all *snakes*!' Swannie shouted, lurching forward, yet held back by the arms of the chair, which were now under his armpits. 'And you're the biggest snake of the lot! You!' He pointed at Malcolm. 'You think you can do what you like, don't you? You think –'

'Swannie –'

'Meneer Swanepoel to you, you bloody snake.' He tried to turn towards the girl. 'You're a bloody whore, that's all you are. You come here for the first time and you've got no shame, you just fuck off into the veld with someone you've never seen before, and you come back stinking like a polecat. You stink! You hear what I say? You stink!'

The girl laughed, standing with her hands on her slight grey trousered hips. 'You're jealous! Why you so jealous, man? What's the matter with you? If you want it so much then you must ask for it; you mustn't sit here talking about books all day.'

'I wouldn't touch you.'

'No, I wouldn't let you touch me. That's why. The only reason.'

Malcolm was sure the girl was right about Swannie's jealousy: the boldness and quickness of what they had done had got under his skin.

'Come off it, Swannie. I wasn't doing anything against you. That other bloke would have a right to complain. But not you.'

Swannie ignored him, and spoke to the girl. 'You think he's bloody marvellous, I suppose. You think he's got such a nice English voice and such nice English manners and maybe he's got a lot of nice English money to go with them. Well, I can tell you that he's nothing. He's got no money. You should read the crap he writes. And you know why he comes here? He's slumming, that's all. We amuse him. He thinks we're funny – funny Boers. Primitive people. Backvelders. Ignorant Dutchies. He thinks it's a joke to hear us talking about books and art, because as far as he's concerned we're just another tribe here in the *bundu*. I know the way these superior bastards think. Don't come here again, Begbie. Fuck off! I don't want to see your face again!'

'All right,' Malcolm said. Then he said; 'Maybe I am slumming – with the others. But not with you, Swannie. You might as well know that. I thought you did.'

He had spoken quietly; but the girl was angry. 'I'm no Boer.' Her mouth twisted in a loop of disgust. 'I'm cosmopolitan.'

Swannie stared at her in silence, for a long time. Then he said: 'You're mad, that's what you are.' He sank back into his chair. 'Ach, leave me alone, do what you like.'

They stood hesitating in front of him. Jacqueline turned to Malcolm and said complainingly, 'I'm dying of thirst.' When he glanced at Swannie she stamped her foot. 'I'm thirsty, dammit, didn't you hear me? It's thirsty work. I want something to drink – water, brandy, anything.'

Her reference to thirsty work made Malcolm smile, and he looked around the room for the water-jug, found that it was empty, and went into the kitchen to fill it up. When he came back into the room the girl was sitting on the arm of Swannie's chair, and stroking his hair. Swannie was in tears. He struggled out of the chair, staggered across the room, and fell into another. From there he begged them not to leave him. He was frightened to be on his own. He was in a hell of a state, he said. Did they know he'd killed, actually killed, his own mother?

This, Malcolm knew from previous experience, was Swannie's way of describing the fact that, two years before, when he'd been away with some of his friends in the Cape, he had ignored a telegram that had announced her illness and asked him to come home immediately. He had thought the telegram to be a ruse to get him away from people of whom he knew his devout, church-going, Bible-reading mother disapproved. So by the time he had come back to the house she was dead and buried. 'But I still see her sometimes,' Swannie said, wringing his hands. 'In dreams, and when I've been drinking too much. And you know what's the most terrible thing when I see her? She doesn't know that she's dead! But I know. She speaks to me just as if she was still alive. And I can't tell her.' Earnestly, imploringly, fixing them with the shining, wet orbs of his eyes, he asked them, 'How can you say something like that to your own mother?'

Later, when he was calmer, they cleared away the glasses and washed them, and put the empty bottles in Malcolm's car – at Swannie's suggestion – so that his father wouldn't see them. 'He's started again, the old bastard,' Swannie explained. 'He comes home stinking, and then he moans about me boozing too much.' They persuaded him to go to bed, which he collapsed into with his suit on; they took off his heavy black shoes and covered him with a sheet, and left the house.

Malcolm drove Jacqueline back to town. She insisted that she be put off at an address she gave him, in Motortown. She had to see what had happened to Barry. Barry was her friend.

'Will I see you again?' he asked.

'You want to?'

'Of course.'

'Then you can phone me.' She gave him her number, and climbed out of the car. The building behind her was an old, shabby block of flats between two wholesalers' warehouses. She fluttered her fingers in farewell, and ran up the steps.

14

'Mind your own business.' 'Ask no questions and you'll hear no lies.' 'Least said soonest mended.' 'Curiosity killed the cat.' It was with phrases like these that Jacqueline answered almost all Malcolm's questions about herself and the way she lived. After having seen her half a dozen times he had learned little more than that she lived in a room in Barry van Tonder's flat but didn't sleep with him because he was impotent; that she had other boyfriends ('Hell, what do you think's so special about you?'); that she had had an abortion three years previously, when she had been sixteen; and that she was half French. Malcolm became more and more sure that this last 'fact' was untrue; not least because she insisted so much on it. Round her supposititious Frenchness, however, she had built a whole theory of national characteristics which seemed to be the one intellectual structure in her head. Frenchmen were best ('sexiest'); then came Italians. Greeks and Portuguese were 'slimy'. About the Jews she was very knowledgeable: Russian Jews were 'all right', but she couldn't stand German Jews – they should never have let so many of them into the country. The English were feeble but they had better manners than the Afrikaners. She wished she had the chance to meet some Americans; they did things in style, you could tell from their bioscope pictures. Kaffirs were beyond consideration, but some

Indians were very attractive; they had such lovely thick black hair. And so on, and so on.

She believed, apparently, in nothing else. Malcolm tried again and again to find in her some scruple or other, some ambition, some shame. But he had no success; the nearest he came to it was to find that she had a kind of wayward, contemptuous loyalty towards van Tonder. She was delinquent, brainless and altogether at the mercy of her own impulses; she prided herself only in her ability to surprise, disappoint and disconcert others. She even lacked greed. She wasn't particularly interested in money or clothes or possessions. She worked when she had to – usually behind the counter of a shop – but for the last six months she had been sponging off van Tonder, whose father was a well-to-do farmer near Potchefstroom. On most mornings she slept late, then she listened to the radio or talked to Barry, or went to a cheap Greek restaurant for a meal, or just walked about looking at shop windows. She spent much of her time in cinemas; she roamed about the town with van Tonder or with one of her other boyfriends; sometimes with Malcolm.

With each meeting his desire for her grew. In a strange, abstract way it fed itself as much upon her stupidity, her availability, her unscrupulousness, her detachment, as it did on the smallness and immaturity of her body, so much used, and so much still like a child's. He was excited to a more intense sensuality by the sight, at unexpected moments, of her small eyes fixed steadily upon him, with the indifferent, uncomprehending curiosity of a child; he learned to anticipate her bouts of sullenness, when she would be as insulting and frustrating as she knew how, as well as the rarer occasions when she would zealously and winningly do her best to please him; he gloated over her imperfections and vulgarities – her too-small eyes, her shiny skin, her wry mouth, her uneducated Afrikaans accent. At night he dreamed about her; by day he thought about her in remembered postures, he imagined grossness he could inflict upon her when he next saw her. There were times when he thought wildly of asking her to marry him; there were other times when he swore he would never see her again. Yet, though she sometimes did, he never failed to keep an appointment he had made with her. If she had allowed him to he would have made one every day.

Yet the knowledge that he was truly obsessed by her came to Malcolm only when his fantasies, for no reason that he knew of, became unremittingly, harrowingly, violent. When he was with her he behaved as he had before; but when he was away from her he pictured himself beating her, pulling her about by her cropped hair, kicking her, strangling her, stabbing her, running her over. And the strangest most seductive thing about these fantasies was the feeling he had, when he indulged himself in them, that in carrying them out he would be doing no more than she hungered for: *then*, in the last moment, she would be whole, transfixed, palpitating, a single being revealed to herself, no longer detached, fragmentary and wondering.

These thoughts and images were grotesque, but they were hardly any more so than so much else in their relationship, including the part played in it by Barry van Tonder; the boring, plodding, inquiring, conversing, car-driving, scribbling Barry van Tonder, who was always ready to sit and smoke while they went into Jackie's bare bedroom and wait for them to come out of it, when he would resume his interrupted conversation with Malcolm about Thomas Mann or D. H. Lawrence, or the advantages of collectivism over individualism, or whether or not God existed, or the origins of colour prejudice, or a hundred other topics as large as these. He was always ready to drive Jackie about, or to make suggestions to get her into a good humour when she was in a bad one; he showed Malcolm his verse and prose in Afrikaans, and English translations of it which he himself had made, in none of which could Malcolm discern the slightest trace of talent. But for all van Tonder's slow verbosity, Malcolm never knew what went on in his mind; whether or not he was jealous, what he felt about Jackie, what he thought about his own impotence. If anything, Malcolm suspected he was rather proud of the last of these, for it set him aside from the ruck who did not suffer from so interesting an ailment; he discussed the various psychiatrists who had treated him for it. He seemed fond of Malcolm; eventually he asked him and Jackie to come to the farm with him for a weekend. 'Meet my parents,' he said. 'They'll like you, even though you are a *rooinek* Englishman.'

Malcolm had no wish to meet Barry's parents, but he did want to spend a weekend with Jackie. It was decided that Malcolm and Jackie would pretend to be married; and at the beginning of the next long weekend the three of them set off for Potchefstroom in Malcolm's car.

15

They were all tired, for they had been working during the day; and at dawn they would have to be up again. The men were all in khaki shirts and shorts; the girls were dressed in blouses and slacks. They sat at ease, relaxed, unhurried, quietly listening to the lecturer, who spoke in emphatic, hissing tones, and twisted his body forward when he made his points. Idly, the eyes of some of the girls watched his performing shadow against the bare, plastered wall of the house; other eyes met and exchanged glances, indifferently, smilingly or seriously. The lecturer's girlfriend – a fine-featured girl with soft, fair hair and intent, dark brows – listened engrossed, one finger touching in turn at each of the brass studs along the arm of the battered leather armchair in which she was sitting; an unshaven youth, deaf in

one ear, sat next to her, his head tilted to one side. Another boy
had the sleeves of his jersey knotted loosely around his neck,
and waggled the ends of the sleeves against one another, as if
he were miming applause of the speech he was hearing. Joel sat
in the doorway, the front room of the house was empty behind
him; his knees were drawn up and his chin rested on them.
When he looked up he saw the dazed yellow light of the oil-
lamps hanging from hooks on the posts that held up the roof of
the verandah; beyond them, as if the light had remained in a
mesh on his retina, there was a vibrating, flecked darkness. The
air was scented with the smell of dry grass and animal-dung,
mingled with the hot paraffin odour of the oil-lamps. The stoep
was open, but for the corrugated iron roof overhead; the black
shapes of the half-ton van in the yard and the outbuildings
were all that stood before the stars. No sound, no wind, no
light, came from outside.

'And so we see that whether we consider the plight of Jewish
youth in the Diaspora from either a Marxist or a Freudian
aspect, we are compelled to the conclusion that only through
collective endeavour can that youth be cured of the social,
economic and psychological sicknesses from which it now
suffers.' The speaker was nearing his peroration. The talk he
was giving them was a rehearsal of what he was going to say to
the Conference of Progressive South African Youth to which
their movement had been invited to send a delegation. 'And
only in a Jewish Palestine can their endeavour be truly
collective. Elsewhere society offers to individuals in our
position only atomization and alienation, a self-defeating hunt
for material goods, cynicism, apathy and despair. That is the
choice before us, *chaverim*; there is no other.'

The speaker sat down: he had started his talk in one of the
wickerwork chairs scattered about the stoep, but halfway
through it had felt the need to get up. The assembled *chaverim*
did not applaud; it was not expected that they should; but

several of them nodded, and others looked simply relieved. Then there was a long silence. Indeed, even while Henry Kramer had been speaking his voice had somehow made little impressions against the vagueness, placidity and warmth of the night-air, and the fatigue of the group listening to him. And Henry Kramer himself, chief spokesman and ideologue of the Hatzofim movement, was glad that he had finished and could sit down next to Riva, his girlfriend, who extended her fingers to him from her chair, as though she had just been introduced. They sat side by side, their fingers loosely touching.

Joel had hardly listened to the lecture. He sat vacant-minded, enjoying his own tiredness. Each time he closed his eyes he saw fragments of the field in which he had been working during the afternoon: the rows of young potato plants with small white blossoms showing among their leaves, the glint off the blade of his hoe, the rusting pipe along which water ran was led from the iron dam and windmill to the furrows. When he had turned the wheel-like tap next to the dam, right at the end of the day, the water had drummed in the iron beneath his fingers; his finger-tips still seemed to tingle with the sensation. He took no part in the brief uncritical discussion of the lecture which had just been given.

Kramer believed in what he had been saying; so did all the others. Nevertheless, out of the fifteen or twenty people on the verandah, only a few were eventually to spend their lives in Palestine, though all of them were to live in the country for a shorter or longer time. One of those who was to remain was a fat, blonde girl with her name, Tamara, embroidered in Hebrew letters across the front of her blouse; she was to marry a Czech immigrant in a kibbutz in the Galilee. Another was a slight, bespectacled youth, whose black hair grew shaggily down the back of his neck and curled over the shafts of his glasses at his temples; he was sitting near to Joel, following the discussion eagerly, moving his lips as though about to enter the conversation, but never doing so. Barely a year later his chest was torn open by a hand grenade tossed from the window of a building in the Old City of Jerusalem, during the unsuccessful attempt to relieve the siege, and the mess of bubbling blood and exposed bone that had been Johnny Magidson was dragged into shelter; and from there, eventually to the calm of the military cemetery on Mount Herzl. Kramer was to become a very successful Johannesburg solicitor; but he was to be made to suffer by the girl whose fingers he now held so loosely and proudly in his left hand. Her intensity, years later, after the birth of her second daughter, was to become what the doctors diagnosed as schizophrenia.

Tamara got up and made her way into the house, followed by two or three of the other girls. When they called out, 'Coffee's ready,' everybody got up and went inside. But it seemed hot and stuffy indoors, and one by one the group came back on to the stoep, with their mugs in their hands. They drank their coffee and smoked; someone said, 'Where's your *fluitjie*, Johnny – give us a tune,' but Magidson shook his head and the others didn't insist. Soon they were yawning and exclaiming 'Who's for bed?'; soon they went off in ones and twos, the unattached girls to their rooms, the unattached boys to theirs; some couples went into the darkness of the yard, to the tents they shared.

16

Joel and Leon stayed behind on the stoep. Leon squatted next to Joel, bearing his great weight on his two small feet beneath him. 'What have you been doing with yourself?' he asked. 'I've hardly seen you all weekend?'

'I've been around.'

They were both silent. Simultaneously they started speaking again; then each halted to let the other go on.

'No, you started first.'

'I wasn't going to say anything.'

Another silence followed.

'Old Henry certainly went on and on tonight,' Joel said.

Leon laughed. 'It does no harm. People like to hear over and over again how right they are.'

'For a while. What's Henry going to do when we're all actually on a kibbutz? Nobody'll want to listen to him there.'

'He'll find something else to talk about.'

From inside the house a girl's high-pitched voice called, 'Joel.'

'Typical!' Joel said with mock disgust. 'Everybody goes to sleep, so Natalie promptly wakes up.'

'That's what she's like,' Leon said, heavily, yet wistfully. 'Perverse.'

He and Joel exchanged a glance. They both looked up when the girl came on to the stoep. Her hair was tousled, her blouse was coming out of the belt of her blue denim skirt, her feet were bare. There was a faint flush of warmth under her smooth brown skin. Her body was sturdy but supple; her short legs were slightly bowed. She stood in front of the two men and looked from the one to the other, smiling at the way they were sitting next to one another, beneath her.

'What were you talking about?'

'You,' Joel answered.

'Were you saying nice things about me?'

'Not very.'

'I'm sure you weren't. But Leon was defending me, weren't you, Leon?' She laughed, and Leon turned his head away quickly, with a look of anger or pain on his face. Natalie put her hand on his head. 'Leon, I'm not laughing at you.'

He jerked his head away from her hand and rose to his feet. 'I don't want your patronage.'

'Oh, Leon,' Natalie said, moving aside, away from them both, with a thrust of her hips. She stood at the head of the steps that led down from the stoep to the yard, looking into the darkness. None of them moved. From the yard they heard someone unseen saying distinctly and quietly. 'Good night,' and the sound of footsteps retreating cautiously. A door at the back of the house slammed shut. For a moment they were suspended in the stillness, as if their own emotions had been taken out of their care. The yellow light wavered, giving a fringe to the darkness.

It seemed simple for Natalie to go to Leon, put her arms around his neck, and say, 'I'm sorry, Leon. I'm not playing with you – or Joel. I think I love him.'

'I think you do,' he answered sadly, but without resentment; almost with a touch of humour or relief in his voice. 'You never loved me anyway, you told me that you didn't. But I hoped –' He turned to Joel. 'I mean before you came. Still, I'm not sorry that you've joined the group. I mustn't think only of myself.'

Joel couldn't help smiling at the remark; it embarrassed him by the self-conscious earnestness of its altruism. Yet Leon had spoken sincerely enough. He said to Leon, and to Natalie, too, 'Anyway, it's a good thing we're speaking out at last.'

'There's nothing else to say,' Leon answered.

Again they were silent. But the impulse of goodwill, of frankness, of reconciliation, had spent itself. Natalie dropped her arms; now she went over to Joel. 'Come,' she said, prodding him with her bare toes. 'Come for a walk.'

'A walk! At this hour? Are you mad?'

'Yes.'

She smiled over him, her eyes bright under her smooth brown forehead. Joel got to his feet with a groan.

'Good night,' Leon said abruptly, and went into the house, hurt, burly and undignified.

Natalie stared after him. Finally she said, 'Well, I'm glad that's done.'

Joel had returned to his place on the floor. 'You're a funny girl. The first time you say that you love me, you say it to someone else, not to me. What's the idea?'

'As long as I've said it.'

Joel lunged at her ankle. But she danced away from him. 'As long as I've said it,' she chanted, hopping about, her toes spreading out with each quick step on the hard cement of the stoep. Her skirt swung about her; her head of hair danced too. 'As long as I've said it.' She hopped through the open door and disappeared.

But she returned a few moments later, with a pair of sandals on her feet and a torch in her hand. 'Come.'

'You're serious?'

'I nearly always am.'

17

They stepped into the darkness of the yard, the torch's circle of white light swinging around them, revealing glimpses of trampled sand, the marks of tyres, the ropes and sloping canvas walls of the tents. Joel took Natalie's bare arm in his hand. Soon they were out of the yard and were walking along the double track that led from the farmhouse to the main road which was the border of the farm. There was no moon in the sky, but the stars were so thick and bright, and the veld was so dark, that the horizon was clearly marked all the way around them. A ridge of kopjes ahead of them brought that horizon comparatively close; behind them the veld stretched away unbroken for such a distance that it looked as though the sky was tilted over to enclose it, at the very end.

They did not speak; they walked steadily together in silence, until they reached the gate that opened on the main road. The metal of the gate was cold on their bare arms. They rested there, side by side. Joel looked at Natalie; her regular features were outlined against the stars, made by them to seem large and austere. When she spoke, saying something about the warmth of the evening, the high girlishness of her voice surprised and delighted him; like a memory it ran through his blood. He moved over to take her in his arms.

'I love you,' he said. 'I heard you say that you love me.'

'I do.'

They stood together, his lips in her hair. The tenderness he felt for her was a pain in his breast: she was so pretty, so troubled, so lively, her voice was so high. Always he had been moved by her frailty and by the largeness of the changes she wished for in her own single life, and the lives of others; now the changes had begun for them both. In the darkness, in the empty veld, where nothing moved and the only sounds were those of their own breathing, rustling, swallowing, the future was a weight he wanted to grasp, to carry, never to surrender. Why had he feared it? How could he have doubted that it would bring such an answer to him?

He felt her hands upon his shoulders, her breath on his face. When they kissed the stars swung about their heads, flared around them, hanging in clusters and bunches – so close a hand could have grasped them, then seeming to spin away with a hiss.

Natalie's flesh was the softest he had ever touched; so soft it escaped from him like water. They came together again, and this time their embrace was strained; her mouth was awkward in its eagerness to meet his. They pressed closer together; still her feather-soft, feather-light flesh seemed to escape from the burden they wished it to bear, and he followed it fiercely in the delusive darkness, searching for it, feeling it gather and scatter before him.

'What's that?'

She had broken away from him with a shock. Behind him was an immense radiance, irregular and wavering, soundlessly growing.

'It's only a car,' Joel reassured her.

He was breathless and disconcerted, unsteady on his feet, hardly knowing where he was. He grasped at the gate to steady himself. They stood a foot or two apart from one another, waiting for the car to go by. The light from it was still wide, thrown skywards, with no single source; then the car appeared over an incline and the light contracted, became a beam racing towards them. Only then, for the first time, did they hear the sound of the engine. The hard metalled surface of the road blinked wickedly. Their shadows, the shadows of the gate, of the fence, of the white, sharp-edged stones revealed on the roadside, of the low acacia trees in the veld – all whirled and raced away from them, stretching longer and longer, until the car burst past. Each shadow was instantly snapped off at the root, the noise of the car swept away, carrying with it a brush of light in front and a receding red light behind. The rest was a single shadow once more, under the sky.

Joel had shielded his eyes with his hand and turned his head away as the car had passed; now he watched it go. The light at the back travelled smoothly, at one height above the ground. Then, inexplicably, Joel saw that red light suddenly swing, swirl high in the air, looking no bigger, no heavier, than a cigarette-end flicked up by a finger. Across the veld they heard a dull, explosive sound, like a cardboard box collapsing, then a second fainter one. The light had gone out.

'They've had an accident,' Joel shouted. He heard Natalie cry out. He groped on the ground for the torch, which he had put down there earlier, took her hand in his and began running along the verge of the road.

18

Inside the car, as the two offside wheels had lifted in the air, Malcolm's last thought had been: She'll never fall back. He was aware of the side of the car rising yet higher, for the briefest instant; then of a blow against the side of his head. It seemed much later that he felt the air rushing past him, he felt its coolness; and another blow struck at him. Where it struck him, or from where it had come, he did not know. He knew nothing, not even darkness.

Brightness assailed his eyes when he opened them, a myriad points of it darted stingingly at him out of black space. The surface he was lying on was cold and hard. He closed his eyes, and opened them again after another lapse of time.

He was fully conscious. He knew what had happened and where he was. The car had turned over, he was on the ground, the points of cold silver light he was looking into were stars in the sky. He remembered the sensation of the side of the car lifting, the bang on his head, his flight through the air, the second blow. He must have been flung out through a door that had burst open. Where was Jackie? How was she?

He sat up, puzzled to find that there were no shoes on his feet. The sky had never before looked as black to him as it did now, the stars had never been so bright. The night air was like another element, like water, flowing over his limbs. The car was a shape a little way ahead. He approached it cautiously, hobbling over the ground in his socks.

'Jackie?' he called quietly. 'Jackie?'

There was no reply. He drew in dread with his breath; then he screamed out, 'Jackie! Are you all right?'

He heard the sound of footsteps, and turned. A light shone in the distance; it was coming closer, people were running towards him. Jackie must have gone to fetch help, he thought, as totally relieved as he had been terrified a moment before. He began hurrying and hopping towards the light. The faint yellow beam appeared to be many yards away; yet he took only a few paces and the people were upon him. One of them was a man, the other a woman. The young woman was not Jackie, but someone else, a stranger.

'Where's Jackie?' he demanded.

'Jackie?'

'Yes, where is she? Have you got her?'

'We've just come.'

The torchbeam was directed downwards, towards the ground. Three detached pairs of feet were visible in its light: in sandals, in *veldskoen*, in socks. Malcolm saw them with the same startling vividness with which he had earlier seen the sky and the stars. They looked absurd and sinister, related to nothing. The beam of the torch swung upwards, it was shining upon him. Before he could bring his hands to his face it was gone again.

'Are you all right? How many of you are there?'

'Just me and Jackie. Barry said he wanted to stay on for a few days.' Malcolm stopped, remembering with difficulty that these people did not know Barry or Jackie. He heard someone tittering at his mistake, and was insulted by the sound. Then he knew that he was the one who had been laughing.

'I'll stay here,' Natalie said, shrinking back into the darkness.

'All right, I'll go and have a look.'

Joel had already moved away before Malcolm called, 'Wait, I'll come with you.' He ran after the other. His feet kicked against something – it was one of his shoes. He stooped and picked it up. On his hands and knees he groped about, looking for the other shoe.

By the time he had found it, Joel was waving his torch and calling to him. He had found Jackie sitting on an ant-heap, a little way inside the wire fence that ran alongside the road.

'Jackie, why didn't you answer? Are you all right?' Malcolm stumbled towards her; when he reached her he picked up her hands from her lap and held them in his. 'How did you get here? Thank God you're all right.'

'I walked,' Jackie answered after a pause, speaking as though she were recollecting something from a long time before. 'I was in the car. It stopped rolling. Then I got out and walked here. Then I wanted to sit down.'

She pulled her hands away and hit at his face, stinging his cheek, one of her fingers bruising his eye. 'You bloody fool!' she shouted at him. 'Why do you drive so fast? I said you were going too fast. You could have killed me.'

'I'm sorry I didn't!' In the pain of the blow Malcolm would have sprung at her had not the stranger held him, pushed him back.

'You're both upset,' he said. 'Don't get hysterical. Everything's all right. You're lucky, you're both lucky.'

Malcolm limped away. He went back to the car. It was standing next to the fence, on all four wheels, as if one could get into it and drive on. But the hood was smashed in, especially over the corner of the front passenger's seat, and the glasswork – safety glass, Malcolm remembered – was in strange, malleable shreds. The driver's door hung wide open, but the others were jammed. It frightened Malcolm to see the car, to grope about it, the shreds of glass underneath him squeaking and grinding. How *hard* all these surfaces were, that had been slammed so violently together; how still everything now was; how irrevocable the smash. There were fragments of glass clinging to his hands, and he brushed them off carefully. His legs and arms were beginning to ache, and he was suddenly very cold.

In the meantime Joel and Jackie had approached; Joel had his arm around her shoulders. He left Jackie standing by the side of the car, and looked inside it for Malcolm's jacket and Jackie's cardigan, and insisted that they put them on. Natalie had also drawn nearer, reassured that there were no horrible sights to be seen.

'Look,' Joel said, 'the two of you stay here and I'll get the van. You can spend the night at the house; there's nothing you can do here. Natalie, will you come with me?'

'If you don't think I should stay?'

'I don't think there's anything you can do. They seem all right, really, but I don't think they could walk to the house. The girl's got a cut on her temple, but it doesn't look anything much.'

Jackie climbed into the car and sat in the driver's seat; Malcolm sat next to her, in the open door of the car, with his feet on the ground.

'Do you mind if we leave you?' Joel asked.

'Mind?' Malcolm made a great effort not to let his voice be affected by the spasms of shivering that were shaking his body. 'You're being very kind. I don't know what we would have done without you.'

Joel said, 'Well, I suppose someone else would have come along eventually.'

Then he and Natalie went off; the light of the torch retreated, the sound of their footsteps grew fainter. Malcolm and Jackie remained in the silence.

'There was a blow-out,' Malcolm said. It was the first time he had spoken to Jackie since she had hit at him. 'I remember now. The wheel just twisted out of my hand. But I was going too fast. I'd have been able to deal with it if I hadn't been going so fast.'

Jackie made no reply. He did not speak to her again. The silence rang in his ears; the stillness made him shiver.

19

When Joel and Natalie returned in the car, together with Martin, a fourth-year medical student who had been roused from his sleep to have a look at the victims of the accident, they found Malcolm on his own. Weary and embarrassed, especially because of the scene Joel had witnessed between the two of them, Malcolm explained that a car had come by, and the people in it had offered their help. He had told them that help was already coming; but on hearing that the newcomers were on their way to Johannesburg, Jackie had said that she would go with them.

Malcolm made the story as brief as possible. He didn't tell them that he had begged Jackie to stay, to be patient; that he had explained to her over and over again why he couldn't leave. He had to see that the car was towed to the nearest dorp in the morning, in any case, he had said, what would the other people think if they returned to the car and simply found no one there? But Jackie had said that all of that was none of her business; she had taken her bag and scrambled in with the newcomers, two noisy grinning young Afrikaners, stinking of drink, who had obviously been delighted to see Malcolm remain behind.

None of the three who had just arrived made any comment on what Malcolm did tell them; Martin merely remarked that he was sorry he couldn't have had a look at her before she had gone. He'd examine Malcolm at the house, he said, just to make sure he hadn't broken anything.

'All I've got is a knock on the back of my head,' Malcolm said. 'And I feel scratched all over.'

In the car, bumping along the winding double track towards the farmhouse, Joel gave his name, and Natalie's, and Martin's, to Malcolm, who responded with his own, and thanked them again for the trouble they were taking. The dark veld went by; occasionally a tree, even darker than everything around it, rose slowly out of the countryside, like some large bird labouring into flight. Malcolm felt utterly exhausted and was constantly afraid he would start shivering again.

He wanted to ask his helpers who they were – they didn't look or sound like farmers to him – but he didn't have the energy. He thought vaguely about the loss of the car: whether the insurance company would write it off, or whether it would have it repaired, how he would manage in town without it.

Just before they got to the farmhouse, Joel said, 'I better tell you – we belong to a Zionist organization. This is our training farm. There's a whole group of us here, some of us live here, some just come on weekends. So don't be surprised at how many people you'll see about tomorrow morning.'

In fact, Malcolm was surprised by the number of people he saw when he came in; word of the accident had brought them from their beds. Someone had made coffee; Malcolm drank it down eagerly, scorching his throat. In the light of the oil-lamps, sleepy, tousled, curious faces looked at him, people asked him how he felt; Joel had to repeat several times the story of how he had seen and heard the crash. It all seemed unreal, fanciful, exotic to Malcolm, as if one life had come to an end in a single thumping, rending moment, and another, after a time of profound silence, had just begun. Martin took him into another room, and examined him carefully; the gashes and scratches on his legs were deeper than Malcolm had imagined, and his trousers were torn. 'They don't hurt at all,' he told the earnest, frowning and determinedly professional young man who was examining him.

'They will,' Martin answered shortly. 'I'm sorry I haven't got anything to make you sleep.' He washed out the cuts with disinfectant, and told Malcolm to go to a doctor the next morning, as soon as he could. 'I don't think any of them will need stitching, though,' he said. 'You're a lucky bloke.'

Then Malcolm was taken into a room with a bed in it, given some blankets, a pillow, and an oil-lamp, and left alone. He did not undress, but simply climbed under the blankets, leaving the lamp burning. He could hear the people of the house dispersing. There was a knock on his door, and Joel came in. 'I'll give you a lift into town tomorrow,' he said; he felt responsible for Malcolm, having brought him there. 'We'll be leaving pretty early.'

'Thank you: I don't know how I'll repay you for what you've done.'

'We've done nothing.'

'You're at Wits, aren't you?' Malcolm asked. 'I'm sure I've seen you around.'

Joel nodded. 'I thought I'd seen you too. Good night.'

'Good night.'

20

Stealthily, Joel and Natalie carried her camp-bed into the tent in which Joel was sleeping; in the darkness they undressed, kissed one another and then lay quietly, their hands linked, their bodies separated by the wooden struts of the beds. Two other boys were fast asleep in the tent; they had slept through all the excitement of Malcolm's arrival. Again and again Joel yawned, grateful to be lying down, grateful for the blankets over him, the feel of Natalie's hand in his own, and the sound of her breathing. The knowledge that she was asleep and the protective feeling this roused in him, was the last thing he was conscious of.

Later he woke, and went out of the tent to go to the lavatory. There was no sign yet of the approach of dawn. The air was chill – he was wearing only a vest and a pair of underpants – and the ground was cold under his bare feet. He moved cautiously across the yard, baffled by the darkness and afraid of hurting his bare feet against stones or thorns. He smelled the lavatory, which was nothing more than a bucket in a little corrugated iron shed, before he reached it, and changed his mind about going into it. Instead, anti-socially, he relieved himself against the wall of the house.

Overhead, the sky seemed further off than before. But the stars were still shining brightly, and there was such a profusion of them that when a breeze blew, pricking his nostrils with the renewed smells of the yard, he almost expected the fabric of the sky to move faintly too, like an embroidered flag. But it remained still; only each point of light within it seemed to flicker, as an insect might flicker and yet remain in one place, vibrant with life.

21

The grass of the highveld was brown, russet, almost pinkish in the light of the morning sun, and the black metalled road ran straight over the slow lifts and falls of the plateau. Iron-roofed farmhouses; small muddy watercourses fringed by willows; fields of mealies and kaffir-corn; herds of grazing cattle; occasional cars approaching or overtaking, each one at first no more than a sharp blink of light ahead or in the driver's mirror, and seconds later a shape, a colour, a rush of wind; new, white, flat-topped mine-dumps, headgear and mine-compounds thrust down nakedly on the veld, with pylons marching towards them and away from them – only these arrested the eye, above the expanses of grass. The sky was high, pale and cloudless.

Inside the car, Joel was driving; Malcolm sat beside him, smoking and looking out of the window, conscious of the continuous, burning pain on his legs, and almost grateful to it, for it distracted his attention away from every slightly irregular movement of the car. Again and again, at the slightest swerve, he involuntarily braced his feet on the floor, though it hurt him to do so, or grasped at the handle of the door. Earlier on the journey Joel had stopped the car at the *dorp* nearest the farm, where Malcolm had arranged with a local garage to have his car towed into Johannesburg. Now there was nothing more to be done. Malcolm was looking forward to getting back to his room and being on his own once more.

The two of them had spoken little since setting out. They had found that they knew a number of people in common at the university; they had mentioned lecturers and choice of subjects, places they had both been to in Italy during the war, the regiments they had served in, their length of service. But they were wary of one another, estranged and yet brought into a curious intimacy by the circumstances under which they had met.

Eventually, Malcolm asked Joel about the group on the farm, and Joel began to describe the organization of the kibbutzim in Palestine, their egalitarianism and collectivism, their nationalism and their belief in the dignity of labour. Malcolm listened attentively and made few comments; nevertheless, Joel found himself adopting a somewhat sceptical, ironic tone, as if to disarm the silent criticism of the other, to get in with his own ironies first. He disliked himself for it; unfairly, he disliked Malcolm more. Why should he describe in denigratory terms the movement, and his own involvement in it, to this stranger? Yet he went on doing so. 'All one's motives are so mixed,' he said. 'I might very well never have joined the group if it hadn't been for the girl I was with last night. She was a member of the group, she's been one ever since she was a kid. And – well – she just had a great deal to do with my decision, I admit it. Of course, I was looking for something – something else – I didn't know what I was looking for. And Zionism was no novelty to me, anyway; I'd thought about it often enough before. My father's been a pretty fervent Zionist all his life.'

Malcolm said, 'It seems to me you can be drawn into worse things by a girl.'

For an instant Joel took his eyes off the road to look at him. Malcolm was staring ahead, and did not meet the glance.

'I suppose that's true,' Joel said. 'And if I'm suspicious of my motives because of the girl, I might as well be suspicious of them for a hundred other reasons.'

'And where would it get you to itemize them? One shouldn't confuse one's judgement of one's motives with judgement of one's actions anyway.'

They travelled some way before Malcolm said, 'But what about ambition – personal ambition, private ambition? You haven't taken that into account, have you? Doesn't it worry you at all?'

He felt frail, detached, confessional; weakened by the quavers of apprehension which ran through his body before his mind was aware of the reason for them. He gave Joel no chance to answer his questions. 'To live, to endure all the bloody ignominies and frustrations of living, and then to be snuffed out, having got nothing out of it except what everybody else gets; and to know beforehand that that's all you're going to get – the thought of it just makes me feel claustrophobic, I couldn't stand it. Don't you want to be – to make yourself – special? God knows, I do. More than ever, after what happened last night.'

By the time he was finished Malcolm was hardly interested in any answer from Joel; he had spoken out of his own need, and felt calmed by the confession he had made. But Joel was irritated, at first into silence, then into an off-hand counter confession.

'If I had some special talent I suppose I'd be a different person.' He watched the surface of the road: dark in the distance, it was a much paler, flecked, molten blur rushing beneath him. 'Besides, I don't think there's anything so ordinary about what I'm – what we're trying to do. We are

215

trying to cure ourselves of all the false, negative ways of being set apart that we suffer from, the wrong kinds of specialness. Or loneliness.'

'Loneliness?'

'Loneliness, marginality – I don't know what the word is. But I know what the state is: to be a kind of demi-European at the bottom of Africa, to be a demi-Jew among Gentiles. Other people have other ways of suffering from it.'

'And if you're a Jew among Jews – then you'll be able to think cheerfully of being snuffed out.'

'I don't know. Perhaps. Perhaps one would be able to reconcile oneself more easily to dying if one felt one really did belong to a living society, instead of just being part of a – of a mad machine.'

The light of the sun lay in their laps; outside the wind hissed and whimpered, the horizon wheeled round slowly. Always at just the same distance ahead of them, the road melted and began its accelerating run towards the car.

After a long silence Malcolm said, 'You know, it was an extraordinary experience for me to be flung among you people last night, especially when I was all so shaken up. It was like a dream, in some queer way: the smashed-up car, the veld, the dark, and that whole crowd of you, jumped out of nowhere, out of nothingness. Your group reminded me of something that a friend of mine – a mad Afrikaans fellow, Swanepoel; he's also at Wits – you reminded me of something he's always saying: that if you want to read about present-day South Africa the only place you can do it in is the nineteenth-century Russian novel. According to him we've got so much that they had. A big unknown, threatening peasantry, for a start. Those chaps,' Malcolm said suddenly, pointing out of the window at a group of African men walking alongside the road. Bundles on their backs, sticks in their hands, their clothes in patches, they were gone in an instant; in the rear-view mirror Joel saw them as so many upright figures, frozen by the speed of the car into an apparent immobility, against the huge, bare, achingly open landscape.

'We've got the space,' Malcolm was continuing. 'We've got the landowners. We've got the intellectuals who sit around talking endlessly about the revolution, and the ones who go out among the blacks to agitate, to plough the virgin soil. And groups like yours – you couldn't be more late nineteenth-century if you tried. We've even got our own kind of Pan-Slav reactionaries, the Afrikaner nationalists. And God knows we've got the tedium, the blankness, the meanness, the crummy provinciality. Look at that place we stopped at to arrange about the car. Look at Johannesburg on a Sunday morning.'

'All we need are the Gogols and the Turgenevs, then.'

Malcolm laughed. 'And a church, and a court, and a language of our own, and a common history.' Then he added, 'But I intend doing my best.'

'Your best?'

Malcolm nodded self-mockingly.

'So that's what your ambitions are?'

'You told me your ambitions, I might as well tell you mine.' Malcolm moved gingerly on his seat, crossing his legs. 'I suppose one other thing we lack that the Russians had, though, is patriotism. Would I be sorry if I never saw that kind of thing again?' Malcolm pointed out of the window once more. 'Never.'

He had pointed at a collection of low, iron-roofed, plaster-walled buildings by the roadside, one selling cooling drinks and fruit, another meat, a third petrol. All of them were covered with enamelled advertising signs. A little further on, a longer sprawling building, as low as the rest, with a gauzed verandah running its full length, had the word 'Hotel' painted in fading white letters on its roof. There were a few bluegum trees at the back of the hotel, a wire fence, the veld.

But they were drawing nearer to Johannesburg now; the traffic was heavier, and Joel was silent, concentrating on his driving. Groves of bluegums and wattles passed by; the mines in the distance were older, their dumps bigger and more haggard than those they had seen earlier. Gangs of African miners, helmets on their heads, their trousers tied with string under their knees, crossed the road, going from the mines to their compounds. Then the road ran through an African township: an indiscriminate, interminable jumble of scraps, tatters, shreds of building materials, in what looked like little heaps, rather than huts or houses. The township was set well back from the road, behind tall barbed-wire fences; on one side, in the open, sandy space between the road and the fence, groups of people waited for buses, or gathered around open-air food stalls. Two meetings were also taking place – one religious, addressed by an African wearing a blue, monk-like cowl and holding up a wooden cross; the other political, for above the speaker's van was a banner with the words 'Democratic South African Movement' painted on it. The crowds at both were small.

More bluegum and wattle plantations, another location; more mines, bridges over railway lines and subways beneath them; then the first suburbs for whites, with their rows of bungalow-like houses, small blocks of flats, shops with neon signs, schools surrounded by rugby fields. It was a landscape in which everything looked new and yet shabby, unused and yet without freshness, man-made yet utterly fortuitous.

'No,' Malcolm said, 'I can't say I'd be sorry never to see any of this again.'

At the entrance to the university ex-servicemen's residence at Cottesloe, Joel stopped the car and Malcolm reached behind him stiffly and took his bag from the back seat. 'A thousand thanks, again. You've helped me so much, I don't know what to say.'

'Don't say anything.'

Were they to see each other again? Joel knew that Malcolm, who was half-in and half-out of the car, was waiting to see if he would make the suggestion that they should. But some instinct of caution, some distrust, held him back. Malcolm read the hesitation in Joel's eyes, and withdrew from the car.

'Thank you again. I expect I'll see you around Main Block some time.'

'Sure. Goodbye.'

Driving away, Joel saw in his mirror Malcolm limping up the little driveway. Partly because he felt guilty about his lack of friendliness Joel decided suddenly that he had disliked the man, and was relieved at knowing what he felt. He turned the car towards Observatory. He would lunch with his parents; then go to his room and finish the essay he had to hand to Viljoen the next day, and for the sake of which he had cut short his weekend on the farm.

It had been agreed in the group that those who were attending courses at the university or elsewhere should continue with them, until such time as the farm could permanently accommodate them all, or they could leave together for Palestine.

22

The meeting of which Joel and Malcolm had caught a glimpse, outside the first township they had passed, was now being addressed by Bertie Preiss. Deliberately, in front of his audience, Bertie made use of the contrast between his harsh voice and his slight frame: he showed a weariness he did not really feel and recovered from it at a phrase he wanted to bring out with particular strength; when he had scored a point he braced himself, as he had always done, with the arm behind his back clutching the other arm at the elbow, and the gesture itself seemed to draw a murmur from the crowd. He had spoken so often in public by now – at meetings such as these at weekends, in the Great Hall and on the steps of the Main Block at the university, on the City Hall steps in town – that he was hardly conscious any longer of the mannerisms he had developed, though at one time they had been an object of much self-study in front of the mirror in his bedroom.

Speaking as simply as he could, for English was half-foreign to his audience, and he knew none of the languages they spoke among themselves, Bertie came to his peroration. He told the people in front of him that the forces that had drawn them into Johannesburg from every corner of the country, that had raised the buildings and factories and sunk the mines in which they worked, that drove the trains which carried them in and out of town every day – these same forces would be theirs to control in the future. How soon this would happen would depend on their own efforts; that it would happen, that it had to happen, was certain. The government, the schools, the laws, the police, the newspapers tried to hide the truth from them; they wanted them to remain ignorant, poor, divided and weak. But for all their weapons and oppressive laws, and for all the ruthlessness with which they used them, the oppressors were helpless in the face of history, they could not reverse the process which they themselves had begun. The course of history would respect the wants of the present rulers of South Africa as little as it had respected the republic of Paul Kruger or the empire of the Zulu king, Chaka. They had gone down, they had been overthrown, by the groups who had had the movement of history on their side. Today, in South Africa, there was only one group whose movement was identical with that of history: 'Your group, you, the industrial workers who are building a new country, a new continent, another Africa.'

There was no applause when he finished, but Bertie stood where he was, his heart beating uncomfortably, a queer nervousness and expectancy in his breast, as if he were only now about to begin his speech. It was always the same: in the stillness, his own voice silenced, standing a little above the small crowd, the township a distant, swarming darkness under the strong sun, he felt himself lifted, held, carried forward through time – time which would mount like a wave, and mount still, and never break.

He jumped off the back of the van and went to Adela, who had been moving through the crowd, peddling copies of the DSAM Newsletter. The man now speaking was an African, Ntuli, a fellow-student at the university. He showed his teeth in a kind of grin when he spoke, but in the pauses between his sentences his face wore a reflective, almost melancholy look; his heavy lids hung low over his eyes, and his mouth, under a nose with wide exposed nostrils, was set square, like that of a middle-aged man. Adela stood next to Bertie and listened for a few minutes to Ntuli, but when he switched from English into Zulu, she began to walk about once more, with her bundle of papers in her hand. The people in the crowd made way for her with a courtesy that was shadowed, that was almost turned into something else, by their curious slowness and lateness of movement, as she passed between them. Most of them were men; a woman, with a baby slung on her back in a fringed blanket, covered her face with her hands and laughed shyly when Adela approached her, holding out a copy of the paper. 'No, missus,' she said, in an abashed, trailing voice, 'I can't read,' and everyone around her laughed at the admission. Few of the people took copies of the newsletter, though Adela was giving them away for nothing.

Ntuli had just finished speaking when a police patrol-van swerved at high speed off the main road, some distance away, and raced across the sandy verge, littered with bricks, tin cans, orange peels, bits of paper. It drew up at the back of the crowd, the skid of its tyres sending up a swirl of dust. An African constable sat in the passenger's seat; a white sergeant, who had been driving, got out of the car. The crowd began to disperse immediately. The sergeant looked hard at Adela, nodded at Bertie, who nodded back in greeting, looked at Ntuli, at Govinda, an Indian, who was with them, and at Vogelman, the only other white there. He approached Vogelman.

'I don't know you. What's your name?'

'Lionel Vogelman.' He was a brightly-dressed youth, wearing a pair of sky-blue flannels, a cream sportscoat, and a white shirt with black stitching around its collar. His hair was so closely cropped it seemed to fit his head like some kind of cap.

'Address?'

Vogelman gave it to him, stammering slightly, in his eagerness to appear unembarrassed and unafraid. But there was a bright red spot on each of his cheeks.

The sergeant wrote it down in his book. He looked at Bertie, smiling. '*Hoekom maak julle Joodjies soveel moeilikheid vir ons mense?*' He shook his head, closed his book, and went back to the van.

It remained there, with the two men sitting inside it, while Govinda spoke; because of its presence only a handful of children stayed to listen to Govinda's appeal to them to ignore the intimidation and terror which the authorities were using, and would use more and more, in their efforts to hold up the advance of the enslaved people of South Africa towards the freedom which was rightfully theirs.

23

Joel and Natalie saw Malcolm again several weeks later, at the inquest on Jacqueline Verster.

The first witness was a young doctor, casualty officer in the Accident Ward of the Johannesburg General Hospital, who stated that the deceased had been admitted to the ward on the evening of the 15th of the previous month. She had been in a state of coma at the time of her admission, and had not emerged from it. There had been a contusion above the deceased's right temple; a postmortem had shown extensive sub-dural haemorrhage, followed by the clotting which was the cause of death. It was obviously impossible for him to say definitely that the death of the patient could have been avoided had she been admitted earlier; but it was certainly most unfortunate that she had not been kept under observation after the accident and had come so late into the hospital.

Apart from the officials of the court, there were in the dim courtroom barely more than a dozen people islanded in clusters on the benches; between each group polished wood gleamed dully. An African witness, a young girl in a smart grey and white frock, silk stockings, and a schoolgirl-like beret on her head, sat behind a barrier on the bench reserved for her. Tall windows went up on one side, showing only a blank grey wall beyond. Though the room was on the ground floor, the occasional noises of traffic that penetrated into it sounded remote, as though they came from a great distance.

In turn, first Natalie then Joel described what they had seen of the accident. Asked about the speed at which the car had been travelling, Joel replied that it had not seemed to him to have been driven at a recklessly high speed, though it had been going fast. Both the driver and the passenger appeared to have been in a state of shock when he had arrived on the scene; he had noticed the cut on the girl's head, but had not thought it to be anything serious, as she was walking and talking in a more or less normal way, allowing for the shock she had suffered. No, he had not smelled any alcohol on Mr Begbie's breath. He had left the scene of the accident in order to get help; when he had returned the girl was no longer there. He understood that she had taken a lift with some passers-by. He had not seen her again.

One of the men who had given Jackie a lift said, in Afrikaans, that the deceased had seemed well and cheerful, until just before they arrived in Johannesburg. Then she said that she was feeling 'funny', and had started shivering; she had said that her head ached and that it had felt to her as if it was 'growing'. They had offered to take her to the hospital, but she had insisted she would be all right once she had had a rest. They had dropped her off outside a building in Eloff Street Extension. They had not seen her again.

The African girl then gave evidence that she had come into the flat in the morning to tidy up, using her own key, and had seen 'Miss Jackie' lying on the bed, fully dressed. She had noticed the cut on her head. 'In the afternoon, master,' the girl went on, addressing the coroner nervously and politely, clutching a handkerchief in her slender, pale brown hands, 'I went to see if Miss Jackie is all right now. I knock on the door. Miss Jackie doesn't answer. I think she is still just sleeping, and I go away. Later I knock again; still Miss Jackie doesn't answer. So I get a little worried, master, and go inside. Miss Jackie is on the bed, lying just the same way, only now she is breathing differently, making more noise, too much noise. I call her and shake her. She doesn't want to wake up, master. So I run out of the room and call Mrs Robinson from next door.'

The girl brought her handkerchief to her eyes and sobbed into it, overcome both by the memory and by her nervousness in front of the court. Her breakdown came almost as a relief; people turned and whispered to one another, and looked out of the windows. Malcolm, who was sitting with Swannie and Barry van Tonder, stared straight ahead of him at the Union coat-of-arms, an ornate blur of green and gold, on the wall behind the coroner's desk.

She was allowed to stand down, and Mrs Robinson, a dishevelled grey-haired Scotswoman, described with many loose dramatic gestures how she, too, had tried to rouse Miss Verster, had failed, and had then called for an ambulance. 'I must say,' she added, one hand upon her bosom, which seemed to stretch all the way down to her waist, 'that I always thought that poor girl would come to a bad end. I never liked what was going on in that flat, and I said so too, to Mr Berliner when he came to collect the rent. But he took no notice, he doesn't care what happens in the building as long as the rents come in.' It was with some difficulty that the coroner persuaded her to step down; she did not do so, in fact, until she had produced a handkerchief from the bag looped over her wrist and had cried affectingly into it.

Finally, Malcolm was called to give evidence. He spoke in a low voice, looking down; he was pale, but did not seem nervous. He said he had been travelling at just under sixty miles an hour when the front nearside tyre had blown out, and the car had been wrenched out of his control. He had been flung out of the car; Miss Verster had apparently remained inside it until it had stopped rolling. He, too, had thought her to be in a shocked state, and had noticed the cut to the side of her forehead. He had begged her not to leave him, but to wait until Mr Glickman had returned; but she had not listened to him.

The coroner was a burly, bespectacled man, who spoke with a thick Afrikaans accent, and put back his head at every question. His face was flat, but for a tiny, pointed nose, emerging between the lenses of his glasses; it was his nose, rather than his gaze, that he seemed to point at the witnesses.

'Did you not feel responsible for her?' he asked Malcolm, his head well back.

'Of course I did. That was why I asked her to stay with me.'

'But you couldn't persuade her to do so?'

'No. She was very strong-minded about the things she wanted to do.'

'And you didn't feel that you should go with her?'

'No. She seemed well enough. And I was anxious about the car. Besides, help was being brought to us – I couldn't just leave.'

Malcolm then described how he had come into Johannesburg the next morning, and had returned to his room at the university ex-servicemen's residence at Cottesloe. He had not seen the deceased again.

'When you came into Johannesburg that morning, you didn't make it your business to find out how she was?'

'No. I was feeling pretty shaken up by the accident. I'd been hurt too. I took some pills and slept all that day.'

'You didn't even phone up to ask what had happened to her?'

'No.'

'Why not?'

'I've told you. Besides, I was fed up with her.' His voice had been low throughout; the last part of this answer he merely muttered.

'Would you repeat that please? We couldn't hear you.'

'Because I was fed up with her,' Malcolm said loudly, looking up.

At this reply there was again a whisper in the room. The coroner stared at him, waiting until the whisper had died down. Then he repeated, as if incredulously committing the words to his memory, 'You were fed up with her!'

'Yes. I'd made up my mind that I wasn't going to have anything more to do with her. Not that that's relevant.'

'Excuse me, Mr Begbie, I'm the one who decides what is relevant and what isn't.'

Malcolm waited.

'So you did nothing? Nothing to help her?'

'No.'

'Very well, you may stand down.'

White-faced, pale-lipped, Malcolm went back to his bench. The coroner then announced that he would be returning a verdict of accidental death, and added that he would be passing over the papers in the case to the public prosecutor, who would decide whether or not, on the evidence that had come before the court, any charge should be brought against the driver of the car. He added, too, that it seemed to him 'utterly deplorable' that a girl as young as the deceased should have been living in such a way – in the flat of a man to whom she wasn't married – that there had simply been no one to take care of her. 'It's a disgrace that the only person who should have been at all concerned about her was the native girl, Alice, who gave evidence here. Mr Begbie, as the driver of the car, should have been particularly concerned; instead, he tells us that he was fed up with her. I can't congratulate him on his sense of responsibility.' With a few more words he concluded his statement, gathered his papers together, and left the court by a side-door, the other officials following him.

24

Malcolm walked out of the court with Swannie and van Tonder; Joel and Natalie followed, some paces behind. The corridor ran past many closed doors, turned several corners, and led at last into a large central foyer. Involuntarily, as Joel and Natalie came into the foyer, and caught a glimpse of the street beyond the tall, folded doors, their steps quickened.

Joel saw Verster, the butter-maker, in the doorway, and recognized him immediately, though he no longer worked in the factory. Standing with him were an elderly man and woman, both of them poorly but neatly dressed. The man, like Verster, had a band of black crepe sewn around the left sleeve of his suit, above the elbow, the woman was dressed in black. Verster was speaking to a uniformed official, who consulted the papers in his hand, looked at his watch, and shook his head. Verster turned to the elderly couple, and said something to them, angrily and reproachfully. He pointed to the clock on the far side of the foyer.

So the dead girl was his sister! Joel realized this at the same moment that Malcolm and his two friends approached the group in the doorway. At once there was a hubbub of raised voices, a flurry of movement and gesticulation; then Verster was pushing back his father, who waved his fist and shouted at van Tonder. Thrust against the glass and gilded wrought iron of the door, the old man puckered his narrow lips, jerked his head, and something white flew through the air. Van Tonder looked down, with an expression that was grotesque in its surprised, enquiring earnestness, at the blob of spittle that had landed on the lapel of his jacket.

Joel heard Malcolm saying to the old woman, as if he had no connection with what was happening a pace or two away from them, '*Parlez-vous français, madame?*' The woman made no response, obviously unaware that the alien words were addressed to her. There was a tight smile on Malcolm's face; the muscles of his upper lip stood out in two tiny, hard bunches, just under his nose. '*Vous êtes Française, non?*'

Joel took Natalie by the arm, and they pushed past the little crowd in the doorway. Van Tonder was wiping the spit off his jacket with a white handkerchief; the uniformed official was now in the middle of the group, expostulating and threatening, waving his papers in the air. Verster took his father by the shoulder and grabbed at his mother, and began hustling them down the steps into the sunlight. His eye fell on Joel, but he did not seem to recognize him. Malcolm was hanging back, the same tight smile on his face.

Joel and Natalie were already at the bottom of the broad, shallow steps that led down from the courthouse to the pavement when Malcolm ran lightly down to them.

'I wanted to say thank you for the evidence you gave,' he said. 'It'll help me with the public prosecutor. I don't think they'll charge me. They've got nothing to go on.' He seemed tense and elated; he swayed a little, like a drunk, in the sunlight. Neither Joel nor Natalie made any reply. 'Don't be so shocked by my friends,' he added, with a jerk of his head towards the building. 'Remember, we don't all have your advantages.' He turned and ran back up the steps, to rejoin the others.

'What did he mean by saying that about our advantages?' Natalie asked Joel much later that day, when he was driving her to her parents' home in Germiston.

'I don't know. Something insulting. Who knows, maybe it was his way of calling us bloody Jews.'

'But what's that got to do with it?'

'What hasn't it got to do with?' It was an unsatisfactory answer; but Joel could think of no other that would be true to the obscure resentment, anger and fear that had been roused in him by Malcolm's remark.

25

Natalie lived in a small house, for her parents were poor; her father was a shoemaker. Joel was always moved, when he visited the house, to see how much of her was still visible in it, as if her parents and the house had unconsciously conspired together to produce the girl he knew. Gestures, inflections of her voice, her mother's straight nose, her father's small, stubby hands, books which she referred to and which were to be seen in the glass-enclosed bookcase in the lounge, tastes in food and clothing – there was so much that had been given to her or that she had learned here, in the years before he had met her. But her ardour and directness were her own, entirely; for both Mr and Mrs Roth were small, timid, weary, defeated people, who spoke English with difficulty and were anxious to be friendly to Joel in a way which embarrassed him, for he felt it was for him to please them, rather than for them to try to please him.

Invariably, when he came in he greeted Mrs Roth, in her flowered dress and apron, and shook Mr Roth by the hand, as he came forward with small steps. Everything about Natalie's father was small, neat and yet wrenched a little out of true, as if at some time in his life he had taken on a task (making the long journey from Lithuania to South Africa? Marrying Mrs Roth? Opening his cobbler's shop in a side-street? Fathering Natalie?) that had proved just too much for him, and the effort of which had left his hands, his back, his features, even the wrinkles on his face, slightly but irrevocably twisted. While Mrs Roth went off to prepare the evening meal, Joel and Mr Roth made conversation about the weather, or about events in Palestine; they each drank a glass of the sweet red wine which Mr Roth insisted on pouring out in Joel's honour. At the table Natalie was always ashamed, subdued and withdrawn, eating the boiled chicken or boiled beef which Mrs Roth usually presented; at these meals Joel would sometimes remember, as if from a dream of another girl, Natalie's quivering, naked body, its secret hair and places, her tears and clenched teeth. What different people we were – not merely from one another, but from ourselves, at different times!

Joel wondered at this; yet he was oppressed, also, by the continuity which claimed, bound, enclosed her, within these bare walls. Sometimes he wanted to ask Mr and Mrs Roth impossible questions about their daughter. Had she always been so impulsive and so shy? Did they worry about her virginity? What had roused in her the irrational terrors which – as he now knew – were so much a part of her eagerness and audacity? Were they, her parents, afraid of her? (He was sure they were.) Did they feel they knew her? Did they feel they could trust her to a man who thought up such questions about her, while he ate their boiled chicken and *tzimmes*?

Afterwards he sat on the stoep with Mr and Mrs Roth until, discreetly, and with embarrassment, they withdrew; then he and Natalie talked and necked on the sofa in the living room, before he left. He never slept there, though a bed could have been made up for him on the sofa; but Natalie did not want him to, and he never insisted. For there was something intensely melancholy about the house, and he was always glad to get out of it, late at night, and to drive on his own through the deserted streets, hearing through the open window of his car the repetitive, empty catch of the wind, as each lamp-post or parked car passed by.

26

When Joel and Natalie were together on the *hachsharah*, they shared a tent which they had to themselves at night. This arrangement had been made without a word having been said to anyone about it; there had been no words to say, for the group prided itself on the complete rationality, frankness and enlightenment of its attitudes towards the relations between the sexes. It was taken for granted that Natalie and Joel were lovers, now, in the full sense of the word. The irony of the situation was that, in fact, they were not; and a further irony was that they would have been extremely abashed, humiliated indeed, if any one had found this out.

Natalie was afraid: afraid, above all, of falling pregnant. It wasn't merely that she was afraid of conceiving a child outside marriage; on the contrary, she said that she wouldn't get married to Joel or to anyone else until this fear had left her. It was the life of the child she dreaded in a way she could not explain, could find no words for, though she talked wildly of being afraid of killing it accidentally, of it being deformed or cretinous, or of simply finding that she hated it. The responsibility was not to be borne, not to be thought of. When Joel spoke of 'taking care', when they agreed that her phobia about pregnancy was a neurotic 'rationalization' of her fear of sex, when he sent her for a consultation to a gynaecologist, she was not reassured by anything either he or the doctor said. Always she came back to it: 'How can you be sure? These things don't work sometimes. And then –?'

Joel, having no one to consult, and being himself inexperienced and lacking confidence, was infected by her fears, and even stirred by their intensity to a feeling of responsibility and adulthood that was a source of unfamiliar pride to him. He could not force her; he did not want to. She would come to it in her own good time, he said to her and to himself; in the meantime she gave enough to him. Enough when they were alone together; enough when they were with the others in the group.

For Natalie's position in the group, Joel had known for a long time, was a special one; inevitably, he benefited from it, and was gratified that he had been singled out to share it. She had no intellectual pretensions, she was the first to admit aggressively that ideological discussions bored the hell out of her, she could be stubbornly mutinous when she was asked to do work she did not want to do. Yet in some curious way – and partly for these very reasons – she was regarded by the others in the group as their touchstone, their flagbearer, almost as their saint, as if she had given up more, and would never hesitate to give up more, than any one else, to become and remain a member of the group. Her prettiness and the smoothness of her skin helped her; so did the childishness of her voice. But none of these would have counted for so much had it not been for the baffled force of her feelings; the sense they all had that she was the one among them who was capable of suffering most deeply, but who was nonetheless determined to seek no shelter for herself because of this. For Joel, who knew more than any of the others about the ways in which she could suffer, there was yet another uncomfortable irony in the fact that had she been as rational, frank and free in her emotions as they all aspired to be, she would never have been admired, courted and honoured as she was; nor would he have been so envied and respected for having been chosen by her.

During the week he attended lectures and met Natalie in town in the late afternoons, when she had finished her work; at weekends they went invariably to the *hachsharah*, where he also spent most of his vacations. The affairs of the movement absorbed him more and more. While in the army he had invariably been one of the youngest in any group in which he found himself; now he was proud to be, with Leon, Henry, and a couple of others, one of the older, more mature members of Hatzofim, whose opinions were respected, whose suggestions were carried out. He was appointed to a committee which was to discuss the possibility of the amalgamation of the training farms which were run separately by the four largest Zionist youth movements in the country; he was much involved in the organization of a three-week camp under canvas for the younger members of Hatzofim. The tone of the conferences, discussions and activities he took part in was always excited, hopeful and conspiratorial; the excitement everyone felt was all the more irresistible for being about a country which hardly any one had yet seen, about a state which did not exist. In comparison with that country of the mind (and, almost every day, as the situation in Palestine became more and more critical, of the newspaper headlines), South Africa seemed null, dry, empty, a place inhabited by strangers, a province. No one in the Zionist youth movement spoke of anything but working on a kibbutz; it was the greatest possible change from the life they had known, they believed they wanted nothing less.

Inevitably, Joel's work at the university suffered; but he did not care. At the end of his second year, he passed all his examinations, but in none of them did he get any grade better than a third. Peter Dewes got a first in History and was invited by Viljoen to take Honours, after he had taken his bachelor's degree. But Joel no longer envied him. He had learned during the year that Viljoen was a touchy, lonely, rancorous, disappointed man; insatiably eager for praise, but never set at rest by it; embittered by the feeling that his work had been insufficiently recognized and appreciated, and yet at the same time always ready with accusations that every other scholar in the field made a habit of stealing his insights and formulations; convinced that he was the victim of innumerable intrigues and conspiracies among his colleagues. So much, Joel thought, for the disregard of self he had imagined Viljoen to live by; so much for the rewards of belonging to the community of scholars! He could not be sorry that he had chosen to belong to another.

'You make sure you don't go the same way as Viljoen,' Joel scoffingly warned Peter one day. 'It's the academic illness. They all suffer from it. He's just more careless about showing it than all the others.'

'I'll believe in you as a tiller of the soil when I see you tilling it – not a moment before,' Peter replied, scoffing too.

'So you'll be visiting us in Palestine?' Joel asked mock-innocently.

They were standing on the steps of the Central Block; they had both come to look up the exam results posted on boards in the foyer. The steps, where the students sat in throngs during term-time, were empty; the long end-of-year vacation had begun. Joel was sure he would not be standing there at the end of the next year, and he felt sorry for Dewes, who would.

27

David chose to leave home, when the time came for him to go to university at the beginning of the academic year; he wanted, he said, to be on his own, and his parents saw no reason why he should not have his way.

So, one morning in February, he arrived at the men's residence of the college he had settled upon. Alert, curious, much less confident in manner than he had appeared to be at home, looking about him as he followed the African houseboy with his bags, David went to the room whose number had been given to him by the matron, when he checked in. There he found the man with whom he was to share the room: a fat, heavily-bespectacled youngster, Langbaart by name, with a rough red skin, and a nose and mouth that were pushed forward as if they were one organ; his upper lip could hardly be seen. He breathed heavily while he spoke, and only a little less heavily when he was silent.

But he was friendly enough, and explained to David, very slowly, what was expected of him as a freshman. He had to wear a white star and green button in his jacket-lapel; he had to bow whenever he passed a senior; he had to walk on the cement strips parallel to the walls in the passageways, and not on the linoleum-covered middle of the passages; he had to find out who his fag-master was and report to him every morning and evening; if any senior shouted 'Fresher!' he had to run to him and do what the senior asked of him. Green buttons and other instructions would be issued by the committee in charge of freshmen, who would probably call David to them after lunch; this committee was called the Assassination Committee – or, simply, The Assass.

They'd give him hell, Langbaart said, between sighs; they gave everybody hell the first time they got hold of them; but afterwards you were left pretty much alone, except on Assass Evenings, twice a week, when all the freshers were brought together to be ragged in the hall. The main thing was to look willing, keep your nose clean, and not be *hardegat* – hardarsed. If you were *hardegat* they'd really lay into you. With gloomy relish, Langbaart told of people being *borseled* – that was, being beaten on the bare bum with gym shoes; or being made to drink a dozen glasses of water; or being held upside down from second-floor windows.

When David went out of the residence, and wandered around the campus his fear of what Langbaart had told him about the initiation ceremonies was lost in everything else he felt: wonder, excitement, expectancy, curiosity. The campus seemed bewilderingly big to him, and filled with people; there were innumerable buildings, lawns, trees, pathways, roads, parking lots; there were so many notice-boards to study and girls to look at. On the closed brown doors to offices in the Arts Block he saw name-plates carrying the names of people whom he had heard giving talks on the radio, and whose articles he had read in newspapers and magazines. He picked up copies of timetables, library regulations, registration regulations, the hand-outs of half a dozen societies in whose activities he thought he might be interested. He was intensely shy of asking his way from anyone, because he did not want to betray his newness to others; instead, by his walk, by the knowing way he looked at the notice-boards, by his forced smiles at his own scattered thoughts, he tried to convince anyone who might have been looking at him that he was an old hand, not a beginner at all. It was disappointing that so few people did in fact look at him; enviously, he saw other people greeting one another cheerfully and gathering in chattering groups. Still, in the freedom of having just arrived, he was sure he had been right to leave Johannesburg. Why should he have stayed at home, now that his schooldays were at last over?

At lunchtime he went down to the hall of residence. While still on the verandah of the building he remembered what Langbaart had told him, and bowed hastily at the first man he saw, whom he thought must be a senior because he wasn't wearing a white star and green button in his jacket lapel.

The man hissed at him, 'Not outside, you fool.'

'I'm sorry,' David stammered.

'Sir, when you speak to me.'

'Sir.'

'That's better. Now piss off.'

Relenting, the man smiled, and only then did David really see him – a blond, fresh-complexioned young man in a sports coat and a pair of grey flannels; he was hardly older than David himself. He felt absurdly grateful for the smile; and went on cheerfully into the building.

Along the side of the passage, keeping off the linoleum, he made his way to the dining room. There were only about twelve inches of uncovered strip on each side of the linoleum in the passage, so progress wasn't easy. But nor, David decided, his shoulder rubbing along the wall, was it impossible.

The dining-hall looked imposing, almost noble, he thought, with its high ceiling, bare white walls and long, heavy tables of black African wood, set well apart from one another. A

Coloured head-waiter, with a sash across his chest, approached him; the other waiters were all Africans.

'Freshman?'

'Yes, I am.'

The waiter indicated a table to him; all the young men sitting at it were wearing large white cardboard stars, with green buttons superimposed, in the buttonholes of their lapels. David felt himself naked without one.

The courses came and went; shyly, the young men talked to one another about the places they came from, the degrees they would be working for, the rooms they had. With lowered voices, they pointed out to each other the dean and sub-dean of the residence at the main table, with the members of the House Committee sitting next to them, and the members of the Assass who sat together at another table. Then the meal was over. Feeling that there was safety in numbers, David waited until a group got up from his table, and joined it in going through the hall.

He was just outside the dining-hall when a moustached man in shirtsleeves stepped in front of him. The man's eyebrows had an odd twist, which made him look as though he squinted. Yet both his brown eyes were fixed steadily and frigidly on David's.

'You, what's your name?'

'Glickman.'

'Sir!'

'Sir.'

'You came today?'

'Yes, I did.'

'Sir!'

'Sir.'

'Room 108. Right away. Double quick. Jig time.'

'Yes sir.'

As David went off, sidling along the wall, the man shouted after him, 'Faster!' Still taking care not to step on the linoleum, David obeyed, conscious that the group lounging about in the vestibule outside the dining-hall were grinning at the spectacle.

There were four or five freshmen in Room 108. None of them was wearing the white star and green button, so David assumed that they had all, like himself, arrived that morning. When he came in they turned anxiously to look at him, but on seeing someone as apprehensive as themselves, they looked away again. The room was a bedroom-study; apparently it belonged to one of the seniors, for it was a single room (only freshmen shared rooms); the pictures on the walls, the drawing-board raised up at an angle from the table and the books on the shelves showed it had been lived in for a long time by the same man. The books were all engineering text-books and a couple of science-fiction paperbacks. David was never to know to whom the room belonged.

'Bow! Freshmen, bow! Lower, scum, lower! Kiss your knees! Heads between your legs! Look up your arseholes, freshmen, and tell us what you see!'

Three men had burst in a group through the door. There was the man in the white shirt whose one eyebrow went up at a different angle from the other; there was a blazered, plump little man, wearing spectacles and a toothbrush moustache; the last one into the room was swarthy, tall, gesticulating, with a long trunk, long legs, long feet, and a tiny head. All three of them were shouting at the tops of their voices; they pushed the freshmen to the sides of the room, against the walls, wedging them between the bookcase and table, the bed and radiator, the radiator and window. The freshmen were bowing deeply, but still the three seniors roared at them, 'Lower! Lower! Lower than shark-shit, you hear?'

Then they paused and turned to each other; after a protracted silence they asked, in suddenly moderate tones, 'How shall we train these monsters, Mr Levy? One by one, or all together?' 'As you wish, Mr de Beer. Whichever will tire you less.' 'An opinion, please, Mr Carnell?' 'It's hopeless, we'll never train these monsters. They're unteachable. They should be destroyed. But not painlessly; not painlessly at all.' And Carnell, the white-shirted one, uttered a shriek, a terrifying, meaningless yell that filled the room.

Later David was to wonder whether it was by accident or by design that the members of the Assass consisted of an Englishman, an Afrikaner and a Jew – a little microcosm, as it were, of white South Africa. Thus there could be no question of there being any 'racialism' in what was done to the freshmen. Probably the precaution had been taken unconsciously at the end of the previous year, by the seniors who, as at the end of very other year, had voted three of their number on to the committee.

The freshman next to David was made to stand in the middle of the room while the others against the walls remained bent double, their eyes strained upwards. The freshman in the middle was yelled at to stand up, to bow, because his face was so ugly the seniors could not bear to look at it; to stand up, to bow, to stand up – ten, fifteen, twenty times, while the seniors thrust their faces at him, and screamed that he was a piece of snot, a lump of shit, a turd, a cockroach, a piss-a-bed. He was asked questions and interrupted by a barrage of yells before he could reply; then his ears were peered into to find out why he couldn't hear the questions he was asked. He was told to stop pulling his wire; to change his face; to sing; to dance; to confess that he had wet dreams about his mother.

This was just a preliminary examination, he was told; later they'd have the pants off him, they'd *borsel* him, they'd hang his arse out to dry; they'd flush him away down the lavatory. All the threats, commands, words of abuse and questions were yelled out simultaneously, often in direct contradiction to one another.

'We're just starting on you!' the three men kept on shouting, 'We're being *kind* to you. And what do you say to people who're being kind to you? What do you say? What? Say it! Say it!'

'Thank you, sir.'

'Thank you, sir, for being kind to me! Say it! Faster! LOUDER! Again! Louder! Softer, you cretin, you pig, I'm not deaf.'

Without warning, the freshman burst loudly and shamelessly into tears. Almost at once he was told disgustedly to go back to the wall.

A second man was called out. Much the same kind of bullying was inflicted on him until he too eventually showed signs of breaking down – though he struggled hard, his facial muscles twitched and quivered for what seemed like minutes before the first tears stood in his eyes. When they at last rolled down his cheeks he uttered no sound, as if he could not believe that it had happened to him. A few final jeers were snorted at him – 'Christ, look what kind of creatures they're letting into hall these days. Give him the tit, somebody' – and he was told to get back to the wall.

The third man, having learned his lesson from the experience of the others, cried early, eagerly, as soon as he possibly could. Then it was David's turn.

28

It was Levy, the swarthy, long-legged one, who called him out. David stepped forward blindly, not knowing what was going to happen to him, hoping merely it would be over soon.

'Bow!' de Beer shouted.

David bowed. 'Again! Again! Again!'

DAN JACOBSON

David bowed, how many times he did not know. Dizzily upright, he heard someone shouting at him, 'Who's your roommate?'

'Langbaart, sir.'

'Langbaart! That abortion! Isn't he the ugliest bastard you've ever set your eyes on?'

'Bow!' Someone else shouted; again and again the floor swung up towards him and retreated. At the end of it he heard, 'Isn't Langbaart the ugliest son of a bitch you've ever seen?'

'I don't know, sir.'

'I say he is! You hear? So what do you say?'

'I don't know, sir.'

'You don't know? You don't know? You say what I say!'

It was Levy who was shouting this at him. David looked up and met his eye. In the brief glance they exchanged David read the message: 'You're a Jew and I'm a Jew, but don't you think that that's going to help you. Because you're a Jew, I'm going to do my worst.'

Had the words been said David could not have been more sure of them. At that moment, with an unwilling dread that was directed entirely against his own foreknowledge, and not against the others in the room, he knew that he was not going to do what these people wanted him to do. He was not going to say what they wanted him to say; he was not going to cry. The decision was like a curse that had been uttered from the depths of himself against himself; his conscious will had nothing to do with it. His fear of the men around him was gone; now he was afraid only of himself.

'So say it!' Levy screamed.

'What, sir?'

Levy danced in front of him, shooting out his arms, tossing back his small, black-haired head. 'You getting *hardegat*? Hey? Hey?'

'Bow!' de Beer shrieked. 'Lower, hard-arse!'

242

Carnell caught the word. 'Is he hard? Soften him, torture him, pulp him!' Now they were all three around him. 'Say it, shithouse: The only bastard in residence uglier than I am is Langbaart! Say it loud! Say it out!' And there was another yell from de Beer. 'Who you staring at like that? Bow! Bow!'

David bowed.

'Now say it!'

'Say what, sir?'

They yelled again in unison, half with joy that they should have found someone really hard-arse; half with fear of what he or they might do.

'*Hardegat*! We'll skin you, flay you, we'll *borsel* your backside, you'll scream for mercy. Say it! Say it!'

David felt the treacherous tears behind his eyes. They had gathered there in an instant; they would fall, he would cry if the shouting went on any longer. And he was not going to cry: it had been decided.

'Say it! Shithouse, fuckface, dog's arse, say it! Say it!'

He could not stop the tears by biting his lips, clenching his fists, standing there in front of them. There was only one way it could be done. Into the faces of de Beer and Levy, who were the nearest to him, David shouted, 'Fuck off! Leave me alone!'

He heard a gasp; then a voice beginning to ascend into a shriek. Now that he had acted, he was terrified once more of the three men. He turned and walked out of the room; at the door he bumped into someone who was coming in, and fiercely pushed the man out of the way. He heard a cry behind him, and then a hurried, half-shouted whisper, which wasn't directed at him, 'Wait! Wait, man.'

David turned the corner, and went on, walking down the middle of the passage now, towards his room. But he remembered that Langbaart might be there; he could not face anyone, Langbaart least of all. So he went into the lavatory, instead. He was in luck: none of the cubicles was occupied. He sat down on the seat in one of them, and put his face in his hands. The tears came at once, briefly, soothing and tiring him; when the spasm was over he got up, feeling comparatively calm, washed his face in one of the hand-basins outside the cubicles and went to his room.

29

In the meantime, the three members of the Assass had dismissed the freshmen who had been with David in the room, and had conferred anxiously together. Initiation ceremonies were strictly forbidden in the residence, though everyone, not least the dean of the residence, knew that they went on; anxious to be thought a good sport by the students, the dean had made it plain that they could do what they liked, as long as no open scandal took place. The members of the Assass did not wish to have this arrangement ruined; and they didn't want to run any risk of being expelled.

So they decided to approach David in a straightforward, man to man way. They would let him off lightly, they agreed among themselves. They would make him apologize; they would punish him formally in front of all the assembled freshmen – they would debag and *borsel* him and they would consider the whole incident closed. That was sporting enough, they decided. Having come to this resolution, the three of them barged into David's room.

They spoke severely to him, but did not shout. 'You're a cheeky little bastard, and you've got to apologize. And we're going to *borsel* your arse, to show you you can't get away with it. And then we'll forget about it, hey? If you don't apologize ... They shook their heads, trying to hide from him, by their threatening, pitying demeanour, how much they hoped he would be cooperative.

But David refused to apologize. His jaw shook, but he managed to bring out his refusal. However, he added, 'I'm leaving residence.'

Relieved, the three men looked at each other.

'Just as well for you,' Carnell and Levy said. 'My God! The sooner you're out of here the better. This is no place for piss-wets.'

But de Beer could not leave it at that. His face suddenly reddened, his round chest swelled out. 'You want to come outside and settle it, hey Glickman?' He crowded himself upon David, clenching and raising one fist, taking his glasses off with the other hand. 'Come on, you're such a big talker, let's see what you can do with yourself. I'm ready. I'm waiting.' David backed towards the wall. His glasses safely in his pocket, de Beer held up both his plump fists in David's face. 'Come on, you yellow little shit.'

But Carnell took him by the arm and pulled him away. 'No, man, leave the miserable bastard.' He pulled de Beer to the door, and whispered earnestly in his ear, gesturing with his hand. Levy moved from leg to leg, looking from David to the others.

'All right, it's your luck, that's all,' de Beer said finally, glowering and breathing noisily from the door. In silence, the three men left the room.

After they had gone David cried again. So this was his first day at the university, which he'd been looking forward to so eagerly! Why hadn't he stayed at home, gone to Wits, as Joel and Rachel had done? No, he'd wanted to be on his own! And what a mess he'd made of it, what a filthy mess! He did not feel there had been anything brave about what he had done; he was simply ashamed of it all, from beginning to end. It seemed to him that it would have been far less degrading to have cried in front of the others, when they had wanted him to, than to be crying on his own now, while he re-packed the few things he had taken out of his bags. He wished the whole affair could remain a secret, known to no one.

He telephoned for a taxi, and went to a hotel. From there he telegraphed to his parents for more money. Later in the evening he wrote a letter telling them what had happened. He wrote it all as fully as he could; he left out of his account only his own tears.

30

Benjamin's response to David's letter was to send long telegrams to the principal of the university, and to the dean of the residence, informing them that on behalf of his son he was suing the university for personal damages and for the financial loss incurred in finding other lodgings. The telegram also demanded to know the names of the members of the Assassination Committee; a separate action, it stated, would be launched against them. This telegram was followed by a letter from a firm of attorneys, confirming the telegram, elaborating on its contents, and giving the figure which was being claimed for the damages done. The lawyers' letter also stated that the press was being put in possession of the facts about the pending lawsuit; and expressed their client's deep sense of outrage that 'such barbaric practices' were permitted in an institution 'which presents itself to the world as a seat of learning'.

The consequences of Benjamin's action were more telegrams, more lawyers' letters, visits by journalists to the halls of residence, a courier to Mr Glickman from the university, meetings of a committee of investigation, and David being made to spend much time in panelled waiting rooms before being summoned to give his account of the events to groups of elderly men.

'Did you,' asked the principal of the university, at one such meeting, his drooping moustache and watery brown eyes coming closer to David, his quavering Oxford voice sinking to a whisper on the key phrase, 'did you say, "Fuck you!" to the others in the room?'

'Yes sir, I did.'

The principal's lips parted and came together several times, with a small, smacking noise, like a man concluding an immense yawn. The other bulky heads around the table stared at David or beyond him, without expression. The version of the incident given by the members of the Assass was that they had merely been explaining to Glickman the traditional customs of the residence and the nominal duties expected of him as a freshman when he had sworn obscenely at them and struck out at someone who had just come into the room.

In the end, an elaborate, artificial procedure was agreed upon. Benjamin withdrew his action against the university and the three students, who were expelled not only from the residence, but from the university. Then, at the previously arranged intercession of Mr Glickman, the expulsion from the university was commuted to a six-months' suspension; but re-admission to the residence remained barred to them. (Carnell was dead, drowned in a bathing accident, before the six months were over.) Formal letters of apology were written by the dean and the principal to both David and his father. Initiation practices were once again condemned at a meeting of all residence students; nevertheless, they continued to take place, though with considerably less violence and obscenity than in previous years.

David was for some time an object of notoriety on the campus. He was pointed out to others; a few times he was hissed publicly by groups of residence men; once, at a dance, a group of them grabbed hold of him and started hustling him outside, but he fought back so fiercely that they let him go, rather than cause a brawl in the middle of the floor. Most of these demonstrations against him came from groups of freshmen: those whom the investigations and expulsions had saved from the full initiation they would otherwise have had to go through. That was precisely what many of them resented; they were convinced that their manhood and valour had been impugned, because they had been prevented from submitting to having their bare arses beaten with gym shoes. And they felt aggrieved because it now seemed unlikely that they would ever have the chance of beating others in the same way.

31

Within a matter of weeks the scandal, which had seemed to David endless in its absurd and shameful consequences, was hardly remembered on the campus. It was almost forgotten by David himself, though he still had spells when for hours on end he went over what had happened, uselessly imagining alternatives to it. The scandal changed nothing in himself; it merely deepened his conviction that he was, inwardly, base and contemptible, without dignity either in his rebellions or conformisms, and that most other people were even worse.

When he went home in April the only person he told the truth of his feelings to was his cousin, Jonathan. To Joel and Rachel he couldn't speak because he didn't want to; to his father, who was simply proud of what David had done, and who had thoroughly enjoyed his own fight with the university authorities, he couldn't speak because Benjamin did all the talking himself.

But Jonathan listened to his, and at the end of his tale Jonathan said, 'Ach, I know what you mean. It's all just a heap of shit. Everything is.'

The two of them were in David's bedroom: it was a Sunday morning and no one else was in the house. Benjamin had gone to a meeting of his Zionist committee; Joel was on the farm; Sarah and Rachel were visiting Adela Klein, whose mother had just died.

'What you've got to do,' Jonathan said, 'is climb right on top of the heap, and let no one push you off. Then only your feet are in the shit, nothing else.'

'I'm the king of the castle,' David sang out. He climbed on to his desk and stood on it; Jonathan made a dive at his legs and began trying to pull him off. They wrestled until David almost fell, then he jumped off the desk on to his bed, and collapsed prostrate on it.

Jonathan staggered back melodramatically, a look of terror on his face. 'The king is dead!' he cried. 'Call out the guards, tell the queen, send the cavalry into the streets. The rabble mustn't get out of hand. The king is dead! Who will succeed him? Will ruin come to our land? Oh woe, woe, woe!'

David had closed his eyes. He lay rigidly still, with his arms at his side.

'Hey, wake up, your majesty,' Jonathan said, 'You can't die now. The enemy's at our gates. The Arabs are attacking up and down the Jerusalem road. There's a general election coming and the Nats might get in. This is not time to die, for God's sake. Pull yourself together.'

David smothered a giggle, and his eyelids fluttered. But he did not open his eyes.

'Christ, I'll revive you.'

From his voice David knew that Jonathan had come closer to the bed. He flinched and put his hands over his crotch, with a snort of laughter.

Jonathan bent his head close to David's and whispered in his ear, 'Hey, your majesty, do you know that I'm screwing your sister?'

'What!'

David opened his eyes instantly, to meet Jonathan's frightened but curious gaze. That look alone told David that he had spoken the truth.

He whistled and sat up on the bed. 'Honestly! Jonathan! But what – what about that other girl you were telling me about? The one in your office?'

Jonathan shrugged and threw his hands in the air, in a gesture that was half-consciously an imitation of his father. 'I'm just too bloody popular, that's my trouble.'

David did not speak for a moment. Then he said. 'Poor Rachel. What are you going to do about her? She's crazy about you, isn't she? She has been, for years.'

'That's why it happened,' Jonathan said in a heavy, remorseful voice. 'It just went on too long for anything else to happen. It had to, sooner or later, if we went on seeing each other. I told her, I warned her. And then it happened.'

'When?'

'About six months ago.'

'As long as that! You're practically married to her.'

Jonathan shook his head.

'You don't want to marry her?'

'No.'

'Does she know that?'

'I've told her.'

'But she doesn't believe you?'

'I don't know what she believes, I really don't.'

'Well, I must say you're a shit,' David said complacently, leaning back against the wall. 'I mean, it wouldn't matter if she weren't so keen on you – but she is. You're going to break her heart, that's what you're going to do.'

'I hope not,' Jonathan said fervently, still speaking in a low voice.

'Does anyone else know about it?'

'I don't think so. Your parents certainly don't.'

'I should hope not! My old man would go crazy if he found out about it. You aren't his favourite nephew, I can tell you. Still, I suppose he'd want you to marry her if he did find out. Why don't you want to marry her?'

'I can't. I don't want to settle down. I've got a career to make.' Jonathan began moodily, but his voice became firmer and more confident as he went on. 'I really am going to be king of the castle, you wait and see. I'm going to England, Rachel knows I'm going, I've told her. I'm not going to tie myself down, I'm not going to take just what's dished out to me. There's nothing here, nothing that I want. Nothing. This is the provinces, man, we live in the back-veld here. Dutchmen and kaffirs, they're the only people who really belong in this country and they're welcome to it, all of it, the whole lot. And mining engineers – it's a great country for mining engineers; they can mine all week and visit each other in their new houses on Sundays.'

Jonathan was walking up and down the small room; he gave David no chance to interrupt him. 'Look, our parents came here, they didn't know any better, they were so busy trying to make a living they didn't know any better, they were so busy trying to make a living they didn't even look around and see what kind of a country it is. But we've got different standards; and they brought enough of Europe with them for us to know that this is the *bundu*, the bloody back of beyond. And don't tell me about the lively little theatrical world of Johannesburg – I know what that's worth. And don't tell me about the drama of the clash of races, or the mystic call of the veld, or our wonderful climate, or any of the other crap that people here like to console themselves with. They wouldn't need such consolations if they didn't know that the bright lights and the real life are over there –' Jonathan pointed to the window, vaguely northwards – 'there, six thousand miles away. Every time you open a book or read a newspaper you know it all over again. And I'll tell you something else: I'm an ambitious shit who's interested only in Number One – all right. And Joel's a big idealist, kibbutznik, selfless, noble, brave and all that – right. But we're going for the same reason. Because there's nothing to keep us here. Because we don't belong, and we don't even believe that there's anything here for us to belong to. And it'll be the same with you, you wait a couple of years and you'll see.'

The certainty of Jonathan's tone impressed David; in comparison he felt himself to be shallow and naive, without ambition or purpose in life. Yet he was flattered that Jonathan should have included him in the roll of restless, cosmopolitan spirits.

'Anyway,' he said, 'it's your business what you do – and Rachel's business what she does. I don't suppose you want her to know that you've told me?'

'I don't know. Perhaps it'd be a relief for her to be able to talk about it to someone. You can make up your mind. I won't tell her that I've said anything to you.'

David lunged back angrily, against the wall. 'You're a lucky bugger!' he exclaimed. 'Do you know – I'm still a virgin?' In his shame at the confession, his voice broke on the last word.

But Jonathan smiled at him so warmly that David could not be sorry he had spoken. 'That's fixed easily enough,' Jonathan said. He sat on the bed and began telling David where it could be fixed, and when, and with whom.

32

At Adela Klein's, Rachel said to Bertie, 'David's at home, you know. He's come for the short vac.'

'Has he? I must go and see him.'

'He'd be glad if you would.'

'I thought his stand against that initiation business terrific.'

'Yes, we were proud of him.'

Rachel was sitting in a deep, velvet-covered, befringed armchair, one of half a dozen that crowded the Klein's living room. The room contained, in addition, a large sofa, also covered in velvet and much befringed; a sideboard bearing a blue and yellow runner, two cut-glass vases, a cut-glass fruit bowl, a pair of family portraits, and a tooled leather booklet of views of Jerusalem; a round, glass-topped table supported by four wide but slender legs that rose in curves from the floor, clasped each other in a fierce confused embrace, and then curved out again to the table's extremities; several standard lamps, a few ash-trays on two-foot high pedestals, and an embroidered firescreen in front of the green marble fireplace. The mirror above the sideboard was shrouded in a white sheet.

Ezreal Klein looked dwarfed by the furniture his late wife had bought for him. He was a spare, small, fine-boned man, with the pouting chest and high stiff shoulders of an asthmatic; the strongest thing about him was his head of white hair, which he wore brushed back in the manner of the Russian student he had been forty years before. The death of his wife, and the funeral two days previously, had left him frail and shaken; but he would not submit to the shock he had suffered. Instead, in a thin, strained voice and with a faintly whistling breath, he tried to talk to Sarah as though nothing were amiss. He had always had a special regard for her, for she was, he often said, one of the few women he had met who appreciated what he called 'literary values'. Ezreal Klein was a successful manufacturer of women's underclothes and infants' garments, and, more recently, a highly successful speculator in real estate, but his true *métier*, he believed, was literature. He contributed articles on literary topics to the *South African Yiddish Weekly*; he was a leading member of the local Yiddish Cultural Circle.

Adela sat at his side on the sofa; across the room was her brother, a plump, bespectacled youth with curly black hair and a frown on his forehead, who worked with his father in Kosiwear, and was quite without literary interests or ambitions.

In spite of the occasion, Adela could not help feeling uneasy to see Bertie and Rachel together. She had no confidence in her hold over Bertie in Rachel's presence, though she could never understand why Bertie seemed still so drawn to her. It was true that Rachel was looking prettier than ever, Adela had to admit to herself; her eyes were bright, her shining hair hung neatly to her shoulders, her ankles were elegant, there was a calmness about her that seemed to Adela quite new. But Adela was sure, Rachel didn't *care* about any of the things Bertie cared about; she was sure that the interest Rachel was showing in what Bertie was now saying to her, the quick way she opened her lips as if to interrupt him, and then closed them before she had spoken, the tilt of her head to listen more closely to him, were all a pretence, an act, a performance. Couldn't Bertie see it?

Adela's eyes filled with tears at the disorder and messiness of everything: of death, which had taken her mother away; of life, which had left her here, incapable of feeling jealousy, envy and anger as well. No one saw the tears; she looked out of the window, blinking them away.

'I must say I find books comforting only when I don't need comfort,' Adela heard Sarah saying to her father.

Mr Klein plaintively replied, 'But that's a terrible thing to say. Then you're admitting that literature is of no use to us when life is most bewildering and painful.'

'Yes,' Sarah answered. 'I suppose that is what I'm saying. Perhaps books can distract us at such times, but that's something else from giving us comfort. And even as a distraction –'

Barney Klein had hardly spoken since the visitors had come into the house. Now he said, 'The only consolation we have is the thought of what a loving mother she was to us.'

He spoke loudly and clearly, like a man who had thought out what he was going to say and was prepared to stick to his position in the face of any disagreement. But there was no disagreement from the others; they were merely embarrassed. Adela looked swiftly from Bertie to Rachel, then down at her own shoes. The two of them, after a pause, resumed their conversation, their heads close together. Again Adela saw a subdued, attentive half-smile on Rachel's lips. What were they saying to one another? She got up, crossed the room, and sat down in the chair nearest to Bertie. At her approach they stopped talking and looked sympathetically at her. Adela brought the back of her hand to her mouth, pressing her knuckles hard against her teeth.

Then she said, in a bright, everyday tone, 'What are you two nattering about?'

The question seemed to embarrass them even more than her brother's remark.

33

When Sarah and Rachel stood up to go, Bertie rose to his feet, too.

'Bertie, you aren't going?'

'I must. I'm sorry, Adela. I promised my mother I'd be back for lunch. I'll come round again this evening.' He stooped and kissed her on the cheek. Adela turned away; but Rachel kissed her too.

'I'll see you soon. I think you're being very brave.'

Sarah said to Mr Klein, 'My husband will be coming in for the prayers this evening.'

'Thank you. Thank you. Everyone is being very kind.' A sigh that turned into a sob suddenly shook Mr Klein's breast. His son came up and took him by the arm.

'Bear up, Dad.'

'I am bearing up,' Mr Klein said irritably, and snatched his arm away.

Out in the street Bertie said, 'I'll walk you home. It won't be out of my way,' he added unnecessarily, for they all knew where he lived. He looked back at the house and saw Adela watching them from the verandah. He waved to her, but she did not wave back.

It was a clear, sunny day, with a hint of autumn in it. The blue of the sky was sharper, clearer, than it had been a few weeks previously; in the gardens they passed the first poinsettias were sending out their flame-coloured leaves at the end of bare stalks, and the lawns were beginning to turn brown. Otherwise there was no sign of the impending change of season: there wasn't the faintest touch of coolness in the air, and the windows of all the houses were wide open, behind their fierce burglar-proofing. From every house there came the commingled sounds of radios turned up, of children calling, of servants chattering. So many mornings like this there were in the year: pure, still, seasonless passages of time and sunlight.

Bertie continued telling Rachel about a meeting he had addressed in the Great Hall of the University a few weeks before – the meeting had been about the admission of non-white students to the university's sports-fields. He did not take the issue very seriously ('How can one? It's one of those ridiculous token battles that you have to fight sometimes'); and

Rachel listened patronizingly to him. Before, she had always felt herself threatened by Bertie's political fervours, diminished by them, made to seem self-centred and frivolous. This was no longer true. She was now confident that she was both more mature and more of a true rebel than either Joel, the Zionist, or Bertie, the Socialist. She was risking more than they were; and, unlike them, she knew what it was she was risking herself for.

So she listened and smiled, shook her head at his description of the boos and yells the 'reactionaries' had raised, congratulated him on his success in being elected on the progressive ticket to the Students Representative Council, and asked him what he thought would happen at the forthcoming general elections.

Bertie surprised her. 'I don't care. Both parties are white supremacists: the one lot is just a little milder than the other. That's the only difference between them.'

'Bertie, how can you say that? The Nationalists are outright Nazis. Look what they were doing during the war. Look what they say about the Jews.'

'Ach, they haven't said anything about the Jews for a long time. I don't believe they'll do anything to the Jews if they do get in. Hitler lost the war, and that's when they lost their chance to settle scores with the Jews. And they know it; they may still be full of anti-semitism but they know the issue's dead, politically. It's the Africans who'll feel it if they come in, and the Coloureds and the Indians, and the whites who've really thrown in their lot with the Africans; no one else. But Lenin had a proverb: 'The worse the better.' If the Nats do get in they'll merely make the revolution come so much the more quickly.'

'Do you really think there will be a revolution?'

'Of course. You suppose things are going to go on like this forever?' He gestured around the quiet, sunlit street they were walking through. 'With the servants in the kitchens and the white folk in their lounges?' He shook his head and laughed. 'Because it won't, it isn't going to.'

'It will in our lifetime.'

'Our lifetime! I hope you'll live to be ... forty, Rachel. That's not a great age, is it? Well, by the time you turn forty you'll have seen the revolution. Perhaps sooner. But certainly not later.'

'Twenty years to go?' Sarah said. 'I think I'll be quite safe then. I won't see it.'

'Mom, you mustn't say things like that!'

'I hope you will see it, too,' Preiss said, smiling at Sarah. 'If I'm right I'll remind you.'

'And if you're wrong?'

'I'll probably be in jail.'

'Perhaps,' Sarah said, 'you'll be in jail even if you are right. Such things happen in revolutions, as you should know.'

'I'm sure nothing's going to happen,' Rachel said firmly, quickening her pace.

She almost ran to the gate of the house when she saw Jonathan and David standing together at it. Bertie hung back, watching her greet Jonathan. Then David came to him and shook him by the hand.

'So how's it feel to be a young gentleman at the university?' Bertie asked.

'Don't be so patronizing.'

'Has your father come home?' Sarah asked David.

'Yes, he has,' Jonathan said cheerfully, before David could reply. 'That's why we're out in the street.' He put his hand on his breast and a vibrant note came in to his voice. 'You know how deep is the love he bears me.'

'Jonathan!' Sarah laughed, amused and unhappy at what he had said. Jonathan pulled a rueful face.

'That's the way it is, alas.'

'Well, I must go inside, I must go and see how Annie's getting on with the lunch.'

'Don't lay a place for Rachel,' Jonathan told her. 'I'm taking her away.'

'Are you?' Rachel asked. 'Where to?'

'You'll find out when we get there.'

Rachel turned to look at the car parked against the kerb. 'Is *this* what you want to take me away in? Is that the best you could do?'

'Don't complain! It'll get us there – in the end. You can't have a Jaguar every weekend.'

'Why not?'

'Doesn't your boss mind you taking all these cars?' Sarah asked.

'My dear Aunt Sarah,' Jonathan said, kissing her on the middle of her broad, lined forehead, 'my boss doesn't know.'

'You're terrible.'

'Yes, I am. Disgusting, unhealthy, criminal, a disgrace to the noble name of Talmon.'

'Mm,' Rachel murmured. 'Well, let's go.' She turned and faced them all, with a dazed challenging smile, as if she saw none of them, but wanted them all to see her.

She and Jonathan drove off, Rachel leaning forward, her head lowered, her arm stretched out – reaching into the cubby-hole for a cigarette or a sweet or a map. Then she settled back in the seat; she was talking eagerly to Jonathan who nodded, keeping his eyes on the road.

34

As she brought her weight down and rose again Rachel was repeating rhythmically, in some distant, exultant corner of her consciousness, 'Riding, riding, riding ...' as if the single word were a song. Her passion, effort and nakedness seemed to her utterly innocent; not since childhood had she ridden so happily as she rode now on the man straddled beneath her. Then, unable to restrain herself, she began to move faster, she jerked, losing her momentum, and gratefully recovered it, feeling the shaft that grew from him, that grew into her, holding her safe. On and on she went, until she was no longer riding but transfixed, impaled, held in a stillness that was also a soaring, a drop, a convulsion, a kind of peace. She crouched over him, her eyes closed, her forehead against his collar bone, her moistures commingled with his. Shudders, quivers of sensation ran through her, and she whispered endearments, nonsense words, she heard her own heavy breathing.

Afterwards, the thought of dressing and going home was always unbearable. But once she was dressed and out in the street, once she became again the Rachel Glickman that everybody knew, the fact that there was another naked, breathing, exploring, singing Rachel, who rode or was ridden, straddled or was straddled, who threshed, hit, writhed, lay still for endless, timeless periods of solemn full pleasure while a hand plucked at her, a tongue licked at her – this secret knowledge of the other Rachel seemed to make it worthwhile being dressed and commonplace once more. No one but she and Jonathan knew how she could be transformed, what she had learned, what she could become; that was the best of it. Jonathan was her secret; she was her own secret, and she loved and cherished it for being secret.

'Would you be very upset, if someone found out that I was fucking you?' Jonathan asked that evening, when they were having dinner in the open air, on the first-floor terrace of a restaurant that looked over the corner of Twist and Coetzee Streets, where the trams screeched when they turned, and sent off sparks from their cables overhead.

'I'd die,' Rachel answered.

He looked at her with shining eyes, a wrinkle of laughter at the corner of his lips. 'Why? Because you're ashamed?'

Rachel pulled at his forelock, not altogether playfully. 'No you fool, because I'm so proud.'

Jonathan did not like having hair disordered. He looked sulky as he smoothed it back. He was about to speak, but changed his mind after a glance at Rachel's watchful, fiercely happy face. Instead he raised his glass of beer to her. 'To our grandfather, the rabbi,' he said.

'*O-main*,' Rachel chanted in response. It was an old joke of theirs. They had decided that their grandfather, the rabbi, after whom Jonathan was named, presided over their lovemaking: he was responsible for it, he had brought them together. '*Boruch shmo*,' Rachel added. 'Amen. Blessed be his name.'

35

Quite suddenly, Joel felt that the days had begun to run out. In Palestine, the British were withdrawing to a few tiny enclaves in Haifa and Jerusalem, and bloody battles were fought between Jews and Arabs to take control of the areas they had vacated. Soon British rule would end entirely; then a Jewish state would come into existence, and the armies of the Arab countries around it would invade. In South Africa, Zionism, which had always had a stronger following among the Jews there than any others in the English-speaking world, became not merely strong but wildly fashionable. Hundreds of young men drilled in secret on farms around Johannesburg; with the connivance of the government, surplus war-stores were bought up and flown or shipped to Europe; registers were made of pilots, of doctors, of engineers who were ready to offer their services. The first small groups of trainees from the various training-farms left for Europe, where they waited with other displaced persons in refugee camps for the boats that would take them across the Mediterranean; some had already, with the collapse of the British administration, managed to enter the country illegally. Among them was Johnny Magidson, from the Hatzofim, who was the first of the South Africans to be killed. The other members of the group waited; the Zionist Federation had promised that they would try to avoid the breaking-up of such groups, and would fly them off together.

Joel still went occasionally to the university; he spent most of his time on the farm, where Natalie was now living permanently, having taken the place of a girl who had gone ahead. But whatever he did, wherever he went, he felt that he was only half-present; the rest of him was elsewhere, in Palestine, in Europe, in a place that wasn't a place at all but rather a time, or a period of history. And this divorce from his surroundings lifted his spirits and calmed him at the same time. It was as if every moment were the moment between two waves of the sea: the current still flowed, the wave that had already broken raced towards the shore, the one following was already gathering itself in an arch before it too broke and crashed, but, in the meantime, he was suspended in a width of creased, hissing water. Calmness, stillness, abstraction, purity: these were the elements of crisis, as the winter came on, the nights grew colder, the air keener. Any day might be his last; the last of this city, with its bristling blocks of flats and high ridges, its miles of suburban houses and mine-dumps, its unchanging poignantly blue sky. The world war, his induction into the army, Egypt, Italy – he felt that then he had been too young, and the events had been too immense, for him to grasp; they had been worlds which had simply swallowed up the previous world. But now everything else went on about him as it always had, and just for that reason Joel felt all the more intensely both the stillness and the speed of the crisis he was in.

Then, within the same month as the declaration of independence of the State of Israel, the Afrikaner Nationalists came into power in South Africa. Joel's reaction to the news of the Nationalist victory was a selfish one; it was almost one of relief. Now he knew he had been right to want to sever himself from this country; the country, in coming into the hands of the Afrikaner Nationalists, had severed itself from him. Everything that was least welcoming in it, everything that was most provincial, most bigoted, backward, barren, cramped, divisive and suspicious, had been given power. He could hardly be bothered to grieve for it. He had turned elsewhere. Back to Europe (for he thought of Palestine as a part of Europe); back to the Jews; away from the haphazard disorder and fortuitousness of the country of his birth, which, he told himself, had never uttered a single, clear word he could understand and attend to with an undivided soul. Instead, he felt, there had merely been estrangement, pity, guilt, fear, contempt, roused at one time or another by every group in it – the blacks, the Coloureds, the Indians, the Afrikaners, the English, the anxious prospering Jews, all brought by chance together, and held together only by their needs and greeds, with no other shared ties of history, culture, kinship, loyalty, or even ordinary human sympathy. The only regret he could feel at leaving the country was at the thought of losing some landscapes and skyscapes, some colours and climates, and some deep but slightly shameful sources of amusement. He remembered Peter Dewes saying to him once, 'In South Africa you're never more truly patriotic than when you laugh at the mistakes each group makes in imitating the others.' It was true that there was far more covert, stumbling imitation among the groups than each would ever admit – in speech, gesture, dress, and notions of manners; and that out of these imitations a kind of unacknowledged, bastardized poverty-stricken nationhood was surreptitiously being formed. But all this wasn't much to lose, or much to miss.

Joel did not try to envisage the new State of Israel; he did not think about the kibbutz to which his group might be posted, or whether or not he might be separated from the rest of the group and drafted directly into the army; he didn't even try to imagine the journey itself, and what it would be like to part from his parents once again. He waited, merely, and was content to wait.

He went for a medical check-up, and was declared fit by the doctors who examined him. In Palestine there was a truce in the fighting. Joel began to get impatient to leave; but when he was telephoned one evening by Leon, and was told that the group would be leaving at the end of the next week, the summons seemed to come to him out of the blue. There would be seven men and three girls in the group, Leon said, Natalie being one of the girls. Leon himself would be travelling with them. They would not be separated on arrival, but would be sent immediately to a border kibbutz; Leon did not know where it would be. But he hoped they would fly straight to Israel, and not be forced to wait their turn at a DP camp in Italy.

So Joel told his parents. His mother's face was as sombre and disappointed as he had ever seen it. 'I can't believe that you're going. I just can't believe it. Why should you go again? Wasn't once enough? And for what? The Jews!'

36

In her misery Sarah blamed herself for not having spoken out months before, for not having protested, wept, persecuted him, blackmailed him emotionally to stay. Other mothers did such things: why hadn't she? She loved Joel no less than they loved their sons.

When she spoke to him again she was filled with a desolate resentment of her own moderation, of the reasonableness of what she was trying to say to him. That reasonableness would be of no help to her at two in the morning. Yet she could speak in no other way.

'It's not just that I hate it so much that you should go and put yourself in danger. Of course I hate it, any mother would. But to feel as well that it's a waste, that you're doing it for nothing … Yes, for nothing. I'm tired of the Jews, I'm not interested in them, or in the country they've got or they haven't got, or in the religion they've got or haven't got, or in the race they belong to or don't belong to, or any of the other things that are supposed to make them so special. Look at you! You, someone like you, with what you've got, you could do anything, you could be whatever you wanted to be. Instead you try to shuffle off the burden of yourself on to the Jews.'

She smiled unhappily at him, her brown eyes filled with tears, her hands working together in her lap. 'It's so small, Joel, it's such a trivial thing to tie yourself to – today, with people on the move everywhere, all over the world, and societies changing while you look at them and the bombs that could wipe us all out. Do you see what I mean? And don't tell me about Hitler and the killing of the Jews. I know what he did. And I say that you can't allow the Hitlers of the world to tell you what should be important to you in your life. Hitler could kill me, he wanted to kill me, and I'd still say to him that being Jewish today is an unimportant affair. It's the measure of his miserable mind that he could kill people for something that mattered so little. I know it's too late, you won't change your mind. I shouldn't be talking to you like this. But if I don't say it now I'll never say it.'

'So what is important?' Joel asked her.

She swayed forward slightly, opening her hands a little. 'You're important. What I feel about you is important.'

Awkwardly, with a wading movement of her arms and a middle-aged gasp of her breath, she got up from the sofa, where they had been sitting side-by-side, and went out of the room. Joel watched her go, pitying her, thinking that he had never loved and admired her more, yet selfishly relieved, too, that if she was going to cry she would do it in her bedroom rather than in front of him.

Benjamin's reaction to the news was much simpler, at first. He was proud. He went to the *shul* and boasted among his acquaintances there that his son would soon be leaving to join the army in Israel. He made a special point of announcing it to those men whom he knew to have sons as old as Joel, who had no intention of interrupting their studies or leaving their businesses to go to a warring Palestine. But the number of men with such sons discouraged him; and when he was alone Benjamin began to be tormented by visions of Joel wounded, Joel dead, himself grieving. Once or twice he even foresaw himself endowing scholarships at the Hebrew University in Joel's memory.

Guiltily, he said to Joel, 'I wish I could go in your place. I can't march any more, but I can shoot as well as anybody else.'

The idea of fighting in a Jewish army stirred him profoundly; and he tried to drive away the thought of Joel's death by indulging in fantasies of himself as a soldier in that army. Nightly he killed his quota of Germans, Arabs, faceless enemies of all kinds; he saw himself running across ploughed fields, shooting from ditches and broken walls; he exacted his revenge for every anti-Semitic remark he had ever heard, for the death of his sister and her family, for those photographs of the naked dead piled in heaps all over Europe.

In the end, however, Joel's quietness and lack of outward excitement made him feel almost as guilty about these fantasies as he had felt about those of Joel's death; and he went about his house and office with a meek absent-mindedness that surprised everyone who knew him.

37

Her own fears had always made Natalie bold; her boldness filled her with fear. But never before had she been as afraid as she was now – now that, after eight years of fervent participation in the Zionist youth movement, she was about to fly away to Palestine, to take part in a war, to make another life for herself. Every conceivable danger occurred to her, in images and fantasies which she followed with an irresistible thrill of the nerves into the recesses of her own mind. She imagined the plane they would be travelling on crashing into the bush in some remote corner of Africa; she saw herself falling ill in a DP camp in Italy or France; she tried to picture herself in a kibbutz that the Arabs were shelling from the ground, bombing from the air, swarming into through the rubble and wreckage. She woke in the middle of disturbed, uneasy nights to a feeling of total, paralyzing incapacity that attached itself to problems she had never considered before, but which now seemed altogether insurmountable. One night it might be the loneliness and helplessness of her parents after she had left them, the next it would be a complete disbelief in her ability ever to learn Hebrew.

As always when her fears most strongly possessed her, it seemed to her that she had always known that these terrors were the real possibilities of her life; that she had never been doing anything more than dare herself, as it were, to come as close to them as she could. At the same time, recoiling from them, she knew that on the other side there was another risk, another opportunity for a boldness whose consequences she could not estimate. She was poised, held up, between her fears: every time she spoke calmly to any one, every time she opened a door, smiled, handed money over a counter, responded to a question, her own action seemed to take place on a height from which all the railings of habit and expectation had been suddenly removed. Around it, beyond the edge, there was nothing but space, darkness and vertigo.

On a Sunday night, three days before she and Joel were due to leave, she had supper with the Glickmans; it was to be her last meal with them. Everyone around the table, except for Natalie, was surprisingly cheerful, largely because of the effort Benjamin was making; he reminisced busily about his own early days in the Zionist movement, speaking of long-forgotten conferences, of the visits to South Africa of men like Weizmann and Jabotinsky. And he told them how he and a friend had once started a Zionist monthly magazine, with a few pounds they had managed to scrape together out of their pockets. He had been a bachelor then, working as a traveller for a firm selling dairy equipment. He and his friend had known nothing about how to produce a magazine, nothing about printing, about layout, or about English grammar. But they had canvassed for advertisements, and they had found a little printer in Doornfontein – a hunchback fellow who wrote poetry – and they had arranged with him that in return for giving them a discount on the printing, and helping them with the layout, they would publish his poetry in the magazine.

'He was delighted with the bargain! So we printed his poetry, though it seemed a lot of rubbish to me. The rest of the magazine we wrote ourselves, entirely. And we laid it on strong and thick. Everything in that magazine was the eleventh hour, a time of crisis, a call for action. We didn't really know what a crisis was for the Jews, in those days. We still had to learn from Hitler. Anyway, we managed to get out two issues, and that was the end of the story, the end of our money, the end of the Zionist Clarion. And I haven't kept a single copy of it and nor has Natie Harsch: I asked him about it when I saw him in Durban last time I was there. The little printer – he's dead, he died years ago. So there's nothing left of it at all, it made no difference to anything. And we were so excited about it at the time!'

Sarah was leaning forward, her hands clasped on the table. 'It did make a difference. It made a difference to me. I can remember how impressed I was when I met you, and you told me you'd been the editor of a monthly magazine.'

Benjamin looked so surprised that everyone burst into laughter.

'You were impressed?'

'Of course, I was very impressed.'

'You should have told me. It would have given me confidence.'

'I think I did tell you. I'm sure I did.'

Joel called out, 'Hey, Mom, you're blushing.'

'Don't tease your mother,' Benjamin reproved him, looking at her with a mischievous, curious expression, inviting her to say more.

'Well, I admired your magazine very much – even though I wasn't a Zionist. I admired the spirit behind it.'

'Did you think you were marrying a literary gentleman then?' Joel asked.

'No, I never thought anything like that. But I did think you were serious about things, and your magazine showed it, even though it was also such a foolish affair in so many ways. It's really too bad that you haven't got a copy of it to show to the children.'

'Ach, the children. The past.' He felt a sad, full happiness, saying the words, and shook his head. 'I remember, just after the First World War, I actually went and made a booking on a boat that was going to Palestine. Everything here was in pieces, it was just after the 'flu epidemic, when my mother died and my little brother, and I had no job, and thought to myself: What are you waiting for? Go! Make a new life in *Eretz Yisroel!* But I didn't have the money for the fare. Booking was one thing, paying another. Afterwards the chance was gone, I was involved in business, in all sorts of things, soon I was married. So I worked in the movement, that's all I ever did. What it would have meant to me in those days if I'd known that a son of mine would be going one day to a real Jewish state, actually existing in the world! I'd have known then that it was worthwhile, it wasn't wasted effort, the little we did – the speeches, the fund-raising, even the *Zionist Clarion*. But who could know?'

'Let the war finish first,' Sarah said, clasping her hands and pressing them together. 'Let there be peace there, before you say that it was all worthwhile.' They all knew that what she was saying was: Let the children not be killed.

'If the Arabs couldn't win in the first few weeks they'll never be able to now,' Benjamin answered confidently; more confidently than he felt when he looked at Joel, who might soon be fighting against the Arabs. But he was determined not to let them fall into a gloomy anxious silence. 'It is amazing,' he went on, 'the way things happen. People get an idea in their heads and run around organizing and squabbling and raising money, and some of them change their lives, give their lives – and so there's something new in the world, there's a Jewish state, for example. Is that how it's done? It seems impossible, somehow. And yet, what else was there? No Zionism, no settlers in Palestine. No Zionism and the settlers would have died in the swamps. No settlers, no *Yishuv* yesterday, no Israel today. Start with an idea, and where can't you end?'

Joel said, 'Zionism's a very special case.'

Sarah added, 'No Hitler, no State of Israel either, don't forget that. You can't isolate anything from anything else.'

'No, I agree, without Hitler there'd have been no Israel. But what was Hitler once except a little *meshuggeneh* bastard of a housepainter running around, organizing and squabbling and trying to raise money? It's the same thing again. We just never know what is really starting or finishing or what it'll one day mean to us.'

'Or to our children,' Sarah put in.

Natalie had been sitting stiffly in her chair, taking no part in the conversation, hardly listening to what was being said; her mouth was set in a stubborn, petulant line Joel knew well. It was some time after Benjamin had spoken that she repeated one of the things he had said – 'Start with an idea and where can't you end?'

They turned to her, she saw them looking at her, puzzled by the tone of her voice. She could not herself recall how she had said the words; but it was obvious to her that she must have betrayed some emotion they were not expecting, or could not understand.

How could they understand? Obtuse, complacent, ugly, the faces around the table crowded on her: Benjamin now sucking at his tea, his eyebrows still raised enquiringly towards her above the rim of his cup, Sarah with her mouth hanging anxiously open, Rachel fingering the ends of her hair, Joel concentrating on the pattern he was making with the tines of his fork on the tablecloth, his dark head lowered. To Natalie they looked grotesque, as if she had never seen people before, and she had to ask herself why they had such chins and noses, such bodies; why they sat on such chairs between such walls. Who were they? What did they want of her? What would they do if she were to scream into those faces of theirs?

She could not bear to look at them. She closed her eyes and waited, not knowing for what she was waiting.

38

Presently Annie came in to clear away the teacups and the group around the table broke up. Sarah said that she was going to give herself a treat and have a really early night; Benjamin went into the living room to listen to the radio and read the

Sunday paper; Rachel went to her room, and Joel and Natalie to his.

Walking down the passage, they heard from the kitchen Jacobus talking in Zulu to the houseboy; from the loud, amused, exclamatory tone of his voice he was clearly recounting some adventure that had happened to him. Jacobus spent every weekend at the house now, and as a result Annie's stomach was just beginning to curve out with the weight of the baby she was carrying. No one knew what had happened to the man she used to speak of as her husband; but Jacobus still conscientiously gave back to his employer a pound a week out of his wages, to be sent to his wife and children in Basutoland.

Hearing him, it occurred to Joel, with a sudden pang, that one noise he would never hear in Israel was that of African servants gathered in the kitchen, after nightfall, to gossip together in languages he had never learned. How many times he had fallen asleep as a child to that deep, leisurely, comforting, incomprehensible sound.

No sooner had he closed the bedroom door than Natalie turned to him, her face smooth, her eyes shining and big with excitement.

'Joel, I've got something to say to you. It's very hard, I don't know how to say it.'

But she said it simply and promptly.

'If I don't go to Israel, Joel, will you stay here with me?'

39

They left at midnight, in a two-engined Dakota chartered by the South African Zionist Federation. The parting from parents, girlfriends, brothers and sisters, and anxious Federation officials, was tense and uncomfortable for practically everyone;

and it was made more so by a group which attempted injudiciously to rouse the spirits of the party by singing the *Hatikvah*. Then the dozen members of the Hatzofim movement and the fifteen others who were going as individual volunteers for the army trooped out of the pre-fabricated departure-lounge and walked across the alternating light and darkness of the tarmac. A cold wind was blowing, carrying with it the smell of fuel, the sound of aircraft engines, and a sense of a flat empty space larger by far than the airport.

Once they were airborne, however, a wild exhilaration possessed them all. Even before the spread of the lights of the Witwatersrand had disappeared into the blackness beneath them, they were standing up, calling to one another, passing slabs of chocolate and a bottle of brandy from hand to hand, singing, flirting with the Israeli girl who was acting as air hostess, joking with the aircrew, demanding food, and shouting encouragement at the pale whirling discs of the propellers, which the plane's own lights lit up. By dawn they were at Salisbury in Southern Rhodesia; a few hours later in Ndola, on the Copperbelt; later still they were flying over Lake Victoria, endlessly it seemed. They spent the night at Entebbe, in an hotel where the waiters wore long white robes, and a smell of moisture, growth and rot was carried off the lake. In the morning they flew on, coming down to refuel every few hours at heat-stricken airports, some of them surrounded by green, humid bush, others by sand and scrub. Their last stop in Africa was Mersa Matruh; then they flew across the Mediterranean to Naples, where they were put on a bus and taken to a DP camp on the coast. The camp, Joel wrote to Natalie (for they had agreed, in the end, that they would write to one another) looked 'like a cross between an army barracks and an African Location'. There, for three long, hot, irritated weeks, surrounded by strangers of every age and sex and language, they remained.

40

Another, more boisterous, departure took place in the central Johannesburg railway station a few months later, on a Saturday morning, when Jonathan Talmon (or Jonathan Delmond as he henceforth intended calling himself) left on the first stage of his journey to England. Rachel was in the large and noisy group that came to see him off. Most of the people in it were strangers to her; but all of them were apparently intimate with Jonathan, who laughed and talked at the top of his voice, gestured wildly, and flung his arms indiscriminately around the men and the women in the group. His cheeks and lips were smeared red from the kisses the women had given him, his collar and tie were disordered, and in his hand he clutched, at different times, magazines, a half-jack of brandy, paper bags of fruit, a teddy bear which one joker had given him, and two rolls of toilet-paper in an 'economy pack' given him by another. Rachel had never seen him so happy and excited before. And he was leaving her! She stood aside from the throng and waited for some word or sign from him; something more meaningful than the hasty kiss he had given her when she had come on to the platform, and his delighted whisper to her – 'They're crazy! What a send-off!'

Right at the end, after the first warning bell had been sounded, Jonathan's mood turned serious, briefly and unexpectedly. He stood on the step of the carriage, holding on to the hand-rails on both sides of the door which stood open behind him, and made a little speech. 'People, I don't want to say anything that will embarrass you. But, all the same, I'm not going to go away without telling you how grateful I am to you. I love you all – I really do – and I'm not –' he paused and swallowed, and his lids dropped over his eyes, as if he were committing to memory the words he was going to utter – 'I'm not going to let you down.' Then he was smiling again, and blowing kisses with one hand, clinging to the hand-rail with the other.

'Good old Jonathan!' his friends shouted. 'Bring 'em back alive!' 'We'll see your name in lights!' 'West End or bust!'

The bell rang twice more, a flag was waved, the train began to move. Jonathan jumped down from the step, while every one shrieked with alarm, and took Rachel in his arms. He kissed her on the lips, kissed the tears that were on her cheeks, and turned and ran down the platform, to catch up once more with his carriage. Rachel saw him leap on to it and turn, waving. Before he was out of sight she had left the group on the platform and was making her way out of the station.

Dazed, frightened and incredulous, she went up Rissik Street towards the Town Hall, simply walking because the street was in front of her. She was aware of the passing of pedestrians and the traffic in the street, of random snatches of conversation, of music from a radio shop; once she stood and watched a driver trying to reverse his car into a vacant bay, and moved on only when she saw the man looking hostilely at her. For months she had known that Jonathan was going to leave; she had even been with him when he had made his final booking at a travel agency and had looked at the bright folders on display there; she had talked of following him at the end of the year; for weeks she had been telling herself that she would do this or that or the other thing 'after Jonathan's gone'.

And now? 'It's over,' she said to herself. 'He's gone. He doesn't want me.' She waited for some movement of grief or despair or anger to rise within herself at these phrases. But there was none. Nothing filled the emptiness within her; and a kind of panic overtook her, at the thought that this blankness would be all she would feel. 'Jonathan,' she moaned under her breath, 'I love you, sweetie, don't leave me.' She closed her eyes and stood still, biting at her lower lip. But no image of Jonathan came into her mind: only the image of herself standing in the dark, waiting for emotions she could not feel, did not have. Then other bare melodramatic, disconnected words came one by one into her mood, assembling there, with emotionless spaces between them. Lost. Broken. Desperate. Punished.

With an insane congruity, as if she were hallucinated, there burst on her ears a harsh, mechanically magnified voice uttering immense words she could not make out at all. The noise was followed by a burst of cheering. She opened her eyes; she was relieved to hear that the sounds still went on, at a distance of a block or two away. She looked around her, and saw that from all sides people were streaming towards the Town Hall, with a look of pleased curiosity on their faces. She let herself go with them.

41

The meeting had been called in protest against the dismissal by the government, under an act it had just passed, of a well-known white trade unionist from his position in the women's union which he had managed to organize on no-racial lines: that was the reason why the government had moved against him. Most of the demonstrators were Coloured and African women, but there were many thousands of whites, too, in the crowd. This mixture of races was in itself enough to make the occasion an exciting one; but what made it even more exciting was the news that the meeting had been banned by the police a few hours previously, and that the committee responsible for it had nevertheless decided to go ahead.

None of this was known to Rachel; all she knew was what she could see and hear. A great crowd of black and white people filled almost the entire space between the Rissik Street Post Office and the City Hall, blocking the traffic in Market and

President Streets, swaying about in a good-humoured, expectant, almost casual frenzy. Different branches of the trade union involved, as well as others that were demonstrating in sympathy, had unfurled banners above the heads of the crowd; the largest banners were yards wide, and on each banner were painted huge defiant slogans in English and Afrikaans: 'South Africa is our Country Too'; 'Down With Apartheid'; 'Hands Off Our Union'; 'We Stand Together'. Because of the movements of the people holding them, the banners billowed out or sagged, were pulled tight or collapsed in wrinkles, so that one might have thought that a strong, irregular wind was blowing; but the morning was warm, sunny and still, and most of the Africans and Coloureds in the crowd, and many of the whites, were in shirtsleeves and cotton dresses. Every now and again a cheer went up from one or another section of it, as a new group of demonstrators appeared around a corner, and those at a distance would turn their heads or jump up and down where they were standing, in order to see what the cheering was about. The speakers' party was at the head of the steps that led to the Town Hall, with the tall brown doors of the Hall closed behind them. People were sitting on the monumental howitzers to the right and left of the steps; several piccanins had climbed up the palm trees that grew near the howitzers, and clung to them with their hands and bare feet. No one looked grim or worried, or fierce; few people in the crowd appeared to be listening to the speeches that were coming from the loudspeakers. Like baffled, ignored, living things, the sounds echoed back and forth between the high buildings.

A woman was speaking now; her voice rose as she came to the end of her speech. 'They've tried to silence our Sammy, but he will not be silenced! Brothers and sisters, our leader – Sammy Levine!' Before she had finished the cheering drowned the name. Here and there heads in the crowd bobbed up and down more vigorously than before, as people tried to see the man who had stepped up to the microphone.

Rachel could not see him at all. But she was taken aback when she heard Levine say his first words. 'Comrades,' he said, 'my friends, this is a sad and glorious occasion for me.' What took her aback was that his accent was so much like her father's: that of an immigrant Jew from Lithuania. It seemed somehow wrong to her, unlikely, undesirable, that such a voice should be booming and quacking through loudspeakers across a great crowd, in a public place. She felt herself exposed, put in danger by it; she did not know why.

But Levine did not speak for long. He had said no more than a few sentences when a noise went up from the crowd quite unlike any Rachel had heard before. It began as a mere hubbub of surprise and consternation, but swelled in an instant into a single shriek which filled the air, and then – incredibly, for there seemed to be no space for it to grow in – rose still higher. A group of about thirty uniformed policemen had burst out of the doors of the Town Hall, rushed upon the speakers' platform, taken hold of Sammy Levine and those standing closest to him, and dragged them into the Town Hall, closing the doors behind them. The arrest or capture had taken place so swiftly that the crowd was able to do no more than shriek before the doors were closed.

Then it thrust forward in a great heave. Rachel found herself in the middle of a group of Coloured women; shoulders, backs, bosoms, arms, faces were shoved against her, someone trod excruciatingly on her foot. 'What's happening?' she gasped. '*Wat makeer*? Don't push like that!' There was a babble of talk and cries in her ears, and a noise beyond it – not the single shriek of rage she had heard before, but a continuous loud howling which seemed to sweep unpredictably in waves across the square.

Rachel had not seen the police, and did not know why the crowd had suddenly turned violent, nor how far forward she had been swept, until she felt under her feet the first of the steps where the speakers had stood. The crowd broke open momentarily in front of her, and she saw that the doors of the Town Hall were no more than yards away. Dark objects were flying towards the building; the missiles simply seemed to rain upwards, like things out of nature, before curving and falling. There was a smashing of glass, a clatter of wood. The crowd closed round her once more, and Rachel could see nothing but the people against whom she was jammed; she felt herself still being carried forward and across. Again, overhead, there was an eruption of dark things into the air; they flew upwards like birds, but fell steeply, heavily, quickly.

Suddenly everyone was tumbling back, pushing back, staggering back. The doors had swung open, they gaped on a dark space, and out of it came the police, carrying long white staves. More and more came, dark blue figures that jostled one another in their haste, and then began to smash out with their riot sticks at the heads and shoulders of the people in front of them. 'They're *hitting* them!' Rachel exclaimed aloud, unable to believe her eyes. She did not run. She could not. Men and women fell, their hands over their eyes, or clutching the tops of their heads, blood spurting between their fingers. Still more police were emerging from the building; they were fanning out freely in pursuit. The crowd was now a wildly fleeing mob. Rachel saw one policeman have his baton snatched from him by a ragged black figure, who was immediately struck down by two others; their staves whirled in the air and fell over the spot where the man had been standing, whirled and fell again. The police were ignoring the whites in the crowd; they were attacking the Coloureds and Africans only. Some of the young white men in the crowd were joining in, chasing the fleeing blacks, kicking out at them, grinning across pale, demented faces.

A policeman ran straight towards Rachel. His stave was broken, it had a sharp, jagged edge, and he held it in front of him as if it were a spear. She opened her mouth and felt the tearing in her throat of her own scream, but did not hear it. An African came between them, with his head down and his shoulder high up. The policeman ran into him, staggered back, and lashed him across the side of the head. He fell sideways; his body hit Rachel in the stomach and she went down, with the man on top of her. The smell of him was in her nostrils; and then it was gone. She fell into a narrow space of darkness, that seemed to have been prepared for her. The sense of the darkness as something fitting her, made for her, was the last thing of which she was conscious.

When she opened her eyes she thought she must have been away, unconscious for a long time. The sky was remote and blue; it looked further off than she had ever seen it. Then a face which was familiar but which she could not recognize came between it and herself.

'Rachel!' she heard. 'Rachel!'

'Bertie,' she answered.

She did not know what part of herself had spoken. Consciously, she recognized him, she knew that he had been speaking to her, only after she had said his name.

'You've been hurt. You're bleeding.'

He was kneeling on the ground beside her. He put his hand under her neck and raised her gently. She looked around unsteadily. Everything seemed to have changed. The African who had fallen on her was gone. No policemen were to be seen. The square seemed almost denuded of people, they were no more than a black, thick fringe around its edges. But there were many dark shapes lying or sitting on the ground, as she was; some of them had one or two men or women stooped or kneeling over them, as Bertie kneeled over her. A number of shoes were scattered about, over the blank paving – women's shoes, for the most part, with an abject, lopsided look to them – and a few handbags, and scraps of torn banners, pieces of broken wood.

The crowd at the rim of the square began to move forward; the sight of it, the darkness and thickness of it, made Rachel feel as though her own vision was drawing in, contracting upon her. Sick and afraid, she wanted to get away. She began to struggle to her feet.

'Help me, Bertie, please.'

His arm was around her; his hand was holding her own. His voice was full of solicitude. 'The ambulances must be coming. Wait here, I'll get a stretcher.'

'No,' she cried, 'don't leave me. I'm all right, I promise you. I'm not hurt.' She saw him looking strangely at her, and lifted her hand to her face. It was wet and sticky, then she saw that her fingers were bright red. A thump of darkness assailed her, left her, and she sat down again. She sat in silence for some time before she was able to say, 'I'm sure it's not me – not my blood.'

Bertie was wiping his face with his handkerchief, and she lifted it up to him, like a child.

When she stood up she found that she ached in all her limbs, and in her chest. Bertie supported her, and she limped along at his side. Some men and women were still lying on the ground, but most of the injured were now sitting up. The blood ran down their faces in streams, or showed itself in heavy, matted patches in the hair of their heads.

'I didn't know that heads could *bleed* so much.' Rachel said; this surprised her as much as anything else she had seen.

They made their way through the crowd at the corner of President and Rissik Streets. Rachel looked back, and saw the square filling with people. At the far corner of it a fight seemed to be going on; some people were running towards it, others running away. Bertie stood on tip-toes beside her, anxiously scanning the square.

'Are you looking for somebody?'

'Yes. Adela. We got separated when the police charged. She's all right, I'm sure, but she may be worried about me.'

'You better go and look for her. I'll – I'll be all right, I can manage on my own.'

'It looks like it!' he shouted furiously at her, jerking his head round, falling back on his heels. She did not know why he was so angry, and stood silently and submissively waiting for him to decide what they should do next.

'No, it's no good, I can't see her.' He put his arm around her waist again. 'Come.'

Several ambulances were approaching. They pulled up just a few yards away, with a long-drawn, reluctant, fading growl from their sirens. Men in peaked caps jumped out of them, both in front and at the back of each vehicle, and began pulling out stretchers.

'You're sure you don't want to get in one?' Bertie asked.

'Quite sure. Have you got a car?'

'No – I'm terribly sorry.' His anger was quite gone; now he was just dismayed and guilty, disgraced in his own eyes because he had no car to offer her. 'I can call a taxi and we can go straight up to Casualty –'

'Let's go somewhere where I can sit down. I'm not really hurt. A man fell on me, that's all.'

42

By chance they went to the café in which Joel and Pamela had sat together, years before. On the way there Rachel stopped to look at herself in a mirror on a shop-front, and wiped off the last of the blood from her cheeks and hands with Bertie's handkerchief. Her face looked hardly any more pale than his. She went straight to the lavatory in the café, then washed her face in a dirty little basin, and combed her hair.

She was struck that she was still carrying her bag; she hadn't noticed it on her arm until she reached automatically into it for the comb.

With its wicker chairs and wicker tables carrying green glass tops, its crammed sweet and cigarette counters, and its knobbly, shiny cream-painted walls decorated with a few murky mirrors, the café looked as though it had been lifted bodily from some forlorn, wayside *dorp*, miles from anywhere, and dumped down by mistake under a fifteen-storey office block. But it was cool, dark and empty, and Rachel sank gratefully into a chair at the table Bertie had taken.

At once she was seized by a fit of shivering. Her whole body shook grossly, intolerably; she was jarred, buffeted, frightened by it. Bertie was trying to attract the attention of one of the African waiters who were lounging against the wall at the other end of the room; he had not yet noticed what was happening to her.

When he did turn to face her, she attacked him before he could speak, before he could see how she was trembling. 'Are you happy now?' The words came out in gasps from her soft, shuddering jaw. 'Are you glad it's happened? It's what you want, isn't it? You're the bloody politician, aren't you?' At last tears sprang to her eyes. 'Oh,' she wept, 'why don't you leave people *alone*?'

She covered her face and sobbed into her hands, glad of the darkness, not wanting to emerge from it, carried away, released by her tears.

Bertie's hands touched at hers, then at her hair. He stammered, exclaimed, apologized. 'We had nothing to do with this morning's meeting. It wasn't anything to do with us. We'd never have … we don't believe it's time for mass action. We're still in the stage of educating people …'

But in the face of the attack she had made, in front of her distress, his words and explanations embarrassed and humiliated him; they seemed so portentous and so irrelevant to her, to himself.

'Rachel, Rachel, please –' he implored her. His hands were still seeking something to grasp, but her face remained covered, she did not yield her fingers to him. He leaned across the table and clumsily took the whole of her head between his hands, bowed and covered though it was.

'Rachel, you've always meant more to me than anyone else. I can't help it. I want you to know it.'

She made no sign that she had heard him. Bertie looked up and found two waiters staring over him, trays in their hands and unabashed curiosity on their dark faces. 'Bugger off! *Voetsak!*' he said furiously to them. 'I'll call you when I want you.'

Rachel's hands had fallen from her face. She no longer trembled; she was smiling strangely. He waited a long time for her to speak.

'Bertie, I think I'm pregnant. The man – he – he left for England this morning.'

She covered her face with her hands again. They sat in silence together. Bertie stared at her, at the dim reflection of her in the glass top of the table. He looked at the door, too, where figures passed and paused and were lost in a shiver of light.

When they got up, hours later, Bertie felt that something had been done to him from which he would never recover; something so deep it was as far beyond alleviation as it was beyond the reach of what he would have called pain. They left the café together.

43

Fifteen months passed before Rachel and Bertie were married. They had decided they would wait until he had written his final examinations for his bachelor's degree. Then he went into business with his father-in-law. He gave up his intention to take law, he gave up his political ambitions, he gave up the ideological beliefs which had sustained him ever since he had begun to read and think for himself.

For what? For what had he given them up? It was a question he asked himself many times in the course of those months, and in the years that followed, until the cynicism of his answer corroded his capacity even to ask the question. The answer was: For nothing. For so many trivialities. For a girl in trouble, for a childhood tenderness, for an impulse of pity, for a notion of honour, for an insecure, vain gesture of strength, for the challenge of matching her recklessness with his own. For the ten-day drama of helping her arrange to have an abortion, and of seeing her through it, while her parents imagined the two of them were camping together in the Magaliesberg. For Rachel's gratitude and smiles, her trust and a share in her passions. For a directorship in the Central Creamery (Pty) Limited.

He told himself, and believed, that these were nothing; yet they were all he had, and he was fiercely jealous and vigilant of all of them. Of none of them was he more jealous than of Rachel herself; Rachel who had acted accordingly to her own desperate notion of honour in not telling her wretched cousin that she was pregnant, lest he should think it was her last device, her last trick, to keep him in South Africa. (Instead, it had become her trick, her device, Bertie often thought with a kind of self-throttling, ironic rage, to entrap him.) He never forgot that she had loved and been despoiled by another man, and that it was because of that that they had come together.

So they were married, and Bertie went to work; and surprised everyone by the eagerness, the hardness, the ambition with which he worked. If he was to be nothing else, he was determined now to become a rich man. Rachel admired his ambition and passionately wanted him to succeed in it. She was more proud of him, more respectful of him, than either of them had anticipated. But this did little to soothe him.

44

Bertie's abandonment of Adela intensified greatly her devotion to the cause they had shared. With Ntuli she left the splinter group of the DSAM, and joined the larger, Communist directed movement that was attempting to rouse the consciousness of the African masses. She said to others that she despised and pitied Bertie for what he now was; but that she would always be grateful to him for having done so much to emancipate her from the contemptible white world of money, self-seeking and insensibility he had chosen deliberately to re-enter.

It was not long, however, before she was saying that the fact that Bertie had belonged to a 'Trotskyist' group like the DSAM showed that he had never really been serious in his politics, though she admitted he had managed to take her in at the time. It was only now, among her new friends, that she had learned what true commitment was. For to her and the others in the movement Communism was more than an ideology and a theory of history to be believed in, more than a way of removing the self-evident, hideous injustices of the society around her, more than a source of intense companionship in danger, more than a side personally chosen in the cold war, in a sense, it was more even than a religion. It was a culture – to which she belonged on fully equal terms with any other member, whether he lived in New York, Rome, Djakarta or Moscow.

The culture had its own shared references in every field of human activity, its own standards of judgement, its own ways of appropriating or rejecting the past, its own hagiographies and festivals, even its own novels and poems, its own music, its own art. Its centres of power may have been physically remote, but their means of expression, their ways of speaking to Adela, never were. After six months in the movement she felt more intimately at home when she read the English language Communist journals published in Budapest or Prague than when she read the Johannesburg newspapers; far more so than when she read the liberal weeklies from England. She was a member of a worldwide community, with a common speech as well as a common struggle to wage; this was a liberation that Adela, Ezreal Klein's daughter, taking her degree in Social Science at Witwaterstand University, hadn't known she had hungered for, until it was given to her.

PART 5

1

Waking to the sound of the clanging bell was always painful for Joel; but once he was awake, once he had washed and had had something to eat, the two-hour stretch of work before breakfast was the best of the day. Morning after morning he watched the dawn break over the Arab-held Judaean hills in the east: as the sky became steadily brighter and brighter, gleaming with a light that had no visible source, so, in contrast, the hills turned a deeper and darker blue, until a single band of purple vibrated against the horizon. Then the sun rose directly over the hills, which immediately began to lose their colour and depth; by breakfast-time they were merely a grey serration in the distance. Only in the evening, in the last calm light of the day, did they appear solid once again, revealing more of themselves than at any other time. You could see Arab villages dotted about on them, the fields marked off on their lower slopes, the finger of a mosque pointing to the sky, the faint lines of ancient, shattered terraces banding them at intervals. Another day was over. On the kibbutz, men and women with wet hair and towels around their necks walked from the shower rooms to the wooden huts and tents scattered on the slope; they sat at ease on the steps of their prefabs; they waited around the door of the dining room for the dinner bell to be rung; they watched the lights beginning to twinkle on both sides of the border.

There were eighty of them on the *meshek*, a little more than half of them English-speaking, the other half from a variety of countries and speaking a variety of languages, including about a dozen native-born Israelis, who had originally been assigned to train and guide the newcomers, and some of whom now intended to remain with them rather than to return to their own kibbutzim. There was also a full-time, paid Hebrew teacher, who gave lessons in rotation and went home over the weekends. Of the twenty-five South Africans who had originally formed the nucleus of the settlement, only ten remained; but they had been joined by a few South Africans from other movements, and a few later arrivals from their own. The other largest contingents came from Canada and the United States. Men greatly outnumbered women, and none of the women was unattached; there were five babies in the nursery.

For Joel the eighteen months he had been on the kibbutz had been on the whole happy ones; and happy for reasons he had not really anticipated. What he had not expected was that the best of life on the kibbutz should have been its ordinariness, its quotidian quality, its physicality, so to speak, and not its spirituality. It had been one thing to talk or to hear others talking of 'the dignity of labour' and 'the normalization of the class-structure of the Jewish people': it was another to flop down exhausted, with pounding heart and closed eyes, on top of a truckload of building sand he had loaded himself, and let the truck carry him half-conscious to the building site; to shovel gravel and sand with a rhythm of idleness and frenzy dictated by the rumble and clank of the mixer that had to be fed; to see boulders crack into fragments under his hammer, revealing their hearts shining as if from the dawn of the world; to loiter through afternoons with a chisel in his hand and a pipe that had to be scraped free of rust laid out on trestles before him; to carry cow-melons to the heaps that made a pattern across the field that was being cleared; to stand knee-deep in a slippery, pungent ensilage of rotten oranges and to shovel it from a truck into barrows, from barrows into the cow-stalls; to ride high on a swaying combine harvester, deafened by its roar, hypnotized by the chaff flying upwards and the grain pouring its bead-like golden weight into the bags he clipped into position when they were empty and shoved overboard when they were full.

Always, while he worked, the sky was above him, around him were fields and wastelands, hills and wide valleys, views of the main road in the distance, with tiny cars flashing by. Within him, if the job he was on was not too taxing, were memories and reveries of an extraordinary vividness and variety. This was perhaps the most surprising thing of all about the work he was doing: that it seemed to set so much of his mind free to speculate and remember, to play with its own images and fantasies, while his body bent and straightened, his muscles clenched and relaxed. He had thought the work might be dulling and stupefying; but once the agony of getting used to it was behind him, he had not found it so. Not yet, at any rate.

Sometimes when he looked up he wondered where he was, what country he was in, what his hands were doing, what had happened to the people whose faces he had just seen and whose voices he had heard just a moment before. Then he would go back to his work. A period of his life to which his thoughts returned with particular frequency was the time he had spent in Italy, in the army; he supposed it was because the communal style of life reminded him in some ways of the army, the colours of the sky and the seasons of Italy. And the sense of disorder and crisis outside the kibbutz was like that of a country still at war, or in a state of siege. He wanted very much to go back to Italy, to look at the riches that the poverty and destruction of war had shrouded from him, that he had been too young, too frightened, too preoccupied, to pay attention to.

Israel was disappointingly less like Europe than he had expected it to be.

His leisure was full, bland, mindless; he thought and dreamed far less when he was idle than he did when he was at work. On Sabbaths he slept, woke, went for walks, helped his friend, Harry, in his amateur archeological explorations in the hills around about, wrote letters, played in scratch games of football and rounders. In the evenings of work-days he enjoyed the rowdiness of the shower rooms, the long bouts of gossip in rooms, the parties given around a bottle of arak and a food-parcel from Canada or South Africa, the irresponsible, schoolboyish excitement that came over them when they took a truck and rode off to see a film in the nearest township, their fellowship in boredom or fits of giggles when some solemn *tarbutnik* from Jerusalem came to lecture to them on child psychology or to play the violin or, on one unforgettable occasion, to perform certain solo Yemenite folk-dances, accompanied by a flute and hindered by an excess of flesh and gauze draperies. It had been one thing to talk or to hear others talking of a restoration of 'the spirit of community'; it was another to find himself living and working among a group of people with whom his relations were amiable, intense, indifferent or hostile, as he or they chose.

Altogether, Joel felt that practically from the moment of his arrival in Israel a great burden of self-consciousness about what he was doing had fallen away from him; he realized how great the burden had been only now that it was gone. For others in the group, it was true, the sudden, harsh, inevitable abrogation of the status they had enjoyed in the eyes of others in South Africa as singular young people, self-sacrificing visionaries, the reduction of the large aspirations and fervours they had nourished into so many small, commonplace facts, had come as a shocking blow, an intolerable affront. They had been the first to leave; Henry Kramer and his wife among them. Others had left later for family reasons, or after quarrels, or simply because they had grown weary of the life.

Joel shirked administrative responsibility, he still had not settled down to learn a special skill, at the bottom of himself he remained undecided as to whether this was what he would do, this was where he would remain, for the rest of his life. Yet, no matter what might happen in the future, the undramatic fullness and arduousness of his routine seemed to him its surest justification; the contentment he had found in it was the surest proof that he had not merely been led there by an infatuation with a girl who had let him down.

2

Joel found the letter from his mother in the rack in the entrance to the dining room; he did not open it until he was seated at one of the long uncovered tables that occupied most of the room, and along each of which, at intervals, were grouped aluminium jugs of tea, plates of sliced bread, saucers of jam, and a collection of mugs, spoons and knives. While he ate and drank, Joel read his letter through, more than once. His mother wrote frequently and entertainingly, and this letter was especially full of news.

As always, he ate steadily, smearing slice after slice of bread with jam; and he went on drinking cup after cup of tea even after he had finished eating. The tea, which was served without milk, was already sweetened, but he secretly put a spoonful of jam into his cup, every time he filled it; his appetite for sweet things was never appeased.

He sat on his own at the end of a bench, and no one disturbed him, though people were constantly coming in and pouring out their first cups of tea before flopping down on the benches. Some sprawled in silence over the tables, littered with crumbs and stained with pools of tea; a few had their heads bent together over the two copies of the *Jerusalem Post* that had come in after lunch; others were busy, as Joel was, with letters; some talked quietly. From the kitchen, beyond the partition that divided the wooden-walled hut in two, there came the sounds of the evening meal being prepared. Bars of strong golden light from the declining sun shone through the uncurtained windows and stretched across the room, above the heads of the seated men; when they stood up their faces were momentarily transfigured, their foreheads gleamed palely, their hair became dark and lustrous, the lines of fatigue around their blinking eyes were smoothed away.

Then another group began coming in: those who had showered and shaved before taking their tea. They were fresher and in better spirits than the people already there, and the volume of the noise in the room rose accordingly. Among the newcomers were some of the Palestinian-born members of the group, the *sabras*, who were soon reading the copy of *Davar* which was delivered with the *Post* but which had not been touched before their arrival. The bench at which Joel was sitting had filled up; he put the letter in the pocket of his shirt and listened to the random talk around him. Leon, who was now called Leib, sat down opposite Joel, across the table. He poured out a mug of tea and spread jam on a slice of bread and began eating and drinking slowly.

Neither said anything to the other until, after a couple of minutes had passed, Joel asked him, 'So, what's new?'

'Nothing. I was in Haifa, wasting my time, as usual.'

Leib was now black-bearded, darker-skinned, harder and less plump than before, yet still giving the impression of having been somehow shanghaied into his own body, and of trying to make the upright, soldierly best of it. He was the secretary of the kibbutz – he took on such responsibilities as naturally as

Joel avoided them – and spent much of his time in Jerusalem and Tel Aviv, raising money, arguing about land-grants, consulting accountants and agronomists, negotiating cautiously with *garinim* which might be 'married' to his group at Ramat Elkan. He was now just back from a trip to Haifa, where he had gone to try and get the release from the docks of a tractor which had been donated to the kibbutz by a well-wisher in South Africa. While he drank his tea he told Joel about the day he had spent there, going from office to office, accumulating stamped and scribbled-upon pieces of paper; at the end of it the tractor was still in its crate in the shed.

'The worst of it all,' he said, in his small, measured, irritated voice, 'is that no one here really sees anything *wrong* with this fantastic load of paperwork you have to go through to get anything done. It's the Eastern European mentality, I suppose – they're just used to carrying around piles and piles of *dokumenti*. And then nobody trusts anybody else an inch, which also means that everything must be written down and stamped and counter-stamped and signed and countersigned until you think you're going out of your mind. And the crowds waiting in every office! And the shouting and arguing – Christ!' He shook his head and drank more of his tea.

'Don't tell me about it!' Joel laughed. 'Sometimes I think in a funny way we're living in a kind of ivory tower here.' He looked ironically around the bare, unfinished dining room, at the exhausted men in their work-clothes scattered about it. 'I know, whenever I go outside at first it's a big holiday – and then I just want to come running back, it's such a madhouse out there. At least here we've got our three meals a day, even if they are lousy, and a place to sleep and room to walk around in, and some kind of order and regularity. But outside –! I really get scared when I leave the *meshek*.'

But while Leib could complain on his own account, he didn't like to hear Joel complaining too. 'They'll get it sorted out, eventually, I suppose. I just hope I live long enough to see it.' He threw a crust of bread into the aluminium scrap-basin in the middle of the table. 'What's new with you?'

Joel hesitated. 'You remember Natalie?'

'Natalie?' Leib said, surprised, 'Yes, of course.'

'She's getting married.'

'Oh.' His eyes opened wide, above the line of his full beard. 'Where'd you hear that?'

'In a letter from my mother. It came today.' Joel touched at the letter in his breast-pocket.

'Who to?'

'Nobody we know. Some *goy* on the mines – an electrician or something. My mother met her in town, and had the story from her. Apparently her people are very upset about it, so they're going to live in Northern Rhodesia, on the Copperbelt.'

'Honestly?' Leib pulled at his beard; each watched the other. Then each began to smile at the expression on the other's face. Joel remembered the evening, in South Africa, so long ago, when Natalie had turned away from Leon, saying that it was Joel she loved. None of them had anticipated this end: he and Leon still together, Natalie marrying a stranger and going with him to Northern Rhodesia.

Joel said, 'You remember, we flew over the Copperbelt, we landed at Ndola.'

'Ja.' Leib dismissed the Copperbelt with a wave of his hand. 'She can keep it.'

With the gesture Joel saw Natalie condemned to a life of suburban boredom in those mining-towns they had glimpsed from the air – tangled bush for hundreds of miles all around them; neat tarred roads, houses, streetlamps and billboards within them. He laughed at this image rather than at Leib's words; then Leib laughed too, a little taken aback by the success of his remark.

'What's the joke?'

It was Ed, one of the Americans. With his dark complexion, thin red lips, and large, long-lashed brown eyes, he was good looking in an oddly dissolute way, rather like a dandy villain in a Western movie. He wore his overalls belted tightly around the waist and tucked trimly into high-laced, rubber-soled paratroop boots. He was standing over Leib with an anticipatory grin on his lips.

Joel had decided a long time ago that Ed was one of the most stupid people on the kibbutz, and he had no wish to tell him anything about Natalie. He was relieved when Leib answered: 'We were just talking about a girl we used to know.'

'Oh?' Ed waited. It took some time before he realized that nothing more was coming from either of them. So he adjusted himself to the situation; he tried to make the best of it, the grin still on his lips. He leaned over Leib. 'You know what this kibbutz needs?' he asked confidentially.

'No. What?'

'A small red-light district.'

'That's good!'

'You're not bluffing!'

Both of them responded with a false heartiness, and Ed went off, satisfied. Then Joel and Leib looked at each other, their eyebrows raised in embarrassment.

Joel stood up. 'I must go and shower.'

Leib nodded. Taking his cup with him he slid down the bench, to close up the gap between himself and his neighbour.

3

The air outside was fresh and cool, after the warmth and reek of food in the dining room.

Long shadows stretched over the ground from every hut and outcrop of pitted, blue-grey stone; the hills in the east had already begun to assume their evening depth and solidity. The soil was still dark with the moisture of what everyone hoped would not be the last of the winter's rains; the grass, which grew in clumps from every untrodden place, was pale green. In the distance the green appeared to fade to a soft, almost silvery grey, which merged imperceptibly with the rock outcrop, giving the slopes and valleys a deceptive look of smoothness. But the young crops in the fields nearby stood out vividly, in stripes alternating with the black of the soil.

Joel walked down from the central group of wooden huts on the top of the hillside towards his own; its roof, well below him, was already in shadow. A man in rubber boots, carrying a pail in one hand, approached him, coming up the path. His boots slapped together as he walked. 'Hey, Yossie,' Joel asked him from a few paces away, 'have you seen Harry anywhere?'

Yossie walked past him with a roll of his eyes in his unshaven face, answering in Hebrew, 'I don't speak English.'

'Ach,' Joel shouted scornfully after him, 'go back to Birmingham.'

Without turning round, clumping heavily up the slope, Yossie made an obscene gesture with his free hand.

Arieh, formerly Lionel, from Montreal, was showing a well-dressed, middle-aged couple around the *meshek*. They had watched and listened to the exchange between Yosef and Joel. Arieh said to them, 'That's what we call socialist solidarity, you see.'

The man laughed and pushed the brim of his pearl-grey hat further back from his forehead. 'Very impressive,' he said. 'Very moving.' He seemed glad of the opportunity to pause; he and the woman with him had been finding it heavy going, uphill, along the rough path.

Arieh was short, sturdy and soft-spoken; his features were clear and small, their only irregularity being the heaviness of his black brows, which met bristlingly above his nose. He introduced his visitors to Joel; they were an uncle and aunt, also from Montreal, who were touring the country. Arieh's uncle lifted his hat when he shook Joel's hand, and his wife smiled and nodded; both of them were short of breath. They said they were most impressed with what they had seen of the kibbutz – most impressed – and Joel said that he was glad to hear it. They talked for a few minutes, the visitors shyly anxious to say the right things, then Joel left them. As he walked away he heard the man asking Arieh how many South Africans there were on the kibbutz.

Joel stopped at the hut immediately above his own. Like the others, it was divided along its length into three rooms, each approached by a little pair of concrete steps. He knocked at the middle door of the three, and pushed it open when a voice called to him to come in.

There were several beds in the room; on one of them, on his back, lay a thin, long-limbed khaki-clad man, his bare feet pointing to the ceiling. He reached out a hand, as Joel came into the room, took up his glasses from the top of a little bookcase next to the bed, and brought them to his eyes. Having seen who had come in, he put them back on the bookcase. His naked eyes had a wide, dark myopic softness; his nose was long and sharp, his straw-coloured hair lay flat on his skull, still wet from the shower he had just taken. All the joints of his body protruded in knobs, bumps, ridges – as frail as they were hard.

'Haven't we seen enough of each other today?' he asked as Joel sat down on one of the empty beds.

'Harry, I've been looking for you.'

'Actually *looking* for me? Since when?'

'Since tea-time.'

'Why? What happened at tea-time?' Harry's voice was harsh and jerky; the words were shaken out under the threat of the stammer which sometimes seized him. He brought his glasses to his eyes again and regarded Joel, sideways on. 'You haven't even washed yet. You're a dirty man, aren't you? Why don't you go and have a wash?'

'I'm going to. First I want to tell you a joke. Then I want to ask you to do me a favour.'

'In payment for the joke?'

'If you like.'

'It better be good,' Harry said gloomily.

'You know what this kibbutz needs? A small red-light district.'

Harry stared straight at the ceiling. 'Is that the end of the joke? I'll tell you another. We're going to throw Ed into the next foundation we dig, and pour the concrete right over him. We'll call that building *Bet Hasimcha*, or the House of Mirth.' He sat up with a series of angular movements of his arms and legs, and put his large bare feet on the tiled floor. 'Have you ever read *The House of Mirth*?'

Joel shook his head.

'So you're ignorant as well as dirty.'

'That's why I'm here. That's why I want your help. You can write Yiddish, can't you?'

Harry had his glasses on now; they seemed to reduce the comic, errant length of his nose. '*For vos villst du schreiben af 'Idish*?'

'I'll tell you. It's something quite extraordinary. I had a letter today from my mother. Among – well, among other things, she told me that much to everybody's amazement they've just found out that there's a cousin of mine here in Israel. From Europe. He's the son of my father's sister – she remained in Lithuania when the rest of the family trekked to Africa. We all thought that whole part of the family had been wiped out, because we'd just heard nothing from them since the war broke out. But this chap's name appeared a few weeks ago, out of the blue, in one of those lists they publish in the Jewish papers at home – you know the kind of thing. A friend of my father's saw

302

it; all it said was that Yitzchak Sklar was looking for his uncles, Benjamin and Meyer Glickman. Of course they wrote at once to the paper, and they found out that he's in a *ma'abara* south of Tel Aviv. Apparently he's been here for only a couple of months. They've written to him that I'm in the country and that he'll be hearing from me. So, with your help, I'll write to him. I thought Yiddish would be the best language to write in.'

'What do you want to say?'

'I don't know. What can one say? I'll suggest we meet in Tel Aviv some day, and see how he answers.'

'That sounds easy enough. Sure, we can do it when we're free in the next day or so.'

'Thanks.' Joel sat in silence, watching Harry putting on a pair of sandals. Then he said, 'You remember that girl, Natalie, I told you about?'

'Yes.'

'She's going to get married.'

'*Mazeltov*.' Harry said dryly.

Joel stood up. 'There doesn't seem much else to say.' And there didn't. So far as he was distressed at all, he knew, it was not for Natalie, but for the emptiness in himself, where there had once been desire and tenderness for her, anxiety and wonder about her. They had long since given up their correspondence. The news about his cousin, whom he had never seen, had disturbed him far more deeply than that about Natalie. When he turned towards the door, Harry called him back.

'Hang on, I want to show you the thing I was telling you about this morning.'

With hardly more than a single stride of his long legs Harry crossed the room and opened a wardrobe which stood near the door. On a shelf inside it, each item neatly labelled, was a collection of coins and shards of pale, curved, jagged-edged pottery. Most of the pieces had been found in the ancient burial chambers – small, musty caverns dug into the stone, with empty stone shelves inside them – which riddled the hills. His latest find was a small, plump-bellied lamp, with a fluted cover and a tiny broken neck. In colour it was darker than his other pieces, pink, almost reddish. He handled it tenderly, and brooded over it even when it was in Joel's hands. It was like holding a pigeon, Joel said, and Harry gave him a grateful look.

'It does feel alive, doesn't it?'

'I was thinking just of the shape, really, this curve here, in front.'

Harry's lips worked; his protuberant, triangular Adam's apple stood out more sharply, moving in his throat. 'It's beautiful,' he managed to say, though with a catch in the middle of the word. He had taken back the lamp, and ran his finger over the front of it, then along one of the flutings of the cover. They stood together over it, Joel held as much by the other's enthusiasm as by the object itself. He felt much closer to Harry, a Canadian, than to anyone else on the kibbutz, and knew that Harry felt the same towards him.

'The guy who made it must have been proud of himself.'

'He had reason to be.'

Reluctantly, Harry put the lamp back on the shelf. They left the room together, Harry going to the dining room for his tea. Joel collected his towel and toilet-kit from his room, walked across the *meshek*, and plunged at last into the steam, noise and pungent wet-wood smell of the shower room.

4

Joel had intended getting up before breakfast and taking a ride to the nearest town on the milk truck; but the knowledge that the day ahead was his own, the luxury of lying in bed and being able to ignore the clanging of the bell, had been irresistible. So now he was walking the four or five kilometres to the main road, where the buses ran. He did not mind the walk, anyway; the morning was not hot, and it was another kind of luxury simply to be on his own.

He followed the double-track down from the elevation on which the *meshek* sprawled, past the shattered, deserted Arab village on the next rise, through the abandoned fields and the olive grove which had once belonged to the Arabs. In the sunlight each olive tree was a gathering of vaguely shining leaves and dark, precise branches. The unsteady roaring of a tractor, somewhere out of sight, now louder, now softer, was the only sound in the air. Between the olive grove and the main road there was a flat, wide, untended stretch of grass and rock, and Joel took a shortcut across it, along a ragged footpath.

He was halfway to the road when a jackal rose suddenly out of the grass and confronted him. It was a brown and yellow creature, as shabby as a doormat. Flies buzzed noisily around its small, half-shut eyes. It stood still, staring at him, until he stooped to pick up a rock. Then it loped off, with a sideways shambling gait, looking back over its shoulder.

Perhaps, Joel thought, it had been a dog from the Arab village, left behind and now grown half-wild, and not a jackal at all. The kaffir-dogs in South Africa, too, had been yellow and brown, and had flinched if one so much as bent to the ground. Still, the suddenness and silence of the encounter had startled him, and he was relieved when he finally reached the main road.

The bus-stop was a corrugated iron hut, with a few bluegum trees behind it. At a distance, on the far side of the road, behind a stretch of ground that had been trodden flat and that was littered with papers, tin cans and other rubbish, there was a big, scattered, squalid *ma'abara*, a camp for new immigrants – bell tents, tar-paper shacks, a few wooden pre-fabs, with pathways running through the sand between them. Some of the people from the camp were waiting at the bus-stop; when they spoke to one another it was in a language Joel did not recognize at all. Russian, Polish, Ladino, Arabic – all these he had learned to identify immediately. But this bubbling, interminable sound was new to him.

'Where are you from?' Joel asked the man nearest to him, in Hebrew. The man was of middle-age, paunchy, unshaven, dressed in a collarless striped shirt, a pair of grey flannels and canvas shoes. He was carrying a baby in his arms, and he jogged it in silence for a few moments before asking Joel suspiciously, 'Where are *you* from?'

'South Africa.'

'Hungary,' the man then answered.

They had to wait a full hour before a bus finally pulled up at the stop; in the meantime almost everyone at the stop begged frantically for a lift from every vehicle that passed by – begging in a desperate, beseeching, bent-kneed manner, with both hands cupped and dangling, that Joel had seen in no other country. But no free rides were given to anyone that morning: the battered express buses, fuming diesel trucks, army cars of every description, rushed by unheedingly. When the bus did stop there was a furious scramble for places, followed by an argument in which the driver, the passengers who were already on the bus, and the newcomers all became involved. Joel, however, was lucky, and managed to get on and stay on.

He stood in the aisle all the way to Tel Aviv. The people in the bus were dishevelled and poorly clad; many of them clutched obscure, misshapen bundles of one kind or another. The Hungarian swayed about in the aisle next to Joel, the wrapped-up baby still in his arms. Several of those who had seats were asleep, their bodies bowed forward, their heads resting on the hands which clutched the seats in front of them. Occasionally Joel stooped to look through the window of the bus. Bluegum trees, shattered Arab villages, small green fields, nondescript, huddled Jewish townships with centres that looked like outskirts and outskirts that looked like builders' scrap, intersections aswarm with people begging for lifts or offering each other trash from trays and barrows or simply standing about in forlorn idleness, stucco walls scarred with machine-gun fire and plastered with political posters, gangs of bearded, earlocked Yemenites working with pickaxes and baskets at the verges of the road, army camps, barbed wire, camps for immigrants, more buildings shattered by high explosive into lumps and heaps – this was the landscape of Israel two years after the state had come into existence. And Tel Aviv was a stupefying concentration of everything outside it: more peeling stucco, more glaring sunlight, less air, more noise, more old men with trays slung in front of their chests peddling shoe-laces and razor-blades. And a slight youth of about eighteen, in army uniform, whom Joel saw as he alighted from the bus, with two articulated metal hooks where his hands should have been.

'Ai! Ai! Ai!' the woman on the step below Joel exclaimed in pity and horror, watching the youth disappear into the throng.

Another long wait in the crowded central bus-station, another scramble and shove to get on another bus, and Joel finally arrived at the Mograbi. From there he walked to the office of the South African Zionist Federation in Hayarkon Street. He was glad to have behind him the journey he had just completed; he loitered, looked into the windows of shops, went into a bookshop and came out of it ten minutes later with a couple of paperbacks; he watched the girls who walked past. It was a painful pleasure for him to see how many of them there were; what skirts and blouses and dresses they wore; what waists they had, what hair, what necks, what bosoms, what backs, what frail wrists; how preoccupied they were, how they smiled, frowned, talked to one another, carried things in their hands. The hardest aspect of living on the kibbutz, every unmarried man on it had many times agreed, was not the work or the food or the housing, but simply the terrible shortage of girls. Ed was right, Joel thought, filled with a desire that, despite its intensity, was somehow absurdly innocent; it had within it so much sheer surprise and wonder at all the various ways woman had of being different from men.

The children in the streets were another surprise. He could hardly say that he noticed their absence on the *meshek*. Yet, having forgotten about them since he had last seen them, he was delighted to see them again, charmed by their diminutiveness and earnestness, by the smoothness of their limbs, the treble of their voices. They were extraordinarily attractive to look at: sturdy, active, lightly clad, always running about in gangs. It was a pity that their adulthood promised to be as hard, humourless and self-absorbed as that of the generation of *sabras* that had preceded them. Joel had lived long enough in Israel to know that the talk of the *sabras* as 'Hebrew Tarzans' was nonsense; yet it was true that one rarely found among them any lightness, softness, or openness of response. They were rather dour, neurotic provincials, more like the Afrikaners than any other group he had ever met. But their hardness was less of a shell, more of a muscle, than that of the Afrikaners, who had had things too easy in an easy country.

At the Federation office Joel greeted the girls at the reception counter, then went through into the little clubroom at the back. There were various notices on the walls, advertising tours, study-courses and rooms to let; there were a few armchairs and tables, and a counter at which one could buy coffee, cool drinks and the chocolate-covered wafer biscuits that seemed to be the only confection on sale anywhere at the time. He ate three of these ravenously. He also drank a glass of syrupy cordial, before settling down to wait with a six-week old copy of the Johannesburg *Sunday Times* that he picked up from one of the tables. It was strange to see the paper, with its distinctive type and layout, and to read the cinema advertisements in it, and the political headlines. He wondered if he would ever again stand on the stoep on which a copy of this paper had thumped down, six weeks previously, early in the morning before Annie had come in to make the coffee and his father and mother had woken to another peaceful Sunday, another Christian sabbath. The picture of the house that the paper brought to his mind was reproachfully bright and forsaken.

5

When the young man came in Joel felt a physical shock that seemed to separate him from his own body, as if it were not his own. Indeed, his body was not his own; the man's appearance was proof of that. He resembled astonishingly those sepia-coloured photographs of Joel's father in his twenties, which Joel had not looked at for years, but which he remembered immediately now. The stranger had the same protruding lower lip as the man in the photographs; the same grey eyes, the same strong cheekbones and large, straight nose. Only his clothes were different from the high-buttoned suits which Joel's father had worn so many years ago. He was wearing a linen jacket and an open-neck khaki shirt; pushed back on his head there was a cloth cap, and on his feet were brown leather shoes with clumsily thick soles.

'Yitzchak,' Joel said, getting to his feet.

'*Shalom.*'

They shook hands, looking at each other shyly.

'We meet at last,' Yitzchak said with difficulty, in English.

'At last,' Joel repeated. Only then did he release the short-fingered, calloused hand he had been holding in his own.

'What do we do now?' Yitzchak asked in Yiddish.

Joel answered in Hebrew. 'Have something to eat.' He looked at his watch. 'It's nearly lunchtime.'

They went to a restaurant almost directly across the road from the office. Tables were set out on a wooden porch, projecting slightly above the pavement, and they sat there in the open, at a rickety wooden table, looking across an empty, rubble-littered plot of ground to the beach and the idle Mediterranean beyond. A cargo boat stood out to sea, and small lighters went between it and the shore. The sea glittered and winked, every little movement producing its own flash.

At first conversation between them was constrained, partly because they had to continue speaking in different languages to one another – Yitzchak in Yiddish, Joel in a mixture of Hebrew, Yiddish and English – and partly because of the kind of bond there was between them. Each had known without hesitation who the other was, and yet they knew nothing at all about each other. So they could ask each other direct questions only.

No, Joel said, in answer to the questions from Yitzchak, he was not married. He had been on the kibbutz for almost two years. Yes, he did like it, on the whole. He had one brother and a sister; the sister had just got married, the brother was younger than himself and was a student at university; neither of them was in Israel. Uncle Meyer had two children; both of them were married. Yes, Benjamin was quite rich, he supposed – certainly rich by Israeli standards. Benjamin owned a butter factory, in which Joel's brother-in-law had just started working. Meyer was in the wholesale produce business, and owned a lot of property as well. Yes, his family did have a big house in South Africa. How many rooms? Joel admitted that he had never added them up to a figure. He did so now: there were five bedrooms, three living rooms, two bathrooms. And there were the rooms for the servants in the back. Yes, they did have black servants: one man and a woman. Yes, his father did have a car, and David had a car too, Joel's old one.

Joel found that there were fewer questions he could ask Yitzchak. Yitzchak told him that he was waiting to be called up into the army; he would like to go into some unit where he could learn a trade. He knew nothing; he was uneducated; he hadn't had time to go to school. He had no relatives on his father's side, neither in Israel nor anywhere else; on his mother's side there was Joel and the others in South Africa. He was quite on his own. Everyone else in his family had been killed.

They were both silent. Joel found that there was now only one question that remained for him to ask Yitzchak. What had happened?

6

What had happened? Yitzchak repeated the question. He swirled round the inch of tea which remained in the glass he was holding, and drank it down. He smiled faintly, pushing his glass to one side, looking out towards the sea, his eyes narrowed against the light. He drew in a breath and began to speak. His hands were motionless, one on the table, the other in his lap.

He had lived. The others had been killed. Within a day of the German invasion, even before the Germans had arrived, the Gentiles in the *shtetl* had fallen upon their Jewish neighbours.

'All day,' he told Joel, 'all day they'd been gathering on the corners, talking about the news, and drinking. And then late in the afternoon, they began. We were in our house: we heard them down the street, attacking other houses. We heard their shouts and the screams of the people inside. Then they were at our house, at the door. One, two, three times they crashed against the door, and it was down.'

He spoke calmly, without gesture or emphasis; and he continued in the same way, though there were times later when he fell into silence, staring away with an ironic, withdrawn, almost scornful expression.

'They stank. The smell came into the house with them. The first one inside was a young fellow, Peter, who had sometimes helped my father in the shop. The man behind him already had blood on his clothes. My father said, "Peter, think what you're doing." My mother sat at the table, saying my sister's name over and over – she lived with her husband and her children in another part of the village. Then my father shouted, "Yitzchak, you run!" he spread out his arms wide, to try to hold them back. I jumped out of the window, into the yard, over the fence. Some of them were chasing me. I heard screams behind me – everywhere screams. And I ran.'

He ran over backyards, over potato patches, under clothes lines, through ditches with water in them. Someone came out of one of the houses and tried to stop him, but he managed to push him over and ran on.

Their house had been near the edge of the village – 'that was my luck,' Yitzchak said. So he was soon in the open. There was a clear space ahead of him, then the forest began. He looked over his shoulder. They had stopped running after him. He went into the woods. Even there he could smell the smoke, and he could hear the noise; it sounded like a fair-day, when the children scream on the merry-go-round. He went deeper into the woods. He didn't come out of them until the war was over.

He had lived. In holes in the ground, in burnt-out villages, in trees; on berries, on raw potatoes, on the carcass of a dog, once; usually by himself, sometimes with small groups of other Jewish fugitives. Finally he had found refuge with a peasant and his wife, living in a lonely spot, who had known that he was Jewish but had taken him in nevertheless. 'Not like all the other peasants, who always ran straight to the Germans or the Lithuanian militia – they worked for the Germans, worked hard for the Germans, you know – when they found a starving Jew.'

The peasant lived in a clearing in the woods, miles from the nearest village, which was itself miles from any main road or railway. He had a few pigs, a couple of goats; he grew potatoes and cabbages and a little corn; he chopped down trees for fuel. They were desperately short of food, of clothes, of everything. Still, it was an easier life for Yitzchak than what had gone before. He slept with the goats, but he had a roof over his head.

Why had the peasant, at the risk of his own life, taken the fugitive in? At first Yitzchak used to wonder. It was true that the old man needed help around the place, for he was old, his chest wheezed, there was something wrong with his left leg; the foot was twisted and he dragged it behind him. After a while, however, Yitzchak decided that the peasant valued him more for the amusement he could provide than for the labour he could do. Before Yitzchak's arrival the old man had had only his wife to bully, beat and torment. A strong young Jew on the run was a welcome change, offered a fresh diversion. He was a humorist, this peasant; that was what had saved Yitzchak's life.

The old man was short and thickset – he must have been very powerful as a young man. His lower jaw protruded and was curved to one side, and his lips could not close fully together, so that he looked as if he was always smiling. He had a tiny nose and bulging brown eyes; on his misshapen jaw there grew a stubble of white beard. When his chest troubled him he would tear open his clothes and scratch and slap at his breast, as if trying to get at the source of congestion with his bare hands and tear it out of himself. 'The devil, he's choking me, he's eating me alive,' he said at these times, labouring for his breath, grinning, scratching at himself spasmodically. He also used to speak to his injured leg as if it did not belong to him and was deliberately hindering him. 'You won't let me run, but I'll stand on you all the same,' he often said to it, banging it down on the ground like a club.

That was one style of his humour. The other was more painful for Yitzchak. Day after day he announced that he was going straight away to turn Yitzchak over to the militia who had a post in the village. 'I'm tired of your Jew-face,' he would gasp. 'You've grown fat on my food. Enough! Enough!' And off he would go, dragging his foot, shaking his head, to return ten minutes or some hours later, smiling with that permanent, half-crazed grin on his face. 'They're coming, my Jew. They're just behind me. They'll be here soon. You better run while you can.'

They never came. But nor did the old man ever tire of his simple joke. And he had many others of a similar kind. There was, for example, the joke about Yitzchak's hidden wealth. It was a well-known fact, the old man said, that all Jews were rich: that was why poor, hard-working peasants like himself had always hated them. Now Yitzchak was a Jew – but where was his money? Where was it? Buried under the floor at home? Hidden in the woods? Or had Yitzchak a few diamond rings stuck up his arse? Where was Yitzchak's fur coat? What had happened to his motorcar? Where was his gold snuff-box? How much of his gold would Yitzchak give to fuck the old man's wife? Well, how much?

Sometimes, by way of variation, he would ask his wife how much she would pay to have Yitzchak fuck her. His wife was an ugly, bony, mumbling creature, whom Yitzchak trusted even less than her husband, though she never threatened him; indeed, she hardly ever spoke to him. She hardly ever spoke to anyone but herself, even when her husband was abusing her, hitting her, or asking her this question about Yitzchak. 'Pay him, pay him!' the old man cried at her. 'You'll get your money's worth. It'll be good with the Jew. His blood's hot, they're all like that. And his prick's naked. Come on, Jew, show her what you've got. Give the old woman something to look at – it'll make her young again. She'll pay you.'

Then there was the matter of Yitzchak's conversion to Christianity. Earnestly, fervently, happily, the peasant tried to persuade Yitzchak that Jesus Christ was the true Son of God, to whom he should go down on his knees to pray. Not, he would add, that this would help him when the Germans came. But afterwards, after the Germans had made 'cold meat' of him, his immortal soul would be eternally grateful that he had accepted the one true religion. He would see all the other Jews – Yitzchak's father and mother and all his relations among them – roasting in hell, suffering tortures far more terrible than any the Germans had been able to practise on them. But he, Yitzchak, would be safe in heaven. And he would be able to intercede with the Blessed Virgin, on behalf of the old sinner who had taken him in, succoured him and shown him the way to salvation. The old man wept, grinned and crossed himself at the thought.

At other times, when he and Yitzchak were working together in the potato patch, he simply marvelled to see a Jew sweat; he offered to cut Yitzchak's throat in the kosher manner; he called his pigs Yankele and Berele and Yitzchak. He also told Yitzchak that when the Germans or the militiamen finally came and killed him, he would feed Yitzchak's corpse to the pigs. 'It's a happier sight to see a pig eating a Jew than a Jew eating a pig.'

But he never struck Yitzchak. This was just as well for him, for Yitzchak had made up his mind that he would kill him if he ever did. He would kill the old woman as well. And the old man seemed to know how far it was safe for him to go, and kept his hands and his feet to himself. This decision comforted Yitzchak and made it easier for him to suffer in silence all the abuse the old man heaped on him. However, there was yet another reason for his silence of which Yitzchak remained ignorant, until one day when he was alone in the woods, he found himself grinning, chuckling, shaking his head, struggling to compose himself and breaking down once more into outbursts of laughter that sounded to his own ears as inhuman and mechanical as the chattering of a squirrel. Seizing hold of his own breast and stomach, fighting to stop the laughter that was tearing him apart, Yitzchak was sure that what was happening to him, what had happened to his family, the life he was leading in the wilderness, had at last driven him out of his mind. For the unspeakable truth was that Yitzchak also was amused by the old man's jokes.

He lay on the ground and roared with laughter; he saw the sky swinging around him, the branches of trees whirling like arms. He beat his head with his fist, he stuffed earth and leaves into his mouth, he sobbed with his forehead against the trunk of a tree and sank to the ground again, scoring his forehead open against the rough bark; he lay with his eyes closed, his shoulders shaking in spasms.

7

Hours had passed before Yitzchak opened his eyes again. It was late in the afternoon and the woods were still; under a covering of moss and dried leaves, the earth breathed forth its coolness and damp. Where he lay it was already dusk; overhead a few dazzling rays of sunlight still reeled among the moving leaves of the trees. Conscious of the calm around him, breathing it in with every lift and fall of his chest, he remembered his own frenzy as if from days before. He felt washed out by it, purged, released. For months, ever since he had fled from his house, he had been telling himself he must live, he *must* live, he must live for the sake of his mother who had sat at the table with clasped hands, saying '*Rivele, Rivele*'; he must live for the sake of his father who had stretched out his arms wide in an attempt to hold up the chase of the mob; he must live because he had run away, leaving them to be killed. Now Yitzchak knew that he was under no obligation to them. It didn't matter whether he lived or died. It didn't matter to them because they were dead; it didn't matter to himself because he no longer cared. Nothing mattered. Nothing at all.

He went back to the cottage, and when the old man opened his mouth in an abusive greeting, Yitzchak took him by the throat and squeezed it until his eyes started more than ever out of his head. The woman sat in her corner, making no move to come to her husband's help. They were all insane, all three of them. The old man clutched at Yitzchak's coat, his legs kicked and twitched. The thickness of the neck between his fingers disgusted Yitzchak. The only sounds in the cabin were those made by the old man's struggling. He was weakening; suddenly his legs collapsed. Yitzchak let him go. 'Now go to the village,' he said. 'I'll wait for you.'

The old man did not go to the village. He made no more jokes, either. Instead, he rested for a few days, then got up and went about his work. One night he beat his wife, because, he said, she was barren, barren as a mule. Why had she never given him a son? What was the good of a barren wife? Even daughters would have been better than nothing; then he would have had sons-in-law to help him and protect him. He should have left her, years before; she wasn't worth keeping, she had nothing inside her that a woman should have. He would have done better to have married a widow with children, or even the mother of a bastard; then he would have had proof that she was fertile. Unlike this she-mule, this blocked-up creature without organs, this Sarah whom God had turned away from. When he had finished with her he told Yitzchak that he had said to people in the village that he, Yitzchak, was the son of his wife's brother: that was why no one had ever come for him, though he had been seen in the woods a few times. And he asked Yitzchak to call him 'Father'.

'Yes – father.'

The old man laughed, slapped his chest, and rubbed his chin. 'And you'll call her mother?'

'Yes – father.'

'Get up, mother,' the old man said and kicked his wife, who was still lying at his feet in a dazed, groaning heap. And they went on as before, except that the old man was subdued and silent for hours at a time, and Yitzchak called him father.

Yitzchak knew nothing of the way the war was going, and could learn nothing from the wild stories the old man brought back from his occasional trips to the village, which became more and more infrequent as time passed. Where they lived there was only stillness, isolation, hunger, the rare sight in the woods of bearded, savage figures lurching north or south, east or west. Once a gang of such people came to the cabin, stripped it of everything edible, killed the livestock, took the ragged clothes off the backs of Yitzchak and the old man, and then made off. The months that followed were almost as cold and hungry for Yitzchak as those he had endured before the old man had come upon him asleep in the woods and led him to the cabin.

Towards the end of an interminable winter the old man's rumours became wilder than ever before: he spoke of having seen Satan in the woods, Stalin in the sky, Germans and militiamen in flight. The horizon gave out noises, concussions, lights at night. One day Yitzchak went out to inspect the rabbit traps he and the old man had set up in the woods; he returned after sunset. The ground was covered with snow; there was a whitish haze in the dark throat of the sky. When he came out of the trees, within sight of the cottage, he saw that the cottage was surrounded by soldiers. In the dim light they looked like the spots a man might see under his own eyelids: dark, squirming, irregular shapes that wavered, disappeared, reappeared, darted to one side. He could not count how many of them there were. He turned and went back into the woods; behind him he heard a burst of machine-gun fire. Two days passed before, crazed with hunger and cold, dreaming when he was awake and waking with shuddering starts from periods of total unconsciousness, stopping to stare obsessively at individual sticks, stones, berries, leaves, he staggered back to the cottage.

He found that both the old man and the woman were dead. The blood that had come out of their breasts was frozen around them. Their eyes were open. Yitzchak danced around the cabin, sobbing and cursing and kicking, shrieking at the old man that he hoped he was in hell, burning there with the Germans and Jews, Lithuanians and Russians, Nazis and Communists, every accursed breed of the whole human race.

8

Then, Yitzchak said, there followed three years in a Russian labour battalion. At the end of that time he and the others in the battalion were put on a train and sent east. How far east it was intended to send them Yitzchak did not know, and did not wait to find out. He managed to jump the train, and made his way back to the *shtetl* in which he had been born. There was no one left alive in it whom he wanted to see again; and it was clear to him that no one there wanted to see him. He was looked at as though *he* were the criminal; as though it were unforgivable that he should have survived and come back to remind them of what had been done.

He went through Latvia and Poland, living under false papers, begging, stealing, smuggling currency and cigarettes;

eventually he found himself in Austria. After living there for some time, working as a day labourer, he at last chose to take the route to Italy, to one of the camps for Jewish refugees awaiting transfer to Israel.

That was how he came to be with Joel now, Yitzchak said. That was what had happened.

The sun had moved, but there was no change in the intensity of the light. On the shore a few hundred yards off, the Mediterranean still slapped down its small waves, making little noise, the cargo boat looked black and flat against the horizon.

There were pale, intersecting stains on the bare, crackling, corrugated plywood of the table-top. As if in a dream Joel knew that the one was Latvia, the other Poland, the third Lithuania. These thoughts moved with such apparent reasonableness through his mind that some moments passed before he was shocked by them into looking up. Yitzchak's eyes were on him. Joel said the first thing that came into his head.

'Why didn't you try to come here before? Why didn't you try to get in touch with us before?' His voice sounded almost angry, accusing.

'I couldn't really do either, until I was in Austria. And then –' Yitzchak did not finish the sentence.

'You must understand,' he said, after a pause, 'I'd got out of the habit of making plans. And once you get out of the habit it's difficult to get into it again.'

'And now?' Joel asked.

'Now? Yes, I think I have plans now.'

'What are they?'

'To learn a trade, to get a flat, to get a wife. I want everything you want.'

Yitzchak spoke with an air of challenge, as if Joel might deny him his right to these things. And deep within himself, though he had no impulse to deny the other whatever he wished for, Joel did feel a pang of an emotion like despair. If a trade, a flat, a wife were all that Yitzchak wanted, why should he have had to go through such experiences before he could think of having them? Having gone through such experiences, should he not be thinking of other things? But of what? Of what?

Because he had no answer to the question, it seemed impertinent and callous to ask it. This was not the first time since his arrival in Israel that he had had to remind himself that it was foolish to expect the survivors of the holocaust in Europe to have come out of the abyss with revelations, understandings, wisdoms; with any hope other than those of finding living-space for themselves, accumulating possessions, doing a job of work, establishing some order and privacy in their lives. Yitzchak was only one among many people in Israel who had asked him, with an intent, almost childishly greedy curiosity about the kind of house his parents lived in and whether or not they had a car. The human capacity to lose and suffer seemed to be equalled only by the capacity to begin all over again the search for what had been lost in suffering, torn away, blown away, turned to smoke and ashes.

Joel had fallen silent; he had no comment to make, no more questions to ask, about the story he had just heard. Yitzchak was staring down, into the road. He did not seem to be waiting for Joel to say anything to him, nor anxious to speak himself. Later, with more hesitation and shyness than he had shown over anything else he had said, Yitzchak told Joel that the work he would most like to do was 'with trees'.

'With trees?' Joel asked, puzzled.

'Yes, I lived so long in the forests – I like trees now. But I don't suppose I'll be able to learn about that in the army. Anyway, there are no forests here, I haven't seen any.'

'Well, they're supposed to be planting them all the time, according to the Zionist propaganda. If you want to go to agricultural college, I'm sure my father and Uncle Meyer will help you. Even in the army, if you say that that's what you want

321

to do, perhaps they'll put you in one of the units that do agricultural work. We've had some of them helping us on the kibbutz. And there must be others working in the Galilee, in the woods they have there.'

'You think it's possible?'

'I'm sure of it. I'll ask people about it, but you must also talk to everyone you can about it. It's the only way you ever find out anything in this country.'

Before they parted Joel repeated his assurance that Yitzchak could count on his uncles in South Africa helping him through any schooling he might want to take after his army service. And he invited Yitzchak to come and visit the kibbutz. 'If you come you can stay as long as you like – as long as you're willing to work. Who knows, perhaps you'll like it so much you won't want to leave, even though we've only got a few tiny trees so far!'

Yitzchak smiled and shook his head. But he promised to come on a visit within a few weeks, after he had appeared before his draft board.

Joel watched him go. Upright, sturdy, trim, lightly clad, glancing about him as he walked, he was no more remarkable than anyone else in the street.

9

All day the boat travelled slowly, alongside a mauve mountainous country. Mist lay in pale coils, between each ridge of the mountains. The next morning, early, through a dim blue and grey light, over a flat sea, Pamela saw the city of Genoa – level after level of it, climbing away steeply from a tangle of cranes, funnels, wireless masts and warehouses. It was her first true glimpse of Europe, and one which she never forgot. The city was so huge, so steep, so still; all its structures were packed closely together, one above and behind the other, built on a scale nothing had prepared her for. She remembered especially one particular wall against the mountainside that her eye was drawn to – remembered it for its great size, for the bluish cobblestones which studded its almost vertical surface, for the arches of masonry that buttressed it, for the road it carried on a terrace, where no traffic was yet moving.

South Africa seemed utterly remote. Was she the same girl who had gone to school in a green gym frock through the makeshift streets of Booysens? Who had just finished her third year at the university at Cape Town, and would be dutifully going back to take her teacher's diploma when the long vacation ended? She did not want to believe it. But her mother fretfully reminded her that she was just another tourist to all the people they would meet. 'All they're interested in is what they could get out of you. Don't forget it, not for one minute,' she impressed upon Pamela. 'Not for one single minute.'

Mrs Curtis clutched her handbag to herself, convinced that every other Italian in the streets was a potential pickpocket, if not a rapist. And while they were having their very first meal, in the glassed-in terrace of a café, they did in fact have an adventure with a strange man: a plump, red-faced, pimpled, light-haired man of about thirty, dressed in a creased blue suit, who approached them politely, begged their pardon for interrupting, said that he had heard them speaking English and wondered if they would mind if he joined them.

'One gets tired of trying to exercise one's Italian,' he said, and laughed, showing a collection of brown teeth and a very pale tongue.

'We're just about to go,' Mrs Curtis replied hastily, reaching for her handbag.

'No, we're not, mom,' Pamela said. 'I haven't finished my ice cream. And I want some coffee afterwards.'

Mrs Curtis indicated that she certainly didn't want any coffee. The stranger snapped his fingers at the waiters and ordered two coffees. Then, with another laugh, he said that he assumed they were Australians.

'No, South Africans,' Pamela answered.

'Really!' He had been in South Africa during the war. Cape Town. Durban. Port Elizabeth. It was a wonderful country. He had been tempted to settle there. But he'd gone back to the old country in the end, though he travelled after the sun as often as he could. Were they going to explore the Italian Riviera? He could recommend some excellent places, places that were a bit off the beaten track.

'No, we're going on to Rome. And then to Venice, and Florence, and then to Switzerland.'

'To Switzerland?' The man's blond eyelashes parted a little more widely than they had done hitherto; he had seemed to find the light of the café troublesome. 'I've got some friends in Switzerland.' He was about to go on, but the coffee came and he was distracted for a few minutes; he stirred and sipped at it reflectively. Then he repeated, 'To Switzerland? You're going to Switzerland? I wonder –' He inspected his fingernails with a slight frown, and then put his hands out of sight under the table, as if displeased by what he had seen. 'I wonder if I could ask you to do a great favour for me. I've got some friends in Switzerland to whom I've got to deliver a parcel. Could I ask you to help me with it? It's a very small parcel, and you could post it to them for me, once you were in Switzerland.'

He was a smuggler! Pamela read the word in her mother's eyes; her mother read it in hers. They stared at one another in consternation.

'Certainly not!' Mrs Curtis managed to bring out. 'I – I don't know who you are, or what you want. Come, Pamela! We must go!'

She got up and began to walk away. But she was overtaken by the waiter, who clearly suspected her of trying to get away without paying the bill. Pamela stood by while her mother fluttered distractedly through large Italian notes in various denominations, one of which the waiter seized and carried away, returning with a pile of very small notes, which he presented individually to Mrs Curtis, with an imploring silence between the offer of each. Only when this transaction was over did Pamela look back in the direction of the smuggler, who had remained at the table. Seeing Pamela looking at him, he winked at her.

Perhaps he was just pretending to be a smuggler! He'd seen how green they were, and had come over to tease and frighten them. Solemnly, Pamela winked back at him; then took her mother by the arm and marched hastily out of the café.

They were in Genoa for only a few more hours, before they took the overnight train to Rome; but Mrs Curtis several times looked over her shoulder, afraid that the man might be following them. For the rest, Pamela remembered of Genoa only pastel stucco walls with stucco medallions on them, narrow streets with many people in them, much wrought iron, a huge grimy railway station, and her own excitement.

10

Rome, Venice, Florence, Geneva, Paris, London: Pamela's excitement did not leave her, though to it was often added a painful fatigue and an anger against her own ignorance and inability to take in all she saw: palaces, squares, galleries, slums, railway yards, formal parks, open markets, elegant shops, children at play in the streets, the ruins of war seen from the windows of moving trains, lips opening to speak in languages she could not understand, arms waving in gestures she had not seen before. There was so much more of Europe, so much more to Europe, than she had ever imagined: such complexities and elaborations, such likeness and diversities, so much grandeur and so much intricate decay, so deep, matted an accumulation of every kind of human achievement that she felt liberated and constricted within herself by it all, enlarged and diminished, instructed and confused at every turn.

She was ashamed of South Africa, for being so bare and simple despite (or perhaps because of) all its miscellaneous varieties of people; for being so poverty-stricken in its inventions, so blank in its surfaces, so random in its styles and dispositions. She was sure that Europe must be filled with people who were better than any she could ever find at home – kinder, less selfish, less limited, more creative. If only she could meet them! If only she could be something more than what her mother had warned her she was, just another gaping tourist! In every city she visited, Pamela imagined that somewhere in the crowds there was a young man who would recognize her, come forward to greet her, take her arm in his, and lead her to one of the cafés, where they would drink and talk together until the streets would be almost empty. Then they would go to his flat and make love. She always imagined the young man to be English or American; sometimes he was a poor student, sometimes a rich actor, often a writer, a painter, a professor, a psychoanalyst, a smuggler.

But she had no luck; and she despised herself for having no luck. It was because she was timid, she told herself, because she was unattractive to men, because she was conventional, because she was travelling with her mother. She wrote some miserable, apologetic, affectionate letters to her boyfriend in Cape Town, Terence Armstrong (*poor Terry, darling Terry*), a slight, fair-haired, unassuming sociology student, a lapsed Catholic who was a few months younger than she was. Terry had bright brown eyes and a reddish, rather lumpy skin, and he liked to sit on the floor and sway to and fro while he listened eagerly to the intellectual conversation of others. He was quite unlike any of the men Pamela imagined meeting in Europe, and she carried each of the letters she wrote him around with her for days on end, and then tore it up, before sitting down to write another. In the end he never did get anything more than a few hectically cheerful picture postcards.

Pamela was also made miserable at times by the many fierce rows she had with her mother, who complained that she was being run off her feet; that Pamela lacked all consideration for others, and showed no appreciation of everything that was being given to her. Their worst argument took place in Paris, where, defeated by the impossible breadth of the streets, the furious chasing of the traffic, and the rudeness and incomprehensibility of the French, Mrs Curtis broke down altogether and said she could go on no longer. She wanted to take the next plane back to South Africa. She had had enough of being homeless, of living out of suitcases, of foreign food and languages, of famous sights and infamous lavatories, of rapacious waiters and indifferent hotel friendships.

Pamela shouted back all the more loudly and scornfully because she, too, was exhausted, dissatisfied and lonely. Later that night she walked alone up and down the Champs Elysées. The great floodlit arch at the top of the street looked idiotic, she thought, a lump of stuff erected for no other purpose than to make an impression of grandeur. All the striped awnings and shining glass of the restaurants could not hide the fact that they were just places in which some people tried to make money and others self-importantly spent it. The underground stations breathed out a vile, metallic odour; the kiosks were festooned with newspapers clipped together like huge sheets of dirty, damp postage stamps; the crowds hurried or loitered past her, faces seamed with individual hungers, blank with a common

327

indifference. For her part, they could catch the next plane back to South Africa; she wouldn't mind.

But the next time she came to Europe, Pamela decided, drawing in a deep, redeeming, satisfying breath, she would not be with her mother. Nor would she be alone. Even if she had to come with Terry, she would not come alone.

They did not go straight back to South Africa: they went on to London, as they had originally planned.

They had no arguments in London. It was a relief simply to be in an English-speaking country once more, though of all the cities they had visited the pall of the war still seemed to hang most heavily over London. It was dark, shabby, grimy, defaced, soiled; its people seemed wearier than those on the continent, their clothes and houses dirtier. With a secretive, triumphant air shop-keepers produced a bar of chocolate or a packet of a particular brand of cigarettes from under the counter; the restaurants were uniformly dingy, and offered jugged hare, reindeer meat, spam and other foods which neither Pamela nor her mother had even eaten before; entire districts were plunged by power-cuts into darkness, at irregular periods of day and night. Yet Pamela could not help assuming, guiltily, all this as well into the risk and richness of Europe.

Then they took the boat back to South Africa. Looking out of the window of the taxi that took them up familiar Adderly Street in Cape Town, Pamela said, 'It's funny, it looks *just* like Australia to me.'

'Pamela, what do you mean? How can you say that? You've never been to Australia.'

11

It was only a few weeks later that John Begbie, looking for capital as always, found Mrs Curtis.

The proposition for which John Begbie was looking for capital this time wasn't sillimanite; it was talc.

Begbie had met a fellow who knew a fellow on whose farm near Barberton in the eastern Transvaal there was a mountain of talc; a bloody great mountain of the stuff, of the very highest quality. On the back of an envelope this fellow had shown Begbie just how profitable the quarrying of the mountain could be. So much per ton for quarrying – right? So much for transport to the nearest railway siding – right? So much for railage to Lorenço Marques, and for loading there – right? So you had an FOB price of so much per ton – right?

Right, right – Begbie nodded, until the flesh under his chin wobbled in affirmation. Well, he was asked, did he know how much they were paying CIF for that quality talc in London? This time Begbie shook his head eagerly, and his companion, who was almost as corpulent as Begbie, and was dressed in an oversize pair of khaki shorts, a pair of dusty *veldskoen*, and a pink, open-necked shirt, looked carefully around the empty bar-lounge to make sure that no one was eavesdropping, leaned forward and whispered a figure into Begbie's attentive ear.

So much! Begbie drew back in astonishment. The other nodded firmly, slowly, proudly, like a man who knew a thing or two. Of course, he added, you had to allow for a royalty to the farmer whose ground you'd be working on. And 'yours truly' was entitled to a cut; that was only fair, wasn't it? But even if you added on these two items, and allowed for extra overheads, it was still a wonderful opportunity for someone who could properly exploit the deposit. You could reckon comfortably on a clear profit of two pounds a ton; and you could pull out five hundred tons a month from the place for the next few years without even making a hole in it. Not a hole that you'd notice, anyway.

'It's just waiting for you,' the man said to Begbie. 'You can't go wrong with it, if you get it going – man with your experience!'

Begbie appreciated the reference to his experience. He took the envelope on which the figures had been written down, and added to it the name of the farmer on whose property stood the mountain of talc. His head was still full of figures when he met Mrs Curtis a few weeks later, in Cape Town.

He met her by chance on the beach at Clifton, when they sat side by side on deck-chairs in the sun, looking out towards the breakers that the Atlantic, as if with the play of slow giant muscles, sent rolling towards the shore – each one gathered to a height of ten or twelve feet, curved over in an arch that was ragged with foam at its crest and pulled sleek behind, while contrary, tremulous movements swirled within it, and then sent crashing down upon itself, obliterating form and shape, turning all to a white confusion. Until the next weight and width of water was shaped, tugged forward with effortless strength, and obliterated in its turn.

The noise of the breakers and the sight of them, the sunlight on the water and the heat of the yellow sand, the cries of the people bathing, playing and sunning themselves, were all mesmerizing, soporific. Begbie and Mrs Curtis would probably never have noticed one another had not a large, clumsy dog run up and begun worrying Mrs Curtis. It put its head on her lap and wagged its tail foolishly, it barked at the toes of her shoes and danced around them as if they were dangerous little animals. She waved her hands and shouted 'Go away! *Voetsak*!' which seemed to please and excite the dog even more. Begbie watched the comedy for some minutes, before he thought of bestirring himself to come to her aid; once the thought had entered his consciousness another minute or two passed before he could translate the thought into action.

But finally he got up, and succeeded in chasing the dog away. It was the best day's work, he was to say later, that he had ever done in his life.

And it did seem to have been a full day's work for him, when he collapsed once more into his deck-chair, sweating and panting, his face mottled red. While he wiped his brow with his handkerchief and struggled for breath, Mrs Curtis thanked him for his help, and told him that she had always hated dogs; they were such clumsy, irritating, unreliable creatures.

Begbie, once he had got back his breath, demurred; he defended dogs. Well-trained dogs, that was to say; dogs that were faithful, disciplined, self-denying, intelligent. Mrs Curtis was impressed by his moral earnestness; and soon he and she were jointly deploring the infrequency with which fidelity, self-denial and intelligence were to be found among human beings. An hour later they took tea together at an open-air kiosk; by that time Begbie had dropped the names of his brothers-in-law (of whom Mrs Curtis *thought* she had heard) and Mrs Curtis had dropped the name of Kraankuil.

They met again, and again, for neither of them had anything very much to do with their time. Just as there had been nothing in particular to draw Begbie to Cape Town in the first instance, apart from a feeling that a change of air and scenery would be good for him, so there was nothing to draw him away from it. But he gave Mrs Curtis to understand that he was looking after certain interests of one of his brothers-in-law – a free translation, so to speak, of the fact that he was living in the hut near the beach that his brother-in-law had recently built as a holiday home. While Mrs Curtis, for her part, as she explained, now lived permanently in Cape Town, with her daughter, Pamela, who had just got her degree and was now doing her teacher's diploma.

'Taking after her father, eh?'

'At least, that's what she says she wants to do, at the moment. But she changes her mind so often – she talks so wildly sometimes. I suppose it's just the age she's at, and I must be patient.' Showing a marked lack of patience, she added: 'With the opportunities I've given her she shouldn't *mope* so much, that's what I always say.'

'She'll settle down, Mrs Curtis, I'm sure she will. Still, I can understand why you're so anxious. You can't be too careful nowadays, with a young girl. You just don't know what to think, do you? You just don't know who to trust, isn't that so?'

'And I feel her to be so much my responsibility; she has no one else,' Mrs Curtis said, with a brave, wistful emphasis.

Begbie's small blue eyes shone with sympathy. He had learned by now all about the death on active service of Captain Curtis; and he had been at pains to let the widow know that it was only because of his bad heart that he had not served in the army. It wasn't through any cowardice or lack of conscience that he too was not lying with Curtis on the field of honour: that he had wanted her clearly to understand. This picture of himself as one of 'the fallen' was vividly in Begbie's mind whenever Curtis came into the conversation. Then, on the spot, in a moment, he resurrected himself, and wished his wife dead and buried instead, so that he could be free to court this wealthy, bored and apparently lonely widow.

And, though his wife remained obstinately alive, Begbie courted Mrs Curtis nevertheless – in the most respectful and respectable way – as they walked up and down the road that ran between the beach and the mountains behind it, or sat on deck-chairs through the long afternoons, or drove in Mrs Curtis's car to her flat in Sea Point. He courted her with smiles, with a carefully shaven chin, with a new linen suit which he made a great effort to keep uncreased, with further passages of stern moralizing about the degradation of the times, with reminiscences of his past experiences as an entrepreneur, and with more and more detailed accounts of the promising new venture he was about to launch. He had been doing some homework, both before meeting Mrs Curtis and with renewed zeal after their meeting, and he had a sheaf of documents to show her. There were letters between himself and the farmer in question, firms of shippers and mineral merchants in London, and some end-users of the talc in England and Holland whom he had approached (with samples and chemical and physical analyses of the article) and who had declared themselves interested in it.

Happily for him, and without his knowing it, Begbie had chosen his time well. Mrs Curtis was unsettled by the trip she had just made, reluctant to go back to the routine of the life she had lived before it, impressed by Begbie's deference and eagerness, and by the apparent prospects of the business.

There was a flurry of visits to lawyers, accountants and bank-managers, the farmer came down to Cape Town, there was much signing of papers; and, to Begbie's incredulity and delight, he found himself the owner of fifty per cent of the shares of the Begbie–Curtis Mineral Development Company (Pty) Ltd. The capital of the company was nominal; the money Mrs Curtis invested, which came to several thousand pounds, was held in a loan account.

Begbie returned to Johannesburg and went boasting all over the town about the fortune he was going to make. Samuel Talmon was among those he boasted to; and Samuel was filled with envy. He begged to be allowed to become a shareholder in the company; and Begbie, in the generosity of his heart – and there was generosity in his heart, just as there was also greed, impetuosity, gullibility and much loose unidentifiable sentiment – decided to sell half his holding to Samuel for a figure that was somewhat more than nominal. Samuel, of course, couldn't pay that figure in cash, but it was arranged that he would do so out of the profits they were eventually bound to make. In the meantime, he became joint manager, with Begbie, of the company, and began to draw cheques on it for his needs. Mrs Curtis accepted him as a partner, for Samuel was presented to her as a man with experience almost as wide as Begbie's own, important connections (especially among the Jews), and unflagging energy.

12

The afternoon faded early into the brown grey vapour of a London evening. In the back garden of the house, fenced in by heavy brick walls, stalks of last season's Michaelmas daisies stood up nakedly from beds of sodden ground; the glistening, tangled leaves of a holly-bush were as sharp-edged and irregular as metal shavings. Eventually the hostess drew the curtains. 'That's quite enough of that,' she said to the group who stood by the window.

She stepped through them, into the middle of the room, moving with her head and shoulders held back and her flat hips thrust forward; her strides were long and she put her feet on the ground with a curious, almost stealthy precision, her toes turned out, as if following a line of marks chalked invisibly on the carpet. The guests obeyed her and turned to look into the room, smiling a little at her imperious and dramatic air. There were about twenty people in the room, most of them dressed informally, none of them negligently.

One of the guests, Neil Hooper, approached the hostess in the middle of the room. The bluffness and openness of his expression was somehow at variance with the ingratiating way he had of moving his thick shoulders and exposing the palms of his hands.

'Congratulations, June,' he said. 'I've just heard the news from Jonathan.'

'What news?'

'About the baby.'

She threw her head back and thrust her hips even further forward. Her long, thin arms dangled, naked from the shoulder to the tips of her painted fingers. 'Oh that! You should be consoling me, not congratulating me.'

Hooper looked at her, his eyebrows drawn together; and the girl said boldly, 'Yes, it was an accident. Of course it was an accident. You don't suppose I want my brilliant career interrupted, do you? Or do you? Do you think I've just found a graceful way of resigning from the battle? Graceful! I'm not looking forward to the next six months, I can tell you.'

'It's a long time. You'd think nature could manage it more economically.'

'Don't you speak to me about nature. I hate nature. To go around looking like a barrel, for months on end –'

'I'm sure you'll make a lovely barrel,' Hooper said, swaying more closely towards her, but not moving his feet. His eye went appraisingly up and down her body, and June let him look his fill. 'You can't help being lovely, whatever you do.'

June gave Hooper a wide, delighted simple smile; she was never more sincere than when she responded to flattery. And because she was generally considered to be handsome, in her fair, silky-haired, elongated way, and because praise obviously gave her so much pleasure, most people were generous in commenting on her appearance. But there was an especial gratification for her in being praised by someone like Hooper.

Deprecatingly, she said, 'Jonathan says I'm already beginning to bulge.'

'Oh, Jonathan ...' He looked around for his host, and dismissed him at the same time with a half-shrug of his

shoulders. 'Jonathan will say anything to be unpleasant. He just
told me that I've got no talent at all.'

'He didn't!'

'He did. Those were his very words.'

June laughed, bringing her hand to her brow. 'You're
impossible, the pair of you. Like cat and dog. Or man and wife,'
she added maliciously, watching Hooper's face. Before he
could say anything she dropped her hand. 'Sorry, Neil, you
must excuse me. I don't know who that man is.' She indicated
the door with a nod of her head, and went to it. Hooper stared
after her, a remote, musing look of disgust on his face. But
immediately he heard his name called by someone else he
smiled and started forward, raising both hands in a gesture of
eager greeting.

13

'Are you – are you Jonathan's wife?' David asked June, who
responded with a tiny curtsey.

'I have the honour to be Mrs Delmond.'

David laughed. 'I thought you must be. My name's David
Glickman. I'm Jonathan's cousin.'

'Well, come in, Jonathan will be thrilled to see you. He told
me you were coming.' She took David by the arm, and began to
lead him into the room. But he held back.

'I didn't know you were giving a party.'

'Call this a party?' She simpered satirically at him. 'No, this
is just a sedate gathering of – um – er – friends, colleagues, you
know, neighbours, people who we think will get on well
together.' David had no idea what kind of woman she was
supposed to be imitating; but he smiled gamely, nevertheless.
'Jonathan and I call them our little At Homes,' she went on, in

the same manner. 'We're At Home every Sunday afternoon. Now –' and with a gesture she dismissed that role, only to assume another: familial, protective, understanding. 'Who do you know here? Who do you want to know? But I suppose you'll want to talk to Jonathan first. There he is in the corner – talking to the girls, of course! Honestly!' And she smiled twice: once in Jonathan's direction and the second time at David, to show that she knew David would understand why her first smile had been so proud and indulgent.

Jonathan stood with his back to the corner of the room; he was holding an empty glass in his hand. He wore a sweater the colour of milk chocolate and slacks the colour of plain chocolate; his hair was cropped short, except for a tight fringe that came over his forehead. His features seemed to David to have grown both larger and more mobile; though he stood at his ease, there was an alert, practised swiftness in his gestures, even in the turns of his head, that was new. He greeted David enthusiastically. David himself had grown taller and thinner since Jonathan had last seen him. His complexion was scarred with the traces of skin eruptions; these faint, bluish scars and irregularities made him look old and young at the same time.

'So you're here at last!' Jonathan exclaimed. 'We've been waiting for you. June! June! The woman's deaf. Never mind, she'll be back in a minute. How are you, man? When did you come? How do you like it here? Where are you staying? Have a drink!'

'Give me a chance,' David protested, laughing and flattered.

'This is my cousin, David,' Jonathan said, turning to the girls to whom he had been talking before David had come up. 'One of the very, very few people I could talk to in Johannesburg. And ha's Jah'birg, men? Wot's nieuw da'n theh?' he asked David in a burlesque Johannesburg accent.

'Nothing. It's the same old place.'

'Same old dump?'

'Worse, if anything.'

Jonathan shuddered at the thought. 'Spare us the details.'

The girls on each side of Jonathan listened to their conversation; one intently, the other languidly. The intent girl wore a pink sweater over her high, tight breasts, which stood out at an angle from one another, as though they had quarrelled and had no intention of ever coming together again. The languid girl, in a black jersey dress, had no breasts to speak of; no face either, but for a pair of immense dark eyes and even darker brows, prolonged on either side by an application of black crayon. 'Julia, Day,' Jonathan said by way of introduction; somewhat to David's confusion, for he thought that 'Day' was Julia's surname. He smiled at her, and then turned to the other girl, waiting to hear her name. But it wasn't forthcoming, until, with an effort, the girl roused herself to say in a surprisingly deep voice, '*I'm* Day,' and then fell once more into the silence of exhaustion.

'Nice girls,' Jonathan said. 'Your father wouldn't approve of them, probably, but he's a long way from here. How is he? And your mother? Have you seen my old Dad at all? How's Rachel?' His eyes met David's. Easily, he asked again, 'Well, how is she?'

'She's fine. She's married, you know.'

'Married! Who to?'

'Bertie Preiss.'

'No!'

David nodded his head, a little uncomfortably.

'Well, I'm damned. I always knew he was keen on her, but I didn't think that she –' He shrugged. 'And has she also become a big radical, then – helping the black chaps, rousing the workers and peasants, bringing on the revolution? Somehow, I don't see Rachel in that role.'

'Nor do I. Nor does Bertie. I think he's more or less chucked it up. He's going into the business, anyway.'

Jonathan laughed with silent satisfaction. 'So he's going to become a Joh'burg business man? What a fate! A prosperous member of the bourgeoisie? God, that's a career I'd go a long way to avoid. And I never went around shooting my mouth off about the revolution. What do your people feel about it?'

'They like him well enough. My father's trying to convert him to Zionism.'

'The only thing your father would ever convert me to is drink. That reminds me – what's happened to Joel? Is he still toiling away in the Promised Land?'

'As far as I know.'

'Better him than me.'

'And me.' Awkwardly, yet pleased to be able to say it, David said, 'I don't have to ask how you've been getting on. I've been reading in the papers at home about you. Another local boy who's making good –'

'Have they really written about me in the papers?' Jonathan asked with an affectation of surprise, though he himself had seen to it that the London offices of various South African newspapers had been kept fully informed of his activities. 'Well, I must say I've been very lucky since I came here. But I haven't really begun yet, I've done nothing.'

'Modest, hey?'

'I'm not being modest. I have been lucky. At least,' he said, lowering his voice, 'I've managed to learn the limitations of my own talents, and that's more than I can say about some of the people in this room. I'm no actor, that much I know. Just three months in drama school and I knew where I was in the league. But I've got other plans, I'll tell you about them. This country's wide open for exploitation, if you ask me. But come and have a drink. That's the first thing.'

He took David by the arm and began to steer him towards the table with the drinks on it, leaving the two girls staring mutely at one another. When they were out of their hearing

Jonathan said intimately, 'A few more energetic, ambitious Jews around the place and we could really make something out of England.'

He grinned savagely, shamefacedly, at what he had said. Then he reached out an arm to Neil Hooper, drawing him from another group, and introduced David to him. 'Neil's a scriptwriter. You want to keep in with him. He knows everybody and everything.' To Hooper he said, 'Maybe I'll be sending David to you for advice one of these days.'

'*My* advice wouldn't be worth anything to him. I'm an embittered old hack, that's all – as you were telling me half an hour ago.'

'Come, come, Neil,' Jonathan chided him. 'You may be a hack, but you're not *so* old – or so embittered, are you?'

Both men smiled. But there was a touch of scorn in Jonathan's smile, anxiety and resentment in Hooper's. Not long before Hooper had been able to patronize Jonathan; now he had merely to look around the room to know that he could do so no longer. A round, pale, prematurely bald young man in a dark suit stood to one side talking to a woman who nodded devoutly at everything he said; he was, Hooper knew, the head of a small, new film company which had recently secured the backing of a City real-estate firm. The woman, with ravaged, bloodshot, protuberant eyes in a face as brown as a gypsy's, held a high administrative job in BBC Television, and, what was more, had once been the mistress of a famous poet. A youth in a roll-neck sweater, speaking in an Irish accent and wearing on his face an expression that grew even more sullen when his smile opened on a mouthful of sharp, crooked teeth, was an actor for whom all the papers had prophesied a brilliant career; the girl he was talking to, Hooper knew, wrote for the *Evening Standard*. All these people, among others, were in Jonathan Delmond's living room; they had all dragged out to Highgate on a rainy Sunday afternoon at his invitation. Hooper saw these things and smiled more anxiously than before; he waggled his shoulders in a gesture of acquiescence. 'If ability runs in the family,' he said to David, 'you won't need much help from me. But what I can give you, you can surely have.'

Then Jonathan relented. 'Don't let Neil's modest ways fool you. He's a first-class man. And a first-class writer, a real pro.'

Jonathan continued across the room, David in tow behind him. 'You want to watch that fellow,' Jonathan warned him. 'He's completely two-faced, like most of his kind. God, the queers there are in this racket! In England as a whole!'

'So I've heard,' David said. He looked back at Hooper with a curiosity which he tried to hide. But Jonathan noticed it.

'I could tell you stories!' Jonathan smiled, lowered his eyelids, and shook his head. 'But they'll shock you. You think such things happen only in books. They don't, believe me. And the funny thing is,' he said with an air of detached thoughtfulness, 'that when they happen you don't find them nearly as shocking as you might have imagined beforehand.'

David stared at his cousin. As if it wasn't enough that since he had left South Africa Jonathan should have got married to a beautiful, sophisticated English actress; that he should have 'discovered the limitations of his own talent' and developed other plans, big plans; that he should have managed to get together in his flat a gathering of people who, though David did not know who they were, were to his eyes theatrically smart and animated, speaking loudly and clearly in English accents such as he had hardly heard before outside films; but that, as well, he should have had secret homosexual experiences and been unshocked by them – !

David took the drink Jonathan offered him. Yet irritation at the other's patronage suddenly flared up in him when Jonathan said, 'Look, I've got to go and play mine host around the place. But don't go when everybody else leaves. We'll have our talk afterwards. I've got a lot to tell you.'

'I won't go. I've also got a few things to tell you.'

14

David had several drinks on an empty stomach, but they did not help him to feel less strange and gauche among Jonathan's guests. He was unfamiliar with the names and references everyone used and laughed at; he was convinced that some of the guests had deliberately slighted him; he resented the way people listened to him speaking and then asked him in polite puzzlement if he came from Scandinavia. So he wasn't an English smoothie – all right! But he wasn't Jonathan's poor relation either. By the time the last of the guests had left, David's initial irritation against Jonathan had become part of a settled, aggressive obstinacy.

June disappeared into the bedroom, to recover from the exhaustion of the afternoon, so he was able to talk to Jonathan without constraint. The fact was, he said immediately the two of them settled down, and before Jonathan could begin boasting on his own behalf, that he was quite on his own in the world. He had had a big row with his father before leaving for England – a really big, final row.

'What about?'

'Everything,' David answered, lying back on the sofa and speaking loudly and swaggeringly. 'We haven't been getting on for a long time. He'd been worrying – I was just doing a B.A., wasting my time – he wanted me to start settling down, to begin thinking about going into business with Bertie, or taking some nice respectable profession, like being a lawyer or a chartered accountant or a doctor or something. And then becoming a good, steady, reliable member of the bourgeoisie, married to a nice Jewish *kugel* and living in a nice Jewish home in Birdhaven or Houghton and bringing up nice Jewish children to be a credit to their grandfather. One son he'd already given for Zion; it was enough for him. And he just shut his ears to anything I had to say – you know what he's like, you know how he can shut his ears if he wants to.

'Anyway, when I came back for the long vac in December it all began again. I had only a year more to go, what was I going to do when I was finished? So tell him, please, what? And I kept answering him, "I don't know yet, I want to find out." "Haven't you had enough time to find out? You've been two years at the university and you want me still to give you more time, more time!"'

David had imitated his father's accent and gestures; he pulled a face, thrusting his jaw forward, like his father's. He wanted to make Benjamin appear ridiculous; then he realized that by doing so he was making his own role in the struggle appear so much less heroic.

'I suppose it sounds funny,' he said, 'but I can tell you it wasn't the least bit funny at the time. It was a real bloody battle. I let him have it back as hard as he tried to hand it out to me. I told him that he was a hypocrite; that he was nothing but a hide-bound, conventional Jewish businessman of the kind he's always pretended to be superior to. I said to him that at least his brother, Meyer, had no pretensions, he didn't pretend to be a reader and a bit of a politician and a man in touch with ideas. Because that's the kind of idea of himself my father's always flattered himself with. "My house is full of books" – that's always been one of his favourite phrases. I told him, "What's the use of having the house full of books if all you want to do is live as your miserable neighbours live?" So he asked me how I proposed living. Like a Bohemian? Like a *schnorrer*? Like my Uncle Samuel?'

'Trust him to say something like that,' Jonathan said bitterly.

'And I said to him,' David went on gleefully, 'that he didn't frighten me by pointing at my Uncle Samuel. That my Uncle Samuel seemed to me to be a more interesting man, and to have had a more interesting life, than ninety-nine per cent of the awful, successful, boring businessmen my father knew. And it was when I said that, that he really went berserk. "Then go and ask your Uncle Samuel for advice! Go and ask him for a handout as well, while you're about it. Let him be your guide and your mentor and your model. Go on! Go on! Get out!" And he added a few loud complaints at my mother, whom he chose to blame for it all – of course. "He's a loafer, that's all, and it doesn't come from my side of the family." So my mother spoke up pretty sharply too, defending me, defending Samuel, attacking him. "Wasn't your father a loafer?" – that's one thing I remember her saying to him. That's the level they were at, by the end … Christ! What an evening it was. It ended in fine style: me packing my bags, my mother crying, my father raging away by himself in the breakfast room, breaking plates, to judge by the noises he was making. And off I went into the night, carrying my bags.'

'Hell!'

Quietly, tiredly, proudly, David sat back in silence at this exclamation from Jonathan.

'How did you manage to get here?' Jonathan asked. 'Where did you get the money for your ticket? What are you going to do now?'

'You'll never guess where I got the money from. Never.'

'From your mother?'

'No.'

'From who then?'

'From your father! I followed my old man's advice; I went to my Uncle Samuel. That same evening. And I told him what had happened. And he asked me what I wanted to do, and I said I wanted to go to England. So without another word he sat down and wrote out a cheque for me.'

'Wrote out a cheque for you!' Jonathan repeated incredulously.

'That's what I said. That's what he did. I went and cashed it the very next morning, just in case it might bounce, or he might change his mind and ask for it back or have it stopped or something. But I needn't have worried. He really was on my side. Or I suppose,' David added, 'he was really against my father's. Anyway he was very pleased and excited about what I was doing and made long speeches about all sorts of things – about how wicked an institution the middle-class family has always been, and about how we must "accept in a positive spirit the anarchy of the times", and how we must submit to loneliness, alienation and exile just as in the olden days people had submitted to marriage, society and work. And so on, and so on. You can imagine the kind of thing he says when he gets carried away. And in between he would have little gloats about my father; he said that he'd always told my father that his children would turn against him in the end, if they had anything in them. And of course, I agreed with every word he said. I had to – he'd just given me a cheque for a hundred pounds. But I'd have agreed with him, anyway.'

'Now where in the name of hell did he *get* a hundred pounds from?'

'I thought perhaps you'd been sending him money.'

Jonathan laughed at the idea. 'Not me. Where would I get money to send him? Did you see my sister? Perhaps she's supporting him. I always thought she'd go on the streets in the end.'

'No, I didn't see her. He didn't say anything about her. But he said plenty about you; he's very proud of you. I don't know, perhaps one of his schemes has come off at last. By the law of averages one would be bound to come off in the end, don't you think?'

'Not my father's. He's not an average man.'

'Anyway, I'm very grateful to him, wherever the money comes from. And I'm not just grateful to him for the money either. He really supported me; he didn't just think I was out of my mind; he didn't try to send me home and tell me to be sensible, as every other uncle in the world would probably have done. It meant a lot to me, that night. It still does. The way he sat down and wrote out that cheque! I'll never forget it. And I'll pay him back one day.'

'He's an impulsive old bugger,' Jonathan said indulgently, shaking his head. The gesture and the tone of his voice claimed a certain amount of credit on his own account for his father's generosity. 'It's typical of him, absolutely typical.'

'I'll pay him back,' David said again promptly and firmly, as if to deny Jonathan the credit he had just claimed for himself.

So Jonathan asked, 'How? What are you going to do? You must be flat broke.'

'I am, just about. I've got enough to live on for about another week or so.'

'And then?'

'God knows. I'll probably get a job with London Transport, or something. Or I may be able to teach somewhere. I've got a certificate from the university saying that I attended courses for two complete years, and passed them all. Or I can always wash dishes. I'm not worried. I'm really not worried. You've got no idea what a relief it is to have given it all up – everything – the family and their approval or disapproval, the whole mad struggle for money, prestige, a place in society, all the things that I used to think I wanted. What society? Prestige in whose eyes? I'm on my own. I've only got myself to please, I can do what I like. Even when I speak to you – well, I don't mind telling you now that I used to admire you, and be envious of you, for looking as though you knew what you wanted and for having the talent and ability to get it. But not now. Not any more.'

From the way David spoke no one could have guessed that he had felt acutely the envy and admiration he was referring to just a couple of hours before, in the room he was sitting in. 'I want to live without limits of any kind,' he went on. 'Do you understand what I mean? Instead of trying to control what happens to me, like you do, instead of saying, "This is what I want, this is how far I go and anything outside of that, is not for me." Even ambitions, no matter how big they may be, are limits, and I don't want them. You – someone like you – you have ambitions, that's fine for you, I wish you luck. But I don't envy you for having them, or for having to battle to fulfil them. I'm out of it, right out of it.'

15

The two cousins parted without much cordiality, and without making any plans to see each other again. Jonathan had been ready, before David had begun to talk, to offer him introductions, 'contacts', ideas for jobs. He had looked forward even more eagerly to telling David how, with the help of some useful people he knew, he was in the process of launching a company which, while beginning in a small way, making advertising and public relations filmlets, would one day do original work on serious film projects, revolutionary stuff which the profits of the advertising side of the firm would make possible. But instead of being able to describe these prospects in the language they deserved, Jonathan had found himself, when it was his turn to talk, insisting defensively that there was nothing shameful about his new ambitions and plans; that he was still as dedicated as he had always been to establishing a name for himself as an artist in his own right; that he despised conventional ideas of success and money-making as thoroughly as David ever did.

In fact, Jonathan said heatedly, he was far more of a threat to the bourgeois order of things than someone like David could be. For the work he was going to do, once the company was truly on its feet, would 'really explore new possibilities of life and art'. Whereas all that people like David could do was sneer and jeer. He knew the type, Jonathan said to himself, falling at last into a grumpy silence. You said 'advertising' and they told you you were corrupt. You said 'financial backing' and they thought you were after nothing but money. You said the word 'public' and they thought you were pandering to it, instead of breaking your heart trying to educate and enliven it.

But what could you expect, anyway, Jonathan said later to June, from someone so ignorant and green and bumptious as David. Hell, he was so ignorant he simply didn't know how respectfully papers like the *Observer* wrote about some of the people who'd been in the very same room with him!

Consolingly, with a limp, dismissive gesture of her hand, June assured him that that was ignorance indeed.

16

Jonathan would perhaps not have needed any consolation at all if he had known that, walking down the hill to the Archway tube station, David cursed himself for being a loudmouth, a fool, an idiot, a child. Why had he made it impossible for Jonathan to offer him help? He had gone to the flat hoping that Jonathan would be friendly and would want to help him; and then, before Jonathan could speak, like a lunatic he had told him that he wasn't looking for advice and assistance, that he didn't need it, he despised it. Why? What had got into him? David knew that he had surprised and somehow bested Jonathan during their conversation, and the thought gave him pleasure. But that pleasure was small compared with his anger with himself, his loneliness and his fear.

It was a dark, cloudy night. The Great North Road glistened in the rain. One after the other, heavy tarpaulin-covered trucks were crawling uphill, the engine of each grinding on a single note, like a strained, oppressive breath being drawn, which you waited to hear the end of, and lost before that relief had come. Below, at the crossroads, there was a turbid confusion of lights and buildings, retreating towards the City and the West End; a mass from which there stood out a few domes and spires, edges of shadow. Immediately on David's right, as he walked down, was a huge, elaborate building – a hospital – rising several storeys, decorated with belfries and cupolas, buttressed by concrete ramps and iron staircases, lights shining in patches from it. It was like a great factory or warehouse for the sick. How many hospitals like it were there in London? A hundred? Two hundred? More?

The journey underground was a long one, through grey, ribbed, rattling tunnels. He came out eventually at Earl's Court. Just outside the Tube station he saw that there had been a road accident of some kind: an elderly man lay in the gutter, in the rain, his bicycle fallen beside him. A knot of onlookers stood around, some of them sheltering under the awning of a shop. The man lay on his back; his eyes were wide open and he did not seem to be badly injured, though there were patches of blood on his face, under his eyes and on his chin. The blood was black in the lamplight. What made the sight bizarre and shocking to David was that whenever any of the onlookers came forward to help him, the man lifted his sodden grey head a few inches off the ground and swore at them – quietly, passionately, obscenely. He would not let them touch him. When they drew back he let his head go down slowly to the ground once more. Some of the people were laughing, others were shocked, all were puzzled; none dared to take hold of him. The man was still lying there, hissing and cursing and raising his head with a snake-like, injured movement at every attempt to help him, when David left the scene.

He made his way back to his room, past terraces of houses with flights of steps resting like heavy stone paws on the pavements in front of them. Light moved obscurely among the pinkish, sagging clouds; it was caught in the shafts of rain; it was gathered together in ribbons and little winking pools on the tar of the street. People passed by, none of them looking at him, all of them huddled and hurried in their movements, under the steady downward sifting of the rain.

At last he was in his room: a shaded bulb, a bare table, a narrow bed, a suitcase on the floor. David flung himself on the bed and covered his face with his hands. What was he to do? Why had he come here? Why had he quarrelled with his father, and spoken as if he intended never to return to South Africa? Why had he been provoked to talk as he had to Jonathan?

Always, always, some perversity in himself mastered him, made him go further than he really wanted to, made him commit himself to notions he didn't know were in his mind until he found himself committed to them, until he had made declarations, policies of them.

He was interrupted by a knock on the door. He went to it, smoothing down his hair with his hands. The housekeeper – an old bedraggled woman wearing what looked like several cardigans, and slippers on her feet – stood in the ill-lit passage. She had come to ask whether he intended keeping the room for another week, as he had said he might, for she had a 'ge'ullm'n' downstairs who was interested in it.

'No, I'll be moving out on Friday,' David said, the decision made on the spur of the moment.

So the gentleman downstairs came to look at the room. He was a bespectacled, emaciated gentleman of about David's age; his face and hair were dripping with rain, but still looked as though he was much in need of a wash. He nodded at David, glanced rapidly around the room, said that it would do, and squelched out, the bottoms of his trousers clinging to his attennuated legs. His long hair and metal-rimmed spectacles had given him the appearance of a seedy scholar; his striped shirt and something indefinably jaunty about his narrow shoulders had suggested funfairs. Where had he come from? How long would he stay in the room? What would he do in the bed David was lying on? Chain-smoke? Pull his wire? Take an overdose of sleeping pills?

London was the place for such speculations. David had been in London three days, and it was here, it seemed to him, that one could enter the heart of darkness he had read of, not in Africa; certainly not in the crudely exposed, thinly populated, suburban Africa he knew. Who would care in these streets, among these houses, in this immense populous darkness, what you did, where you went, how you lived? Who could trace you if you fell into the great tide of brick and asphalt that carried indifferently on its surface a scum of advertisements, torn newspapers, vehicles, people? Here, in front of him, around him, was the place where, if he truly wished to do so, his perversities could be explored and known; here he could throw off the shames that inhibited him, the scruples that hindered him, the affections that weakened him, the name that labelled him, the background that conscribed him. He could stop being a Jew, he could say that he came from Australia or Denmark, he could find a job under another name, receive no letters, send no letters, begin another life unlike any ever imagined for him. Could he do it? Did he have the courage?

Lying on the bed, David found that he had begun to pray. At first this frightened him more than anything else that had happened to him since he had left home; it was something he had never done before. He had no forms in which to pray, he didn't know to what or whom he was praying, he couldn't believe that his prayer was being heard or attended to. But his lips still moved, he uttered words aloud into the squalid room. 'Help me, make me better, let me do the right things, don't let me make a mess again and again, please help me.' It was like a madness; in shame and fear he put his hands over his mouth, but the words still ran through his mind – words of appeal, of apology, of promises for the future, of renewed appeals for help to keep the promises he was making.

Then his hands dropped from his mouth. He had wanted to throw off shame and inhibition and scruple, to make himself over, to become another man. Then why shouldn't he pray? Because he had never prayed before? That was no reason; not for him, not any more. On the contrary: was this the beginning of a change greater than any he had ever dreamed of? Greater, deeper, more transfiguring, more dangerous to everything he had been? In his excitement at the thought he got up from the bed and walked about the room; he opened the window that looked over the sunken back garden of the house and leaned out, breathing the damp, smoke-tainted air. Overhead the illuminated clouds followed one another still, in an interminable shifting and streaming; in his ears there was the subdued hoarse whisper of the city's noise, so sustained that it might have been the sound of his own blood; on his hands, at the sill, fell drops of rain. Grateful, incredulous, filled with a fear that was different from the one he had known previously, for it was a fear not of himself but of the living response he might evoke, of the force which he felt streaming through the clouds and his own body, he began to pray again.

He said the Lord's Prayer in English and the *Shema Yisrael* in Hebrew, for these were the only two prayers he knew right through; then as much as he could remember of the twenty-third psalm. He was sorry that he knew no more than fragments of other prayers; and that the one he had uttered was Christian, the other Jewish. He would try to do better, he promised himself, to be a little less clumsy, ignorant and confused the next time; though how he would manage this he did not know.

17

If this was illness, Joel asked himself, why did it have the power to make all the other times of his life seem a thin, foolish, disgusting delusion, a wretched scurry for shelter – shelter in work, in talk, in the huddled, flimsy community of the kibbutz, in enlightened 'views', in girls or thoughts about girls, in books, in fantasies, in notions of success or failure?

If this was health, why was he alone in it? How did everyone else manage to carry on? Why had it come on him again like a seizure, a cold, a fever?

It had begun with nothing more than a deep, persistent depression after his meeting with Yitzchak. Then, one night, he dreamed luridly, horribly, endlessly. He was Yitzchak, he was himself, he was killing, he was hunted. Trees were in his dreams, and snow, and a man with a twisted chin, his mother and father in attitudes of alarm, wild laughter, obscure effort, his hands dragging through thick, moist, living matter. Until the bell clanged and it was daylight; confusion shrank to the sight of the brown wooden walls of the room, of his feet going into his boots on a tiled floor.

Confusion shrank, but daylight brought less relief than he had hoped. Confusion became commonplace, habitual, true, no dream; that was all. His depression extended itself, ramified, it reached everywhere within him. He went out to work. Later he slept, eagerly, dreamlessly. The bell clanged; he went out to work. What for?

He found no satisfaction in it. He remembered finding satisfaction in it; but there was none now. It was as if from memory that he spoke, smiled, listened to others, strained at his work; he knew from before how to do such things, so he did them. But everything around him had receded to a distance; he had been severed from his own responses. He had no appetite for his food or leisure; when he looked at the hills at morning or evening their beauty and calm meant nothing to him. They were calm and beautiful; what was he?

What was he? What for? What did it matter? He was tormented by questions and reflections that he told himself were banal, cheap, adolescent, boring, portentous, poverty-stricken. This did not make them any the less tormenting. Nor did his fierce efforts to silence them, to shut them up, by telling himself that his own weakness or illness, revealing itself once more, merely seized upon them as a kind of rationale, as a means of self-inflation, as a secret cause for self-admiration. Everyone on the kibbutz, except for the patrolling *shomrim*, slept at night: but he, Joel Glickman, sensitive, compassionate, imaginative Joel Glickman, lay awake thinking about the six million dead Jews of Europe!

As if he had the power or courage to do it! As if it would help them or himself if he did. He was safe in his bed, conscious always of what was reassuringly and distractingly around him – the shadows of the room, the movements of the others in their beds, the coolness and freshness of the air he was breathing into his untouched lungs, the maniacal whoops and yells of the jackals in the hills. While the gassed and machine-gunned Jews of Europe were gone; they were as silent as the dead Hebrews and Samaritans whose burial chambers he and Harry had explored and had found to be empty.

In their time those vanished people had also seen the sun come up over the mountains in the east, and had lived through wars and massacres, or died in them. Alive, they had lain awake at night, worrying, scheming, arguing with themselves, fretting for what they could not have, listening to the cackles of the animals in the hills, who knew nothing of the past or future.

How could time be measured? The onrushing, silencing indifference of succession; the fixity of repetition and re-enactment: they were the same, they were one, they made a futility of what they revealed: futile birth, futile death, futile pain or gratification between.

Futility was not an abstraction, a notion; it made heavy every shovelful of earth he lifted, ugly or ridiculous every face he saw, remote every voice he heard, tiresome every response that was demanded from him, disgusting his preoccupation with himself. He felt futility built into his bones, circulating in his blood. It was the truth, festering always within him, as lies were supposed to do.

18

Joel was awake before he knew what had woken him; and his first consciousness was one of resentment at having been woken before it was time, when it was still dark. Then, in what seemed a single burst of sound, he heard shots, yells, a loud explosion. He jumped out of bed and groped at the foot of it for his trousers; the others in the room were also pulling their clothes on in a fever of fear and hurry. Joel opened the door, and stood aside from it for a second. The air that came into the room was cool. He lowered his head and began sprinting towards the central group of buildings, where the kibbutz had its armoury. He did not know from which side the firing had come, but instinctively tried to put the buildings he passed between himself and the east, as he ran. Others were running in the same direction as himself. A door burst open ahead of him, a dim light shone, several figures emerged carrying Sten guns and ran past him in the opposite direction. They shouted something, he did not know what.

A torch was burning on the floor of the armoury, which was just off the entrance to the dining room. By its light, Arieh, small, neat and methodical, was handing out weapons to each of the men who came up, and telling him as he did so where to go. 'Main gate ... cowshed ... workshop ...' Joel took the Sten gun and the magazine of cartridges that was given to him; it smelled of metal and oil, a clean, distinctive, machine-like odour, unmistakable. He clipped the magazine into place.

Arieh had directed him to the tractor shed; he and Sam, a Dutchman, who was going to the *bet yeladim*, ran part of the way together. 'I think we're too late,' Joel panted hopefully. The words were hardly out of his mouth when there was another burst of firing somewhere on their left; the sound of it seemed to knock holes in the darkness, as if into something solid. He and Sam checked their stride and swerved, not knowing whether they should go in the direction from which the firing had come. Then Sam broke away, towards the *bet yeladim*, and Joel ran on by himself towards the tractor-shed.

The shed had been made by using one of the sharp, quarry-like declivities of the hillside; its three walls were of rock, the fourth side was open. Its roof was made of corrugated iron, and was level with the ground from which Joel came. He ran straight on to the roof, and then jumped down into the darkness. The earth hit him sooner than he had expected, and he sprawled, trying to hold the gun clear of the ground. There was a strong smell of diesel-oil everywhere. Someone else clattered over the roof and dropped down beside him. 'Raffi,' he said, and Joel answered, 'No, it's Joel.'

'*I'm* Raffi,' the man whispered in Hebrew, with such irritation in his voice at the misunderstanding that Joel couldn't help laughing. But he thought, Good, I'm laughing, and the laugh was cut short by his consciousness of it.

In the darkness they took up their positions by memory, rather than by sight. The double track to the tractor shed curved away to the right; on the other side of the track was a bank of earth that looked over a ploughed field. To the left of the shed the ground was rough, and sloped down more abruptly. Raffi lay behind the bank facing the field; Joel clambered cautiously down the hillside and took up a position behind a spur of rock. Farther to the left were the cow-sheds, the sheep-pens, the poultry-sheds, and a workshop, in a semi-circular arc which followed the curve of the hillside and was several hundred yards from end to end; in front of these buildings there was only broken rock and grass. The firing had seemed to come from the very tip of the arc on the left; but there was none now. Far off, there was the faintest thread of light running along the top of the hills in the east; overhead the stars still shone.

Joel had slipped off the safety-catch of the gun. He lay on his stomach, the barrel of the gun resting on a rock, his elbows digging into the earth; the roughness of it on his skin was slightly painful and somehow reassuring. He heard voices from the central cluster of buildings, the violent lowing and bleating of the cattle and sheep, a door slamming. His eyes strained forward, but none of the small humps he could see ahead of him changed their shape or moved.

He was astonished and incredulous when, at what looked like an immense distance, points within the darkness suddenly scratched into life, into flame, sparks flying off as if from a grindstone. There was some rifle firing in answer; the attackers were too far off now for automatic weapons to be of any use. Obviously they were going. Joel wondered what damage they had done, and whether they had wounded or killed anyone. In the last raid the kibbutz had suffered the marauders had simply crept up, thrown their grenades and then fled; the buildings into which they had thrown their grenades had been uncompleted and empty. He hoped they'd had the same luck this time.

Someone whistled softly. It was Arieh. He and Raffi were standing together in the oil-soaked space in front of the shed. Joel had not heard any of their movements behind him.

'Listen, Joel,' Arieh said, 'will you stay on duty? I'm sure they won't come back, but still –'

'Sure,' Joel said. 'If I can sleep late tomorrow morning.'

'Bargains, at this hour! What are you, a Jew or something?'

'That's right. You've found me out.'

Raffi, a *sabra*, either did not understand their exchange, or was not amused by it. 'So I go to sleep,' he said with sombre accuracy, and began climbing up, round the side of the shed. He disappeared from sight almost at once.

'Is everything all right? What did they do?'

'They killed four calves, that's what they did.'

There was the sound of a single, muffled shot from within the *meshek*. The two men listened. Arieh said, 'Five calves, from the sound of it.'

'But everyone's OK?'

'We thought Gingie was hurt, but he seems all right now. I think he was just knocked out by the blast. He's bleeding something horrible from the nose.'

'He was on *shmira* last time they came, I remember.'

'It's the colour of his hair that attracts them.'

Joel was relieved when Arieh left him; alone, he could abandon the light, strained casualness of demeanour which each had demanded from the other. His body's recollection of fear was stronger than anything he had felt in the unreal confusion and activity of the raid itself. He shivered slightly from time to time; when he heard a footfall behind him, his whole frame became instantaneously a single chilled stiffness. Then his heart started beating within it.

It was Arieh, again.

'Knock off as soon as it's light.'

'What do you think?' Joel whispered gruffly, after two attempts to speak had produced nothing but creaks of sound from his throat. 'You think I'm going to sit here all bloody day?'

Arieh punched him lightly on the shoulder and went off, leaving Joel ashamed and angry with himself. Philosopher! Pioneer! Cunt!

19

Joel did not know how far he was from the *meshek*. The thread of light along the crest of the hills looked hardly any nearer than before, but it was brighter and sharper; below it, like a stain in the darkness, was a faint purple infusion, the colour of a dark grape. Though he knew it could not be so, it seemed to him that only a few minutes had passed since he had simply walked out of the kibbutz perimeter, into the darkness.

He remembered running at first, once he was outside the *meshek*, the roughness of the ground shaking the breath out of his body, bushes and rocks starting out of nowhere, at angles under his feet; then resting on his back in a damp, cool, grassed-over hollow, from within which the stars had shone more sharply, the sky had looked blacker than they had outside it; then his slower, more cautious progress eastwards. Twigs whined across his trousers, sand and pebbles scuffed under his boots, the dew was chill around his ankles; he moved forward as steadily as he could, baffled by the darkness and yet feeling himself sheltered by it, too. The stillness and silence were trancelike; so was the contrast between the vividness of what was most distant from him, the stars and the ridge of the hills, and the total obscurity of what was immediately around him. In his mind, as if it had always been there, was a destination: a small, empty valley that he had seen many times when he had gone out with the sheep. It was right on the border, at the very foot of the hills, its entrance on the west protected by two flanking elevations. The kibbutz grazed its sheep in the nearer valleys, but not in that one, which had always looked serene, secret and inviolate, a pocket of rolling grass under walls of blue-white stone, untouched between two hostile armies. It seemed to Joel that ever since the first time he had seen it he had known he would visit it one day, and stand in it; he thought about it now as if it had been created for just that purpose, no other, and thought about nothing else.

In his trance of alertness and detachment, he had all but forgotten the emotions with which he had set out on this ramble through the dark: chagrin, boredom, self-disgust, a childish bravado, a perverse determination to neglect a duty that had been assigned to him, a wish to prove to himself that he wasn't all despairing speculation on the surface and self-regarding cowardice beneath. He saw the sky beginning to grow pale, in slow, irregular washes of light, that reached further to the west and then seemed to recede, like the coming-in of a tide, each shallow wave of light washing away more of the stars. The change was so slow, so large in scale, that it appeared to have nothing to do with his realization that he could now, before his hands or feet touched them, tell outcrops of rock from shrubs, hollows from inclines. He felt frail, disburdened, almost disembodied; he was grateful for the physicality of the dawn's sharp chill, the hard heaviness of the gun he was carrying across his back. Occluded within him, like a flaw in a crystal, was a sense of reversal that he hardly dared to hope was also one of renewal.

The sound was at first hardly a sound at all, it was a mere trembling of the air. Instinctively, Joel dropped behind some boulders; slowly he raised himself on his hands to listen again. Now it was louder, but he still could not make out what it was: it quacked faintly, hissed, quacked again; it sounded neither animal nor human. Then it ceased abruptly. Had he really heard anything?

He hunched himself in the hollow behind the boulders. Then he heard someone saying, in Hebrew, very clearly and peevishly, at what seemed to be a distance of only a few yards, 'Wait, I've got a stone in my boot!'

Joel lay still. He felt embarrassment, above all, at the thought of revealing himself to the men ahead of him, at having to explain what he was doing there. They would certainly think him mad; and in a way they would be right. He was disappointed that his adventure had already come to its end.

'*Shalom!*' he called softly. His voice sounded bold, almost impertinent, even though the silence had already been broken by the others.

No one answered. Nothing stirred. He might have imagined that casual, complaining voice in the half-darkness. Then he heard a metallic clink somewhere on his left.

Joel called out again. '*Shalom. Ani yehudi m'kibbutz Ramat Elkan. Mi zeh?*'

'*Mi zeh?*' a voice shouted out.

Joel stood up. '*Ani yehudi. Mi atem?*'

A savage blow hit him on the chest, and he wondered as he fell why he had been struck like that, what kind of rough foolishness it was. He was on his back. The brightness and size of what was overhead astonished him. Flares and streamers of light hung curled and languid, in a great stillness, under the polished, all-encompassing dome of the sky.

20

The patrol which Joel had come across consisted of a dozen border-guards; the sounds he had heard in the darkness were those from the earpieces of a walkie-talkie radio which the signaller of the patrol had taken off his back and put down on the ground while they were taking a rest. They had been to the south at the time of the raid on the kibbutz, and had been told on their radio from the base-camp to move north on foot, in an attempt to cut off the retreat of the Arab marauders. They had moved as fast as they had been able to; and were just about to move forward again when Joel had stood up and called to them. One man only had fired.

The dawn came up clear; the hills in the east filled the horizon with their rich purple solidity; the rest of the countryside revealed itself in its dry sallowness of colour and rolling irregularity of contour; the sun, though still hidden, sent out an ever-greater intensity of light. The members of the patrol sat and smoked and talked to each other, or tried to sleep with their helmets over their faces. Two men were on guard, on top of a nearby rise. Someone had cut open Joel's jersey and pyjama jacket and stuffed a dressing into the wound in his breast. He breathed labouringly, a pinkish froth on his lips, and occasionally muttered a word in English. His gun had been propped up on a rock. The man who had shot him – a youngster with a thin neck and a large, floppy blond head of hair, who had been in the army for only a few months – kept looking over his shoulder at Joel. He felt some awe at what he had done: he had actually shot a man, and when he looked at Joel it was as much to confirm this extraordinary fact as out of guilt or anxiety. The others in the patrol were unhappy about what had happened – the wounded man was clearly a Jew, and they knew they would have to go through endless enquiries before the incident could be forgotten. They felt sorry for him, but they were irritated with him, too, for having landed them in trouble. And they were bored and hungry.

When two jeeps came bumping across the open country they loaded Joel into one, and then jumped on to the vehicles themselves, in spite of the expostulations of the drivers who protested against the weights their vehicles were being made to carry. Then, whining, groaning, bumping, the two jeeps made their way to the nearest settlement – not Joel's – where a puzzled, stricken Harry confirmed that Joel was from Ramat Elkan; where he was transferred to an ambulance and taken to hospital; and where the members of the patrol had a breakfast of bread, tea, green salad and *lebeniyeh*.

21

It is astonishing what money can do, when it is spent to some purpose. It can rent office-space, print notepaper, buy machinery, hire trucks, employ a white foreman and a host of Swazi labourers; it can produce talc.

Happier and busier than he had been for years, his clothes in sweat-drenched swathes around him, Begbie drove between Barberton and Johannesburg, frequently phoned Cape Town, typed innumerable letters with his own podgy fingers, drank with a clear conscience through entire evenings, mystified his brothers-in-law by the patronizing cordiality he showed to them, made large promises to the fellow who had originally told him about the deposit, and secretly marvelled at the fact that 'the thing', as he put it to himself, 'was actually working'. A red-necked Afrikaner lit a charge of dynamite and so many tons of rock collapsed from the wall of the quarry; half-naked Swazis, smelling of sweat, powdered with dust, chanting rhythmically while they worked, loaded it on to trucks;

railwaymen signalled to one another and the trucks clattered towards the coast; a tramp steamer was moored to the quayside in Lourenço Marques and the lumps of talc were stowed aboard; the steamer butted its way northwards, then through the Suez Canal, across the Mediterranean, up the coast of France and discharged its cargo in Liverpool. There the talc could be ground, it could be despatched to manufacturers of paint or linoleum, textiles or cosmetics, refractory materials, paper or insecticides.

It had happened, the thing was working, the first shipment of two hundred tons had been sent off, and the buyers had accepted it, paid for it, and asked for more. They were negotiating now for a long-term contract. As much as the money that this promised him, after his years of failure, Begbie prized the feeling that he had become once again a full member of society: that his activity was part of the irresistible momentum of production, that he was an initiator and a worker in a great assembly of processes which was interminable and planless, and which yet operated and cohered in a way beyond all comprehension. It made you think, he said often to Samuel, to anyone who would listen to him; at the same time it had you beat what to think. That hole in the ground near Barberton, those people, ships, documents, distances, trains, factories, oceans ... amazing!

Begbie did not know that something else wasn't working as it should have. One afternoon, in Eloff Street, he suffered a sudden shortness of breath that embarrassed him while he was buying a packet of cigarettes from a girl in a kiosk. He fumbled for the change she had given him, failed to get it between his fingers, and left the coins lying on the counter. He had begun to walk down the pavement, unconscious of what he was doing, as if to leave behind whatever it was that was stifling him. He pulled vaguely, with frightened, disordered gestures, at the tight ring of his collar around his neck. The sunlight flickered in his eyes; noises louder than those of the traffic roared in his ears, the pressure within him mounted unbearably. For the briefest moment he was reassured by the thought, which broke like a bubble in a corner of his mind, that this was just a nightmare; he often had nightmares in which he couldn't breathe. Then he found he was lying on the pavement. Faces leaned over him; he opened his mouth to beg for help. But he could not speak, there was no air in his lungs to speak with. The paving-slabs were warm and he tried to sink more deeply into them, for comfort, as in a bed. He opened his mouth again and uttered a sound which reached the people over him like the faintest, saddest of sighs. His face went blue, his eyes rolled upwards, he was dead.

22

Begbie was buried in a new burial-ground near Northcliff: an exposed, sloping piece of ground, beyond the suburb itself, overlooking and overlooked by a scatter of smallholdings. Fowl runs, mealie patches, wire fences, dirt roads, and signs advertising fruit and tomatoes for sale met the eyes of the mourners when they looked up, over the low brick and wrought iron fence around the graveyard. The only people who saw the coffin being lowered into the ground were Mrs Begbie, Malcolm, Begbie's brothers-in-law, Samuel Talmon, a robed, supercilious Anglican priest, and a wizened, red-skinned, filthy-fingernailed little man in a threadbare suit much too big for him, who had simply joined the mourners at the gate. This stranger watched the proceedings with what appeared to be a deep reverential satisfaction, and insisted on shaking everybody by the hand before walking down the hill to one of the homesteads nearby.

Samuel returned to his room in a mood of deep dejection. Poor Begbie! Gone, just like that – a boxed-up weight, thrust into the earth.

Poor mama! It was only two months since he had been at her funeral, too. He had been little affected by it at the time; this made him all the more wretched now, in recollection. Guiltily, he remembered how irritated he had been with her for being so frightened, so childish, at the end; he had been positively pleased, at the same time, that her religion, over which they had quarrelled so much in earlier years, had finally been of no use or comfort to her.

He stood at the window of his room, looking down on to the foreshortened trees and parked cars along the pavements, eight storeys below. His thoughts moved slowly, erratically; he felt very tired. His feet had ached at the funeral and he wondered, without moving from the window, why he did not sit down. He remembered how strange it had felt, at the graveside, to stand bareheaded while prayers were being said. He was still that much of a Jew apparently.

He wasn't much of a Jew. He wasn't much of a businessman – he was sure he must be the only man in the world who actually owed Begbie's estate money. He wasn't much of anything. What had he done with his life? Where had it gone? Talking, arguing, studying law, throwing it up, selling ladies' handbags, running around like a *meshuggeneh* looking for sillimanite, kyanite, spodumene, silcrete, talc – importing corks, buying feathers. What rubbish he had busied himself with! Any new rubbish would do for him, as long as it kept him busy, kept him from making any order out of his life or finding any purpose in it. Now, he jeered at himself, now he was sorry for all the time he had wasted in his life. But for how long would he be sorry? Until the next bit of rubbish was dangled in front of him; then he would reach out with both his hands, then he would open his mouth to swallow it. He leaned his head against the window and sobbed spasmodically, with gasps of sound; in between there were long intervals when he stood quite silent, motionless, dry-eyed, watching a car drive down the road, a cat make its stealthy way down the gutter, an African nursemaid wheeling a pram into the foyer of the block of flats opposite. The abrupt ringing of the telephone interrupted him; he let it ring for some time before crossing the room to answer it.

'Hullo, yes? What is it?'

Benjamin's voice sounded frail and hesitant, like an old man's, or like someone speaking from a great distance. 'Shmuel,' he said, and the Yiddish form of his name made some point of emotion within Samuel quiver and then lie open as if it had been touched by a whip, 'Shmuel, I wonder – you think you could perhaps come to the house? We've had bad news about Joel, Sarah is terribly upset, and I thought –' His voice faded away altogether, then came back. 'You think you could come? It might help her.'

'What? What bad news? What's happened to Joel?'

'We don't really know, we just had this telegram saying that he was hurt in some border shooting – I don't understand it –'

'How badly? He's not –'

'It says seriously. That's all we know. Bertie's trying now to fix up for us to fly to Israel – both of us.'

'I'll come right away.'

Benjamin rang off immediately.

'All we need!' Samuel exclaimed fiercely at the black instrument he held in his hand. He drove to the house like a man distraught, lifting his hands from the steering wheel in gestures of rage and helplessness.

His rage left him at the sight of Benjamin's face, when he opened the door. All he saw at first were Benjamin's eyes: they were quick, timorous, curious, startled in their glance, not like those of a man who had had bad news, but of a man anticipating it, without knowing of what kind it might be. Their quickness contrasted painfully with the heavy, frozen set of his jaw. Samuel stretched out his hands, and took his brother-in-law by the shoulders. 'Ah, it's a world!' he exclaimed strangely in Yiddish, his own face puckered, his nose standing out, his dry, lined, bald forehead moving above the tufts of his brows.

'Sarah –' Benjamin said, gesturing for Samuel to come into the house, to go to her.

'How are you?' Samuel asked, his hands still on the other's shoulders.

Samuel felt the weight of Benjamin's body rise in a slow shrug. 'I told you what we heard,' he said.

Sarah and Rachel were in the living room. They were both shocked, quiet and tearless, though Sarah's lips trembled when she greeted Samuel, simply saying his name.

'I'm glad you came,' Rachel said, coming forward and kissing him on the cheek.

'What else could I do?'

Benjamin had come into the room behind him, and Samuel turned to ask him, 'When is there a plane?'

'Not until the day after tomorrow.'

'You've booked on it?'

Benjamin nodded, his eyes darting from one to the other in the room. 'Bertie's seeing to it. Perhaps we can go sooner, flying first to Athens – I don't know –' He gestured vacantly.

'Have you got the cable?'

Rachel took it from the mantelpiece and showed it to him. It said what Benjamin had told him over the phone: it was signed 'Leon'.

'I remember that Leon,' Samuel said, giving the paper back to Rachel.

They were silent; three of them standing, Sarah seated on the couch. She began to rub her hands together. 'Joel will be all right, I'm sure of it.'

'Of course,' Samuel said. 'It doesn't even say "critically". Seriously is something else.' He sat down on the couch and took his sister's restless hands in his own. 'You'll go to him, you'll see him, he'll be all right.'

Sarah hardly seemed to hear him; but Benjamin listened as if Samuel must know what he was talking about, could be relied upon, wouldn't speak unless he was sure. In the state he was in this confidence did not seem surprising or remarkable in any way. And it was to Samuel that he cried out suddenly, 'Why Joel? Why not me?' He struck himself on the chest. 'I said when he left me that I was ready to go.'

'What do we want with Palestine?' Sarah cried out. 'Who talked about Palestine? What for?'

Samuel quietened her. 'Don't ask such questions. It's no use blaming each other. There's nobody to blame. Joel chose his own way. You must be proud of him. It's something to be able to choose, to have the strength to do it.'

He held Sarah's hands tightly in his own, and brought them to his forehead, hiding the tears that were in his eyes. 'It's a world, I tell you,' he said, his voice breaking, tears running down his drawn cheeks, 'It's such a world, we have to live in it.'

23

Later Bertie came from town with the news that he had managed to book his in-laws on a plane leaving early the next morning for Rome, where they would get a connection for Lydda. This would bring them to Israel well before the next direct Johannesburg–Lydda flight.

'Of course we'll take it,' Benjamin said. For a half-hour he had been sitting in an armchair staring at the same page of a newspaper.

'I got your passports, too,' Bertie said, taking them out of his pocket and putting them on a small table near the door.

He was proud that he had managed to arrange everything satisfactorily; and told Samuel and Rachel about the trouble he had had in getting the passports issued without delay. 'No, man,' he imitated the Afrikaner official he had dealt with at the passport office, 'twenty-foor owerrs uhss the muhnuhmum forr emuhrrjuhncy ishoo.' But the man had been proved wrong. 'One of these days I must put in for a passport,' Bertie said, 'just to see what happens. I wonder how long it'll take me to live down my radical past, as far as they're concerned.'

He knew Rachel disliked him mentioning this, which was one of the reasons why he often did.

But she ignored the provocation this time. 'Will you have something to drink, Bertie – whisky?'

'Please.'

'Dad?'

Benjamin had not been listening to Bertie's story. He roused himself slowly from his newspaper. 'What?'

'A drink?'

'Yes, I think so, a little whisky.'

Presently, a very subdued Annie called them in for their meal. Only Bertie and Samuel ate with any appetite. After the meal Rachel and Annie did some packing; both Benjamin and Sarah tried ineffectively to help, but succeeded merely in hindering them. Annie also made up a bed in Rachel's old room, for she and Bertie had decided that they would spend the night in the house, instead of going back to their flat; they had to take Sarah and Benjamin to the airport at five-thirty the next morning. Sarah then went straight to bed; Benjamin sat in his corner of the living room, first with the same newspaper in his hand, then a book, then, finally, just a drink, while Rachel, Samuel and Bertie sat at the other end of the room.

Usually, Samuel and Bertie were awkward in one another's company. Samuel did not know how far the affair between Rachel and his son had gone, but was sure it had gone farther than either of the young couple now wished to remember; for Bertie it was humiliating to imagine what this man might be conscious of when he saw him with Rachel. But tonight, the gravity of the occasion made their talk easier, in a curious way, than it had been before.

Bertie felt the burdens of the family on him, and was determined to carry them like a man; Samuel's spirits were recovering from their earlier low ebb of humility and compassion. He and Bertie talked business together, Bertie at first doing most of the talking. Samuel was impressed by the way he spoke, and was anxious to impress him in turn. Soon he was boasting about the prospects of his mining company as though nothing untoward had just happened; or, at least, as though Begbie's family would want the business to carry on and would rely on him to see that it did – which their behaviour to him at the funeral had done nothing to suggest.

'You must come and see the quarry, next time I go,' Samuel invited Bertie expansively. 'You'll find it interesting. It's something to see.'

'I'd like to.' Bertie was genuinely curious, willing to learn from anyone about any aspect of the world of production, sale and profit he had entered.

'I'll fix it up then, when things have settled down, when we're all in a happier mood.'

Samuel looked from Bertie to the silent, shrunken Benjamin, who sat in his chair like an old man – no longer in command, someone for whom things were done.

So! Joel was in Israel, perhaps dying there; David had run away to England, like a lunatic; if he should ever want anything from this family, Samuel thought, Bertie would be the man to whom he would have to come. The reflection surprised him, then pleased him. Precisely because of the kind of uneasiness there had been between them, he might find it all the easier to work on Bertie, to win him over. You could never tell what might come up, how useful Bertie might one day be to him.

He got up to go. 'You must go and try to get some sleep,' he said to Benjamin. 'You really must look after yourself.'

'Yes, yes, I will.'

'I'll hear from Rachel how you find Joel. And I'm sure I'll hear only good news.'

'Thank you, yes, I hope so.'

Rachel and Bertie saw him to the door. There he said to them with a meaningful look, 'I can't tell you how much it means to me that the poor people have the two of you to look after them, at such a time.'

'We can do little enough,' Bertie answered.

Samuel shrugged, in the doorway. 'Little is all any of us can do. I know you'll do what you must.'

They watched him walk down the garden path to his car. When they came back into the living room, they found that Benjamin had already left it. They stood in the middle of the room, looking around them. Rachel began collecting the dirty glasses, then changed her mind and left them for Annie to clear away, in the morning. She was exhausted.

'Let's go to bed.'

'Ja.' He was tired, too, but restless. Now that Samuel was gone, he felt more ill-at-ease about him than he had in his presence.

Rachel came to him and put her arms around his neck.

'Thank you for everything you've done. I'm sorry my family's dumped all this trouble on you.' Her face was pale; her brown eyes were enlarged, the surface of their whites had tiny irregular patches on them, that looked almost as if they could peel off. 'I don't know why my family's so hopeless,' she said sadly.

'Hopeless?'

'We are. We are. We're incompetent, really. We aren't one thing or another. Joel – Mom – Dad – David – Uncle Samuel – all of us. Me too. I'm sorry.' She put her forehead against his chest. She began to cry. 'Poor Bertie,' she said, between sobs. 'I'm sorry for you too, Bertie.'

'Ah, I've joined you, have I?'

'Haven't you?' She drew away; she reached in the belt of her skirt for a tissue and blew her nose. He had been standing with his hands on his hips, in a stiff, unresponsive posture, holding himself erect rather than holding her away from him.

'Millions of people would envy us. If Joel recovers you'll have nothing to complain about.'

They looked at each other. 'Then why are you so unhappy, too?' she asked. 'Why are you so sorry for yourself?'

'Because I've got a weak character, I suppose.'

He had intended his answer to be a rebuff; but once it was said, he was afraid that he had spoken the truth. He held out his arms to her. 'Don't be sad, Rachel. Don't be cross. I'll look after you – always. I've said I will.'

24

Annie, the Glickman's maid, and Nicholas, the servant from the house next door, were enemies of long standing. Nicholas was a lonely, greying man, much given to talking to himself, who had been working for the Lowther sisters for many more years than Annie had been working for the Glickmans. He was devoted to the timid, elderly, unmarried, identical twin ladies who employed him; everyone else, black or white, he resented and suspected. He never left the backyard of the Misses Lowthers' house, and no one ever visited him there. Annie insisted, often, that Nicholas was mad; what he thought of her he showed by the scowl which came upon his round, lined, black face, and his more than usually vehement mutterings and head-shakings, whenever he saw her.

While Benjamin and Sarah were in Israel, their house was left in the care of Annie and the latest houseboy, Charlie; on the fourth night that they were alone in the house, Annie gave a party for some of her friends in the backyard, just outside her room. Nine or ten men and women, most of them servants from other houses in the street, gathered to sit and talk around a brazier, to drink from the bottle of brandy that Jacobus had brought with him, and to listen to the records played on a hand-operated portable gramophone that belonged to a man who had come with Jacobus. Through the thick cypress hedge that divided the two yards, Nicholas tried to see from his side what was going on. The hedge was so thick that one could really see through it only at ground level, and eventually Nicholas lay down on the ground and peered between the trunks of the hedge-plants. He had lain there for many minutes before the whites of his eyes were seen by one of the women around the brazier.

She gave an affected shriek of alarm, clutched at the man nearest to her and pointed at Nicholas, who lay quite still, gazing unwinkingly forward, as if there were nothing unusual about what he was doing, or as if his best hope of escaping detection by the rest of them lay in remaining just where he was. For the sake of a laugh, Jacobus, who knew all about Nicholas, crossed the yard and stretched himself down on the ground, putting his face just a few inches in front of Nicholas's own. They stared wordlessly at one another, until Jacobus opened his mouth and uttered a roar from the depths of his chest, like a lion. Then Nicholas got up and went away, shaking his head, gesturing, talking to himself; Jacobus returned happily to his place at the fire.

But Nicholas had not gone back to his room. He was knocking on the kitchen door of the house, to call his employers. The kitchen door was double-locked from inside, once Nicholas had finished his work for the evening, so he could not get in. But he persisted with his knocking until he had brought the two women into the kitchen.

'What's the matter, Nicholas? What is it?'

The Misses Lowther stood in the middle of the room, their gowns clutched around them, their brushed, fading, reddish hair down to their shoulders, alarm on their long pale, droopingly refined faces.

'Madams, listen, next door.'

They listened. They had heard the noise of the party from the front of the house; it sounded much louder now that they were in the kitchen.

'Yes, we can hear it, Nicholas, what about it?'

'Madam, they *tsotsis* next door. Baas Glickman is gone, so that girl, she brings *tsotsis* to the house, every night. They drinking, madams, they bad people, they want to fight Nicholas.'

'Nonsense, Nicholas, go to bed. We know that Annie, she's a good girl.'

Nicholas stood outside and grumbled obscurely. Then his grumbles became words, became a request. Could he come inside and spend the night on the kitchen floor? He was too frightened to sleep in his own room because of the *tsotsis* that girl had there. He knew they wanted to kill him.

'Nicholas, stop talking like that! They won't do anything to you. If they worry you, call us, and we'll call the police.'

They switched off the light and began to make their way back to their bedroom. They had barely reached the door of the room when the knocking began again.

'What's it now, Nicholas?'

'Madams,' Nicholas said, in the sincere dogged tones of a man to whom the expected worst had happened, 'they worrying me.'

'You know,' the one Miss Lowther said to the other, 'I think he's as drunk as the rest of them.'

'He must have been drinking with them.'

'I'm sure of it.'

'Just listen to them!'

The Misses Lowther fled to the front of the house. The knocking went on; so did the music, the voices, the laughter. With every minute that passed they sounded louder, uglier and more threatening to the two frightened white women. On an impulse one of them picked up the telephone and dialled the number of the Flying Squad.

A few minutes later a police van, with dimmed lights, drew up in front of the Glickman's house. Out of it climbed four policemen, two white, two African. They made their way round the side of the house, to the backyard.

'*Wat makk julle hierso?*' they shouted, turning the beams of their powerful torches on to the group around the brazier.

The women screamed with fright, the man who had the bottle of brandy in his hands flung it away from him, Annie got up, stumbled over the step to her room and crawled towards her bed. The brazier was knocked over, its coals poured out in a heap on the ground. One man tried to flee round the side of the house, another was clubbed down by an African policeman while trying to scramble over the back fence. Annie was pulled out of her room, and she and the others were lined up.

When the police left, ten minutes later, they dragged with them, handcuffed together, Jacobus, the friend of his who owned the gramophone, and a houseboy from a neighbouring house, the one who had tried to jump over the fence. The women and the other men were allowed to go after they had shown their papers and sworn they lived nearby.

Nicholas had lain on the ground and watched the scene through the hedge; no one had seen him. The Misses Lowther had merely heard the shouts and cries. They hoped the police would not call on them, that they would not become 'involved' in any way, that no one would ever know who had asked the police to come. They did not breathe freely until they heard the police van drive off. Then they went to bed, each of them taking a couple of aspirins with water before doing so.

Because she was frightened and ashamed, Annie did not immediately go to tell Rachel what had happened. Some days later Rachel and Bertie came to the house to see that everything was in order; and Bertie asked her if she knew where Jacobus was, for he had not been to work at the factory for some days. Annie confessed that the police had come to the house and taken him and some others away.

'What was going on? Why did they come? Were you having a party? Making a noise?'

'Yes, master.' Annie hung her head. 'Not so much noise, master.'

'I'll try to find out what's happened to him.'

It took several weeks before Bertie was able to find out that Jacobus had been summarily tried and convicted on charges of being unable to produce all his documents on demand, and for being in illegal possession of 'white' liquor. He had been sent to a farm prison in the Bethel district.

He never returned to Johannesburg. Annie never heard from him again. That too was one of the results of the shot which had been fired at Joel in the hills of Samaria.

25

The bullet had shattered one of Joel's ribs on entry, and a portion of the shoulder blade on exit; it had gone straight through his lung. In the hospital in Tel Aviv, to which he had been transferred from the local institution, his chest had been opened and the external and internal wounds repaired; the blood spilt within his chest had been drained; after a week the drain had been removed. Of all this Joel was unconscious; all he was intermittently aware of was pain.

Sometimes his pain was part of a gross, laboured, pitiable, nerve-wracking noise, which he heard without knowing who was making it; often it was a weight which every inward breath was a struggle to lift from his chest and every expulsion of breath another failure to do so. It was a needle and thread passing through him with slow, deft, unbearable strokes which were somehow also connected with his breathing; it was a disc whirling within him at such speed and with such steadiness that it seemed quite still and harmless until the footsteps of someone passing jarred his bed, jarred his pain, and he knew how viciously it was moving. In his dreams the pain became landscapes which he was compelled to enter, so that he wandered through rooms of pain, climbed hills of pain, was trapped among rocks of pain.

Often he dreamed that he was dead, or had been dead, or was dying once more, having died insufficiently the previous times. Death became familiar to him, a visited place, a known state, spacious, painless, vacant, silent, dark, cool. It was life, not death, that choked him and hurt him; and he wanted only to escape from it. He crawled away from life when it wasn't attending to him, he hid from it, he composed himself as inconspicuously as he could and waited for death to take him in. At other times, when all the rest of him was alive and in pain, he simply held his death in his hand. It seemed to him that it had always been there – a help, a promise that he would never forego.

Once he dreamed that he had been transformed into a tree; his right leg had sprouted branches, twigs, and leaves; and even after some part of himself had woken, he lay quite still, afraid that if he moved those twigs would tear the sheets between which he now knew himself to be lying. He woke fully at last from the dream and was surprised to find himself wholly a man: he might as well have been a tree, he thought in confusion and yet with a sense of total logicality, before he had been a man.

Waking from that dream or from some other, he was astonished to see his mother and father by his bedside. 'What are you doing here?' he asked – surprised not because they were at his bedside, but because of the strange places in which he had last seen them in his dreams. Then he forgot that they had been near him, and dreamed he was writing letters to them, explaining where he was, and what had happened. But where was he? What had happened? He could not read what he had written, and stared at the blurred, disintegrating words that had made everything plain just a moment before; he saw Leon's face, and Harry's and Yitzchak's, and the faces of others from the kibbutz and elsewhere; but if he saw them once a day he saw them innumerable times in places neither they nor he had ever been in, regions, provinces, countries of sensation he had never visited before.

So time, or what would have been time had it been measurable, passed. The same night recurred again and again, mysteriously demanding to be lived through repeatedly; there were days that were no more than a space of light between two swiftly closing excluding curtains of darkness; others that began before dawn and were still waiting for dawn after lapses longer, deeper, than time could span. There were gaps and crevasses out of life into which he was rolled down, tumbled, bruised, abrased; he was dissolved into levels of himself that were not himself, that were stone, root, grain or sand, branch of tree, pure wind, water, anything. Pursuing consciousness and pursued by it, inhabited by alien beings and vacated from being, lost, dead and reborn, he was cast out at length on an ordinary white bed in a white hospital ward. The curtains, he saw, opening his eyes wide to the light one morning, were checked with red and white.

26

Rapidly, as the days of his recuperation passed, Joel realized how little new was the world around him; the time that had immediately followed his wounding ceased to be a cataclysmic end of days and became instead merely a brief, implausible, vaguely recollected interval of pain and delirium. Yet many things had changed – how or why he did not know. Decisions had been made within him, ambitions had been surrendered and acquired, he had become both more patient and less so. He couldn't speak of any of this; he was still too weak, too uncertain, too surprised by his own recovery.

In fact, he spoke very little; when he did speak it was usually to his mother, who sat by his bed for as many hours of every day as she was allowed to. Sometimes she talked quietly to him, and sometimes, in Yiddish, or in her long-unused, formal, literary Hebrew, to the other patients in the ward; often she just read the books which she brought with her, while Joel slept.

Sleep was the third stage of his recovery, after the delirium and his return to consciousness. He slept copiously, accepting gratefully the drugs that were given to him when he asked for them; he slept through mealtimes and visiting hours, through the hundred loud noises of the hospital; all he looked forward to during his periods of waking were the profound immersions in sleep which awaited him. It was another lapse of his consciousness that he was surrendering to; but this one was calm, like a return to childhood, and all the more so for his awareness of his mother's presence at his bedside.

27

Once Benjamin was sure that Joel would recover, and he could look up, as it were, from the hospital bed and his own anxieties, he spent much less of his time in the hospital than Sarah; he busied himself in trying to see as much of the country as he could.

He walked about the Tel Aviv streets when his rheumatism permitted him to, he went on guided tours with busloads of tourists, he spent a day wandering about the *ma'abara* in which Yitzchak had lived before he had been called into the army – asking questions, staring, poking, frowning, shaking his head; he hired a car and travelled with a driver through the Galilee, and to Haifa and Jerusalem and Beersheba.

He said little to the others about what he was seeing and learning outside the hospital. He found it too difficult to describe either what he saw or the truth of his own reactions to it. After so many years of thinking about a Jewish state in a Jewish Palestine, after having read so many Zionist books and papers, having attended so many meetings, given so much money; after having relied so heavily upon Zionist achievements as a moral and emotional recompense for the humiliations, estrangements and insecurities he had suffered in his own life, and for the unimaginable horrors of what had been done to the Jews of Europe – after all this, Benjamin felt cheated, thwarted, baffled and disappointed everywhere he went. Was this the Zion he had dreamed of, comforted himself with, propagandized and given money for, been so proud to have his son work in and fight for? This? *This*?

How could he speak about it to his wife, who had never been a Zionist; or to his son, whose life had been put in danger from a Jewish bullet, as a result of a lunatic escapade which no one could account for or excuse, and which Joel himself had never offered any explanation for? Could he tell them that he found Tel Aviv hot and crowded, filled with rough-mannered and poorly dressed people? That he saw strained, unhappy and unfriendly faces everywhere? That there was so much haste in the streets and so much idleness; so much noise and so much inefficiency? That the buildings all looked so unspeakably rubbishy to him? That the Hebrew he had learned a lifetime before, in *talmud torah* and *yeshivah*, was of so little use; and that there were tens of thousands of people in the street whose Hebrew was no better than his own, and who spoke in a babble of languages he couldn't understand? That food was in such short supply, and that what there was of it was so ill-prepared? That there were no big factories, no department stores, no wide thoroughfares, no railway stations – nothing that made up what he thought of as a city, a real city? And what was he comparing it with, after all? Not Paris, not London, not Rome: just lousy Johannesburg!

Outside Tel Aviv the small towns were hideous; the kibbutzim were for people who could put up with wooden huts, flies, heat and communal feeding; the refugee camps were worse than the locations for Africans in South Africa – he couldn't help thinking them worse, simply because most of the people in them were white, were Jews. Only in the south was there any real sense of available space; and the south was nothing but a desert, like the Karroo, the backside of a country. Elsewhere there was rock, uncultivable hills, stretches of barren sea-sand, and, here and there, green pockets, pouches, tablecloths of fields and orange groves. The promised land! It filled his heart with grief and pity, and with a kind of anger, too, a rebelliousness and defiance which, to his own surprise, were directed chiefly against the pale, recumbent silent Joel – so far as they were directed against anybody, and not just against God, fate, or Jewish history.

Benjamin could not forgive Joel the panic and confusion which he had felt when he had heard that Joel's life was in danger, his sense of utter, black helplessness and dependence; and that memory was linked inextricably in his mind with his present raw disappointments and fatigues.

'What do you expect?' he said once or twice to his wife. 'It's a poor little country, it's hardly two years old, the refugees are pouring in by the hundreds of thousands. What do you expect?'

But to Joel he said nothing at all, though wild accusations, words of reproach and self-assertion rose from his breast to his tongue and were swallowed down again, sometimes with a visible effort. 'What were you looking for? Why must I come to Eretz Yisroel to find you like this? What did you want – to finish us both off? I have a life of my own, you hear? I won't let you spoil it!'

He had said none of this, yet the silence between them had been without peace since Benjamin had asked, in furious bewilderment, 'What were you doing there, in that no-man's-land?' and Joel had given the cold, off-hand reply, 'I went for a walk.' Neither of his parents had asked him the same question since.

28

Everybody in the ward, with one exception, looked with interest and curiosity at the excited, happy, talkative family group around Joel's bed. Among the people in the ward there was a *sabra* who had had his appendix out and another who had fallen out of the back of a moving truck; there was a Roumanian cook from a café near the Mograbi who had been operated on for piles, a German bank clerk with a heart condition, a Yemenite policeman who had had his head cut open during a demonstration by unemployed immigrants, a jovial Russian builder with a broken leg and an immense set of gleaming steel teeth, a boy of about fifteen with a wasting disease who looked eight or nine years old. All of them knew a great deal about each other, perhaps because of, rather than in spite of, the difficulties they had in communicating with each other or with the staff; one or another was continually being called upon to translate for the next, sometimes in order to get a message across to a third.

Now while the Glickmans stood together, laughing and exclaiming, the word about David was already being passed from patient to patient, in a variety of languages. 'It's his brother. The one who was in England.' 'They're from South Africa, who says England?' 'He's younger, you can see it.' 'He looks more like the mother, if you ask me.' 'No, that's his brother, I said, *bruder, acho ... ken? Ata mehvin? Verstehst du?*'

The one patient who had not looked up was in the far corner of the ward. He sat on the edge of his bed, with one leg lifted in front of him and crossed over the other. The pyjama trouser of the leg in front of him had been rolled up to the knee, and with the tips of his fingers, his eyes fixed upon his hand as it moved up and down, he was gently stroking the length of his fleshless, hairless, yellow shin. He was a concentration camp survivor: that was all that was known about him in the ward. He never spoke to anyone, and moved from his bed only to go to the lavatory. Each time he did this he carefully rolled down his pyjama-leg and stood up, revealing himself to be surprisingly tall and large-boned, and not much past middle-age; then he limped through the ward, looking neither to the right nor left.

When he returned he took up his position on the edge of his bed, rolled up his trouser-leg, and with the same, light soothing touch, began once more to stroke his shin, up and down, up and down, endlessly, tirelessly. Even when the ward was in darkness, late at night, he sat there; in the mornings, when the others awoke, they found him sitting bowed and absorbed over his moving hand. No one ever visited him. He should obviously have been in a psychiatric ward, but the other patients accepted his presence there without comment or complaint.

29

Benjamin was smiling with pleasure at the surprise he and David had given the others. 'I went into the Federation office,' he explained, 'to look if there was any post, and the first thing I see, if you don't mind, is this young gentleman leaning over the counter and asking if they knew what hospital Joel was in. I don't know who was more astonished – me when I saw him, or him when I tapped him on the shoulder.'

'Tapped? That was no tap! You knocked the breath out of me.'

He and David had made up their quarrel: that was obvious. They had made it up on the instant, before they had known that they were doing so, having met so unexpectedly and having felt so much happiness in seeing each other. It hadn't seemed possible for them to feel anything else.

'I wasn't even sure that you were in Israel,' David explained. 'Let alone that you were in the Fed. Office, all ready to punch me in the back!'

'Who punched? What punched?'

'You didn't get our letters?' his mother asked.

'The last letter I got was the one Rachel wrote me, just after you left. For all I knew you might have been and gone. Or Joel –' he turned and looked at his brother, his eyes shining with relief and remembered fear. There was no need for him to finish the sentence.

'So you came?' Joel said, gratefully.

David nodded.

The silence that followed was broken by Benjamin. 'How did you manage it?' he asked. 'Where did you get the money for your fare?'

'Well, I travelled rough, I can tell you – third-class to Marseilles, and on the deck from there, on a Greek boat. I took on board a whole lot of chocolate and fruit and condensed milk, and lived off that. We went first to Genoa, then to Piraeus, then to Nicosia, all over the place. But I can't grumble, actually I had a good time, except for being anxious about Joel. There was a crowd of American boys on board and I fell in with them, they used to smuggle me food from the dining room.'

David's animation and pride in his adventures made it easy for them to overlook the fact that everything he said referred indirectly to his quarrel with his father. He told them of the job he had had in a Lyons tea-shop in London, washing dishes and wiping tables; he described the room he had taken in Camden Town; he told them about Jonathan's flat and Jonathan's wife.

'One visit to them was enough for me,' he said scornfully, 'I never went back.'

Benjamin heard him with satisfaction. Then he said, 'But even to travel on the deck costs money. You didn't manage to save up so much from your dish-washing, did you?'

'No, that's not where I got the money.'

'So where did you get it?'

'Well, when I got Rachel's letter, all I thought about was how to come here as soon as I could. I didn't want to go and ask Jonathan for anything. I really wasn't keen on that. I didn't know what to do. Then I remembered Uncle Samuel telling me that there was some kind of a cousin of his – of ours – in London, a psychoanalyst, Dr Rosing. So I looked him up in the book, phoned him up, and told him who I was, and asked him if I could come and see him. Once I was there I asked him to lend me fifty quid, and explained to him why I needed it. I told him you'd pay him back. And he gave it to me, what's more! He said he was glad to – he said he did it for my mother's sake. I didn't know he was an old flame of yours, mom?'

'So first you borrow from Samuel, then from someone you've never seen before! What kind of way is that to travel around the world?' Only then did Benjamin say to his wife, 'I remember, you told me about that Rosing fellow.'

David laughed at the tone of his voice and the expression on his face. Sarah laughed too. 'I'm glad he still thinks so kindly of me,' she said.

'Oh, he does. He certainly made me wonder what went on between the two of you. He asked me all about you, about all of us, he kept on saying how well he remembers you, and what an interesting girl you were.'

'You think that's impossible?' Sarah exclaimed, still amused, yet a little incensed, also, by David's tone of voice. She was sitting in the armchair next to the bed, David was standing beside her. He took her hand in his.

'He told me it was like another life for him – Cape Town, Dors River, South Africa altogether. He's never been back. But he's still got a bit of a South African accent, it was funny to hear it coming out.'

'What's he like?' Sarah asked curiously. 'How does he live?'

'Very comfortably, from what I saw of his place. He's got a big Victorian house somewhere in Hampstead. It looks a bit grim from the outside, but inside it's pretty luxurious – all white-panelled woodwork and Persian rugs and bits of antique furniture here and there. And vases of flowers. His wife's

English, I think, not Jewish anyway – a big, smart-looking kind of woman. I hardly saw her. And they have just one son – he mentioned only one, doing law in Oxford. "Reading" law, as he said. That's how they live, anyway. As for what he's like –'

David pulled a face, and spoke cautiously at first, glancing down at his mother. 'Well, he was really very nice to me, giving me the fifty quid and everything, so I suppose I should be nice to him in return. But I can't say I took to him. He didn't seem anything special to me. He's a bit dried out and self-satisfied; pretty smug, really. We got talking about things in general – to listen to him talk you'd get the idea that serious thinking about life just didn't exist in the world until people like him appeared on the scene. Then, plonk! in 1903 or whenever it was that Freud started writing, it began. And a few people like himself have carried it on ever since. He's got it all worked out, he knows all the answers, he can see with his wise, trained eyes through all our little delusions and religions and ailments. It's a kind of smallness, knowingness, cocksureness – I don't know what the word is – anyway, he's got it. I'm quite sure it never occurs to him that anyone would be perfectly sane and intelligent and still think his way of looking at things one-eyed and boring.'

He broke off with a gesture, half-apologetic, half-indicative of how much more he still had to say to them. But this wasn't the place or the time. 'Hell, all I've done is talk about what's been happening to me. I want to hear about you people, all of you.'

'Bevakashah, bevakashah!' A small, fat nurse waddled towards them, gesturing, pointing at her watch; it was time for the evening meal.

The visitors began to leave. When David and his mother and father had reached the door, Joel called out, 'Hey, David.'

He came back eagerly. 'Ja.'

'Coming here like this – you make me feel – I've never been much of a brother to you.'

'Balls! You have, you have – don't talk like that. You know, all the way here I was thinking about when we were kids – the games we used to play, the things you used to tell me, the way we used to feel when Dad got mad with us and we'd hide in the garden until he'd got over it? You remember? Why do we ever forget that kind of stuff? When I heard you were sick, in danger, I realized just how much I've always relied on you. You were always there; and I was freer and stronger, I was safe, because you were there. When I was a kid I knew it, too; there was nothing in the world I knew better. Now I had to learn it all over again. That's why I came, you understand?' Then he said, astonishing Joel: 'I tried to pray for you.'

'*Bevakashah! Bevakashah!*'

'Here she comes again. You better go.'

'Sure, see you tomorrow.'

30

On his first Friday evening David went by himself to a tiny synagogue in a street running off from Allenby Street, towards the war-devastated area that had once been the border between Tel Aviv and Jaffa. The synagogue was simply a room on the ground floor of a run-down building which had crazy staircases and verandahs of wood, iron and gauze hanging from its unpainted front. Lights burned in rooms, the air was scented with the smell of food cooking over primus stoves; in the sandy little space in front of the building children played and shouted while the members of the congregation gathered together.

David had gone out to look for a synagogue; he had never imagined that he would find one so small and shabby. There were two steps down into it; the place was lit dimly by a few unshaded bulbs and by candles in tarnished holders. Over the ark hung a threadbare, dusty piece of green baize, attached by rings to a brass rod, and the ark itself was merely a wooden cupboard; the platform for the reader was a schoolmaster's dais, on which stood a decrepit household table, covered with an imitation silk cloth. From cracks in the plaster of the walls the low ceiling dust seemed actually to sprout forward, like a kind of growth.

In these surroundings, benches creaking at every movement, the dozen or fifteen members of the congregation went through the service that David remembered unwillingly attending with his father, when he had been a schoolboy in Johannesburg. Their voices holding in a sigh or cry to one interminable syllable, or rushing unpredictably over a hundred, the congregants uttered the Hebrew words that were familiar to him only as noise, not as meanings, and that roused in him a melancholy, slightly resentful nostalgia for what he had never known: for the synagogues of Eastern Europe in which his forebears had prayed and which he was sure this place resembled; for the piety which was not ashamed of the meagreness it tenanted; for a God so humble as to enter a room like this one, to be satisfied with so little.

And yet how much that God had been given! This was how Jews had always prayed, lifting discordant plaintive voices in an eternity of supplication, across wildernesses of space – Russia, America, South Africa, everywhere. What a people the Jews were; how entangled in the sadness of their history was their God! They had thrown that net of suffering over Him; and, all-powerful though He was, He could never escape it. An imprisoned, suffering God: David's mind clung to the words.

In a suffering world only a God who suffered could be respected.

There were several bearded old men in the congregation; the others were more or less middle-aged, more or less shabbily dressed; there was no one of David's age. One of the old men, with red watering eyes and a strange fatty odour on the miscellany of clothes he wore, asked David in Yiddish if he wanted to be called up to the desk, and David shook his head hastily, when he understood what was being suggested to him; he wouldn't have known what to do, he wouldn't have been able to read the prayers. The old man left him, the shuffle of one foot carrying him further than the shuffle of the other. David sat there, a tattered *siddur* in front of him, the black archaic letters on its pages staring up at him. He rose to his feet when the others did, and sat when they sat. Then the service was over. Outside, most of the children were gone; in the dusk, on one side, the ruins stretched away, each shattered wall or heap of rubble seeming to rise to no height at all against the sky and the dark space around it. On the other side, though all its lights burned, the city was strangely hushed.

Of course – this Sabbath wasn't just his and those of a few other Jews; it was Sabbath for the whole city. The streets were almost empty of traffic; through half-drawn curtains, he saw candles burning in first- and second-floor windows; the letters on the shopfronts were the same as those he had seen in the *siddur*; the people who passed him in the streets spoke the language of the prayers he had just heard. Here there was nothing freakish or suspect about going to *shul* on a Friday evening, or walking home from the service after having been there. Not that he was going home now; he was merely going to an hotel. But he imagined himself walking back to a home of his own; settled, secure, returning to a waiting wife, a pair of burning candles, a festive tablecloth, children perhaps; and he quickened his pace, as though these were already waiting for him. The evening air was mild, and the graceless, peeling, repetitive, narrow streets of the city seemed to him safe, already known.

He remembered his grandmother, and wished she were walking with him, and that he had known her better, had taken the chance to learn from all she had had to teach him, instead of dismissing her as a remote, antique survival. And he also said to himself 'Jewboy – hooknose – Yid –' testing the words out to see if they still had the power to hurt him, in these surroundings.

David had often wondered how difficult it would be for him to speak to his family of the change that had begun to take place within him; he had anticipated embarrassment, apology, laboured explanation. But once he started to talk to them, on his return to their hotel, all the doubts, insecurities and hesitations he actually felt; his sense of tentative hope and speculative wonder; the nostalgia, resentment and yearning that had filled him in the little synagogue he had just left; the loneliness and unreality of the hours he had spent in London in and out of stone-pillared, marble-tabled churches, churches luminous with stucco and gilt, churches ugly and forbidding with varnished wood and tortured Christs; the shock of fear and deprivation that had gone through him when he had heard of Joel's wounding; the fantasy of marriage and homecoming in which he had just indulged himself – all this was translated, when he opened his mouth, into a firm, almost boastful confession of faith.

'I want to become a real Jew,' he told his mother and father, in the half-empty hotel lounge, with its beige paintwork and dispiriting decorations. Gilt wires were twisted across entire walls in the shapes of Stars of David, of kibbutz watchtowers, of vague skyscraping cities (unlike any in Israel), of half-human figures dancing the *horra* and holding up Scrolls of the Law. The three of them were sitting there over their coffee-cups, after the meal, waiting for Yitzchak, who had earlier left a message that he would call, as he was in town with a weekend pass.

'I don't suppose,' David added, with a smile that gave his face a mocking expression, though who or what he was mocking none of them could have said, 'there can be a better place to do it in than Israel.'

His parents were as astonished as Joel had been when David had spoken of prayer to him. They were more than astonished; they were worried. 'Why? Why?' they asked. 'Do you believe in God?'

'Yes.'

'Why?' Sarah asked.

'Because I believe He exists.'

It was comic as well as serious; but it was not embarrassing.

'A Jewish God? The Bible, the Talmud, everything?'

'I don't know about everything. I know nothing at all. So how can I say? But I want to find out. And to try to become a Jew is the obvious path for me; at least until I know more I should try to go the way that all the other Jews have gone along. I'm not a Christian, I never could become one; quite apart from anything else, I could never forgive the religion for what it's done to the Jews. But I feel that if I try hard it's possible, it's conceivable, that I could become a Jew. Some kind of Jew. And I want the help that belonging to the group can give me – the guidance, the instruction, the experience.'

Benjamin was more disturbed and at the same time more sympathetic than Sarah. She found it difficult to take David seriously; while he felt some obscure part of himself both vindicated and challenged by what David had said. 'When did you begin to feel like this?' he asked, wondering if the quarrel he had had with David had perhaps been a cause or a symptom of David's alteration.

'In London,' David answered. 'One night there – something happened to me – I began to ask questions I hadn't asked before.' But the memory of the confusion of that evening silenced him. He had said enough. He was relieved that he had spoken at last, and that it had been so easy. He was proud, too, of the surprise he had caused. To go on would merely weaken its effect.

31

Joel progressed from his bed to an armchair next to it, from the armchair to being able to walk about the ward, and from there at last to coming out of the hospital and going to stay temporarily at the same hotel as David, near that in which his parents were living. During this time suggestions were made and decisions were taken which were eventually to lead to the dissolution of the way of life of the Glickman family, as it had been previously taken for granted by them all, even when they had been separated from one another – with its centre the sprawling, iron-roofed house in Observatory, Johannesburg, and its income from the butter factory in Pritchard Street Extension.

There was much argument, but no drama, during those three weeks; much vehemence but little persuasion. Each felt he was doing no more than make explicit what had already happened within him; at the same time each thought the talk of the others idle, wilful, and self-deluded. To all of them the period was one of tedium and scepticism, spent in the unreal surroundings of hotel-lounges, of restaurants and pavement cafés, finally in the departure lounge of Lydda airport. They were relieved when it was over, when they had had the last of the many discussions that had begun with Benjamin's announcement that he wanted to retire to Israel.

'That we're all together here is an opportunity we must grasp,' he said, his hands closing in the air above the restaurant table at which they were sitting. 'Me and your mother can do it, we can manage. We wouldn't live as comfortably as we do in South Africa – there'd be no Annie or John to do everything for us. But, all the same, we're both keeping well, and we could make a life for ourselves.'

He had been talking, he said, to some people he'd met in the Federation Office, who had bought some land about fifteen miles outside Tel Aviv and were planning to lay out a township there. 'But a good one – not like the rubbish you see in other places. Big plots, with decent houses on them, and a club for the people who live there, and so on.' They wanted to attract people like himself who were thinking of retiring, as well as younger business and professional people who were settling in Israel and had some capital behind them – South Africans, Americans, people from England, who were used to a high standard of living. 'Manny Bresloff – you remember him from Joh'burg? – he told me the names of some of the people from South Africa who've put themselves down for plots, and I already knew half a dozen of them. So we wouldn't be lonely, that's for sure.'

As for the business in Johannesburg: there were two possible alternatives. The first was to let Bertie run it for him; he would be keen enough to have it as his own responsibility, and he was competent enough, too, or would be when he had had a little more experience. The other possibility was simply to sell the place. He'd already had invitations to sell from farmers' co-ops; it was the type of business they were itching to get their hands on. Well, if they really wanted it he would let them have it. But they would have to pay!

He wasn't afraid of the cost of the move, of the cost of buying the land and building on it, even though prices in Israel were crazy. Things had been going well in the business in South

Africa. Since he'd bought out Meyer he'd had the best years ever in the creamery; he'd gone into partnership with Ezrael Klein and a couple of others in putting up a block of flats and shops in Hillbrow, and the venture had turned out well, better than he'd anticipated; what he'd invested in the Stock Exchange had lately come splendidly right. He had never done so well in his whole life as he had in those last few years, even though none of the children had known anything about it, they'd been so busy running around with their own affairs – university, England, Israel, whatever they liked.

If all he wanted in the world was money, he would stay in South Africa. But instead of using the money to make more money, he'd rather use it to please himself. Perhaps (who could tell?) he might bring over enough to make an investment in Israel, too; something that might help them here.

There was no one who could reproach him for leaving South Africa, he added – though no one had offered any reproach. The country wasn't a poorer place because he'd lived in it. In any case, what feeling could he have for it when it was ruled by people who'd prayed for Hitler to win the war; who'd waited for the day when they could send the Jews to concentration camps? They now talked differently, they wouldn't touch the Jews, he was sure, they now tried their best to make everyone forget what their past was like. But he had not forgotten. And how much better was their present – when all they knew was to hound the blacks with new laws, new restrictions, new penalties? It wasn't for people like that to tell him what to feel about South Africa. He would miss the country, it was true. He'd spent nearly fifty years in it; it was his life that had passed there.

'But if I can live in Israel for the years I've still got,' he said firmly, 'then this is where I must live. They talk about building a nation here. But the Jews are already a nation, they always have been. A nation's a memory, that's all, a longer memory than any of us can have on our own. And what's the Jewish memory? Does it bear much thinking about? I don't want to leave it to others to make the memory a different one, now that I have the chance, at last.'

'But what's the good of talking like that?' Sarah protested. 'What you've got in your head won't help you in your actual living here. Benjamin, why are you pretending, what are you trying to tell us? I know that you don't really like it here.'

Benjamin's face wrinkled in a queer expression of amusement and chagrin. 'If I choose to live here then I bloody well have the right – the right, do you hear? – *not* to like it!' he said loudly, bringing his hand down with a bang on the tabletop.

32

They all laughed at this answer, but later Joel surprised the others by telling them that he wanted to leave Israel, that he wanted to go back to university and finish his degree in history. This merely made Benjamin more obdurate.

'You suit yourself. It doesn't matter to me, I have my own life.' The phrase he had swallowed down several times before came out almost casually, without Benjamin noticing it until it was said.

Besides, he said, David would be staying in Israel; and David agreed, yes, he would, he wanted to stay. At any rate, he didn't want to leave.

Sarah's dogged, distressed opposition to the idea of the move also had no apparent effect on Benjamin. He didn't care what she did. If she didn't like the idea of living in Israel, she could go and live with Bertie and Rachel; she could keep house for Joel in Johannesburg; she could go and live with her brother,

Samuel. She could do what she liked. But he knew, he added later, that she would come with him; she always did in the end what she was told, though never with any grace, never so that a man could feel himself helped and supported.

That outburst was followed by silence. Then the talk began again. Talk about the costs of building, talk about David going on to one of the *ulpan* courses to learn Hebrew, talk about nationalism, talk about religion, talk about countries, careers, ambitions, talk about currency transfer regulations.

There was Joel asking David, 'Doesn't it put you off – the whole thing – *kashrut*, keeping the Sabbath, all those fanatics in Jerusalem in their kaftans and fur hats?'

David laughed. 'I shouldn't think I'll become one of them. But they don't put me off, no. Why should they? Why shouldn't they believe that God is interested in us keeping our milk and meat separate? Why shouldn't that be a way for us to show our willingness, our obedience to Him? It's too bad if it offends your idea of your own dignity; perhaps you have the wrong idea of it. What are we, after all? What's the whole bloody human race worth? How much better can we do? You know I remember once in London I was sitting in one of those Wren churches, and I thought, here's one of the greatest architects the world's ever seen, his buildings are a marvel to us. But say there *is* a higher intelligence than ours, watching us. Some spirit as intelligent in relation to us as we are to a child who makes a little building out of blocks, a good building for a child of his age. We say, "He's a clever boy." But what do we really think of his building? Do we take it seriously? Don't we pity him in a way for being proud of it? Do we take it more seriously than his table manners, or anything else about him? You see what I mean?'

'No.'

David was annoyed. 'All right, I'm not proselytizing. If you don't want to see it, you don't.' Yet he asked, on another occasion, 'So what do you believe? Or do you think you can get along fine without believing in anything?'

'Oh, I don't know,' Joel answered wearily. 'I just feel that beliefs and justifications and all that kind of stuff aren't as important as I once thought. Or not important in the way I thought they were. They don't last, anyhow. Nothing lasts. We change, so they change.' He looked around for more to say, provoked by the condescension he read on David's face, and found some words. 'It seems to me that we should just be content to be mediators, and not try to be judges.'

'Mediators? I don't understand. What do you think we mediate between?'

'Practically everything. Everything that we're part of and that's part of us. Life and death. Matter and consciousness. Past and future. The tiniest cell in my fingernail's doing it, as much as my mind or my consciousness or any other part of me.

'I told you,' he went on, suddenly vehement. 'I'm tired of trying to find justifications for myself and for what I do. I've had enough of it. The hell with it! I don't owe anyone any explanations or apologies for being alive, or for being a Jew, or for being five foot eight and having brown eyes, or for living in the middle of the twentieth century, or for being white and having a father who made some money in South Africa. I don't have to exonerate myself in front of anyone. Not the *goyim*, not the six million dead, not the blacks, not my father, not the Israelis – no one! I'll do what I like. I'll live where I like. I won't go round telling myself that I can't do this and I can't do that, that I'll be too lonely, that it's too late, the world's too wretched, I'm too guilty. Look, I was nearly dead, I thought I was dead: I know how easily I can be dispensed with. What's true of me is true of everybody else – OK, I don't want to pity myself for it or to admire myself for knowing it. I just want to explore my margin while I can, to take my chances – all of them, including the ones I've been handed on a platter, as well as the ones I may be able to earn for myself. Nobody in the world can do any more, and there's no group or society who can do it for me.'

'You sound like me,' David said, 'Like me some time ago. That kind of thing won't carry you very far. Either you'll realize it and start looking for something else again or –'

'Or I won't,' Joel interrupted, irritatedly.

'Or you'll stop caring. You'll live like most other people do – so busy with themselves that they're never really aware that there's a whole world outside themselves.'

Joel kept to himself his unkind opinion that that, perhaps, was what ailed David. And David wondered at how things had changed since his boyhood, when he had always believed Joel to be wiser than himself.

Talk, talk, talk. When Sarah and Benjamin left for South Africa everything was decided and undecided. But Benjamin had put his name down for one of the plots in the village of which he had spoken. David went to his *ulpan*, which was on a religious kibbutz near Haifa. Joel went to Ramat Elkan to tell the others there that he was leaving, and to collect his things.

33

Leaving the kibbutz was a more painful experience for Joel than he had allowed himself to anticipate, lying in hospital and knowing that that was what he wished to do.

It wasn't easy to leave for good a place where he had put in so much work, and where the results of his work, together with that of all the others, had made so great a difference. When they had come to the hillside after six weeks on a border kibbutz in the Galilee, there had been nothing on it but grass and rock; in those days they had slept under canvas and had had their water brought up to them by tender each day. They had put up every building that could be seen on the crown of the hill; they had laid the pipes that brought their water to them; they had cleared the rocks from the fields round about, that were now real fields, instead of so many tracts of wasteland; they had planted the little trees, still swathed in sacking and tied to stakes, that would one day shade all the paths on the *meshek*. To an outsider it might have looked like an ugly collection of hutments, sheds, vehicles and heaps of building materials; but, though he tried to do so, Joel could not see it as an outsider. It occurred to him that perhaps never again would his work produce such tangible and effective results as it had done here.

The people on the kibbutz were hurt by his defection, as he had known they would be; he had been hurt in the past by the defection of others, and he remembered how painful had been the disappointment and self-doubt he had felt when he had seen the departure of someone he liked or whose work he had valued. Now it was his turn to inflict that pain on others. Raffi, the *sabra* with whom he had guarded the tractor-shed on the night he had been wounded, asked him, 'What for you go? It's no better any other place,' and Ginger from London, whose hair was a wild tangle of coppery red waves and ringlets and errant locks, and whose face beneath was as mild and as plump as a baby's, paid Joel the compliment of saying simply, 'Oh, shit!' – not to Joel, but, as it were, to the world – and turning away so that no one could see the distress in his round, blue eyes.

His courage having failed him, Joel had given out that he might be leaving only temporarily; but most people knew immediately that this was a fiction. Leib, for one, at last felt free to express some of the hostility there had been between them for so long, and which both of them had always been careful to try to conceal.

'I always knew you'd pack in,' he said, making no attempt to hide the reproach – and the satisfaction at having been proved right – in his voice.

It was curious in fact that those who were most reproachful, who were most ready to look at and speak to Joel as if he were some kind of traitor, were those with whom he had got on least well, and who would not miss him at all.

Harry took it for granted that Joel would not be coming back.

'I knew something was going on,' he said. 'Otherwise you'd never have gone out like you did that night. And before – you were in a state.' He laughed abruptly. 'It's the kibbutz cafard.' Then he said, 'If you're going I'll probably go too. I don't think I'll be able to stick it out here without you.'

They were walking together through the olive grove of the abandoned Arab village. Harry walked with stiff strides, his long legs opening and closing like the blades of a pair of scissors. The grey, twisted trees looked more wraith-like than the black shadows they cast on the ground; the grove had an appearance of age, almost of antiquity, to which its neglected, desolate air contributed. The ground was littered with twigs and tiny leaves, with shreds and stones from fallen fruit; and branches had fallen, too.

'What'll you do if you do leave?' Joel asked.

'I don't know. But I don't think I'll leave Israel. I don't fancy the idea of becoming a Jew again.'

'It makes me nervous sometimes, to think of going back among the *goyim*,' Joel confessed. 'But it's funny – what you've just said – my brother's all keen on Israel because he thinks he's become religious, he says he wants to be a real Jew.'

'Well, it's a free country,' Harry answered ironically. 'We admit all types.'

At the end of the grove was a small ditch or gulley, with a tumbledown fence of stone on the other side of it. They jumped over the ditch and sat down on the ground, their backs to the pale sun-warmed stone, their feet dangling above the ooze of mud that glittered in the hollow.

'No,' Harry said, 'I'd rather be an Anglo-Saxon among the Israelis, any day, than a Jew among the *goyim*. I had enough of that.'

Joel threw down a pebble and kicked it away with his shoe before it had reached the ground. 'It wasn't only disadvantages we wanted to get rid of by coming here. It was advantages as well. We wanted to get rid of the advantages of being lucky Jews, Anglo-Saxon Jews, rich Jews, Jews who escaped.'

Harry looked up, frowning, his lips thrust forward in a characteristic, pouting smile, the skin around them drawn smooth and tight. Joel knew he was going to stammer: that smile was almost a part of it. 'But now – but now, you've learned to value those advantages – is that it?'

'In a way, yes. I want to use them, somehow, if I can.'

'Well, I can't say I envy you. Neither the advantages nor the disadvantages.'

But he was making no reproach, passing no judgement. Calmed by the sunshine and the silence around them, by the friendship they felt for one another, by the melancholy of knowing that they would not again be together for many years, if ever, they sat talking together. Then, from far off, they heard the sound of the bell clanging on the kibbutz for the midday meal. Joel was leaving after he had eaten.

They got up to go. The grove was still; the trees held up their dim, wistful branches to the sun.

Harry stood without moving, his head lowered thoughtfully. 'You know what's the worst thing about being a Jew among the *goyim*?' he said. 'I'll tell you. They don't hate us because we killed Christ. They hate us because we produced him, it was from the Jews that he came. Came with all his impossible demands – give all you have to the poor, turn the other cheek when anyone strikes you, look not after a woman with lust in your heart. How can ordinary, hitting, fucking, greedy people do it? So they hate him for asking it of them, and the more they hate him the more they hate the Jews, who're responsible for him.'

'Are you trying to make me stay here?' Joel asked.

'No. I'm just thinking of what you're going back to.'

PART 6

1

Denys Warrenton's small, rapidly blinking, dimly blue eyes were set closely together, his lips were thin and pale, his shoulders were slight, and his legs were short. However, he made up for the lack of distinction in his appearance by the alertness, interest and ingenuousness which he conveyed with every lively movement of his body, every cock of his head, every gesture of his hands. When he was seated he always sat on the very edge of his chair, like an excited schoolboy; when he was on his feet he often rose eagerly on to his toes. He expressed amusement by lowering and shaking his head in a silent laugh; surprise by swaying back and holding up a hand, as if to take an oath; seriousness by nodding repeatedly with a stiffened neck and blinking his eyes even more rapidly than usual; affection by putting his head so much to one side that it almost rested on his shoulder; determination by bringing his hands together in front of his chest and shaking them as though he held a pair of dice concealed within them. Generally he listened and responded with these gestures far more than he spoke; this gave him a reputation for being not only eager and alert but for being deep and sincere as well.

He was sincere, in his way – a way which had always been profitable to him. He was sincere in making mock of his title and the whole institution of the House of Lords; sincere in deploring colour prejudice, the hydrogen bomb, organized religion, English conservatism and English cooking, the famous public school at which he had been educated and the philistinism of the British public; sincere in the modesty with which he pronounced himself to be a man whose only meagre talent lay in spotting the talents of others and nursing them to fruition; sincere in anticipating that the goodwill he showed to the world would be reciprocated by the world; on those sad occasions when this faith was betrayed he was sincere in the dismay and disappointment he showed. Above all, he was sincere in the esteem and adoration with which he regarded his wife and their three children.

The Warrentons' marriage was a famous one. The Warrentons' marriage had been written about in several journals, more than once by one or the other of the Warrentons, who ascribed its success firstly to the love they felt for one another, of course, and then to the similarity of their interests and views, to the frankness with which they thrashed out their problems between them, to the fact that Lady Warrenton (or Meg, as she was referred to in the articles that Denys Warrenton wrote) had never allowed the arduousness of her duties as the mother of the three Warrenton children to come between her work and herself, and had also never allowed her work to come between her and her children. The Warrenton marriage had been on television; so had the Warrenton children, who were famous (among those who went to the Warrentons' parties) for their delightful, barefooted, pyjama'd appearances among the Warrentons' distinguished guests. These appearances were typical of the artlessness and sincerity of the Warrentons' family life, which had always remained extraordinarily little affected by the publicity it had received or by the strains of the many social and intellectual demands the work of the Warrenton parents made upon them. After ten years of marriage Meg and Denys Warrenton were still like young lovers. They held hands in public, they smiled tenderly at one another across rooms full of guests, they spoke to each other in scraps of gibberish meaningful only themselves and bewildering (but charming) to their friends; they played private games together on railway journeys and at dull dinner parties and in their office. They shared their office (the two desks in it, side by side, had been photographed); they shared their bed (that, too, had been photographed); they shared their talent for spotting the talent of others.

They had met while they had both been working for the BBC during the war; since the war they had together revitalized the old-established publishing firm of Kenworthy and Rose. Meg was black-haired, sharp-toothed, even smaller and slighter than Denys, but fully as energetic. Everyone (that is, everyone who knew the Warrentons) agreed that no photograph did Meg full justice, for photography could not reproduce her warm, dark complexion and the mobility of her face when she talked. She was almost as good a talker, people generally agreed, as he was listener.

2

It was in the Warrentons' large, high-ceilinged, ornately-corniced drawing room, with its tall windows overlooking Teviot Square, that Joel and Pamela met again. They found themselves jammed together, facing one another, each with a glass in hand, neither recognizing the other and yet both knowing that they had met before.

There was such a crowd in the room, and the noise rose so deafeningly around them, that they might have done no more than smile fugitively at each other, if they had not been held where they were by the crush, and if Joel had not been feeling so ill-at-ease at knowing so few people there – among the hundred or more who were drinking, talking, smoking, grimacing, laughing, bending forward to hear one another and altogether raising a noise that ascended to the ceiling and seemed to echo from it with a high, sustained, independent, ringing note.

Of all the people Joel had seen, Pamela was the first whose eyes had not slid uninterestedly over or to one side of him, whose face had not worn a strangely blank, abstracted look of excitement that broke abruptly (though not for him) into a hundred creases of amiability, complaisance and gratification. Instead, the young woman looked at him curiously, with half-recognition, with a mouth turned down humorously as someone behind her forced her more closely against him.

You had to shout to be heard. So he shouted, his lips almost touching her ear, half-concealed under the line of her black hair, 'Haven't we met before?'

'Have we?'

'I don't know, I'm asking you.'

She smiled and shook her head to show that she did not know, she could not speak.

'Is it always like this?' Joel shouted at her.

'Every time I've been.'

'God!'

It was impossible to say more. They lost sight of each other. Pamela was taken away by Meg Warrenton, who dragged her through the crowd to meet 'such a sweet, clever man', as she shouted into Pamela's ear, 'an Amewican Anthwopologist who's just spent two years in Kenya and is going to wite the book on the Masai for us.' Pamela found herself in front of a plump, young man in a curiously crumpled and shiny suit, whose face, like his suit, was much creased and yet somehow quite unweary.

No, she shouted at him, she had never been to Kenya. She was from South Africa. Oh, he shouted, he guessed they had problems of their own down there. Yes, she shouted back, they had.

The conversation came to a halt. The American pursed his lips reflectively; as if coming to a decision he took a drink from his glass. Then he pondered for a moment longer.

'Quite a crowd here,' he shouted.

'Isn't there?'

'Yes, there is.'

That was settled.

Pamela said suddenly: 'I've just seen somebody I haven't seen for about eight years.' She hadn't shouted these words, so the American's face expressed total incomprehension. Then, bravely, he made his attempt to reply to her.

'You've been in England how many years?'

'No –' But it was too much of an effort to repeat what she had just said; she had spoken only in the surprise of remembering who Joel was. She looked around the room, seeing again its walls papered in alternating panels of white and royal blue, its tall draped windows, the cubes of lozenges of the cornice thrust out like white teeth under a series of gilded horizontal convexities, the dark-suited men, the bare-armed women, the smoke ascending to the ceiling. Joel Glickman! What on earth was he doing here?

'Excuse me,' she shouted at the American. 'I must go and find my husband.'

But it was in hope of finding Joel that, to his relief, she left the American anthropologist and began to struggle through the throng.

Joel, too, had remembered who Pamela was only after she had been taken away from him; like Pamela about himself, he wondered with much curiosity what she was doing here. He felt that very little time had passed since he had last met her; yet he knew it was hardly less than eight years before, and in another country, another world. He did not know which was the more surprising – how long ago their last meeting was in fact, or how recent it seemed to be.

When she reappeared in front of him he said at once to her, 'You're Pamela.'

'You're Joel.'

'That's right. Joel Glickman?'

'I know.'

'It's fantastic.'

'Isn't it?'

Once again the noise silenced them. They remained smiling at one another.

'It's impossible to talk here,'

'Let's find a quieter place.'

'Where?'

She began to make her way towards the big open double-doors to the room. They passed a struggling, grey-haired waitress with a tray of drinks in her hand, and Joel took one from her and put his empty glass on the tray. 'That's it!' the waitress hissed out; he could not tell if the exclamation was ironical or not.

The crowd thinned out a little near the door. A small, bald, dapper man, a look of concentrated impatience on his face, was taking three tiny, rapid, almost running steps forward and then the same number of steps back, while listening to a much taller and older man, who had a grey fringe of moustache on his upper lip, spectacles on his nose, and a savoury in his hand. The man slipped the savoury under his moustache and went on talking, without apparently noticing the food now in his mouth or his listener's charges and retreats across the little space of carpet between them. 'The whole thing is preposterous,' he was saying. 'If Jesus really couldn't find a place for him we'd have taken him with pleasure. And we said so. We did say so. But –'

In the little hall outside, the hot reek of smoke and gin became quite suddenly a smell rather than an atmosphere; the noise, receding, sounded like a simple roar in the background. Coats were piled on chairs against the walls, men and women were continually passing, from the far end of a carpeted passageway there came the noises of cutlery and glasses being washed. It was possible to talk rather than shout, and as a result Joel and Pamela were shy with one another; they had nothing to say.

'Well?'

'Well!'

'Did you hear that bit about Jesus?' Joel said, looking back. 'And did you see the two men talking! The pair of them!'

'I suppose it was Jesus College they meant. In Cambridge.'

'Or Oxford. I'd worked that out for myself.'

Joel's tone was sharp. Pamela stared at him. The whites of her eyes were large and clear. 'It's all right,' she said mildly. 'I'm sure you know as much about all this as I do.' She gestured towards the room they had just left.

They had lost some of their shyness in the exchange, but none of their wonder at meeting again, in surroundings so different from those in which they had known each other before. With a roughness that betrayed his own curiosity and self-distrust Joel asked her, 'Don't you mind – that I can remember you when you were my father's typist?'

'Why should I mind?'

'Because you've been keeping such grand company since.'

'Do you call this grand company?'

'Don't you?'

'I thought it might be, before I met it,' she admitted.

'And now?'

'Now –' Her shoulders rose, the corners of her mouth went down.

'Still,' Joel said, 'it's much more satisfactory to pull faces about them after you've met them than when you've never had the chance of doing so.'

'Of course. But it would be nicer still if there was no need to pull any faces at all.'

Joel laughed. 'Now you're asking for a lot. Who are they, anyway?' he asked.

'God knows. I've spoken to an American who was writing a book about Kenya. There was nothing very grand about him. I suppose there's the usual lot of people –'

'I saw Professor Transome. He looked just like he looks on television.

'They all do.'

'I mind,' Joel said suddenly, 'that you can remember me when I was at Wits.'

'I thought you did, or you wouldn't have gone for me like that.'

'It makes me feel exposed somehow. I look back and feel I was so stupid and raw and easy to see through, when I knew you.'

'And what are you now?'

Joel laughed. 'Stupid – and raw – and easy to see through. That's what I mind most of all.'

Pamela was smiling; when he saw, between her painted, parted lips, the edges of her teeth, he remembered how white they were.

'You weren't so bad,' she said.

'Thank you. You were very nice.'

She nodded quickly, acknowledging the compliment.

'I remember we always got on well together.'

'Always? We only met about twice.'

'Both times, then.'

A woman wearing on her head a dusty-looking, pale green, scalloped velvet object, came between them, peered shortsightedly and impolitely from one to the other, presenting to each of them in turn a good view of her hideous hat, and went down the passage. They looked at one another, each trying to match doubtful memory with a presence that effaced all but itself. Joel knew that whatever memories he had of Pamela were of a girl, and the person in front of him was plainly no longer a girl. She was still unlined, her colour was high, her eyes were clear, so where the difference lay he could not really tell: it involved her whole appearance, all her features – they were moulded emphatically now, finally, as it were; her skin had lost its gleam, and lay tightly against the bones of her face. He was sure that her hair was much shorter than it had been; he didn't remember it brushed loosely over to one side, rather high off her head, the effect of it being both rough and smart. Pamela saw only that he had put on weight, and his face was pale, under the sallowness of his skin. At the corners of his eyes were a few lines which deepened when he smiled, but never entirely disappeared.

'We did get on well together,' Joel said, and added, as if with an air of apology, 'Every time.'

Pamela stirred. 'I've got to find my husband. I really must.'

'Who is your husband?'

'Malcolm Begbie.' She said the name as if she expected him to have heard of it. But it meant nothing to him.

'Pamela! I was beginning to wonder if you'd come.'

It was their host: small, quick, alert, shaking Pamela's hand, kissing her on the cheek, drawing back to look at her again, his head to one side. 'What a pretty dress.' Only then did he turn to Joel. 'Have we met? I'm Denys Warrenton.'

Joel put out his hand. 'I'm a gatecrasher, I hope you don't mind.'

Warrenton looked at Joel from quite another angle. 'May I ask who you crashed my gates with?' His eyes blinked humorously, but he evidently wanted an answer to his question.

'Peter Dewes.'

'Peter Dewes? Peter Dewes? Oh, Peter, of course. But I really can't let you monopolize the pretty wife of one of my most promising authors. You must come inside, both of you, come.'

He led the way; Joel and Pamela followed. Once they were inside the drawing room they were separated. Joel found he was still carrying his drink in his hand and emptied it at a gulp. He felt he had carried off his part of the meeting with Warrenton rather well; yet he was sorry that he had been exposed in front of Pamela as an interloper, someone who was not there by right, as she obviously was. He was sorrier still that he was weak enough to give the matter any thought at all. 'The pretty wife of one of my most promising authors' – he remembered the phrase. Little Pamela had done very well for herself. She was not to be monopolized by insignificant, uninvited Joel Glickman, guest of Peter Dewes. Peter Dewes? Peter Dewes? Oh, Peter, of course.

He smiled slightly, his eyes half-closed, smarting a little from the smoke in the air, his ears filled with the noise of the party, his body buffeted by the movements of the people around him. He had swallowed his last drink too quickly. The effect it was having on him made him feel like having another.

3

Later they came together again, but this time Pamela was with her husband; Joel was with Peter Dewes and Peter's wife, Sally.

'Malcolm, this is Joel Glickman – Joel –'

Pamela began to make the introductions. Peter and Malcolm knew each other, but Pamela had not met Peter before, and Sally had met neither of the Begbies. So the introductions seemed to take a long time. But it had taken no time at all for

Joel and Malcolm to be staring at each other with complete recognition and great wariness.

'You have met Joel?' Pamela exclaimed at a mutter from Malcolm. 'Where?'

'On the Potchefstroom Road,' Malcolm answered, amused by the obscurity of his answer. His gaze lingered on Joel for a moment longer, before he said to Pamela, 'Come, we must go. The party's breaking up.'

The room was quite suddenly emptier and quieter than it had been for the past hour; the people who were still there stood in knots and clusters, with naked spaces of carpet between them.

'Joel, will we be seeing you again?' Pamela asked.

Joel shrugged. 'I live in London.'

'I haven't even asked you what you're doing. What are you doing?'

'I'm at LSE. Doing research. I'm supposed to be working for a doctorate.'

'That's nice,' she said inanely.

'Is it?'

'Isn't it?'

'I don't know.'

The emptiness of their talk did not matter, for each saw in the other's eyes the meanings that their words lacked. It was that silent, curious, cautiously sympathetic exchange to which they both attended.

Malcolm had been standing aside with Peter and Sally. 'Come on, Pamela,' he called out. 'It's time we were off.'

'On our bicycles!' Peter said.

Malcolm laughed out loud at the phrase. 'What's all this about bicycles?' Sally demanded. 'What's the joke?'

Peter did not explain it to her. Instead he asked her, 'You feeling spare?'

Malcolm laughed again. 'Dead right, man! You can see how *skaam* she is.'

'*Lelik is niks, maar stupid – !*'

The pause that followed was somewhat dejected, though men still smiled. Malcolm moved away. 'Pamela, go and get your coat. I'm waiting.'

'I'm going now. Where do you live, Joel?'

'West Hampstead. Behind John Barnes.'

'We're near Primrose Hill – Regent's Park – it isn't far from you.'

'No.'

'We're in the book.'

She took a pace or two, looked back, and went on towards the door. Joel watched her go. The room was a long one and she walked slowly, soft-footed, across the carpet, her dark head tilted a little forward, her bare arms drooping.

'I didn't know you knew my wife,' Malcolm said, at Joel's aside.

'Yes, we knew each other years ago, in Joh'burg. When I was at Wits.'

'Weren't you supposed to be going to Palestine, or something like that?'

'Yes. I did go. But it's a long time since I left – about four years.'

'What have you been up to since then?'

'I went back to Wits for a couple of years. Then I came here.'

'This suits you better, does it?'

'I suppose so.'

Malcolm nodded, rubbing the blond bristles that had begun to appear on his chin. The hollows of his face were deep, the protuberances stark and hard. His blue eyes were hot, inflamed, prominent.

'And you?' Joel asked, feeling that it was time the other answered rather than asked questions. 'You prefer it here?'

'Sometimes – sometimes not.'

It was clear to them both that neither was going to give away much to the other.

'Are you off?' Joel asked Peter.

'Sure.'

Malcolm walked with them to the door. Pamela was waiting in the hall, talking to Meg Warrenton. Minutes passed before they made their way down the stairs and on to the pavement. Somehow Joel and Pamela found themselves together again. But they did not speak at all. Everybody waved and smiled, and Joel went with Peter and Sally to the car that Peter had parked around the corner.

'Darling, do you think you're sober enough to drive?'

Peter ignored her.

'So – where do you want to go, Joel? You want to come back to the flat with us? There'll be something to eat there.'

'I don't know. Perhaps you can just drop me at the Tube. I think I'll go on to Dora's.'

'Well, I'll take you as far as I can. Come on.'

4

Sally Dewes worked on a fashion magazine; and so made a point of dressing simply, of using no make-up except for some thick, inexpertly-applied lipstick, of wearing her long straight hair like a schoolgirl, with an alice-band to keep it in place. Because of the weight and length of her hair she seldom turned her head without turning her shoulders too; when she threw back her head it seemed to go a little further, always, than might have been expected. These simplicities and easy expenditures of energy were matched by a clear skin, sharply defined features, a straight back, a tall figure, and a complacent conviction that she was entitled to, and would always get, a full share of whatever nourished, sheltered and pleased her.

She and Peter had met in Oxford, where he had been doing research. It was because of her that Peter had abandoned his academic ambitions; Sally had said that she wasn't prepared to be a don's wife, thank you very much, and that had been that. So instead, he had worked miserably for a time in the publicity department of an enormous chemical company; and had then managed to get a job in the publicity department of Kenworthy and Rose, where the pay was less good but the work and prospects more attractive. Just a few weeks before he had at last got the transfer he had been hoping for, into the firm's editorial department. Sally was satisfied with his progress; Peter was satisfied with her satisfaction.

Now, while he drove towards the West End, Sally talked in her confident voice about the people who had been at the party – about so-and-so's dress, and the amount that someone else had been drinking, and what Meg Warrenton had said to her about Peter's work. She asked Peter about Malcolm, whose novel they had both read, but which Joel had not.

'I think he's terribly attractive,' she said. 'In that bony sort of way. He looks much more like a son of the wide open spaces than either of you do, I must say.'

'It's just because he's taller than we are,' Peter protested.

'And bonier,' Sally said, pleased with the word.

Joel let the car carry him, hardly noticing in which direction they were going, hardly listening to Sally's talk. There was still light in the high, firm sky, light in the streets; as if on a level of its own darkness hovered, just above the trees and rooftops. Cream-coloured stucco terraces, with all their scrolls and flutings, sills and pilasters, arranged themselves into squares, were tilted into crescents, ran alongside the car in long straight streets. The rows of black spear-headed railings flickered, vaguely importunate, like something gone wrong on a cinema screen. He felt much drunker now than he had at any time during the party, perhaps because of the fresh air, perhaps because of the movement of the car. He was warm within, but the skin of his face and on the backs of his hands was chilled. Something good and something bad had happened tonight, he thought childishly, without knowing what either was: it seemed minutes later that he understood the good thing to be that he had met Pamela, the bad thing that she was married to Malcolm Begbie.

'What did you think of my boss?' Peter asked him.

'I hardly spoke to him. I can't say I liked what I saw. But I suppose I'd have it in for him, anyway, because he's rich and English and a lord and everything.'

'He's a terrible little fellow, there's no doubt about that.'

'Darling!'

'Well, he is. I don't have to love the man just because he gave me a job. Or his wife.'

'They're not so bad,' Sally insisted. 'Meg's been sweet to me.'

'I hope it's OK that you brought me along,' Joel said. 'He didn't look too charmed when I told him I was there under your patronage.'

'It's all right,' Peter assured him. 'I'll tell him you're writing a book.'

Joel laughed at the idea. 'Will he believe you?'

'Oh, he'll believe anything – for a while. If you ask me, gullibility's the secret of his success. He couldn't push all those books of his so hard if he didn't believe that he was really making a contribution to art, literature, history, modern politics, anything you like, everything that's on his list.'

'Darling! Then anyone could make a success in publishing.'

'Perhaps anyone could if he had the capital and the connections. But the thing is, the important thing is, that you must keep your gullibility liquid, you must always be ready to invest it in something absolutely new, the very latest thing, in any line. It's a valuable asset, you must see that it turns over quickly. No one turns it over faster than Denys Warrenton.'

'What's going to be the secret of your success, then?' Joel asked, knowing the question to be unkind.

'Of mine? My wife!'

'Dar*ling*!'

Sally had taken his reply for a compliment. Peter did not correct her. He concentrated on his driving. They came out just below Hyde Park Corner to a sense of great flat spaces between the gates and monuments; of dangerously tiny, changing spaces between the scurrying cars and buses. The darkness seemed to have ascended, deepened, in the sky.

'Dora's just off Baker Street, isn't she?' Peter said. 'I'll take you there. It isn't out of your way at all.'

The trees in the park were erect, bearing as if with outstretched arms great weights and widths of foliage. Between them were level expanses of turf, and, further back, dark blue air becoming night. Then the squalor and confusion of Marble Arch; another square, a narrow street of brick, with dirty shops and doorways opening directly on the pavement.

'Won't you come in? I'm sure Dora will be glad to see you.'

Sally and Peter consulted together and decided against it.

'Thanks very much,' Joel said. 'For the lift, and for everything else. I enjoyed myself at the party. It was interesting.'

Peter grimaced humorously. 'It's an attraction for tourists.'

'I certainly felt like one.' Then Joel said, 'Can I order a book from you? I'd like to read Begbie's novel.'

Don't be funny. I'll lend you my copy. It's rather good, actually, I think you'll enjoy it.'

'OK. I'll pick it up next time I'm at your place. Good night, Sally. So long, Peter.'

The car drove off. Joel crossed the pavement and rang one of the bells on a door constricted between two shops; each bell had a name on a slip of cardboard pinned up to the side of it. *D. Magid*, said the card next to the bell Joel had pressed.

'Hullo, D. Magid.'

'Joel – Oh, you do smell. Are you drunk?'

'A little.'

5

Dora turned and began making her way up the stairs, which were hardly wider than the door. When Joel closed the street-door behind him the staircase was filled with a brown gloom, lightening to grey only at the landing windows. He followed her, several steps behind, his eyes on the pallid glimmer of her stockinged ankles. Her flat was on the second landing: a large, low-ceilinged untidy room, with a divan bed in a corner, two windows overlooking the street, between them a crammed bookshelf, on top of which were scattered some lumps of rough, uncut semi-precious stones, and a desk with a reading-lamp directed on to a couple of opened books. There were a few shabby rugs on the floor; a few prints stuck with drawing pins on the walls. Two doors led off to the bathroom and kitchen.

'Have you eaten?' Dora asked. Her voice was small but incisive, with a strong South African inflection.

'I had bits of stuff at the party.'

'Enough?'

'I'd like some coffee.'

She made two mugs of Nescafé, and while they drank it – Joel sitting at the desk, Dora on the divan, her back against the wall – he told her about the party. She listened with a detached, musing attentiveness, her small, triangular face raised, except when she bent her head to take little sips at her drink. Her face would have been pretty, with its high, flat cheekbones and drawn cheeks, had her skin not been so tired; had there not been so much care visible on her forehead and about her brown eyes. She was slightly built; her shoulders were childish, the sinews and veins of her hands stood out, even when they were clasped around her mug.

'Have you ever heard of a novelist, Malcolm Begbie – a South African?' Joel asked.

'No, I don't think so.'

'Nor had I. He was there with his wife, and the funny thing is that I knew them both. I'd known them both, anyway, years ago. Years and years ago. His wife used to work for my father, in the creamery, of all things; she was a typist, secretary, something like that. Then she came into some money and went to Cape Town. It was queer seeing her again, really queer, I couldn't get over it. And him, too – he was at Wits the same time as I was.'

'Did you speak to them?'

'A little – I spoke to her – Pamela.'

The name was oddly clumsy on his tongue.

Later Dora worked and Joel lay reading on the bed, looking up occasionally to see her at the desk. The intensity and stillness with which she could work always impressed and touched him; even after the many months he had known her, he still found it difficult to associate her femininity and frailty, her emotional vulnerability, with ambition, heavy books, pads of notepaper, a public role, a career. But she was truly ambitious; often, in comparison with her, he felt himself to be shiftless, restless, a dawdler, a dreamer, no worker at all – someone who walked about the room, smoked, fidgeted, looked up, when he was supposed to be working. Even now, the book he was reading was one of his own, which he had left there on a previous occasion; and what was he doing with it? – looking at her, bent over her books.

He got up and crossed the room, and touched the hand which she had thrust into her cropped, brown hair.

'Time for bed.'

'Is it?'

He kissed her on the cheek. Her eyes remained on the bright black and white page in the lamplight, but she was no longer reading it. She leaned back and put her arm around his waist.

'It would make everything so much simpler if you loved me,' she said, as if she had been thinking of nothing else all evening.

He was silent; sorry for her, ashamed of himself. She sighed and closed her books, one by one, awkwardly, with her left hand, keeping the other arm around his waist. Joel read the titles of the books: Cheshire and Fifoot's *On Contract Law*; *Casebook on Contract* by Chitty, Smith and Thomas.

In bed her body was agile, frail, quickly moist in many places. He was tender towards her, until neither looked for tenderness from the other, only oblivion.

But after she had fallen asleep he was possessed by a shallow, familiar tension that let him doze but did not let him sleep, and in and out of which were woven a host of preoccupations of a shallow, familiar kind: about Dora, about his work, about whether or not he had said the right things to the right people at the party, about his parents' forthcoming visit to London, about how fast time was passing.

More than once during the last year he had woken from such a doze to tell himself in a confused way, 'What's there to worry about? You're only twenty-three,' or 'The war's been over just a few years' – only to remember with dismay when he was fully awake that the war had ended many years before, that in fact he was already twenty-seven. Twenty-seven! It seemed an immense age to him. And the worst of it was that as he grew older the pace of time appeared to increase, each year went by faster than the one before. Instead of time somehow accumulating, thickening, as he had imagined it would, so that it could be moulded into firm, known shapes which would be his life, time was more elusive than ever, it escaped any grasping, it left him dissatisfied and empty-handed, a girl he pitied and exploited asleep at his side, street lamps sending cracks of yellow light between drawn curtains into his sleepless eyes, an alcoholic dryness in his mouth, too much activity in his stomach.

What had he done with himself, where had he been, since he had last seen Pamela? The time in the movement, the time in Israel, two years back in South Africa taking the Honours degree he had disdained before, and now almost two years in London – how, Joel asked himself, overlooking all that had sustained and absorbed and distracted him, how had he endured it all? He was where he had always been: in the dark, still asking himself how he should live, why he didn't live better, still afraid to acknowledge to himself that the shapes his life had indeed assumed were those of failure, lack, dissatisfaction, irritation. How Pamela would despise him if she knew how much the same person he was as when she had last seen him. Only older; unforgivably older.

6

The shrieking voices of the children dropped suddenly, when the bell rang, then rose again, in a final outburst. Pamela, who had been on playground duty, began to cross the stretch of asphalt towards the corner where her class queued up before going into the classroom; around her and in front of her, children darted and swerved in all directions. The retreating patches of moisture on the tar gleamed and sparkled so brightly under the scurrying feet of the children that it was a relief for her to look up, when she could, and see how mildly blue the sky was, how much white cloud hung in it, how small and weak the sun really was, above the low, ugly, Gothicized school building.

There were thirty-five six-year-old boys and girls in her class. As always after break, she read a story from a book to them, for she had found nothing settled them so quickly; then she issued arithmetic cards and went around the class looking at and marking the children's attempts to deal with them. She sharpened many pencils and blew some noses; she traced and confiscated (until the end of the lesson) a missing Dinky toy which one boy claimed had been stolen from him and another insisted had been given to him; she praised some children for the work they were doing, reproved one or two others, and sat down, for the sheer pleasure of it, next to Mickey Pentopolous, a recent arrival from Cyprus and her favourite in the class – not for any aptitude he showed in his lessons, but simply for the size of his black eyes, the length and curliness of his black hair, the sturdiness of his chest and the gruffness of his voice. He, like many others of the children, called her 'Miss Bigbee', under the impression that that was her name, which gave Pamela a vision of herself as the kind of giant, flying monster she must sometimes appear to them to be.

The last few minutes of the lesson were spent in reciting, in chorus with them and with accompanying hand movements, some of the little rhymes she had taught them.

> Five little ducks went out to play,
> Over the hills and far away.
> Old mother duck said quack-quack-quack,
> But only FOUR little ducks came back.

The ringing of the bell sent a quiver through her, through the entire class; at once a general shuffling, banging and chirping began. She still had to see her class into the cloakrooms, where they went to the lavatory and washed their hands; then she led them into the school hall for lunch. Her responsibilities for them ended there; usually it was at that moment that the fatigue of the entire morning's work overtook her. But she hurried back to her classroom, tidied it up for the teacher who took over from her after lunch every day, packed into her case the books and papers she was taking home with her, and set off at a quick pace across the playground towards the gate.

She was already at the gate when Mr Dinwoody, the headmaster of the junior school, called her. 'Mrs Begbie, Mrs Begbie, can I have a word with you?'

Mr Dinwoody's word became ten, became a hundred; they all dealt with the absolute necessity of Pamela not failing to hand in, by ten o'clock on Friday morning, the cash and unsold tickets for the combined infant and junior school concert due to take place the following week. Mr Dinwoody had a small, pallidy shining, bald head, attached to a thin neck, and an ingratiating smile which didn't for a moment conceal his fussy determination to have his way in every particular. Pamela, who had agreed to be responsible for the infants' sale of tickets, listened to him in a quiet frenzy of impatience, her eyes fixed madly on the widening and narrowing gap between his neck and collar button. At the first chance he gave her she assured him that she had not forgotten, that she had everything under control, that she wouldn't fail him. But Mr Dinwoody remained unconvinced. It was most important, he repeated for the third or fourth time; they had to know just how many tickets had been sold so that arrangements could be put in hand for the teas to be served afterwards. And he wanted to be able to announce on the night of the concert, just how much money had been raised; it always made a good impression ...

At that point, mercifully, it began to rain. Pamela turned up the collar of her raincoat; Mr Dinwoody looked up with displeasure at the sky, looked down with greater displeasure at the grey sleeve of his suit, on which a few dark drops had fallen, and with a final, 'Friday morning – mind!' busily made his way back to the building.

Then she had to wait for a bus, on the main road, while the rain came down, held off, came down more lightly, stopped altogether and the sun broke through once more, all within the space of a few minutes. Bright drops slid down the side of the bus-shelter, hung from the panels of every passing car, shivered on the hedges and rose-bushes of the gardens of the houses opposite. The sky looked mild and innocent again, with clouds moving casually across it.

7

When she saw the bus approaching, Pamela decided that she was mad, cracked in the head. Every day it was the same: she fled from home to school as if her life depended on it, and then fled from school back home again, as if she had betrayed herself by staying away from it for so long. Or as if she might find, when she got there, that something of great importance had happened while she had been away. But nothing would have happened; all she would have betrayed during her absence, in her absorption in her work, was her own unhappiness.

That you could develop a loyalty to unhappiness, that you could look around for it when it had been forgotten for a spell, that you could shake it, poke it for response, be reassured when you felt its movement within and alongside yourself, was one of the things Pamela had been most surprised to learn from her experience. Another had been that unhappiness could be intense and persistent, affecting everything she did, and yet not be disabling. She could be unhappy and yet remain a competent teacher, cook the food that she ate, read newspapers

429

and books and have opinions on what she read, meet people socially and converse with them, sleep night after night with the man who was the cause of her unhappiness, make love to him, and write reasonably cheerful letters home to her mother.

All of which went to show, she often felt, that she lacked depth of feeling, lacked strength, lacked passion, was incapable of being truly, profoundly unhappy. Was unworthy, in fact, of her own unhappiness, particularly and generally; which was in itself another reason for unhappiness.

Unhappiness was circular in all its movements; it neither advanced nor retreated, led neither forward nor back. Unhappiness sapped the heart and life out of all her responses, made all she did appear trivial and insignificant; and found in the triviality and insignificance of her actions another reason for unhappiness. Then it jeered at her for being so trivially, so modestly, so civilly unhappy, unhappy in such comfort.

How wretched did you have to be, she sometimes wondered, before you ran screaming into the streets, or talked to yourself and waved your arms about on the tops of buses, or thrust your head into a gas cooker? It was only at moments that she could imagine herself doing any of these things; but she felt that she understood far more deeply than ever before those who did. Unhappiness was egocentric, interested only in itself, it was true; yet what had happened to her had brought her an appalled, intermittent consciousness of the individuality of suffering that she had never had previously. Pain, failure, madness, imprisonment were not, as she had always unthinkingly imagined them, an abyss, a darkness, an undifferentiated mass: each sufferer, of whatever kind, had to bear his portion by himself, in all the weight, sharpness and length it had for him. 'It must come to an end!' she exclaimed within herself; it was intolerable that there should be so much individual wretchedness and pain in the world, and that it should just go on, from one person to another; and her exclamation made no difference to herself, or to all the others.

The bus jerked up the Hendon Way; the repetitive, semidetached houses with their scab-like, red-tiled roofs went by, unreal in their repetition; an inch or two from her forehead the drops of rain on the moving window vibrated, or one or another of them suddenly ran down at an angle, becoming a trickle, then nothing at all. She saw and did not see what was before her open eyes; a line creased the middle of her brow, her lips were pressed together and their corners were turned down, slightly, girlishly, sullenly, as if to contradict the openness of her eyes.

She had, in all seriousness, with the conviction that this was the rational thing to do, proposed terms, periods, to her unhappiness. It would come to an end by Christmas; surely it would be gone when they went on their holiday to the continent in spring; it would end when Malcolm's mother came to stay with them. But each of these terms had passed, and there had been no change. She and Malcolm were left confronting each other in the same silence, or with the same recriminations; she looked up from her meals or her books to see Malcolm looking at her with the same clenched hatred in his expression, as if she were the worst enemy he had ever had. He pestered her still at times with the same nagging, derisive questions about her innocent past, harrying her obsessively about the school she had gone to, the jobs she had held, the degree she had taken, the books she had admired, the boyfriends she had had, the money her mother had come into, the man her mother had recently married, the letters her mother wrote to her, the opinions she held about people, London, life, anything. He made unreasonable demands of her time, of her body, of her patience, and despised her when she gave in to him and shouted at her when she refused to; he told her that he did not love her, and had never loved her, that he

431

was incapable of loving anyone; he invited her to be unfaithful to him and assured her that he would not hesitate – he had never hesitated – to be unfaithful to her.

Yet they went on living together, with remissions of calm indifference, stubborn neutrality, or exhaustion; they had done so for far longer than she would ever have thought imaginable. Months, indeed, had become years – well, almost two years. For she could more or less date the beginning of their unhappiness, even if she could not put a term to it; it was after Malcolm's first success, after his publishers had enthusiastically accepted the manuscript of his first novel, that he had turned against her. But while that success may have precipitated his anger with her, it had not caused it: of that she was sure. His anger must have been there all the time; it must have been there before they had married, and in their first happy period together in Johannesburg; perhaps he had felt it the very first time he had seen her in the flat in Sea Point, when he had called to talk about his father's estate with her mother, and she, Pamela, had come in from a game of tennis, dressed like a fool in a short, white tennis dress that left her thighs bare, her racket in her hand, shouting at the maid to run a bath.

The bus turned, and Pamela's thoughts swung heavily with it, away from the past, away from what she had thought of him then and later, the impression of strength, detachment and rigorous ambition he had made upon her, the admiration she had felt for what he had shown her of his work; away from speculations about what she might have been to his imagination, what she might have represented among his aspirations; away from speculations about his relations with his mother. There was no point in thinking about the past, in trying to remake it, to look in it now for warnings of events that had already taken place. In any case, the lessons of the past were never those one thought one was learning when one most needed them.

She did not know what depressed her more outside the window of the bus: the weighty, meaningless confusion of what she saw, or its simultaneous, meek orderliness. The bus was in the Finchley Road now; the houses on it were much bigger than those on the road they had left, older, more elaborate, built to last longer, with flights of steps going up to ponderous hooded doors. But just because they were so much more solid they looked as though they were lived in solely by nomad electricians and carpenters, always busy at the task of sub-dividing them. Soon there would be the first of the blocks of flats, then the traffic jams around the Tube station. In fifteen minutes she would be home once more.

He hated her. She knew it, though he had never used the word to her. He did not need to. The way he looked at her was worse, almost, than the words he used about her; his eyes shallow and watchful, always following her. Only recently had it become possible for her to face the idea of his hatred without panic. Yet what she now believed was more hopeless than her earlier notions that she must have deserved his hatred, that she must have failed or betrayed or misunderstood him. Panic was irrelevant to belief of the kind she now had.

What he hated was what she was: it was her life, her vital principle, that threatened him and that he felt he had to overcome, to extirpate. Simply by living with him, by wanting to live with him, by accepting that she could do no better for herself than live with him, by offering again and again to love him, she challenged and enraged him. He was a man who never escaped from an exacerbated sense of defeat; that was precisely why he was a success.

Poor Malcolm! She groaned inwardly at the thought of the torment of his ambition. In South Africa things had appeared to be so much simpler, they had been so much younger and less experienced. There, if you wanted to make money, if you wanted to have your name in the papers, if you wanted to marry this or that girl, if you wanted to write a book, if you wanted to come to London, then you considered yourself ambitious, everyone thought you were ambitious. But here, in London, surrounded by an infinity of streets, a never-diminishing surge of population, by distractions and opportunities which appeared everywhere as unpredictable as the views the city offered of itself through its own thick atmosphere, she had seen his ambitions lose their hardness and simplicity of outline, become diffuse, strange to him, always unsatisfactory, but never moderate. She knew what snobberies he had developed and what acute, trivial shames; how much he despised both his own past and the meagreness of the ambitions that had helped him to sever himself from it (she, too, among them); how much he felt betrayed by his work, which did not increasingly sustain or support him, as he had once expected it to, but which instead he had to drive on, drive on, day after day, for an end which was so uncertain to him, and which the work did not itself contain; how he was filled at times with an absurd envy and rage at the success of others, in any field – lawyers, businessmen, scientists, actors, academics. 'The ambitions of a Tamburlaine and the habits of a toady'; that was how he had once described himself to her, pleased by the phrase. But it had helped him little to formulate it.

And to think that she had imagined it would be simple to put in the service of his ambition whatever she had had in the way of spirit, money and health; that she had believed that through him, all her privileges would find not only their form but their justification, too! She hadn't known then how much the world could be hated by those who wished to remake it, or add to it. She had thought that on one side lay kindness, generosity, constructive endeavour and love, and on the other hatred, destructiveness and frustration; and that the two sides could never be confused. Now Malcolm had taught her that there were no sides, there were only interpenetrations, mutual dependences, dark concurrences. By that lesson or vision, even more than by her own incredulity at finding herself hated, she had been rendered incapable of decision and movement.

What were they to do? What was she to do? She was not surprised to step off the bus with that last interminable question unanswered.

8

She hesitated on the pavement, trying to make up her mind about a much simpler question: whether or not to cross the stream of the traffic for the sake of going to a delicatessen shop just off the main road, or whether to go on to one of the smaller, less interesting shops which were more directly on her walk home. The problem was complicated for her by the fact that she did not know whether or not she would find Malcolm at home for lunch; ever since Swannie had arrived on his visit, Malcolm had more or less given up any pretence to be working seriously, and had gone on an orgy of sightseeing, gallery-visiting and general, aimless wandering about with his visitor.

Finally she decided to go to the delicatessen; the most she could hope to get from the other shops would be a tin of steak and kidney pudding or a tin of tomato soup, and she felt like treating herself to something a little better. She would buy some of the cold meats and ready-made salads at the delicatessen. And some olives. If Malcolm wasn't there she would have just a bit of it and leave the rest for their supper that evening.

She stood on the corner, waiting for the lights to change, the entrance to Swiss Cottage Tube station behind her. The traffic went by, glittering, stinking, whining; over to the left was the great dark red structure of the local Odeon, like a fortress or a prison. So many busy roads met at this point that she was never quite sure just where or when she should cross, which traffic light she should watch for.

'Don't look so worried,' a voice said to her.

She turned, startled, and saw Joel. For an instant she thought he knew what she was truly most worried about; and that momentary feeling of guilt and exposure made her voice, when she answered him, emphatic and breathless.

'It's the traffic!' she cried. 'I never know how to get across here.'

'I'll help you.'

He was smiling cheerfully at her; the sunlight glinted off his plump, sallow cheeks and he stood with his arms a little apart, hanging down, as if forced to do so by the thickness of his own figure. When he moved to her side she lost the sense she had of him as someone thick, dumpy, boyish, in a jacket too tight for him. The lights changed and they began to cross the road. It was perfectly simple, after all. 'There we are,' he said, when they reached the opposite pavement. He had not touched her, but he seemed to relinquish her all the same, drawing back. 'Things always happen in pairs,' he said. 'I knew I'd meet you again.'

'If we hadn't met last time we wouldn't even have known each other now.'

'That's why a benevolent Providence sees to it that things happen in pairs.'

They were smiling, pleased to have met one another; it seemed a small triumph over the size and turmoil of everything around them. Through an aperture in a glassed-in tobacconist's kiosk, the face of a sad, captive, bespectacled, hairy-chinned woman stared at them.

'Perhaps we've passed each other in the street lots of times,' Pamela said.

'Perhaps we have. Or in John Barnes, on a Saturday morning.

She laughed. 'You go there too? Anyway,' she said, taking a step forward, 'Providence was guiding me to that delicatessen over there. I must get a move on.' Then she stopped. 'But we must fix something, Joel. We can't wait for Providence every time. It takes so long, apart from anything else! Why don't you come round one evening? I'd like to see you, I want to find out what's been happening to you.'

'Thank you, I'd like to come.'

'Come for dinner. Or for coffee. We're in most evenings, really. What about next week – say, today a week?'

'Do you mean it?'

'Of course.'

'I'll come for coffee, then. Thank you very much.'

'Not for dinner?'

'No, why should you bother? Coffee'll be fine. About half past eight? Nine? What's the address?'

When he had written down her address on a scrap of paper which he took from his wallet, she said, 'I'll put it in the book that you're coming, first thing when I get home. So I'm definitely expecting you.'

'Then I'll definitely come.'

'Good.' She smiled at him, he at her; each of them lifted a hand at the other and turned away.

Five minutes later Pamela had all but forgotten about the meeting, except for that small part of her mind which still retained the intention of writing down in her engagement book the appointment she had just made. The frown was back on her brow; her thoughts were again moving backwards and forwards along the grooves they escaped from so seldom and returned to each time with such guilt, with such self-abasing relief.

9

'So what does your literary sensibility say, when it's confronted with all this – with this process of process that's taken us over? In a special trembly voice it says: More than ever we are the guardians of what is essentially private in human experience; we remind you that consciousness remains an individual affair and always will be; that no technical revolution can affect the truth that each of us is forever alone with the inwardness of his own fate.' Malcolm abandoned his special, trembly voice. 'And you know what the world answers to that?'

'It tests another hydrogen bomb.'

'Exactly. And having done so, satisfied with the results, it says, Say that again, you literary gentleman, say it controversially, say it sensationally, and we'll make you our Personality of the Week. Last week we had a racing driver, next week there'll be an Indian who lives on water and monkey-nuts, and the week after that we're going to have another controversial and intransigent writer who says that the industrial world is a stinking corpse and he is a gift from God. And most of the literary gentlemen are only too eager to oblige – for the fee, for the fame, for the good effect it'll have on the sales of their next book. Perhaps there are a few really incorruptible spirits who don't oblige, who won't perform and prance and simper and pull terrible faces. But they're very rare, very rare indeed. And perhaps they're even less capable than the others of admitting that something irreversible has happened – to the world, and so, also, to them, to the place they can occupy in the mind of society, to the kind of attention their audience can spare, to what their audience has become.'

'So where does all this lead you to?' Swannie asked.

'Well, I certainly don't believe in running away from it, or in pretending that it isn't happening. Or in shuddering at it and crying out, Ooh it's so ugly, it isn't nice, I wish I'd been born an eighteenth-century gentleman with a landed estate. What have we got to lose? A particular notion of what's important in history and what isn't? A literary culture? Most people have never known anything about them, anyway. A sense of localness, a variety of styles of living? Too bad! As for that individual consciousness that's supposed to be so threatened, it's a burden most people would be glad to get rid of. They don't feel threatened by the process I was talking about; all they're afraid of is that they might be left out of it, they're disappointed because they're not totally absorbed into it – into the business of production and consumption and disposal, which is the one true passion of the soul everyone shares nowadays. And who's to blame them? Not me. Certainly not me.'

Malcolm leaned back and grinned suddenly. 'Christ, you want to know how insupportable human beings are? In their private, natural, inward, individual state? In detail? Then get married!'

'No thank you. I don't like women.'

The confessions had not been difficult for them to make; each knew the other to be already aware of what he had said. Looking at Swannie, seeing again his round face, which was smaller than he had remembered it and which was still a little unreal in these surroundings, even after the many days they had spent together, a strange thought occurred to Malcolm: How much more friendship was like love was supposed to be than love itself was.

'I've been thinking,' Swannie said. 'You should come back to South Africa. This place doesn't need you. We do.'

Malcolm answered jeeringly, because of the affection he had felt a moment before. 'What makes you say that? Patriotism? Or do you think I should just settle for being a big fish in a little pond?'

'You say you don't want to run away from the real world. Well, you could count, Malcolm, you could make a difference in a country like South Africa. You'll never be anything but a hanger-on here. And a hanger-on to what? To what you go around saying every day is dead and meaningless and played out! Not the England of consumption and production, all right, but the England of – of high culture and –' Swannie waved his hand in the air – 'literary resonances. The England James and Eliot came looking for. You can't have it both ways. Either you mean what you said about the way things are going, or the whole harangue is just your way of consoling yourself for being another provincial, another colonial outsider. An outsider to what you must believe still exists, after all, and which you want to sniff and lick and hang on to, whatever the cost.'

In another tone of voice Swannie said, 'Besides, South Africa isn't such a little pond. Sure, in comparison with England maybe it looks drab and makeshift and confused. But that shouldn't scare a prophet of the new order like you. And it's already managed to produce some pretty big fish: that's one of the extraordinary things about the place. I was thinking about it just the other day – Rhodes, Kruger, Smuts and Gandhi were all alive and active in the country, all at the same time. That's a pretty big fishery for you, by any standards. It's happened once, it can happen again.'

'They were all in politics.'

'Well?'

The two men remained staring at one another.

'It's up to you,' Swannie said. 'It's up to you to decide whether you're going to make the maximum effect you're capable of, or whether you're going to be just someone who's – who's affected. By this stuff, among other things.'

He gestured over his shoulder towards the buildings of Hampton Court behind him. The two men were having lunch in the open-air section of the tearoom; they were sitting at one of the wobbly tin tables scattered about near a space of shaven lawn. It was a grey, clouded rather heavy morning, yet the air was full of a light that gleamed in haphazard suspended patches, above the grass, the twisted crab-apple trees in formal rows, the hedges and thick brick walls that divided one section of the grounds from another. The palace itself was hardly visible among the bigger more distant trees; in the complication of the light, its pinnacles and chimneys looked no more substantial than the foliage which obscured them.

'You reckon I should get back my roots?'

'I haven't used the word. I'm not going to either. It's much too late for that kind of stuff. I see the whole thing so differently from you in some ways. I agree, what you call the process of process is taking over, but the result is that we're all being forced into our own individuality more than people ever have been before; intolerably so. No absolutes for each of us outside our own feelings; no scale of time even imaginable outside the passing moments of the process. But we can't live like that – we're not birds, or dogs!'

'So?'

'So we need people who'll take risk for us. They need them here in England, we need them there – people who know what's going on and who're prepared to work with it, without just sinking into it like all those others you were talking about. Leaders, if that's the word you want to use. And the biggest risk *you* can take as a writer – as the person you are, altogether – is to go back. That's why you need us. That's precisely why I'm telling you to do it, not because of any crap about roots. Or you can play it safe here and live like some kind of metropolitan literary gentleman, whatever that means nowadays. You know better than I do.'

10

Swannie was now a lecturer in comparative literature at the Afrikaans university in Pretoria; he was travelling for a few months in Europe on a Government scholarship. He was quieter and more subdued than Malcolm had ever known him to be; he also drank far less. All this he ascribed to the fact when Malcolm commented on it, that he had finally accepted his own nature and its inclinations. But he said the words with aversion, cutting under their truth even as he uttered them. He also told Malcolm that he taught his students from memory; he found the books he admired too depressing to read. 'You read Dickens or someone, and you see all that vitality and depth of feeling going on, and you compare it with yourself, with what you're capable of feeling and seeing, with the way you live – no, it's too much, I'm not prepared to do it.'

Yet with what risks, in how much loneliness, Swannie lived! In Pretoria! Malcolm returned again and again to the thought; and he returned, too, to the challenge Swannie had thrown out to him. It had been a great relief to hear Swannie talk, after listening to all those supposedly clever people in London who solemnly asked him, sooner or later, 'Do you think you'll be able to go on working, now that you're cut off from your roots?' As if he hadn't been goaded into his ambitions, hadn't chosen his career, precisely with the intention of leaving behind what they were too smug and stupid ever to think of as 'roots' – humiliations, isolations, angers, hatreds, frustrations …

But what if they could never be left behind? If they were the ground of his being, the mode of his understanding? If the incurable singleness of his body among so many millions of others was one aspect of them, its mortality another, the limitations of his mind a third? He had worked hard, for many years; he had been determined to do work that would stand out, stand apart, individual, meaningful, distinctive and recognizable by others; only in that sense had 'art' been his intention. He could say that he had succeeded; at least, that he had begun to succeed. But wasn't it time that he, like Swannie, 'accepted' his own nature, and ceased to hope that some success he hadn't yet attained – some book he hadn't yet written, some recognition he hadn't yet had, some wealth he hadn't yet earned – could assuage his angers? Shouldn't he rather try to provide them with a worthy object? Worthier, for example, than wretched Pamela; smaller, more manageable than the world in general and all the people in it? Especially as he was now sure of two things he had only suspected before: that the kind of work he was trying to do would mean less and less to fewer and fewer people, as he had pointed out to Swannie, with a kind of rhetorical glee; and that he would continue to work at it, he would never give it up.

The day after Swannie had urged him to go back to South Africa it seemed to Malcolm that he had been thinking of the possibility for weeks. Carefully, he dwelt upon the least attractive features of the country – its racial and cultural confusions, the crass racialism of its rulers and the oppressiveness of their rule, its provinciality, the drab lack of style of its cities, the narrowness of mind that all its peoples shared, with the blacks shut off from real education or enlightenment, and gross, prized, material comforts the only adornment of the life enjoyed by the whites. Of its compensations, its beauties and potentialities, he chose not to think; they were not directly to the point.

'What would you say,' he asked Pamela, 'if I were to say that we should go back to South Africa?'

'I'll wait until you say it,' she answered, wearily pert.

Less evasive replies had infuriated Malcolm in the past. She waited for an attack from him, but it did not come.

Instead, he told Pamela that he had hired a car and intended doing a bit of a tour with Swannie – Oxford, the Cotswolds, Stratford. Then Swannie would be off, Malcolm would go back to his work, everything would return to normal.

11

Arriving at Meyer Glickman's house in Cape Town, Sarah and Benjamin found only his wife, Roise, at home. She made them welcome, kissing each of them in turn, chirping out words of Yiddish and fluttering her hands in eager, inefficient movements, so that the loose sleeves of her dress fell back to reveal her thin, blue-veined arms. She issued instruction to the servants to carry the suitcases Sarah and Benjamin had brought with them into the guest bedroom, and then to make tea, *gleich, gleich*. Having given these orders, Roise made sure they were carried out; she pursued the servants down the passages and into the kitchen, her head craned forward shortsightedly at the end of her long neck.

Sarah and Benjamin were left in the large living room, the windows on one side showing a view of the rough flank of one of the Twelve Apostles, and the windows on the other looking over a terraced garden, and over the roofs of a few houses scattered at a distance, to the width of the Atlantic beyond – blue-grey, faintly rippling, gleaming not at all, under a cloudy sky. Benjamin looked out of one window, Sarah out of the other; they met in the middle of the room, and sat on a couch, waiting for Roise's return.

'She's looking well.'

'Yes, she doesn't change. And she still keeps everything beautiful, doesn't she?'

Roise came in, following the tray that a white-capped, white-aproned Cape Coloured girl was carrying. When the girl had put the tray down on the table, Roise hovered over it, inspecting it once more, to make absolutely sure that everything that should have been on it was there. Satisfied by her inspection, Roise told the girl, '*Bet Alfred arein kummen.*'

Alfred, white-jacketed, yellow-skinned, with a sardonic slant to his black brows, came in.

'*Heitz ain dem faier,*' Roise directed him. Alfred knelt and lit the fire, which had already been laid in the grate. Soon it was burning cheerfully; the curtains were drawn; the tea had been poured out; and Roise sat down with her brother-in-law and his wife. But she did not sit for long. The dinner, the dinner, she had to go and see what was happening to it.

The fact that her husband had been a very rich man for many years, that she lived in a house she would have thought a palace as a girl in the old country, and that she had servants to do all the work for her, had never in the least affected Roise's view of herself or her duties. She had to cherish her heavy, gleaming furniture, present enormous meals at the right times, bicker over the price and quality of every item that came into her house, and generally carry on in the manner of a frugal, conscientious *berye* from any *shtel* in Lithuania.

Sarah heard the sound of a car on the little asphalted driveway. 'I think they've come.'

Benjamin went to the window, drew aside a corner of the curtain and looked out. Yes, they had come. The car had pulled up at the front door. Morry Glickman and the driver, who was dressed in a white coat and peaked cap, got out of the front of the car, and the driver opened one of the back doors.

A light aluminium crutch appeared through the open door, then another, both of which the driver handed to Morry. The driver thrust his head and shoulders into the car and pulled at what appeared to be a great weight. Meyer emerged slowly, one arm around the driver's neck, the other grasping for support on the front seat of the car, then the door column, the door itself, and finally at Morry, who put his crutches in his hands. Only when Meyer was firmly on his feet, supported by his crutches, did the driver withdraw.

Meyer stood still for a moment, looking up at the dozen steps which led to the front verandah of the house – because of those steps he was now trying to sell the house; he wanted to move to a block of flats which would have a lift and no steps to its foyer – and then, slowly, hobbling heavily, made his way round the side of the house. There was a slope on that side, and he found it easier to manage than the steps.

He had not seen his brother watching him; but Morry, who ran up the steps, letting his father make his own way into the house, noticed Benjamin at the window and waved to him.

Morry was in the room first: he was a handsome, hard-featured, rather taciturn man in his mid-thirties, who still bore very visibly, in the way he carried his shoulders and head, the mark of the five years he had spent in the army. He greeted his uncle and aunt, in a rather rasping, unwilling voice.

'We'll be fellow-travellers, hey?'

'It's good to have company on board, among a crowd of strangers,' Benjamin said.

'Depends on the company,' Morry answered grimly. But that, as people often said about him, was only his way. He and his wife were taking their younger son, Selwyn, to London so that he could be examined by specialists there; the boy's left leg had been in irons for the past few years.

'Where's your wife?' Sarah asked.

'She'll be here soon, with the children.'

The rubber tips of Meyer's crutches were heard on the polished parquet of the hall, before he came into the room. He was dressed as carefully as ever, but his clothes no longer fitted him; his body had grown smaller and had changed its shape since he had fallen and broken his thigh the previous year. His skin no longer fitted him either; it hung dry, loose and colourless from the bones of his face and tendons of his neck. His eyes swam towards the recognitions they made.

'*Nu,*' he said, nodding his head ironically and looking from one to the other in the room, 'we make progress.'

12

Seated around the table for dinner that night were Meyer and Roise; Benjamin and Sarah; Morry and his wife, Rina, and their two sons, Ivor and Selwyn; Meyer's daughter, Ethel, and her husband, Max; and Yitzchak Sklar, who was working as a storeman in the mill owned by Meyer.

There was little conversation during the meal, for Meyer's family treated their food with considerable respect, and the food – a cold *gefilte* fish, clear chicken soup with a baked *pirogen* inside each plate, roast beef with prunes and three vegetables, and fruit salad – was declared by everyone to be excellent, even by Roise's standards.

Halfway through the meal the two boys became restless, and were allowed to take their plates into what had once been the playroom for Morry and Ethel, where they settled down to play a game on the pocket-billiard table which still stood there, and was one of the great attractions of the house for all Meyer's grandchildren. Ivor and Selwyn had been brought to the meal as a last special treat before the leavetaking the next day; while the others were away, Ivor was to stay with his uncle and aunt. He was a strained, silent boy, resembling his father, and was used to being overlooked in favour of his much younger, plump, petulant, bright-eyed brother, whose lurching, clattering walk and knowing demeanour had always secured for him the watchfulness of his parents and kisses and caresses from everyone else.

'There are two *kailikes* in the family, you see,' Meyer said to Benjamin, when the door had closed behind the two boys. 'One old one, one young one.'

'Dad!' Ethel reproved him, from her end of the table.

'Which one musn't I call a *kailike*? Me? Or the little one?'

'Both.'

'So find me another word.'

447

'Leave him,' Morry interjected. 'Let him talk. He thinks I listen to him?' He jerked his head to one side, to show how little he listened. Rina, with lowered eyes, attended to the food on her plate.

Immediately after the meal, Morry and Rina got up to go; they had to finish their packing, and it was time the children were in bed anyway. Selwyn protested loudly at being taken away from his game; then limped clumsily but determinedly around the table, exacting a goodnight kiss from every adult there, while his parents and brother waited for him at the door.

'I've told Morry he's wasting his money,' Meyer said, after they had gone. 'You think they can perform miracles in London? Nowadays everyone wants to run to London if he cuts his finger. The doctors are doing everything they can, they won't learn anything different in London.'

'Our medical standards are very high,' Max said, hoarsely eager to please. 'There was an American professor visiting the other day – I read in the paper – he said we don't take second place to any other country in the world.'

'Listen to the expert. Listen to the reader of newspapers.'

Sycophantically, trapped by his own bulk between his chair and the table, Max laughed. Ethel, who shared her family's low opinion of her husband, smiled more sincerely. She sat upright, almost as large as Max himself, but supported externally by a carapace of corsets, and internally by a determined, managerial nature. Max had no such props to sustain him, so year by year his face and belly expanded, his voice retreated further down in his throat, his eyes grew more humid and sentimental in expression.

'And how's Joel?' Meyer rounded on Benjamin, the contemplation of his son-in-law having confirmed him in his ill-temper. 'Is he a professor yet?'

'Not yet. But he seems to be doing quite well, from what he writes us. We'll be able to tell better when we're there.'

'He's another one that South Africa isn't good enough for. He must also go running to London. You think he'll be able to make a living?'

'I don't know,' Benjamin replied unhappily. 'He doesn't ask for money.'

'He's working,' Sarah said. 'If that's the kind of life he wants for himself, I'm perfectly happy.'

'What work?'

Sarah was less certain than she had been before.

'I think he teaches part-time. And he's writing a thesis, doing his doctorate. After that – I don't know – I suppose he'll be able to find something.'

'A lerrind boy,' Roise said, impressed; for which she earned a glare from Meyer.

'And how's your other lerrind boy, David? Is he still in Haifa?'

'Ja.'

'Still learning?'

'Ja.'

Max struggled anew to make his contribution: 'They say the Haifa Tech has become one of the best schools of engineering in the world.'

'Listen to him! Opinions on all subjects! The only thing he knows nothing about is the milling business, where he earns his living.' Meyer turned again to Benjamin. 'How old are these professors of yours?'

Sarah answered. 'Joel's twenty-seven. David's twenty-three.'

'They're taking their time.'

'I'm not so worried about David,' Benjamin said. 'He seems to have settled down, he's changed.'

'Is he still *froom*?'

'I don't know, so much.'

'A *froom* engineer – that's something strange, something new in the world.'

'Perhaps that's why David has become one,' Sarah said.

Meyer stared at her, not sure whether the point that had been made was directed against himself or against David. He grunted, without animus. 'Ring the bell,' he said peremptorily to Roise. 'We'll go to the other room.'

The bell was rung, the servant came to clear away the things from the table. Max brought his father-in-law his crutches, and he and Yitzchak stood by to help him out of his chair. It was a laborious business, that left Meyer panting for breath. Then the labour was gone through again in the living room, when he sat down in his armchair near the fire.

Benjamin sat at his side; Max, Yitzchak, Sarah and Ethel sat together at the other end of the room; Roise was in the kitchen, making sure that the servants took for their supper only what they were entitled to.

The fire had been built up again, while they had been at dinner, and the logs burned brightly and noisily. Meyer put up a hand to shield his face from its glare, but he did not move away from it; he found the warmth and agitation of the flames comforting, he enjoyed the extravagance of the blaze.

13

Only then did Meyer say something to Benjamin of the journey he was about to make; previously, at dinner, he had avoided the subject. 'So it's goodbye to South Africa for you too?'

Benjamin hesitated. 'Not altogether goodbye. There's still a lot that keeps me here.'

'I know how much. You got a good price for the creamery, hey? Better than you paid for my half.'

'It's a long time that I bought you out. And money isn't worth what it was then.'

'I know how much money is worth –'

'Who knows better?'

'And I tell you that you got a good price. I was a fool, I should never have let you talk me out of it.'

'That was a long time ago, Meyer, let's not go over it now. Anyway, how do you know how much I got for the factory? I never wrote to you.'

'People talk, I listen.'

'People exaggerate.'

'I allow for that, also.'

Benjamin laughed. 'Perhaps not enough. But I'm satisfied with what I got, I'm not complaining. A funny thing you know this Boerre Ko-op that bought the place from me – they've put in that fellow Verster as manager. You remember him? He used to work for me years ago. Then he went to a creamery somewhere in the Free State. You should see him now: smart suit, very respectable, very keen, still young. He'll make a go of it, I could see. And there he sits in my office!'

'I remember him. Well, it's their country, more and more they're taking such positions.'

'Ja, sure, I wish him luck. It's not my business, anyway, what happens there. What I hope is that this new company of Bertie's will turn out all right, and that he'll be able to manage on his own. It looks promising, and he's energetic and hardworking. I've got a lot of respect for that boy, he's got more ambition than Joel and David put together, in some ways.'

'What is the business?'

'Minerals, industrial ores –'

'What? Mining them?'

'Maybe later mining them. But at the moment, no – he wants just to merchant and ship the goods, and build up his connections, learn his way into business. There are minerals in this country that the whole world needs and that ordinary people have never heard of. They're just starting to be developed properly, they've only been scratched so far. So Bertie got this idea from talking to Sarah's brother, Samuel, and he's decided that something can be made of it. And I'm backing him, all the way.'

'Is he taking him in?'

'Who?'

'That Samuel, with the waving arms.'

'Taking him in? God forbid! Anyhow, Samuel's all right, he's found what to do with himself at last. There's a firm of Germans, real Germans from Germany – they're trying to get into the market in a big way with their typewriters and adding machines and all that kind of stuff. Gelingen Office Equipment they call themselves. Well, they've taken a good look around and they've seen there's a lot of Jewish businesses in this country, plenty, plenty, of every kind, with lots of money to spend. So, for public relations, to show the Jews that they're not Nazis any more, that they're kosher democrats, they've decided they must have a Jew in the company. And they've found my fine brother-in-law. He's their show-Jew. They pay him well for it, and he's happy. You should hear him on the subject of how such a thing as Nazism was just an unfortunate accident that can never, never happen again!'

On her side of the room, Sarah was talking of her two grandchildren, Rachel's little boy and girl. 'Lovely, lovely children,' she said. 'The little boy's such a bright little monkey. And the baby's a beauty, so fat and peaceful.'

'Bless their hearts,' said Max, who was easily moved, even by the thought of children he had never seen. 'When you're a grandparent you have all the *nachas*, hey? and none of the anxiety. That's what I'm looking forward to being – a grandfather, with no troubles.'

'I haven't managed to feel as though I've got no troubles,' Sarah answered. 'I still worry, all the time – about the children, and their children, and so on, it's endless, until you're in the grave.'

'Don't use such words!' said Max, who was easily shocked. Yitzchak sat by quietly, taking little part in the conversation, though Sarah made a point of trying to draw him into it. He was polite, but shy – especially shy because he knew that Benjamin had still not forgiven him for accepting Meyer's offer of a job and a passage to South Africa, after he had finished his army service in Israel. Benjamin had been furiously indignant at the thought that he, who had all the comforts he wished for in South Africa, should be moving to Israel; while Yitzchak, the refugee, the one who had suffered most at the hands of the *goyim*, chose to leave the Jewish state and come to South Africa – just fifty years too late, fifty years after the rest of the family! Benjamin had been especially indignant because he suspected that Meyer had engineered the move 'to stick his finger in my eye', as he had said at the time to Sarah.

Sarah had no patience with this attitude, and wanted Yitzchak to know it. In reply to her questions Yitzchak told her that he was living in a boarding house in Wynberg; that he did not find it difficult to get to and from work because he had bought a motor scooter; that he enjoyed the work in the mill. Was he good at the work? He smiled; he could not answer that question. Perhaps Max could?

'First class, first class,' Max said enthusiastically.

'And you like the country?'

'Very much.'

'And the politics?'

'Not so much. But I'm so new here, I haven't really got opinions.'

Max approved of this caution even more than he had approved of Yitzchak's work. 'Quite right! Quite right! It's a complicated situation here. I don't like the way the government goes about things, it makes me sick sometimes, but they also have a case. Without the white man there'd be nothing here.

And when the white man goes under it won't be justice that rules the land, believe me.'

'It isn't justice now,' Sarah said.

'No, of course not. But all the same, the country is being built up, it's becoming richer every day, and everyone is getting a little more for himself, the blacks also.'

'It's true,' Sarah said. 'These people in the government – with one part of themselves they want to be rich, to have a flourishing country, and with the other all they want is to drive the blacks down into the dust. And they can't really do both, the two things don't go together, even though they try their hardest to make them do it. So there is a little hope. Still, I do feel that I know what it was like to be a good German, who did nothing against Hitler.'

'No!' Max rejected the comparison with many shakes of his head. 'We can still vote against them. Hitler didn't even let the good Germans do that. But anyway, why are we talking about such a depressing subject? Tomorrow you'll be gone, and then you'll be able to look down on all the white South Africans, like they do overseas. Won't that be nice?'

Sarah smiled. 'No.' Yet she couldn't help feeling that it would be nice to take part in fewer of such endless guilty conversations.

The evening passed by quietly, with talk and tea and the handing round of bowls of chocolates and crystallized fruit. Yitzchak was the first to go. After he had left Sarah was told in confidence by Ethel that he was known to be courting a respectable widowed woman, Jewish, poor, a couple of years older than himself, who lived in Cape Town and had a little daughter 'I've met her once,' Ethel said, 'and she seemed to me a very nice person. Suitable. Quiet, you know.' She nodded sagaciously, confident of the correctness of all her judgements. 'And the little girl is sweet, he can be a father to her.'

Then it was the turn of Max and Ethel to leave. 'And what will we find when we get home?' Max asked. 'Sleeping children? No! We'll find fighting children, arguing children, children up to mischief, I know it. I tell you, I can't wait to be a *zeide!*'

'Go! Go!' Ethel pushed him towards the door.

After they had gone no comment about them was made by anyone.

The fire had burned down to a mess of grey ash, black charcoal, shreds of bark fallen clear on to the tiled hearth. Roise yawned three times, with an apology for each yawn, and went to make a final inspection of the guest bedroom.

Benjamin yawned too, rubbed his eyes, sniffed deeply. 'I tell you, Meyer,' he said, leaning over the arm of his chair, 'if I'd known it was all going to take me so long, this plan of mine, I don't think I'd ever have started. Now, I've sold the business, I've sold the house, I've had that house built in Eretz – and what a job that was! I'll never build again from a distance, I can tell you – I've consolidated my investments here, and seen Bertie into the new business, I've packed – everything. And what do I feel? I just don't believe it! Not from beginning to end. Am I really leaving South Africa? Don't tell me such a thing! I know I'll get on the boat tomorrow and I'll be asking myself, What am I doing here? Where am I going? What am I looking for? What kind of a dream is this? Better I should wake up tomorrow in Paget Street and find everything the same. Yet the boat will carry me away, I won't be able to stop it, I'll find myself in London, then on another boat, then in Israel. Perhaps I'll never see Paget Street again. But it seems impossible, like a dream.'

Meyer had listened, expressionless. Then he said, 'Perhaps it's good that it's like a dream, otherwise you'd get the fright of your life and run home.'

'Home? What is my home? I feel as if I've never had one.'

'And you, Sarah?' Meyer asked, with a lift of his chin towards her.

Her fingers began to beat on the arm of her chair; she tilted her head in a quick, doubtful, bashful movement that was neither a nod nor a shake, but something of both. 'I was the one who wasn't keen on the whole adventure, you know that. I was quite happy to spend the rest of my life in Paget Street. But now I don't feel like Benjamin does, at all. I'm impatient, I'm excited, I'm ready to go. I want to see Joel and David again. And for the rest – I don't feel we've got so much to lose, at our age. If we don't like it we can come back and take a flat; we'll live somehow.'

'Three children, three different countries,' Benjamin said, holding up three fingers of one hand. The thought dismayed him and yet was a source of pride to him.

Meyer made no comment. But the next morning, on the docks, near the foot of the gangway which he could not climb, the great pink swell of the hull of the Union Castle liner above him, he cried out loudly to Benjamin, with a heave of his chest that made him stagger between his crutches, 'Ach, why did you never ask me if I wanted to come with you?'

'To come with me?' Benjamin repeated in astonishment. The idea had never occurred to him.

A moment later he understood that it had not occurred to Meyer before, either: that this was just his way of protesting against his own age, illness and powerlessness. Morry shrugged, more indifferent than embarrassed by Meyer's cry. Roise hadn't even heard him, for she was repeating over and over again to no one in particular, 'You must hurry, you must hurry.' Max stood with his arm around Ivor's shoulder, already feeling himself to be *in loco parentis* and anxious to show everyone how responsibly he would carry out his duties. Ivor, for his part, kept on taking ostentatiously from his pocket a comic that someone had brought for him earlier in the morning and looking fixedly at it, for a few seconds at a time.

'You'll come and visit us in Eretz Yisroel,' Benjamin said to Meyer.

'No I won't.'

'Then we'll visit you here.'

People were coming out of the large black mouth of the customs shed and crossing the quay to climb up the gangway; other groups, like the Glickmans, were gathered in huddles of farewell, or were shouting up at the passengers who already lined the railing of the boat. Two young policemen patrolled up and down, their revolver holsters gleaming, their faces vacuous, their booted feet splashing in the puddles of water which shone here and there on the grey concrete. It had rained earlier in the morning, but the sun was shining now, and the sky that showed between the fast-moving clouds was a very bright blue. The bulk of the boat sheltered the quay, but beyond it, on both sides, the shirts of workmen were blown out behind them by the wind, canvas tarpaulins pulled at the ropes that lashed them down over heaps of baggage, the pennants flying from the offices and warehouses of shipping companies were strained to landward. It was going to be cold, out at sea.

Morry, Rina and Selwyn drew aside to say goodbye to Ivor. The boy's face worked, but he did not cry. He stooped and kissed his little brother goodbye. Then there was a flurry of kisses and handshakes all round.

'You go first,' Benjamin said to Morry. 'You can climb quicker than I can.'

Morry picked up Selwyn and began to carry him up the gangway, followed by Rina. Uncertainly, very slowly, Benjamin and Sarah began to ascend, Benjamin groping in his pocket for the boarding card to show the officials at the top of the incline. Halfway up he turned to look behind him. The others had retreated a little; they were all staring up, Max and Ethel waving, Roise moving her head from left to right, no longer knowing where to look, Meyer leaning on his aluminium crutches, immobile, his white collar a distinctive mark in the middle of the group. Bereft and incredulous, Benjamin felt his arm was too heavy to lift in a wave of farewell.

14

By the time Benjamin and Sarah had had their tickets cleared, had been shown down to their cabin, and had come up on deck again, Meyer and the others had gone. Ethel said Rina had arranged that they should leave immediately, as it would be too much of a strain for Ivor, they had agreed, to remain on the quay any longer than was necessary.

Ivor had made his own plans, however. Somewhere between the quay and Max's car, he simply disappeared, leaving his frantic aunt and uncle, and eventually a large force of harbour police to scour the docks for him. Max almost went out of his mind, his eyes almost fell out of his head; quite apart from his anguish about the boy, he suffered unspeakably at the thought of what his wife's family might do to him if the smallest part of his fears proved true.

Ivor turned up at his grandfather's house late that afternoon, drenched to the skin and ravenously hungry. (Meyer and Roise, who had left the docks in their own car, did not learn of his disappearance until then.) Ivor offered no explanation of where he had been: partly because he knew his silence would distress the grown-ups, and partly because he was ashamed of having done nothing more exciting than hide in a shed in a deserted corner of the docks where he had read his comic, cried a great deal, eaten a slab of chocolate and worked out elaborate fantasies of startling his parents by suddenly appearing in front of them in their hotel in London. Then he had walked through the rain to his grandfather's house in Camp's Bay.

After this escapade he settled down quietly with his uncle and aunt, and their children, in their house in Gardens.

15

For the first two days the sea was pale green and white, running heavily, and the boat rolled and pitched, creaked and shivered; the cabins and public rooms seemed groaningly to expand and contract with every heave; wind hissed in the ears of the passengers who ventured out on deck, and rain spattered down every now and again, small drops of water falling into a waste of water. But during the third morning the weather improved; by mid-afternoon the sky was clear, the sea was blue and calm, except for an occasional deep swell that rocked the ship sedately and then passed off. Deck quoits began to slap down heavily on the games deck, and passengers who had previously remained immured in their cabins now leaned complacently over the rails and exchanged remarks with one another, each sizing up the others as possible companions or as people to be avoided during the days of travelling still ahead. The waves that ran off from the hull of the vessel were regular now – almost diminishing as they grew wider, always renewed by the steady forward thrust of the prow. Farther out there was no regularity: only the haphazard movement and light of the water, ringed by the horizon slowly falling and rising. Now there was nothing to be done but to wait for the arrival in Southampton, eleven days hence; and everyone was at once bored by the prospect. By the end of that first afternoon of sunshine and calm seas, the passengers were eager for distraction of any kind.

They were given one. At dinner, over the public address system the master of the vessel announced that a stowaway had been found on board, and that the ship would be meeting a southbound liner, at dawn the next day, in order to transfer the stowaway for return to Cape Town. For the rest of the meal, and for most of the evening, hardly any of the passengers could talk of anything else. Everyone in uniform was seized upon and questioned for details. Disappointingly few were forthcoming. The stowaway was a Cape Coloured. A young fellow. He had been found in one of the chests for storing lifebelts. It was the invariable policy of the Company simply to transfer stowaways for return to their port of embarkation, rather than to carry them to their destinations and prosecute them there. The Company believed this procedure to be the most effective deterrent it could use.

At dawn the next morning the two liners met. Enlarged rather than diminished by the emptiness of the sea around them, the featurelessness of the sky, the distance of the full circle of the horizon, the two huge boats swayed lazily, a few hundred yards apart from one another. Erect black fins of sharks moved at random between the two hulls. The sea was calm, its surface heavy, its colour grey with a sliding, oily undersheen of pink. In the east there was a sudden spill of light as the sun broke through two bars of cloud, and a single, empty patch of sea, miles away, was illumined theatrically, as if for some special purpose. The light fell steadily upon that patch, then faded; once it was gone no one could have said just where in the grey, restless width of water it had been.

The lifeboat carrying the stowaway was lowered forward of the ship, where passengers were not permitted to go. The stowaway sat in the middle of the boat; he was young, swarthy and slightly built. He was wearing a blue suit, a white shirt, a tie; his hair was neatly combed. He looked like a clerk or insurance salesman. The seamen manning the lifeboat worked vigorously, pumping away at the upright levers that served as oars; but their progress was slow and toilsome, the little boat rocked and bobbed more violently than the onlookers, at their height, would have expected. The stowaway sat motionless, his hands in his lap, his face lifted towards the ship he was approaching. He had not looked back once. There was no sound on the liner he had left but for the slap of water against its hull and the faint hum of the wind. At last the lifeboat was hooked against the side of the other's hull, and the stowaway stood up warily, grasped at the rope ladder hanging against its side, and began his climb, followed by one of the crew members; they went through a breach in the rail of the lowest deck, and were immediately surrounded by a small group of men who had been waiting for them. A few minutes later the sailor who had gone up descended the ladder alone. Slowly, the lifeboat made its way back; an outburst of cries and shouted orders broke the silence as it was brought under the davit, tilted at an unfamiliar angle, from which it had been lowered. It took only a few minutes before the boat was hauled up again.

The engine began to throb, the decks to vibrate. Each of the liners gave a blast on its siren, and the sound seemed to bounce sharply off the water, fall and bounce once more, much farther off, and fall again, for the last time, very faintly, at a great distance. The passengers went down for breakfast.

But no one mentioned the stowaway. A kind of collective shame seemed to have come over them at having watched the failure of his attempt to make the journey they were permitted to continue in comfort; at having seen him delivered over, like a felon, for return to the place he had wanted to leave; at having photographed the scene with their shiny, leather-boxed cameras. It wasn't until evening that he was spoken of again; and then the rumour went swiftly around the ship that he was a Cape Coloured student who had been denied a passport for political reasons.

16

Having good trip all well love mom dad. Rachel put the cable on the mantelpiece, so that Bertie could see it when he came in; then went through into the kitchen, where Annie was giving supper to Mark. The table between the two of them appeared small when you looked at Annie, large when you looked at Mark, whose round head seemed to be balanced just over the edge of it. He held a spoon of his own, but most of the food that actually went into his mouth came from Annie's spoon. 'Four more,' she was saying, as she gently put the spoon between his lips, and Mark, with a full mouth, repeated the sounds, drawing them out into a kind of song.

'I've just had a telegram from the master and the madam,' Rachel said to Annie. 'From the boat. Everything's fine.'

'That's nice Miss Rachel.'

Rachel stood behind Annie, next to the stove, and pursed her lips at Mark, in a kiss, in a sign of encouragement.

'Four more,' Mark sang.

'Three more,' Annie said, slipping another spoonful into his mouth. He chewed, with swollen cheeks, clowning a little, his eyes fixed on his mother.

'You spoil him, you know, Annie. He's quite capable of feeding himself. He's old enough.'

'But then he takes so long, Miss Rachel.'

'Don't I know it!'

'Four more,' Mark said proudly, pleased to be the subject of their conversation.

'Three more, you dope,' Rachel said to him. Restless, reluctant to say to Annie what she knew she had to tell her, Rachel watched him eating the last spoonful of the stew. She waited until Annie had peeled an apple and was giving it to the boy in quarters; then, as casually as she could, Rachel said, 'Oh, Annie, I've been meaning to tell you. I spoke to Mr Brunton this afternoon. It looks pretty hopeless. He says that there's a rule in the building that all servants have to live in the dormitory upstairs and that they can't make any exceptions. He says it's in our lease.

In fact, Mr Brunton, the building superintendent, had been most unpleasant when Rachel had suggested to him that Annie should live with them in the spare room of their flat. 'Look in your lease, Mrs Preiss, and you'll see what the owners have had to say about that.' His pointed features had been tilted venomously up to her, from his seat at his little desk; Rachel had looked down with loathing into his long narrow nostrils, filled with ginger hairs. She had at least had the satisfaction of seeing that her gaze had forced him to turn away, to lower his head. 'Besides there's the Group Areas Act. The government wouldn't have it, even if the owners would. Even if you would. Either she stays in the dormitory or she goes somewhere else. Who does she think she is, anyhow? What's so grand about her? Why can't she sleep with all the other girls?'

Rachel told Annie none of this, though the scene was still raw in her mind, though she still felt degraded by it. But Annie seemed to know, nevertheless, how the conversation had gone. The expression on her broad, flat pale brown face was one that Rachel had seen on many such faces – sadness, resolve, patience, and a profound knowingness, a perfectly firm awareness of what was being done to her, and by whom. In her quiet, trailing voice, Annie said, 'That Mr Brunton, Miss Rachel, he doesn't want to help, always he tries to make trouble.'

Mark had listened patiently to them; now, deciding finally that this conversation was not about himself, and feeling that it had gone on long enough, he threw his last piece of apple across the table; it skidded off the plastic surface and hit Rachel just below the hem of her cardigan. 'No more,' Mark cried. 'I'm full up.'

'I should think you are, too,' Rachel answered, stopping to pick up the bit of apple from the floor. 'Come on, let me wipe your face. Then we'll give Sharon her turn.'

Mark came round the tale and stood by the sink, presenting his face for the wiping. His complexion was olive, his eyelids paler than the skin around them, his lips had a moist, bluish tint. Rachel adored him; she could not keep her hands off all the smoothnesses and smallnesses of his limbs and face. For the pallor of his eyelids alone she thought she would have loved him with all the passion she was capable of. He held up his face to her and she wiped it lingeringly, gently. Then she said, 'Go and play in your room, Mark. See what Sharon's doing. I want to talk to Annie.'

Obediently, Mark trotted out of the room; Rachel watched the little workings of the backs of his knees. Annie was still sitting at the table, staring down at the apple peelings in the dirty plate in front of her. Her patience irritated Rachel suddenly; she felt that Annie was using it as a weapon, as a reproach, as a way of pretending that the entire responsibility for her life rested upon Rachel – she was helpless, at the mercy of others.

'So what's going to happen?' Rachel asked, to provoke some response from her. But it was only when Rachel sat down on Mark's stool that Annie got up, gathered together the plates, and carried them to the sink. Rachel turned on the stool. 'You definitely don't want to stay in the dormitory?'

'No, Miss Rachel. I don't like it there. I like better a room of my own.'

'I know, you've told us. But you can't have one here.'

'I'm used to it, Miss Rachel. All the years I was working for the master and the madam I had a room of my own.'

'I know, Annie, I know.' Rachel ran her hand through her soft, brown hair; then, irritated by its softness, scratched hard at her scalp. 'Look, Annie, we always said that when they left you should come and work for us. And you always said that you wanted to. And you know how glad I am that you've come; I would have hated it if you'd had to go and work for some other family, when you've been with us for so long. It's nice, it's right, that we should stay together. Master Bernie and me will do anything to see that you're happy. But if you don't want that dormitory then you can't live in, there's nothing we can do about it.'

'I don't like it there,' Annie repeated, with an unaltered note of patience and obstinacy in her voice, as if she had heard nothing of what Rachel had said.

She was now washing the few plates she had brought to the sink; her hands moved and came up gloved in foam, carrying a foam-covered plate. Annie had always been wasteful with detergents; and this added to Rachel's exasperation when she asked, 'Why didn't you tell us before?'

'I didn't know what it would be like, Miss Rachel.'

'Well, all you can do then is take a room in Alexandra or somewhere, and come in every day. At least you'll be able to see Nigel more often, if you do.'

Annie ignored the proffered bribe of being able to see her son more often than she now did; he was boarded out in a kind of baby-farm run by an old woman in a tumbledown shack at the edge of Alexandra Township, and Annie visited him only on her afternoons, off. 'If I live there what will you do about the baby-sitting, Miss Rachel?'

'I don't know. We'll have to make some other plan. Perhaps we can get one of the other girls from the building to sit in, some evenings. We – I don't go out so much.'

'Also, it takes so long, Miss Rachel, on the bus, to come in every day. They make you wait in the queues there, sometimes hours. And it costs too much.'

'So what *do* you want to do, Annie? You must also help us, you know, if you still want to work for us.'

465

Annie said quietly into the sink, 'Maybe I should go and find another work, Miss Rachel.'

Rachel sat quite still; only her lips moved, in a kind of snarl. '*Et tu, Brute*?' she said, laughing at herself for throwing a Latin tag at an African servant girl who had perhaps managed to pass Standard IV thirty years before. With a single indrawn breath her laughter changed into a shout of anger and injury. 'Then go! I don't need you! I don't know what's the matter with everybody – going, going, going – I haven't got the plague, have I? You can go, if that's all we mean to you. What do I care?'

She got up and ran into the bedroom. Slowly, her face showing no emotion, Annie finished washing up, then went to fetch Sharon from her play-pen, to give her her supper.

17

When Bertie came home from work he found both women subdued and yet self-important as a result of their quarrel. As soon as she could – after he had gone into the children's bedroom to say good night to them in their cots, and had helped himself to a drink – Rachel began to tell him what had taken place. She spoke in a low voice, so that Annie, silent in the kitchen, would hear nothing, and passionately, so that Bertie would realize how hurt she was. His legs were stretched out to the electric fire; he relished the taste of his whisky and soda, and looked from Rachel's gleaming, injured eyes to the busy bubbles in his glass, chasing one another to the surface of the liquid.

When Rachel had finished her story, he finished his drink. 'I'll go and speak to her now. You should never have begged her to stay. Put people in a position where they think they can do you favours and they may do you the favour – or they may not – but either way they'll take advantage of you, whoever they are. And especially people like Annie. How many chances does she get to throw her weight around?'

Rachel listened submissively to his rebuke. 'I was upset, Bertie. Not just by Annie. Or by that awful Brunton man. Oh, you know how I've been feeling –'

He interrupted her. 'I know all right. You've told me often enough. So they're gone – so what? You're the one who always wanted to stay here and have peace and quiet and – and – continuity. Well, this is as much of them as you'll ever get. What more do you want?'

'Perhaps some sympathy,' she flared up.

'OK,' he agreed tiredly, pacifyingly, 'you're entitled to that. And you've got it too. You really have, Rachel.' He stood up, and handed his empty glass to her. 'Now to deal with Mistress Annie.'

Rachel did not follow him into the kitchen; she was frightened she might do or say the wrong things, or what Bertie might later tell her were the wrong things. She heard his voice, and Annie's soft replies, without being able to make out their words. He came back a few minutes later, looking satisfied with himself.

'She's staying. She says maybe the dormitory won't be so bad. She says she'll try it, anyway, and if she can't stand it then she'll try coming in every day from Alexandra. But I think she'll stand it all right. She's had her little fling.'

He straightened himself, standing in the middle of the room, looking down at the carpet. 'You must try to be patient with her. She's also been pretty upset by your people going away. I think so, at least.' Again he moved his thin body, bringing a hand to his hip. 'It's so difficult to know what they really feel. We're the masters and they're the servants and they feel they can't afford to let us know too much – ever.'

'You make it sound so sinister.'

'In many ways it is. Hell! Don't you know what kind of a country our glorious fatherland is?'

'I must say it gets me down more and more, the whole thing. Old Brunton was so *awful* this afternoon, I could have strangled him. And the worst of it was that he was so sure he was on the right side. He just knew he was, in that little sundried pea of a brain that he's got. The master bloody race! Brunton!'

But the portentous atmosphere in the flat that had greeted Bertie had been dispelled. Annie served them their dinner in the little dining room; she was cheerful, as relieved as they were to have the matter settled. Outside it was already dark and cold, but they left the curtains open, for the sake of the view. Their flat overlooked a small sloping park on the other side of which the ground rose so steeply that much of it had remained unbuilt-upon and unlit. So the tall blocks of flats on that side of the park looked as if they were suspended, hanging with their lights above spaces of darkness. Cars drew up to them and pulled away, each one like a messenger, silent, mysterious and somehow discreet at that distance, in spite of their shining headlights. The sky behind was black.

18

During the last couple of years Bertie had acquired and abandoned several enthusiasms. He had had a phase when he had spent a large part of his free time learning French – he had gone to lessons at the Alliance Française in town, he had listened every night to his Linguaphone records, he had gone around the flat reciting aloud the conjugations of irregular verbs and individual lines from the Romantic poets he was battling through (*Le jeune homme, devant les laideurs de ce monde/Tresaille dans son coeur largement irrité*), he had listened regularly to the news on the radio from the Belgian Congo.

Then there was his enthusiasm for chamber music; he had bought expensive reproduction equipment, a large library of records, books on the subject, and tickets for the concerts occasionally given in town by visiting quartets from Europe; he had filled the flat with the howl of violas, the pleadings of violins, the minatory tones of cellos, all at full volume, driving Rachel out of the living room into the bedroom, where, at times, she lay with her fingers to her ears. Then there had been his bookbinding spell; though he was really rather clumsy with his hands he had, once again, bought books on the subject and all kinds of equipment: shears, sheets of fine leather, sheets of gold leaf, pots of glue which he melted on the kitchen stove, stinking up the whole flat, sets of punches, needles, threads, tapes; he had turned the spare room into his workshop and torn off the covers of some of Rachel's favourite books in order to rebind them, he promised her, exquisitely. But that had been the least successful of his enthusiasms – except perhaps for his bouts of photography and of a special kind of therapeutic deep-breathing – and Rachel's favourite books were still without bindings or covers, lying in the cupboard where he had thrown them with the rest of the gear he had collected.

His latest enthusiasm was poker. Though Rachel begged him not to almost every time, he had been going for several months at least once a week and sometimes more often, to play at Wolfgang Leverkuhn's flat. However, he insisted that he was not truly a gambler; it was not the chance of winning or the danger of losing big sums of money that really attracted and excited him. He was actually a cautious player, and was often mocked by Leverkuhn for his caution; the most he had lost so far in a night had been about thirty pounds. What he found irresistible was the fact that when he played he thought of nothing but the game; his consciousness was altogether filled by the hard light over the table, the busy hands, each pair so different in its appearance from the others, the cards coming and going in all their permutations, the tension accumulating and finding its resolution only to accumulate once more, the faces of the players frowning, laughing, expressionless, yet with eyes always watchful, always on the move, the guessing, the calculating, the smoke, the glasses of beer, the disconnected snatches of conversation.

On this evening he had his usual argument with Rachel and then went off expectantly, after dinner. But the game proved to be disappointingly quiet and ragged. 'The rhythm,' Leverkuhn said later, 'was missing.' Bertie had brought with him, for the first time, Barney Klein, Adela's brother, who was now married, plumper than ever, and persistently, mildly, naggingly good-humoured on every topic, except when he talked of his 'mad sister' who had been arrested during the Defiance of Unjust Laws Campaign the previous year, and who had learned nothing, Barney said, from her experience – she still ran around with Natives and Indians, talking about the revolution that was always coming tomorrow but never came today. The other two players were a wholesaler of artificial jewellery, by the name of Markus, who was a neighbour of Leverkuhn's in the building and a loud-mouthed, soft-fleshed advertising man, with yellow pouches under his eyes, who kept on making remarks about being a poor *goy* fallen among Jews, at which only Barney Klein laughed loudly. Markus, dressed in an ash-littered blue cardigan, was bald, heavy, hunched, and many years older than anyone else there; he did not laugh once in the course of the evening; he hardly spoke, except to make his calls, and to mutter, each time he examined his hand, '*Kinder*, let me see, let-me-see, letmesee.' When he had seen what he wanted to see, he thrust out his lower lip and waited for the others, his hairless, round head bowed in concentration over his cards.

By common consent the game broke up early, at about half-past twelve; no one had won or lost anything much, and they did not spend as much time as they usually did anatomizing the hands they had had. Instead they talked about cars and money, the career of a defaulting stock-broker who had bankrupted scores of his clients and whose trial was taking up much space in the papers, and the latest of the Government's interminable pieces of race legislation. Markus and the advertising man left soon afterwards; Bertie and Barney Klein remained a little longer. As always, after the game, Bertie left glum and depleted; he knew at such moments that the chief attraction of these evenings for him was their quintessentially wasteful quality – they were by design wasteful of time, wasteful of money, wasteful of the self that was expended in them. No wonder, he thought, that Freud had said people gambled as a substitute for masturbation.

But Leverkuhn was depressed only because the game had demanded so little of the players that evening, had wasted so little of them. 'The rhythm was missing.' And Barney Klein was not depressed at all. He had come out best in the evening's play, which naturally pleased him and Leverkuhn flattered him adroitly – to no real end except that of seeing Barney rise unsuspectingly to the flattery. Soon Barney was talking about his little victory as though luck had had nothing to do with it, and Leverkuhn encouraged him, going on to refer knowledgeably to the 'lines of psychic force' which had radiated from Barney and had compelled the game to go the way it had.

This Leverkuhn, who talked so easily of rhythms and lines of psychic force, was a great boaster and romancer: Bertie had no doubt about it. He was in his late thirties, a divorcee, a refugee from Germany. According to his own accounts he had, since coming to South Africa, been a diamond buyer, a teacher of languages, a salesman of sewing machines, and an intelligence agent who had worked under the direct command of General Smuts during the war; he had also spent some time farming on a smallholding just outside Johannesburg, where he had used a revolutionary method for the growing of tomatoes and potatoes. He had grown his crops out of rocks, out of heaps of pebbles, as far as Bertie had understood his explanations; it was an adaptation of a system, Leverkuhn claimed, that had been employed in antiquity by the Nabataens. Now he was a correspondent for the German press, a literary agent, a scout for English publishers, a tourist courier, a host of things. Bertie never knew how much to believe of what Leverkuhn said about himself; quite apart from the implausibility of his claims, there was the implausibility of his appearance to contend with. Full-face, he had the look of a sly, harmless, wrinkled, amused monkey, with a flat, wide-nostrilled nose, nothing much in the way of a chin, and a bald, curved brow. In profile the cast of his face was sombre, authoritarian, hooked, avaricious. Bertie had spent much time trying, without success, to put together Leverkuhn's two faces.

But you could pass the time entertainingly in Leverkuhn's company. He was a reader of Reich, a reader of works of Zen, a believer in what he called 'the X-factor' ('So that you won't confuse my conception of divinity with your sadistic Jahweh or your masochistic Christ'); he said he had been a Spartacist in Germany, but knew better now than to try to work out his 'inner disharmonies and disequilibriums' by inciting the Africans to revolt, especially as the overwhelming mass of the Africans were deeply acquiescent in what was being done to them, and any attempt at revolution was certain to fail. (He had what he called a 'psycho-historic' explanation of the political submissiveness of the African masses. In tribal society women had done all the work, while the men had merely hunted, herded cattle and prepared for war; now because the men had become wage-slaves, because they did repetitive manual labour, 'they have been womanized in their own eyes, you understand, they have become convinced that their role must be a feminine one of passivity, compliance and caution.') He spent most of his nights playing poker; he said he was working on a book which would establish the theory of 'sensetime' as a dimension comparable to the space-time of physicists; he spoke with a deliberately challenging, calm open-mindedness about flying saucers.

Barney listened to him open-mouthed, with round eyes; Bertie with a sceptical smile on his face. But it was in Bertie, not Barney, that something baffled, embittered and yet hopeful rose in response to Leverkuhn's words. And it was Barney, not Bertie, who dismissed Leverkuhn when they were on the pavement outside the building. 'That bloke, he's off his head if you ask me. Where d'you pick him up?'

If Barney had spoken with respect of Leverkuhn, Bertie would have been scornful and derisive. As it was he said, 'I don't know, I think he's on the track of some things that most people prefer not to think about.'

He drove Barney home. Now that Benjamin Glickman had left the country, and Ezreal Klein was more or less confined to his bed, with one asthma attack after another, the two young men were effectively in charge of the block of flats in Observatory owned by Benjamin and Ezreal, and they had much in the way of business to say to each other.

19

Bertie was surprised, and a little irritated, to find Rachel still awake when he came home. He leaned over her in the darkness, feeling the warmth of her body coming from the bed. 'Sweetie! why aren't you asleep?' he whispered, trying to anticipate and render harmless with his display of solicitude the reproaches he feared she was ready to make.

'I couldn't sleep,' she said. 'So I stopped trying to.' She spoke in a normal tone of voice, which made his whisper appear childish.

'Well, perhaps you'll be able to, now that I'm back.'

He undressed in the dark; the only light in the flat came from the night-light in the children's room, through the open door. Stretching, yawning, sighing, he climbed between the sheets; Rachel hardly moved to make room for him. They lay in silence for some time.

'So you want to say something to me?' Bertie asked finally.

She answered him, after another long silence – 'I've been thinking – I want to take a job. I want to do something. I don't need to be with Sharon all the time, especially if Annie's staying with us. I could do something half-time.'

Bertie was relieved that what she had said did not – at any rate, not directly – concern him: his absences, his coldness, his poker games; his lack of love for her, and all the rest of the accusations and reproaches she wearied him with.

'Of course,' he said, trying to put some interest and encouragement into his voice. 'Why shouldn't you? What sort of thing are you thinking of?'

'I thought I'd like to do some voluntary work – something with the Africans – I don't know. With the Blind Society, or the Legal Aid, or the Institute of Race Relations – something like that.'

He lay quite still, between one breath and another. 'I see,' he said. 'Charity. Good works.'

'They're better than nothing. If we're going to be on our own here, I want to make my own connexctons, instead of just feeling caught in the ones that other people have made.'

He did not answer her. But a few minutes later he laughed, not because he was amused, but because he wanted her to ask him what the joke was. She did not oblige, however, so he lifted himself up on one elbow and looked down into her face, a paler shadow within the shadow of her hair.

'You're so obvious! Suddenly you must do good works! Who're you trying to reproach? Who're you trying to justify yourself in front of? Me? Your parents? You think your old man could go off to Israel if he didn't know that I was here, looking after everything he's left behind? And the same thing goes for Joel and David: the last thing you have to be is ashamed in front of them. They're going to draw plenty of benefit one day from the work I'm doing – or so they hope, anyway, I bet. And so are the Africans you're suddenly so concerned about. They don't stand a chance unless this country becomes really rich and developed. If they want to cut my throat then, I'll say good luck to them. If they're capable of doing it.'

'There's no need for you to speak like that. You're drawing your benefits already, aren't you?'

'And you're one of them! Thanks very much!'

He had the satisfaction of seeing that this made her cry, as he had intended it to.

He lay beside her, letting her sob, finding in her tears a justification for his anger. Lying still, swallowing his rage, he remembered one of Leverkuhn's dicta: In modern, middle-class society more deaths are caused by the restraint of violent impulses than by their expression.

It was another reverberating lie, of course. Or was it? He fell asleep with the question unresolved. Much later, Rachel fell asleep too.

20

Professor Viljoen had warned Joel that graduate students in arts subjects were, in England, a permanently depressed and neglected class; that by and large the university authorities were indifferent to them, that they were thrown upon their own resources and left to shift for themselves as best they could.

Joel, of course, had disbelieved him. It was Viljoen's bitterness that was speaking he had told himself, his resentment of being stuck forever in the provinces, his envy of the superior status and facilities of the universities in Britain. However, Joel was now convinced that though Viljoen may have spoken bitterly, he had spoken the truth.

It had been one thing to open an airmail letter in Johannesburg and to read, with much satisfaction and pride, that he had been accepted by the London School of Economics to work for his doctorate on the dissertation he had suggested ('Studies in the Origins of the Theory of Imperialism, from Seeley to Lenin') under the direction of Professor Michael Davidson; it was quite another actually to come once every few weeks or so to the School, tucked so improbably and inconspicuously in a bent, sunless little side street off Kingsway, and spend there a half-hour or a little longer each time in Professor Davidson's office, making conversation with Professor Davidson and listening to the sighing and bubbling of Professor Davidson's pipe. There were also, it was true, coffee-parties at Professor Davidson's home in Twickenham, which he attended together with a dozen others at a time, and where he drank coffee and admired the legs of Professor Davidson's wife. But not even these occasions altogether assuaged Joel's feelings that he was, academically speaking, a neglected body.

Professor Davidson was a modest, busy, genuinely kindly man, a Leeds Jew by origin, who had written a great deal on British imperial history before the war and very little since then, and who now served conscientiously on many academic committees. Personally, Joel found him as unfathomable as all the other middle-class Englishmen he had met; they were a strange, intricate race, much less reserved than they were reputed to be – they were in fact immensely given to gossip – and yet at the same time self-absorbed, broodingly in-turned.

But he had the impression that Davidson liked him and for some reason was amused by him. Intellectually, Davidson was acute and fatigued; this too seemed to Joel characteristic, even while he suspected that the fatigue was something of a pose. Socially, the most striking thing about Davidson, perhaps, was his wife, Lily. She was not just an American heiress – she was a member of a well-known department-store family – but a beautiful one as well, being tall, pale-skinned, black-haired, light-eyed, youthful in her appearance and voice, and imposingly dignified in her movements and manners. Joel's admiration of her legs was wholehearted.

For the rest, Joel was left pretty much on his own. Now that he was halfway through his thesis he had decided, inevitably, that it was the wrong topic for him to have tackled; he was no theoretician. But the subject engaged his curiosity at many levels; he felt its scope to be as wide, ultimately, as he might dare to make it; and he worked at it as hard as his own somewhat indolent and always divided and self-doubting nature permitted him to. He drew some comfort, also, from the fact that this approach to the subject was positively 'anti-theoretical', anyway; it seemed to him that the theoreticians, whether they supported or attacked the imperialisms of their time, had never done more than try to offer rational explanations for what was essentially an irrational political process, an 'objectless expansion', as Schumpter had described it, a compulsive movement of power of a kind which, under favouring internal and external circumstances, would always find its excuses and presumed objects, and would always manage to generate the heroism, exaltation, and ruthlessness it needed. In a curious way, Joel suspected that a romantic, cynical, posturing dandy and exhibitionist like Disraeli in fact knew better what he was about than those who imagined his postures and absurdities to be a mask for calculation. Though he found many of Disraeli's views, and the whole of his personality, embarrassing and repellent to a degree, Joel vaguely promised himself that if his work went well he would one day 'do something' on Disraeli.

Such promises he made only in his more cheerful daydreaming moments, when he saw his thesis completed and received with acclamation, and offers of lucrative, undemanding and prestigious jobs being thrust upon him. More often he saw himself as a perpetual graduate student, a drifter, a nagger, a tenth-rate *luftmensch*; not handsome, not talented, not industrious, unable to earn a living, a failure.

In order to earn some kind of living he taught twice a week at a night-school, giving a course in nineteenth-century British history (his misgivings about teaching such a course had disappeared when he had seen that most of his students were as little British as himself), and he marked innumerable history papers for a correspondence college which advertised widely in African and Asian newspapers, charged its students heavily for its services, and paid him meagrely. The first job he had got through Professor Davidson; the second by answering a notice that had been posted up on the board at the School.

21

'And that's the way I get my bread
    A trifle, if you please.'

Pamela laughed at Joel's facetious, apologetic conclusion to his account of the way he lived. They were on Primrose Hill; below them was the simple geography of London, a wide flat valley, between two ranges of low hills.

They stood on one side, and many miles away vague stripes of mauve and brown against the sky marked the hills of Surrey. The larger, nearer buildings stood out distinctly; others were reduced to angles of darkness, flanges of light; the rest were nothing more than so much occupied space, from which a faint vapour rose into the sky. The view reminded Joel of that of Johannesburg from behind the main block of the university, but this one was wider and less dramatic; less dramatic because it was so much more immense, because at no point was it gathered together in a single heap or pile. It simply filled the valley as a dream fills the mind – seen and yet not known, experienced yet hardly to be believed in. Bald, stony, dusty distances, the ache of interminable roads, the secrecy of squares and alleys, the oppression of traffic and of crowds on the pavements, the irregularities and disorders of hundreds of years of buildings, canals, bridges and railways, were all reduced to a sound in the air, a vapour, a brown and black growth or stain that had spread everywhere.

'What about girls?' Pamela asked, turning from the view to look at Joel. Her voice was light, strained, defiant. 'You've told me about everything else, but you haven't mentioned them. You're not married – or anything – are you?'

Joel hesitated. 'Or anything? I suppose that's more or less what I am. I've got a girl, we –'

'What's her name?'

'Dora. She's South African. From Port Elizabeth. Then Wits, and now the Middle Temple. She wants to go back when she's finished.'

'And you?'

'No, I don't want to go back.'

'Why not? Because of the politics?'

'Because of the politics and everything else. Because I like it better here than there.' He added, adopting exaggeratedly the posture of a defeated politician, his hand on his heart, 'Because I've retired altogether from public life.'

'And you think this is the place to do it in?'

'Don't you think so?'

She did not answer; she just said emphatically, 'I don't want to leave.' She moved away at once, having spoken; as if, Joel thought, the exposure of their position on the skyline challenged them to justify their choice. How could it be done, in the face of that vast indifference, the city sprawled immeasurably beneath them? Yet that indifference was surely one of the reasons for their choice.

She had moved hardly a yard or two away from him, but the baldness and height of the slope made the distance appear greater; they seemed to be calling to one another rather than talking. 'So what's going to happen between the two of you? If she wants to go back and you don't?'

'She'd stay if I asked her to.'

'But you don't want to do that either?'

'No.'

'Poor Dora!'

He resented the way she flung out the remark, like some kind of joke. 'You don't have to be patronizing – just because you're all right.'

Her flat-heeled, black, skimpy shoes were in the grass, the rays of evening sunlight were blurred against her legs and skirt. She rocked a little, backwards and forwards, taunting him; watching her he was dizzied by the steep green decline at her feet, with formal tarred paths running down, and the tops of the trees far below. 'You still feel so sorry for yourself, Joel?' she cried. 'After we'd met at that party I remembered how sorry for yourself you always used to be. You haven't changed, have you? You told me so that evening, you said you hadn't changed.'

'That's right, I'm still sorry for myself. And you're still pleased with yourself, aren't you?'

'Oh, very. Why shouldn't I be?'

Her breath caught on the question, and he looked curiously at her, before stooping and picking up the raincoat she had put down on the grass.

'So what do you want to do now? Are you satisfied with the walking we've done?'

She did not answer; instead she began walking away slowly, in the direction of Hampstead. He fell in beside her. 'Would you like to meet Dora?'

She flinched away from the suggestion. 'Not after what you've told me. Not tonight, anyway.'

The sun went; the sky slowly lost its golden greenish hue, became paler, clearer, more distant. They wandered through the streets, following no particular direction. The peeling stucco pillars and porticos of Swiss Cottage gave way to the red brick of Hampstead. In a street neither of them had been in before they came upon a house on which a plaque announced that Freud had spent the last year of his life there. The house was modestly expensive in appearance, its garden neat and luxuriant, its windows white-sashed, its brickwork firm and discreet under a bright green creeper. They stared at it like tourists, standing in the narrow street that the dying exile had looked out upon. The height and ponderous ugliness of the houses opposite spoilt the street, made it dark and prison-like.

Then they walked on. They had spoken little since leaving Primrose Hill, though before then Joel had talked laboriously, as if explaining or excusing himself, determinedly, out of his embarrassment at finding Pamela alone when he had come to her flat – her husband, she had said, was motoring in the country with a friend from South Africa. It was at Pamela's suggestion that they had gone out for a walk, and Joel had conscientiously filled the silence between them with topics and explanations: the place of the graduate student in British universities, Professor Davidson, Hobson's *Imperialism*. Now

481

he had nothing to say; everything he had said before seemed shamingly pedantic, boring, pompous, beside the point.

But what was the point? Where were they going? He wanted to hear Pamela talk; but she walked silently beside him, her hands in the pockets of the flimsy raincoat she had taken from him a little earlier. The sway of her walk was womanly, unfamiliar, purposeful; she carried her heavy black head of hair upright, as if she were sure of herself. But Joel did not believe that she knew any better than he what they were doing together, so far from where they had first met, after so much had happened to them both.

Yet when she did speak it was to ask him, merely, as of an acquaintance, 'Why did you leave Israel?'

Because he had hoped for more after her long silence, the first word that came to his tongue was, 'Disappointment.' Then he added, 'In myself as much as in the country. Shock. Discomfort. Restlessness. The language. I suppose I just didn't like the place enough, basically.'

'Are you sorry about it now?'

'At times, I feel guilty to the people there – and to some part of myself – for having left. But I think I might have betrayed some other part by staying.' He walked on a few paces. 'The strange thing is that both parts seem to me equally Jewish.'

She answered severely, 'I don't know what that means.'

'Nor do I. If I knew then I'd no longer be the kind of Jew I am.'

'I don't know what that means either.'

'I'm sorry,' Joel said, with more irritation than regret. When he spoke again it was in his laborious, plodding, explanatory vein. 'You're a Gentile, Pamela, so your problems are your own in a way that mine aren't mine. Jews are always forced to generalize about their problems because they never know just how much is Jewish in them – that is, how much is imposed or accidental in a way – and how much is common, ordinary, human, necessary. I mean Jews like me, of course; Jews who've been brought up in the Gentile world – not Jews like my grandparents were. Mind, I'm not saying that that makes our problems or your problems easier or harder for either of us; that's something else again. It makes them different, inwardly, that's all.'

Pamela thrust her head forward suddenly, in an ugly aggressive movement, her fists clenched in her raincoat. 'God, I wish I could generalize my problems. I wish I felt they weren't just private and personal and insignificant. I suppose it serves me right for never really thinking about anything except myself – my life, my happiness, my decisions. So now that I know they're all good for nothing I've got nothing else. Nothing. Nothing.'

They had stopped walking. Pamela was not looking at him; she still stared angrily ahead. Joel did not know why she had spoken so passionately, what she meant by what she had said, but he reached out and touched her hand gently, as if from a distance, acting without thought; a gesture more of placation than of tenderness. Long after he had forgotten the expression on her face, the set lines of her features at that moment, he remembered the pattern made by a wall of reddish bricks and crumbling grey mortar behind her head.

'You're crying,' he said wonderingly. It was at his touch that the tears had come into her eyes.

She nodded, admitting it, lowering her head, her mouth trembling for what seemed to him an unendurably long time. Then she turned away from him, put her arms against the wall, and sobbed into them. She remained standing like that even after her tears were exhausted, making no sound, her shoulders still shaking in spasms. Joel watched her, all his curiosities already sated and self-disgusted, warning voices within him telling him that he should see her home quickly and quietly and never return.

He might have obeyed them had it not been for a sense of the lightness and absurdity of fate which held him there, and yet held him detached, in the sloping anonymous street, under a sky which as it darkened was acquiring colour once again, a deep, tense blue, everywhere at once. Was this what they had been aimed at, unknowingly, through the years, across the distances of the world? It might never have happened, easily enough.

22

'I was in the same camp in Egypt, just after the war,' Joel said. 'So I know exactly the place he's describing. He's got it beautifully – or horribly, rather – just as it was. And everyone shared the moods he deals with: now the war's over, now real life's going to begin again. But one of the things he shows in the book is that life's always real, wherever it's going on. That time in the camp was real, so was the place itself – and so was everyone's delusion that they weren't. It was a real delusion, if you see what I mean, one that we're always bound to fall into. The way he puts that across is what makes the book so strong. I thought it quite an achievement, I must say.'

Joel had found it easier than he had thought it would be to speak fairly of Malcolm's work; what had distracted him was not any impulse to denigration, but simply the strangeness of talking in this way to the author's wife, after what she had told him, at such length, with such shame and hopelessness, about her marriage. They sat in the isolation of his room, Pamela inexpertly smoking a cigarette, her feet curled under her in the armchair, her shoes lying on the carpet; next to the ash-tray was an empty coffee cup she had put there earlier. She answered him calmly, thoughtfully, with the same fairness of tone.

'The trouble is he really doesn't believe that achievement of that kind matters very much any more.'

'Do you?'

She said, less calmly, 'All I feel at the moment is that if the price of achieving anything is what he's had to pay – then who wants achievements? It's just too much, it isn't worth it.'

'And the price of not achieving anything?' Joel exclaimed. 'You think that's cheap? Believe me, it isn't. You pay, you pay, anyhow.'

He got up from the chair at his work-table, crossed the room to the window, looked out restlessly, then came back to sit on his chair. The desk lamp burned brightly, the only light in the room, its shade turned so that it lit up with a white glare one section of the wall to the side of him, leaving the rest of the room in shadow.

'No,' he said, speaking as if at random, moving his hands, 'I sit down to do my work – say, to show that you can't explain imperialism in this or that way, to show how much of it is compulsive and irrational. Fine. It's a useful job to be done. It's what I believe. I think there'd be less mischief in the world if more people believed it. But the trouble is that when I go on – or back – or into myself – I don't see any reason to believe in anything but compulsion and irrationality, whatever I deal with, wherever I begin or end. And *that* thought makes me miserable and incompetent; it makes the whole thing seem a waste of time. So the work suffers, and I pay more than ever for it in guilt and worry. Not that I haven't got simpler, lazier reasons for not getting on with it … It's like morality in a way, isn't it? Animals hunt for protein, we hunt for protein and prestige. That's what you must always begin and end with. But to complain because it's a vicious predatory universe is in itself to adopt a moral posture. So we're stuck inside it, inside morality, whatever we do. Which doesn't, God knows, begin to make us moral creatures.' He looked directly at Pamela, his hands falling into his lap. 'You know, one of the things I thought when you were crying in the street – I thought, well, I'm glad that I'm not the only one of us who's made a balls-up of his life. It gave me great satisfaction to think that, while I was standing by so kindly.' Then he said: 'Do you mind?'

'It's not very nice.'

'No, I didn't think so either. But that's me. That's practically every one of us, I'm sure. So go make sense of it. Go bring up your children to be responsible; respectable citizens, as kind as you can make them. But see they get their animal proteins.'

His own words reminding him to do it, he took her cup and his and went behind the beaverboard partition which cut off a corner of his room, and which hid a basin, a small gas-ring, and a tiny food cabinet. He made more Nescafé for them both and took out a packet of biscuits from the cabinet. When he came out he found her sitting in the armchair, as he had left her; only now she had her handkerchief in her hand. Despite the dim light he saw at once that she had been crying again. He put the tray on the floor and leaned over her, his hands gripping the top of the chair, his arms on both sides of his head. She looked up. Fatigue had made the colour of her face patchy, had changed its contours; her tears had reddened her eyes.

He spoke harshly, yet he intended to reassure her, to show her he had no wish to exploit her, or what she had told him. 'So we aren't going to go to bed with one another?' he said.

She stirred, captive between his arms. 'No, it doesn't look like it. Did you think we were?'

'I didn't know. I thought, probably, when I said we should come here and you agreed.'

'It seems hours ago.'

'It is.'

She looked at her watch, and what she saw made her yawn at once, childishly. She brought up her hand to cover her mouth. 'I'm sorry if I've disappointed you. All I've done is tell you my troubles.'

'Have I disappointed you?'

'No – I didn't know either – what we were going to do. I suppose it's just as well.'

He felt no desire for her, he was too tired, he had heard too much, been too surprised and agitated by some of what he had heard. It was only because he was afraid he might hurt her if he did not make some token advance to her that, leaning over her, he slowly lowered his head. Their foreheads met gently, and they smiled, their eyes wide open, each looking into the vague dark gleam of the other's. They kissed, without pretending to passion.

Joel stood up and gave Pamela her cup of coffee. 'No, if we were going to be lovers we should have done it a long time ago.'

'A long time ago tonight, or along time ago – really?'

'Either.'

She took the cup from him, added sugar to it, and began to drink from it. Joel went to the chair at his table, where he had been sitting before. For the first time since they had come into the room they were conscious of the silence of the streets outside – a silence broken at long intervals by the sound of a car passing along the main road a few blocks away. They could hear that each car was travelling fast, and that in itself was a reminder to them of the lateness of the hour. But they sat on, neither speaking, neither disturbed by the other's silence.

Eventually Joel said, 'So what are you going to do? Just carry on?'

'Or try to. I suppose so.'

'Do you still love him?'

'I could, if he'd let me.'

'What about children? Haven't you wanted them?'

'At first I did – very much. But I had a couple of miscarriages, one after the other, when we were in South Africa, and then, what with coming to England and everything, we decided not to try again. Since then things have been ... I just haven't thought about it. Except,' she added, with a shake in her voice, 'to worry that I can't anyway, that there's something wrong with me.'

The thought distressed Joel; he felt great pity for what the full, female line of her hips and thighs contained, under her thin cotton dress.

'What do the doctors say?'

'They don't really know why it happened, those times,' she said. She looked at him, as if asking for forgiveness, and he gave it to her readily, a queer, self-forgetful grimace of encouragement wrinkling his brow, drawing lines about his mouth.

After another silence she asked him when he had met Malcolm. He replied briefly – 'After an accident, just on the road' – but then the whole encounter became vivid to him, he remembered Natalie and the emptiness of the veld, the darkness, the fast-moving car, the strange, shattered desultoriness of his encounter with Malcolm and the girl, the return to the farmhouse. He described it all for her, and the inquest too, though he could recollect less about it; and Pamela listened intently.

'Malcolm never told me anything about it,' she said sadly, without surprise, when he had finished. 'Not a word.' Presently she asked, 'And your girl? What happened to her?'

'She didn't want to go to Israel, in the end. She married another bloke and went to Northern Rhodesia. Then he divorced him. I saw her in Joh'burg a few years later, in the street. She had a little blond kid, he was pulling at her hand. We stood and chatted for a bit, and that was that.'

23

Joel put Pamela into a lone taxi they found at a rank a few blocks from his room. She was shivering and soft in the corner of the cab, her face pale. He kissed her, but they did not speak of seeing each other again. Then he walked slowly back to his room. The air was chill and metallic, the streetlamps burned with a shallow, fatigued appearance, as if they knew how soon they would be superseded by the approach of dawn; there was dew on the metal of all the cars parked alongside the pavement, dulling their gleam. The tall terraces of houses were silent, with black doorways, lightless windows, roofs humped against the sky which had only just become a faint, visible surface, rather than an indeterminate darkness.

Only when he reached his room did Joel become aware of what had happened to him; the knowledge of it took possession of him the moment he opened the door. His desk-lamp still burned, throwing its white glare in a patch on the wall; his chairs, his bed, his books were where they had always been. But they would never be the same again, for upon them all was the impress or breath or taste of Pamela's presence. They contained her now; they reminded him of her.

She had stood here, looked there, picked up this; there was where her shoes had lain after she kicked them off, here was where she had been standing when she had turned her head in that remembered way, said those words, asked that question. Her pale stockinged legs, her pointed feet, her cotton dress, her arms, the black head of her hair he remembered these with a desire he had hardly felt at the time; but even his desire was merely a part of his sense of change, of being surrounded by her presence, of containing its power and wistfulness within him. Her cup was on the floor, next to the armchair, and he picked it up and stood with it in his hands looking at the coffee stain within it, looking at nothing.

Just outside the window a bird chirped, a peremptory, unhesitating utterance, a bright flicker and slither of sound, which was followed after an interval, from a distance, by an equally precise response. Joel found he was still holding the cup in his hand. He took a pace or two towards the little kitchenette, then changed his mind and put the cup down, next to his own on the table. The day would come soon enough – it was already coming; more birds were singing; the sky was looming brighter – and his changed room would change again, would be cleared, littered, cleared again, losing what it now had. He would rather fall asleep with everything in it as it had been when she had been there.

But he took a long time to fall asleep. Over and over again in his mind he went through some of the things they had said to each other, remembering her words and his, remembering especially her face in profile, seeing it always in calm, level movement through an element that existed only in his thought of her. It seemed incredible to him that they had done nothing but talk to one another, all the hours she had been in his room; yet he could not imagine them having done anything else, or anything more; he was content with what they had done.

He woke to the sense of change; it was still with him. Even the sky had changed in the few hours he had been asleep; he smelt the damp smokiness of the clouds in the air before he went to the window. That pungency in the nostrils was for him the very smell of London. Low, unmoving, soft, silent, a single gleaming grey in colour, the clouds filled all the sky that he could see, above the bulging and sloping roofs of the houses opposite, abolishing the glassy serenities and recessions of the previous evening. They were gone. This was another day beginning. Standing at the window, he felt that his own past, all that had gone before, was as unknowable to him as what he was going to do or become; the present was always ceaselessly altering the past, making another unexpected order or disorder out of it. And so it would be, until the end.

How extraordinary love was! This congested dizziness at the thought of her, this yearning wonder, this ache of incompletion because she wasn't there, this foolish conviction that all mysteries and the resolution to all mysteries were contained in the crook of her arms, the swell of her breast, the knuckles of her fingers – from where had they come? For how long would they last? How could he think of letting them rule his life, change it altogether? They would pass, they would be gone tomorrow.

'Of course. That's why I must act on them today,' he said to himself, and stood when he was at the window, as if in the stillness made by the certainty and decisiveness of his own response.

He was so filled with wonder that time passed before he realized he was taking it for granted that she, too, knew of the change that had taken place, that she shared his mood of tender comprehension and certainty. Then he was touched by the thought of her ignorance; he felt sorry for her, he wanted to reassure her, to break the good news to her. He looked at his watch. She was already at school; he did not even know the name of the school at which she taught. Well, he would phone in the afternoon, when she would be back from school.

And if, when he phoned, her husband answered – What then? Inevitably, with a horrible rapidity, his mood began to change once more. Later he sat over his books, trying to prepare the lecture he was supposed to be giving that evening; instead he kept himself busy itemizing the multitude of his weaknesses and stupidities, convicting himself of trouble-seeking, chivalry, neurosis, escapism, Jewish self-hatred, romanticism, shallowness, irresponsibility and megalomania. The English, he had often thought, were strange and foreign to him. What, for God's sake, did he imagine Pamela to be? She was a *shiksa* and another man's wife – nothing less! And what was he? Sir Galahad Glickman? With a great flamboyant crusader's cross upon his breast, doubtless, and his circumcized cock discreetly hidden? Dora, poor Dora, who came from a home like his own and who thought and felt about so many things so much like himself, he could not love. Pamela, when she had been young and free, he had not loved. No, he had to wait until she was worn, married and miserable; he had to hear that she had had a couple of miscarriages and was afraid her woman's organs were defective; he had to satisfy his appetite for failure: then he chose to say her name aloud into the empty room, then he stood mooning over her at the window, then he closed his eyes and tried to visualize her presence. He could no longer succeed even in doing that; all he saw was a pale, uncertain shape against the darkness, a shape that narrowed to a waist which he stretched out his arms to grasp, before letting them drop upon his papers on the table.

The morning seemed interminable, exhausting; it pulsated strangely, somewhere behind its light and sounds, its rhythms unlike those of other days. Tormented, he sat in his room with his books, then threw them aside, went out walking, stared around him at the crowded, busy pavements, the shop windows, the vehicles surging in the streets – unseeing and yet looking for something, he did not know what, among them; deafened by haphazard noises yet hoping to hear some meaningful sound, private to him, among them. He returned to his room and fell into a doze from which he awoke with a furious jerk, his heart beating, a bitter taste in his mouth, his head full of vague reverberating words that disappeared the moment he opened his eyes. But the confusion of his thoughts – meaner and more outrageous than ever – returned at once.

Did he suppose, he asked himself, did he suppose, fool that he was, that this sudden, overwhelming rapture of love he imagined himself to be feeling was not connected, for example, with the fact that his parents would be arriving in London within a few days? What was he trying to prove to them, what kind of pitiful, utterly childish assertion of his own adulthood was he planning to make – at his age, at twenty-seven? 'Look, I'm involved with a married woman! And a *shiksa*, too! So don't think I'm still your little Joel!' Was that it? He groaned at the thought; and struck his head like a lunatic at another. 'It's the times, it's the times we live in – such times of dislocation and loss – and see how Glickman, with a little bit of adultery, a bit of divorce, a bit of mixed marriage, conscientiously does his little best to embody them!' Was that his ambition? Every Sunday scribbler knew what a tragic figure he could cut by invoking the times, how he could put his profundity on show by mentioning the concentration camps. And now bankrupt, hysterical Glickman came to get his secret charge from the same vile source – was that it?

He read again, standing at his desk, the quotation he had intended using in his lecture that evening and had copied out for that purpose on a piece of paper: 'Chained, belted, harnessed like dogs in a go-cart, black, saturated with wet, and more than half-naked crawling upon their hands and feet, and tagging their heavy load behind them the children present an appearance indescribably unnatural and disgusting.'

That was not a description of a scene in a concentration camp, but an extract from the Children's Employment Commission, First Report, Mines, 1852. The children had been aged between seven and nine; they had worked down in the pits from four in the morning until half-past five in the evening. There were your times – all your times. There was your human race. And in all times the race had never been short of its Joel Glickmans: compassionate, but not too compassionate; indignant, but not too indignant; worried about others, but always, invariably, most worried about himself.

He was some catch, no doubt about it. How could she possibly resist his splendid self-confidence, his brilliant career, his glittering prospects, his habit of seizing hold of her and nagging her again and again with his daring views and mighty speculations?

'Pamela!' Joel imitated himself, calling to her in his empty room. 'Pamela!'

Once it had been his ambition to learn from the world rules, reasons, meanings; he had wanted to know from scratch how he should live; to know why he should live in one way rather than another. He had failed. Having failed he had consciously and deliberately decided to try and remain modest, cautious, demanding little for himself and expecting little from everyone else, living as quietly as he could, trying to do a job of work without asking of it that it should either change the world, or explain it. But even that, it seemed, was too much for him to manage. No, he had to try to live by romantic delusions, in the midst of crises which did not concern him, by proxies, by fanciful surrenders to fanciful passions, by utterances into empty rooms. 'Pamela!'

He had intended his cry to be self-taunting once more, derisory. But it came out as something else, and he sat quietly, for the first time in what seemed to be hours, the note of tenderness and appeal he had sounded still echoing in his ears. He visualized her perfectly clearly, and his heart opened at the precious, living singularity of her: her black hair, her white hands, her tired mouth.

24

Pamela saw Joel before he saw her; he was leaning with his back to the window of a men's outfitters, behind him an array of shirts, ties, and socks on truncated waxworks legs. He watched a bus pull up a little further down the road, and discharge a few passengers; from the way he looked at it she knew he was wondering if she were among them.

She came forward hesitantly.

'Joel.'

He turned, and she stiffened against the look that she feared might be on his face. But when she saw how surprised and irresolute was his expression, she ran forward the last couple of paces. 'Joel, don't be cross with me.'

'Cross?'

Tentatively, waveringly, they kissed, holding each other's hands, then looked anxiously at one another.

'I'm sorry I was so muddled on the phone. I'd just come home – I wasn't expecting you to phone – I didn't think you'd want –' She laughed, or tried to laugh, tightening her grasp on his hands, then withdrawing her own gently. Beyond him she saw the road going away, narrowing, the movements of the traffic within it seeming to grow smaller and smaller in the distance, until at the end there appeared to be only a dark, crowded stillness, filling the space between the buildings. 'Joel –'

As if the dazed weight were sunk far beneath his words, he asked her quietly, 'Pamela, will you marry me?'

For a long, silent moment she stared forward, her eyes dilated. Then she scolded him, waving her hands in agitation. 'What are you talking about? Why didn't you ask me before? When you could have? It's too late now.'

'No, it isn't.'

'It is. It is.'

Passers-by were looking at them. She broke away and began walking down the pavement not knowing what she was doing. He followed and caught up with her. She walked faster, refusing to look at him.

'Please go away, Joel.'

'I won't.'

'You must. You're talking nonsense. I'm married already.'

She fled, staring straight in front of her; still he walked alongside her.

'You can't go on living with that man. You can't leave me.'

'I can. I will.'

'You can't!'

'Why not?'

'Because I love you, Pamela. Can't you understand what I'm telling you? I want to live with you, I want to give you another life, I want to share with you everything I've got, and everything I do. I've never met anyone like you.'

'You don't know what you're saying. Joel, please stop it, please, please.'

'I do know what I'm saying. I've never known anything so well in all my life.'

'You feel sorry for me, that's all.'

'I don't. I love you.'

'You don't.'

'I do. I do. But if you don't want me to I suppose there's nothing I can do about it. Except,' Joel shouted, suddenly enraged by their stupid walking wrangle, and giving vent in his rage to the torment of all the other emotions he had suffered throughout the long morning, 'except to ask you never to come into my room and tell me your bloody miserable troubles ever again! I don't want to know them! Do you hear?'

In Pamela's sight the street was a single, undulating, wormlike expansion and contraction, shining in random gleams, showing darker and lighter patches, faces, trade names on shopfronts. Joel had stopped walking, she was leaving him behind. All she had to do was go on. Looking over her shoulder, she saw his face, hanging still among all the moving faces in the street – angry, accusing, swollen. What had she wanted from him? Why was she running from him? She remembered his kindness to her the previous night, the sympathy with which he'd listened to her, his sad irritation with himself; she thought of the vein of impulsiveness in him which had always touched her and had brought him now to his wild proposal; she saw herself, flustered and graceless, running back in fear to her familiar misery. What was she running from? The danger of happiness?

It was when she decided that her chances of happiness were remote indeed, whatever she did, that she turned and walked slowly back towards him. All she had thought while staring at him had been compacted into a single reflex, a single shock; yet she felt that many minutes had passed since the last words he had shouted at her.

She spoke humbly, with difficulty. 'I'm sorry I told you my troubles, Joel. I had no right to do it. I shouldn't have come this afternoon either, when you phoned.' But she still had not made her confession. 'Joel,' she said, 'when Malcolm went away, and I knew I'd be on my own when I saw you, I was hoping that something would happen between us. I didn't think what, I didn't want to. But I was excited about it and glad, because I'd always liked you so much, and I thought you were so nice when I met you again. So I can't just run away pretending I don't feel anything about you, or wasn't hoping … But now I don't want it. I can't listen to you. I truly cannot.'

'You want to stay with him?'

'Joel, what else can I do? I'm married to him. You don't understand what it's like.'

'What? Marriage?'

'Yes.'

'I should have taken you to bed last night. I don't know why I didn't.'

'Perhaps if you had you wouldn't be asking me to live with you.'

'Perhaps not.' He drew in a breath. 'Either way, I'd be better off than I am now.'

Pamela knew exactly what she was going to say. 'I'm sorry, Joel. Goodbye.' She opened her mouth and tried to speak. Her throat contracted, she bowed her head to him. 'I know I can love you too, Joel. If you really want me to.'

25

That night, because she had nowhere else to go, and because she was afraid of what might happen to her or what she might feel if she were separated from him, Pamela went with Joel to the rundown building in Kentish Town, where he was to give his lecture; she sat shivering in spasms, her stomach hollow with anxiety, in a classroom together with twelve or fifteen others, listening to him talk. He was a better lecturer than she had thought he might be: less hesitant, more assured, more provocative. She did not know how many of his most effective mannerisms were those he had learned in Johannesburg from Professor Viljoen; but she did notice, listening to him in the presence of others, how much stronger his South African accent sounded to her than it did when she heard him alone. At the end of the lecture she could hardly have repeated a word that he had said, though she believed the particular dingy shade of the yellow-brown paint on the walls to be stamped forever on her memory.

They had decided that she should spend the night in his room; what would happen the day after, or three days later when Joel's parents were due to arrive, they simply did not know. But, while they were on the bus travelling from Kentish Town, Pamela suggested that they should go to her flat, just to see if Malcolm had come home; they had agreed that he should be told as soon as he returned, by them both if possible, that Pamela was leaving him. They dreaded the meeting, not having the faintest idea of what to expect – though each of them had his own vivid, frightening imaginings – and for that reason they were eager to get it over with. Nothing could be worse than waiting, they had said; yet both of them, as they went up the stairs of the building, were inwardly praying that they would find the flat dark, silent, deserted.

Malcolm was back; he and Swannie were together in the living room. Joel and Pamela came blinking into it; it took Joel some seconds before he could see how spacious and lightly furnished the room was, cushions of bright red and blue standing out against the darkness of the edge-to-edge carpeting and the bare whiteness of the walls. Pale, striped curtains were drawn across the windows at the far end of the room.

'Hullo,' Malcolm said, when they had come in. 'What's this?' Swannie had got up, but Malcolm sat on the couch, his legs stretched in front of him.

'You know Joel,' Pamela said. 'This is Swannie.' Her voice was high and clear; for the moment she felt lucid, confident, forgiving, no longer at all afraid. Swannie and Joel nodded at one another. 'Malcolm, Joel and I would like to speak to you.'

'What about?'

Before she could answer, Swannie said, 'You want me to go.'

'No,' Malcolm answered, turning his gaze from Pamela for the first time since she had come into the room. 'You don't have to go.'

'I'd rather, Malcolm –' Pamela said.

Jerkily, embarrassed, Swannie began to make for the door. But Malcolm called him back. 'What's the secret? That you've been up to something while I've been away? I knew it as soon as you walked in. It's all over your faces. Yours especially,' he said to Joel. 'You look like a thief.' He added a little later, 'A slightly defiant thief.'

499

Joel moved, planting his legs apart, clasping his hands behind his back. His left knee was shaking uncontrollably; he hoped it could not be seen through the flannel of his trousers.

He and Pamela were side by side in the middle of the room, Swannie was behind them, near the door.

'Sit down,' Malcolm said, with a wave of his hand.

'No,' Joel answered. It was the first word he had said.

'Joel has asked me to live with him. I've said yes.'

'I see.'

They waited, in the bright light, between the bare walls, as if to be told what they should do or feel, each staring straight ahead. Pamela said, 'That's all.'

She turned towards the door.

'Jesus Christ is that all?' Malcolm said, watching her, his voice rising. His face, his whole body, expanded visibly, as if more air or blood than it could contain were passing through it. He did not move. None of them moved, then they saw the spasm diminish within him; he did not struggle either to quell it or to call it back. At last it was gone, and he could speak again, quietly, rid of passion or surprise, almost with enjoyment.

'All for love, hey. Not me, then him. Not him, then someone else. But always chasing it, hotfoot. You should have seen her when I met her, Glickman. Panting for love, dying for love, always ready to wallow in it and then come up for more. She could love anyone.'

Joel said: 'I know.'

'Even you.' Malcolm nodded his head. 'She'll drive you mad with her love, before she's finished with you. You haven't got enough love in you for her: no one has. She thinks the whole world was made to love her and to be loved by her, for no other purpose. And it's wicked, it's wicked to suggest anything else. Is that what you think, too, Glickman? Are you also a lover of the world – a lover of love?'

'No.'

'You don't look like one. But you're ready to run off with her, right away, all the same? Well, go on, get on with your loving, your kissing, your fucking, your raptures. I'm not going to oblige you by staging a big dramatic scene, so there's no point in waiting around for one. I'm not going to help you feel heroic and splendid about what you're doing. You'll have to dig up your own splendours. Dig them out of her, if you can. I've been working there for long enough, I can tell you. All for love!'

He rose suddenly to his feet, and Joel started. Malcolm looked him up and down. 'You're not such a hero. What do you do with yourself, Glickman, when you're not falling in love with other men's wives?'

'Come,' Joel said. 'I think we've heard enough.' He took Pamela by the arm. But Swannie stood in the way.

'You've just been asked a question,' he said. 'Answer it.'

'I don't know who you are. I don't have to say anything to you.'

They stood facing one another, breathing through dry, open lips.

'Swannie!' Pamela cried out, in a chiding, fearful tone. At the same moment, clumsily, heavily, like a man pushing at a door, he swung out at Joel.

Malcolm had started after them. Pamela was against the wall, her hand to her cheek, a sound coming from her throat. There was blood on Joel's lips, on his teeth; he stood still, his eyes wide open, as if listening. Malcolm pushed Swannie back. 'When I want your help I'll ask for it,' he shouted. He held him, in an embrace that was furious and affectionate. Swannie did not resist. Seconds passed, scraping by to the sound of their breath.

Joel took Pamela by the arm again. The door of the room closed behind them. Then the two men heard the slam of the outside door.

Malcolm let go of Swannie's shoulders. 'I want your help,' he said.

26

Out in the street Pamela asked Joel, 'Do you still want me to come with you? Or do you want me to go back inside?'

He stood under a streetlamp wiping his lip with a handkerchief. 'It's shameful,' he said. 'I was wondering why I felt I'd got off lightly. It's because no one made any anti-Semitic remarks.'

Pamela began to cry. She cried all the way to Joel's room; she was still crying when she took off her dress and she got between his rumpled sheets, in her white petticoat.

He threw her dress over a chair; it fell softly, crumpling, a flake. Then he went to lock the door. He stood over the bed, looking at her round dark head thrust into the pillow, her face hidden from him. His lip felt swollen and tasted salty; it stung sharply when he passed his tongue over it. He couldn't have kissed her even if he had wanted to. He began to undress slowly. When he looked again at Pamela he saw that she was watching him.

She tried to smile. It was so little, a movement of her lips and eyes, but it was more than he could bear. He switched off the light and got into bed with her; she passed her arm under his neck. They lay together for a long time, tense, wakeful, silent, still, the warmth of their bodies filling the bed. Neither had any faith in the future each had promised the other.

27

On board the *Johannesburg Castle* the days had drummed, swayed and quivered by, each morning and evening like the last, the centre of the circling horizon always the solitary, moving boat. Sarah and Benjamin shared their dinner-table in the cabin class dining room with Morry and Rina, and with two elderly widows who had made the cruise to South Africa for the sake of their health, and who were now returning to Eastbourne and Leamington respectively. One of the widows was soft and shrinking and quite without opinions; the other was of a sterner sort, and towards the end of the voyage was telling her table companions about the truth of certain prophecies which could be deduced on mathematical principles from the measurements of the Great Pyramid. These, she suggested, should be of especial interest to those who claimed (fallaciously, she believed) to be descended from the Ancient Hebrews. For the rest, Morry and Rina played bridge and canasta in the evenings, after Selwyn had gone to sleep, and the Glickmans found that they were far from being the only Jewish couple on board who were going to meet their student sons in London.

Few other vessels were seen, until the last two days of the voyage; then, crossing the Bay of Biscay and steaming up the Channel, other boats were always in sight, so that a sense of the closeness and populousness of Europe came to the passengers even before their first sight of land. On the last night the liner stood idle in the Southampton roadstead, waiting for morning; lights shone softly in the darkness around it, far off, low down, scattered in every direction.

Joel was waiting for the boat train at Waterloo the next morning. Standing over them, he couldn't really believe in the presence of his parents on the platform, in the first, confused moment of greeting; and this feeling of incredulity recurred several times later during the day. This was his context, not theirs, he felt these crowded streets and soot-stained buildings, this soft, complicated sky, the strained tortuousness of his own feelings. Several times, amused and challenging, he found he wanted to ask them, 'Hey, what are *you* doing here?'

What they did on the first morning, was to say goodbye amidst the bustle of the station, to Rina, Morry and Selwyn, as well as to several others of their fellow-travellers, and then to go by cab to the service flat off Portland Place that Joel had taken for them. (Rina and Morry had booked a room in the Cumberland Hotel.) By the time they had unpacked a few of the things they needed immediately, and had washed their hands and brushed their hair, it was time for lunch, which they had, with Joel, in a restaurant in Marylebone High Street. During the meal the eagerness and uncertainty of arrival still on them, the steadiness of the ground under their feet making them unsteady, they gave Joel their news about the family, about their trip, about conditions in South Africa; Benjamin spoke about the business arrangements he had made and Bertie's prospects. Then they returned to the flat, and Joel left them to have a rest, while he went to University College library to enquire about some books he had been told he would be able to find there. But he couldn't remember what they were, he couldn't pursue his own enquiries; he was too restless, too much shaken inside by the reunion – by the love and pity he felt for his parents; by their dependence on him; by the reality their talk had given to his memories of South Africa; by what had changed in their appearance, and by all he saw in them that for him hadn't changed since his eyes had opened to the world; by his thoughts of Pamela, of whom they knew nothing. By the clutch of life, and its incessant, swift unreeling.

He was also desperately, almost drunkenly fatigued. Since Pamela had moved into his room, into his single bed, they had had no more than a few hours sleep; all the rest had been talk, tears, some love-making, a little laughter, scraps of food at unlikely hours, no work – an existence that seemed nocturnal even during the long hours of daylight.

With sore, tired eyes he looked at the backs of many books, he opened many journals and glanced into them, reading paragraphs of articles here and there, then went to the students' refectory for tea. It was near the end of term, the examinations had started, and there were few people about in the long corridors and the great Italianate quadrangle outside; even the tearoom was empty. The stillness was familiar but not soothing; it seemed to contain within itself all the tedium and desultoriness of the kind of life he seemed to have chosen for himself. Yet the sweep of the building lifted his spirits, when he looked back on it, on his way out: it was self-consciously, deliberately imposing, but its builders had felt themselves securely entitled to the assertions they had made, more than a century before. While the children crawled on their hands and feet in the coal mines.

Then back to the flat, to find Sarah and Benjamin much refreshed, and a little shyer than they had been previously.

'So, are you ready to go sightseeing?' Joel asked.

'You're the sight we want to see the most of,' Sarah answered, smiling.

'Is there anyone else you want to get in touch with?'

'I must phone Rina tomorrow evening. Selwyn goes for his first examination in the morning, already, and I'd like to hear what the doctors say. And there's Jonathan, your cousin. How is he? Do you ever see him?'

'Only on television – once.'

'Really – you've seen him doing his programme?' Sarah was most excited. 'It's wonderful that he should have made such a success over here. What is it, exactly, this programme of his?'

'Some kind of daft game – he gets famous people and they tell about the most embarrassing moments in their lives, or the happiest, and that kind of thing, and the audience votes who was most embarrassed or whatever it is by pressing buttons. Jonathan's master of ceremonies, and doesn't he just love it! Honestly, from what I saw of him I don't think he'll be much interested in you or me or any of us. He's in the big-time.'

'Well, he deserves to be. Samuel told me that he had a lot of heartache when all that film business collapsed. It's wonderful that he's so versatile and ambitious, that he can go from one thing and be such a success in another. And Samuel tells me that he's still got an interest in films, he hasn't altogether given it up.'

'All right, Mom. Phone him if you like. You'll never change, will you?'

'Never!' Benjamin said disagreeably.

Sarah did not attempt to defend herself. 'We'd also like to meet some of the people you've mentioned in your letters, Joel. If you think you can bear to introduce your unfashionable parents to them.'

'Oh, I think I can summon up enough social courage for that.'

'Dora?' They both said her name, eagerly.

It was an effort for Joel to speak calmly; both because of what he was revealing to them, and because of what he was keeping hidden.

'I'm afraid we've bust up.'

'Oh.' They were disappointed, but did not ask any questions. They could not hide from their faces, however, their anxiety to see him married, settled, safe within the bulwarks of domesticity. Joel was moved by their concern; their marriage, after all, had not been such a happy one. But he knew that their private experience was somehow beside the point. In its history the race had found few enough bulwarks of any other kind against the menace of the world.

There were, it appeared, a few other people in London they wanted to see, including a family by the name of Pogrund with whom Benjamin had lived in the East End for a few weeks on his way to South Africa, fifty years before. The old people were dead, but he remembered the children and he had always promised himself a return visit to them.

'We'll draw up a programme, then: people, shows, sights, shops – whatever you want.'

When they set out for dinner Benjamin insisted that they go to a Jewish restaurant of which he'd been told by someone in Johannesburg. He had its name and address in his notebook. It turned out to be a rather large bare place, scantily patronized considering its size, with portraits of Herzl, Weizmann and Ben Gurion hanging from its shabby walls; but Benjamin sniffed the air appreciatively when they walked in.

'After fourteen days of that Union Castle cookery, this smells right to me.'

'Then you better eat as much as you can. They don't serve Jewish food in Israel.'

'It's a most extraordinary thing,' Benjamin agreed. 'Still, they say the food position has improved out of comparison with what it was when we were last there.'

They settled down, examined the menu, and placed their orders with a small, swarthy, middle-aged waiter, who made no response to Benjamin's demonstrative greetings and remarks in Yiddish.

'What's he?' Benjamin asked, after the waiter had left. 'A snob?'

'No, just a tired old man,' Sarah said.

'You've never been here before?' he asked Joel.

'No.'

'I'd have thought you'd have found a place like this for yourself.'

'I can't say I've gone looking for Jewish restaurants, especially. I've been to Bloom's in the East End a couple of times.'

'We must go there, too, I know about Bloom's. I want to go to the East End, anyway, to see if I can still recognize some of the places there. I hear there isn't much left of the old Jewish East End, they say it was knocked flat in the bombing … One hundred and eleven Mile End Road – that's where I lived with the Pogrunds. It was all the English I knew, when I landed. I wonder if the house is still standing. They moved long ago. The one son lives now' – Benjamin again pulled out his notebook from his breast pocket, continuing to talk in the way of a vigorous, garrulous old man while he opened it and went carefully through its pages, with his bent, brown fingers – 'I had the address from Burgin, he keeps in touch with them, he visited when he was here last – ah – here it is – Clifton Gardens, St John's Wood.'

'That's a long way from Mile End Road.'

'Yes, he became a big man, in furniture. The other son's a lawyer, I think. Perhaps it'll be useful for you to come with us and meet them. It may be a house for you to visit, where you can meet people, or have a meal sometimes.'

Joel believed he knew the drift of some of his father's remarks, even if Benjamin himself didn't. Joel was not mistaken. Towards the end of the meal, Benjamin asked him, 'Tell me, do you keep in touch with Jewish things, with any Jewish organization, with Jewish people?'

'Oh, Benjamin,' Sarah protested wearily. 'Leave him alone. What does it matter?'

'Let him answer for himself.'

'Well, most of the people I know are Jews. What else should they be? But with Jewish organizations – no, I don't.'

'And this doesn't worry you?'

'Not any more than a lot of other things.'

Benjamin's eyes moved restlessly. But he did not want to argue with Joel, on their first evening. He was somewhat surprised – almost disappointed – to find that he did not want to argue with Joel at all.

28

Both Sarah and Benjamin slept badly that night, though they went to bed peacefully enough, after doing a little more unpacking and exchanging a few casual remarks. Sarah slept badly because she always did, especially in new places; Benjamin because he was disturbed by many obscure dreams, which culminated in a vision of himself running under the trees of a wide boulevard, in some nameless European city which he knew in his dream to be occupied by the Nazis. Softly, gently, dispersed at random in the darkness, yet always at a distance from him, streetlamps twinkled; he ran, knowing it was too late, he should have fled before; then, directly in front of him, among the lights and leaves and shadows, he saw black uniformed men waiting. He woke on his back, his heart pounding, his neck sweating, his hands folded in a heavy corpse-like position across his stifled chest. It seemed to take him minutes to find out that he was in bed, to remember that Hitler was dead, to realize that he was in London. London!

Sarah called him by name from her bed. 'You've had a nightmare.'

Some time passed before he answered her. 'Yes.'

'I was asleep. But I thought I heard you call out.'

'The lights,' he said, 'they were the lights we saw from the boat.'

She knew he was still caught up in his dream. 'Go to sleep again.'

'Yes.' He breathed out heavily, and swallowed, smacking his lips. 'Yes.' But he passed the rest of the night in a slow pale doze; he was afraid to sink deeply into his sleep once more. He was surprised to see how early, in this long-unvisited latitude, the dawn lightened the sky.

Joel, too, saw the beginning of the day filling his room with light. Pamela slept nearest the wall, one loosely-clenched hand leaning against it. The very root of him had been aching for her, when he had woken to her heat and closeness; but once he was awake, his desire receded, his flesh shrank; he remembered, in the dreariness of the dawn, how upset she had been when he had come home and told her that he hadn't spoken of her to his parents. 'What are you afraid of?' she had cried. 'You've got to tell them, if you mean any of the things you've been saying to me. You've got to, you've got to.'

He remembered also, his thoughts returning obsessively to it, the scene between themselves and Malcolm. He felt he had been worsted, made a fool of, degraded; Begbie had turned what might be one of the greatest events of Joel's life into a tiresome, contemptible disagreement, hardly worth more than the notice of scorn and relief; and he had stood there, letting the man do it, even agreeing with him, positively grateful, in his weakness and cowardice, that nothing more was asked of him. Now, for the hundredth time, Joel imagined himself uttering passionate denunciations of Begbie and irresistibly persuasive, final, meaningful explanations of all that he himself was and had done; he clenched his fist and with one blow sent Begbie flying; joyfully he came upon Begbie stark dead on the Potchefstroom road.

Then it was time to get up.

29

The doctors in London confirmed the diagnosis of Selwyn's condition which had been made by the doctors in Cape Town: he was suffering from Perthes disease, a crumbling of the head of the femur. The caliper he was wearing was of the right kind, the London doctors said, that he should continue to wear it; there was nothing more that could be done. They confirmed also that the Cape Town doctors had been correct in their prognosis that the degenerative process should come to an end, without any further treatment; but that the joint would not reform in its original shape. Selwyn, they said, would be left with a limp; and he would almost certainly develop osteo-arthritis in later life.

Morry and Rina showed only on their faces how much they were disappointed; they said little about it, even to each other, both for the sake of the child and because neither now wished to remember the blind hope they had invested in their trip. In his disappointment Morry was ready to return at once to South Africa; but Selwyn insisted, once the examinations were over, that he wanted to see all the famous sights of London before they left – he wanted to see the Tower, Madame Tussaud's, St Paul's, the Changing of the Guard – and so they put off their departure.

Morry went to the Midlands and the North on his own, to look at some milling plants and factories which made milling machinery. He came back unimpressed by what he had seen. Then the sad, well-dressed, wealthy, tense little family group left by air for South Africa.

Their plane left in the afternoon, and Joel and Sarah went to the terminal to see them off. Benjamin was asleep in the flatlet; it was now his invariable rule to sleep after lunch. Coming back from the terminal Joel told his mother about his affair with Pamela.

Sarah walked with her arm through his. It was a whitish, glaring, gusty day, and the curls of her hair were blown over her forehead, even over the lenses of her glasses; her mouth hung slightly open with the effort she was making, though he was careful to suit his pace to hers. They were going towards Victoria Station, where they could get a bus back to the flat.

'That's why you're not seeing Dora any more?'

'Yes.' Then he asked her, 'Are you upset?'

'Upset? Of course. How much happiness can you get from such an affair?'

'I don't know. There hasn't been very much so far.'

'Why didn't you tell me before?'

'I didn't want to upset you. Besides, I wanted to be surer of myself before I spoke to you.'

'Are you surer now?'

'I decided I couldn't be surer until I'd told you. I'd got it the wrong way round.'

They walked for a few paces, along the pavement, the black, ruled-off, busy street to one side. The clothing of passers-by was blown out or blown flat against their bodies by the wind, women walked with their hands up to hold on to their hats, a large piece of newspaper on the pavement seemed to rouse itself awkwardly and shuffle like a living thing across the road, before being squashed flat under the wheels of a car.

'Joel, you and Dora – were you – lovers?'

'You mean, were we sleeping with one another? Yes.'

His answer reassured her, in a small way; at least he had made a choice that had been dictated by something more than physical frustration, which had been her immediate fear or speculation. She did not remember Pamela at all, except vaguely, as a name, and was somewhat surprised that she felt so little hostility towards her. Rather, she felt a great curiosity about Pamela; and indeed about Dora, too – these girls who did what she had never done, who slept with men to whom they were not married. She supposed they felt desire as men did, as women in books did, as she never had.

She said, with a faltering step, 'I'd like to meet Pamela.'

'She'd like to meet you. She's very nervous about it, though; she's afraid of what you'll think of her.' He tried to reassure her. 'She isn't what she might sound like to you, I promise you that. She isn't hard or assured or calculating, really she isn't. She was in a mess, and now she's in another. But she's a good girl – I

512

mean, she wants to live as well as she can, and as much as she can. I suppose it's her eagerness that I really like her for, if there's any one thing I can say that about.' He gave up the task he had taken on; he said, 'I can't talk you into liking her, but I'll be so glad if you do. So will she.'

'You want to marry her? If she's free?'

'Yes, I said I did. It's funny – the only lawyer I knew I could ask about a divorce was Dora. She was very decent about it, and she's going to put us in touch with a man she knows, a South African who's practising as a solicitor here. It's all pretty complicated, the legal side. As far as I can see it mostly depends on Begbie. But we're doing nothing about it in the meantime, anyway, and she hasn't heard from him. She hasn't seen him. He wasn't there when she went to the flat to collect some of her things.'

Joel went on talking busily, until they were sitting in the bus. Then he fell silent, suddenly exhausted. When he looked at Sarah, her plump body shaking with the movement of the bus, her hair disordered, her bespectacled face grave, he wanted to unsay all his words, if only because he felt so little surer in himself as a result of them; only deeper in the affair. But perhaps that was as much certainty as he might hope for.

Presently, Sarah said, 'I'll have to tell your father about it. It isn't fair for me to keep secrets from him.'

'I thought you'd feel like that. Then I better tell him. Do you think he'll take it badly? Start ranting and raving?'

'I don't know. He would have, five years ago. He isn't going to be pleased, that's for sure.'

'I wasn't expecting either of you to be pleased.'

'Which is perhaps why you've done it.'

'I don't know, mom, honestly I don't know. I've asked myself that so many times, and still haven't come up with an answer. The nearest I've managed to one is that if I went to Israel for dad's sake, perhaps in some mad way I want to marry Pamela for your sake.'

'For my sake?'

'Well, it's a way of putting it.'

'A very strange way,' Sarah said, displeased.

'You really think so?'

Sarah thought before she answered him. 'You must do what you do for your own sake.'

'I'm trying to do that too.'

30

Benjamin did not rant and rave; on the contrary, he behaved with great circumspection and firmness. He declined to meet Pamela; he said he would not do so until it became certain that she and Joel would marry. He did not hide his hope that this would never happen. Then he made no further mention of the matter.

Sarah and Pamela, however, met several times. They were quiet and uncertain at first, then suddenly at their ease, almost triumphantly so, delighting in the implausibility of the straightforward affection they felt for one another. After she had seen Sarah for the last time, Pamela told Joel that she had felt a greater warmth towards herself from Sarah than from any other woman she had ever known, including her own mother.

For the rest, Joel rediscovered, in attendance upon his parents, the weariness of visitors' London: of the constant pressure of being always in public places; of the distances that had to be traversed daily from one sight to another; of the visitors' having nowhere of their own to go to except the impersonal service flat whose walls and furniture gave forth almost the same odour of transience as an hotel room might have done; of the need to have, in these circumstances, a good time, under pain of failing one another and wasting the money that was constantly being spent. Yet there were also, for all of them, occasions when they did have a good time, when they felt their efforts to be fully rewarded.

One such moment came for Benjamin when they visited the house he had lived in, in Mile End Road, and found that though the bombing had levelled almost everything around it, that house still stood. The only change he could see in it was that the shop on the ground floor had been boarded up. But there were still curtains on the windows of the upper floors, where he had lived with the Pogrunds, before setting out with Avrom and Meyer for Africa. Another most successful excursion was when Benjamin and Sarah went as members of the studio audience to watch Jonathan's show being televised. For, in spite of Joel's expectations, Jonathan had come to see them and had been courteous and thoughtful towards them. On the night of the show he sent a car to call for them; after the show he introduced them to the famous don, the famous general, the famous footballer and the famous nightclub singer who had made up his panel for that evening's performance. He seemed, Sarah reported to Joel, pitching her words as modestly as possible, very happy in his work. Benjamin added, his old grudges forgotten for the moment, 'And very good at it too! They were eating out of his hand, all those Englishmen!'

Before they left, Benjamin had what he called a serious talk – not the first in Joel's life – about Joel's future. If Bertie's business proved successful, he pointed out, really successful, the firm might well be able to use a man in London. It wasn't a prospect for the immediate future; but he thought that Joel should bear it in mind. Joel, his responsibilities as a possible husband weighing upon him as much as his dissatisfactions with himself as a research student, promised earnestly that he would do so.

31

'They've settled down better than I thought they would,' David wrote in his diary, two months after the arrival of his parents in Israel. 'Their coming has changed things less for me than I thought it would. Which is a good thing, both for their sake and for mine. For their sake because it means they're able to manage for themselves – they've got friends in that "California-style" village of theirs, the house is comfortable, they've found fat Masha to work in it, Dad is busy with his schemes and talk, Mom with pottering around the house and writing letters. For my sake because I know how much I value my privacy. I didn't want it disrupted. It hasn't been.' The fact that David kept a diary was just one aspect or symptom of the privacy he cherished so greatly. His most intense experiences were those he had when he was alone.

At times this worried him; then he made an effort to see people, to go out with other students in his classes, to invite the other lodgers in Mrs Beilinson's house into his room for coffee or to listen to his records. But he didn't find that he got much out of such attempts at sociability, and they had become less and less frequent. It was enough, he usually felt, to be in the company of others in the classrooms, laboratories and workshops of the Technion, or to drink coffee with them during breaks, or to work with strangers on the jobs he was obliged to take during his vacations. In any event, there was so much swotting to be done for the course that he would have had to be on his own much of the time, whether he liked it or not. So it was just as well that it was what he positively wanted.

Of the three Glickman children David had always been the best at maths and science, the one who had most enjoyed messing about with Meccano and chemistry sets as a child, and with machines and motor cars as an adolescent; he had always been the neatest and most deft of them with a pencil. When he looked back now it puzzled him that he had never seriously thought of doing a technical course until he had come to Israel, and had decided then to take his diploma in civil engineering at the Tech. But this puzzled him no more than so many other things about the self he had been in South Africa. Looking back, it seemed to him that he had never been anything but a fool, a snob and a weakling, always self-indulgent, even in those periods when he had been self-hating as well.

Snobbery had told him, for example, that engineers were invariably philistines; snobbery, again, had told him that he shouldn't think of taking medicine, because the profession was intolerably overcrowded with nice Jewish boys who had proud Jewish mothers. And to make his life's choices for such reasons had not merely seemed to him sufficient; they had been a source of inward pride to him! Imagine being proud of not living up to the expectations of the *goyim* – as if that in itself were not a form of slavery to them! Imagine turning one's back on the satisfactions of what he had learned to do at the Tech for the sake of some vague, empty notion of 'culture' or 'refinement' – as if true, individual culture and taste were not derived from one's knowledge of what it was like to be devoted to, and absorbed in, the tasks one set one's hand to.

He had been a social slave, nothing more. Most people were. They would willingly endure boredom and falsity rather than be alone for any time at all; they would clutch at any distraction to avoid recognizing their true needs; they denied what they felt or lied about it to themselves, zealously, devoutly, in order to agree with (or at least not to be discommoded by) the lies of others. The intellectuals were no better than the bourgeoisie – look at the books the intellectuals read, the plays they jabbered about, the fashions they followed – and the bourgeoisie were no better than the workers. The great chain of lying held them all together; it also burdened them, twisted their moral limbs out of shape.

517

All this David could say he had experienced from within, having been a liar and a hypocrite himself, for so long; he knew what it was like. Now, by contrast, if he felt that it helped him to pray at regular times at the neighbouring synagogue, if he was glad to be a member of the religious-national group to whom the land had belonged epochs before and to whom it miraculously belonged once again, if he was proud of the useful, professional skill he was acquiring, he believed that these participations in the life of the community did not bind him or restrict him at all. They differed from the others he had known precisely because they set him all the more deeply free to be on his own, without guilt, anxiety or shame.

He had long since given up the attempt to make an orthodox Jew of himself. He rode in taxis on the Sabbath, he worked on some of the feasts and fasts, he did not care if his meat were kosher or not. But he remained a believer, and, on his own terms, a believing Jew. These terms were defined for him in a text from Deuteronomy to which, having undergone in his own body and mind again and again, what they spoke of, he gave total, unconditional assent. When he had read the verses for the first time he had trembled in his chair, overwhelmed by the sense he had of being seen and recognized by the words, rather than of recognizing them:

> *It is not hidden from thee, neither is it far off.*
>
> *It is not in heaven that thou shouldest say, Who shall go up for us to heaven, and bring it unto us, that we may hear and do it?*
>
> *Neither is it beyond the sea, that thou shouldest say, Who shall go over the sea for us, and bring it unto us, that we may hear it, and do it?*
>
> *But the word is very much nigh unto thee, in thy mouth and in thy heart, that thou mayest do it.*

32

Very nigh. In solitude, in concentration, in devotion, in submission, in patience, the truth moved through his heart and mouth, within his whole body. Not in words and visions, not in exhortations and instructions, not in lights and darknesses; but in what he could think of only as a pressure: a pressure of response that was at times no more than a touch, a brush of being, and that was sometimes much more. Then his rhythms ceased to be his own and became another's; he did not breathe but was breathed in and breathed out, as his breast rose and fell; he pulsed with soft, slow strokes which were not those of his heart only; he was filled in his limbs with a weight they contained but did not possess. The only measurement of the pressure was its intensity; he was told nothing of it by his watch, which raced forward or stood at one point, leaving him with a vague recollection of having done nothing more since he had last looked at it than close his eyes, or of having laboured, swooned, babbled, waited in stillness, before the response was upon him, within him.

Such experiences were not the only rewards of solitude; often they did not come for weeks on end, and during those weeks he did not feel himself deprived or abandoned. There was his work, which gave him a pleasure that was almost as much sensuous as intellectual; he enjoyed even the ache in his back that came after he had been stooping for hours over his drawing-board; he relished the sight of his pencil drawings on the white sheets of drawing-paper, and the bold black ink of his tracings on the pale blue tracing-sheets, which had to his nostrils such a strong, distinctive smell; he felt physically relieved and gratified every time a maths or physics problem he was working on came at last to its solution, its ineluctable order and coherence at last revealed. There was his reading: he read a great deal, sitting on his little balcony or lying on his bed with a pillow under his neck – going slowly through the Old and New Testaments, parts of the Talmud and the Zohar, as well as Buber on Hasidism, or Newman's *Apologia*, or Nietzsche, and others that came to hand; he read Tolstoy's *Religion and Morality* and *What I Believe*, but was bored by *War and Peace* and did not finish it. There was his diary: when he had nothing of his own to write in it he transcribed sentences and paragraphs from what he had read. There was his music: he seldom went to the concerts given in town, where he found the people around him and the faces and antics of the musicians a distraction, but he had become addicted to listening to it on gramophone records. His favourite composers were Bach, Schubert and Vaughan Williams; and he liked to imagine that people who knew about music would be unable to make sense of such a selection.

There was also, at all times, the view from the little balcony outside his room – a tiny courtyard or garden just below, and the stony gulleys, valleys and ridges of the back of the Carmel falling away to the east, with flat-topped houses of stone perched on them at angles here and there, and a new *shikun* for immigrants dominating the brow of the nearest hill to the left. The *shikun* was of a dirty grey in colour, with hideous red-tiled roofs, but most of the other houses were made of stone, and their sallow colours blended with those of the hills. Biblical colours he thought them to be: yellow, brown, white, pale blue, the green of slender cypresses and straggling carob trees. In the distance were the hills of Galilee, silver at dusk and in the early mornings, hazy at mid-day; softly green for three months of the year, like unreal, unmoving hills of water. He spent as much time as he could out on his balcony; many nights, in summer, he dragged out his mattress on to its tiled floor and slept there.

Another reward for his solitude – though he told himself it was one he did not desire – was to see how much respect it won for him from others; it was a source of power. The other people in his classes thought of him, he knew, as a bit of a puzzle, an odd fish, a strange, reserved 'Anglo-Sax', not to be trusted. But he knew, too, that he disturbed them, that they were, in their offhand, begrudging Israeli manner, eager to please and placate him. Even more eager to please him was Mrs Beilinson, his landlady, on whom he depended greatly for his comfort, and with whom he had much the warmest relationship of any among the people around him.

She was an Austrian woman, childless, widowed, past middle-age, foolish and sentimental; she fussed over all her lodgers, but she fussed most of all over David, who was the only one for whom she prepared meals. He paid her more than the others, it was true; but it was not for the sake of the money, as she frequently and truthfully told him, that she prepared his breakfast-tray so carefully every morning and often brought to him in the evenings, last thing, a snack of some kind. Mrs Beilinson was plump and round-chinned; her eyes were an innocent blue and her hair was dyed a villainous blonde; her fingers were stained with nicotine and her social manner combined helplessness and jauntiness in varying proportions. But she ran her house efficiently enough. With David she was coquettish, self-pitying, motherly, reproachful; she told him long stories about her childhood and the habits of Mr Beilinson, about all the hardships she had endured as a refugee, then during the troubles at the time of the Mandate, then during the war against the Arabs, then during the period of austerity that had followed it, now with the new immigrants still pouring in. David listened patiently to her, and patted her hand whenever she was overcome by emotion in the middle of her stories. There were occasions when he had fantasies of putting his head in her lap, like a child, or of making love to her; and he suspected that she indulged in such fantasies, too. But nothing of the kind ever happened between them.

521

Desire tormented him unendurably in spells; tormented him physically, and tormented him also because it made nonsense of his belief in his own self-sufficiency. Sometimes he masturbated, sometimes he went to a place where you could get Moroccan girls, sometimes he struggled against it. He thought much of getting married, but met few girls, and had never met one that he wanted to marry. Perhaps he would meet one, he thought, when he went into the army, after the completion of the course.

'A God of Auschwitz!' he wrote in his diary. 'A God for David Glickman! Who can believe in such a Being? I can. I do. "He is the Place of the world," says the Talmud, "but the world is not His place." Like everyone else, I'm free to ignore Him to deny Him, to do what I like with the world He's given us. But He isn't free to ignore me if I call on Him. That makes the bondage of God worse than ours; it means that He needs our pity more than we need His. But we won't give it to Him. We'll go on for another million years as we are, being free to do so.'

PART 7

1

After her sixtieth birthday Sarah's health began to fail. She was troubled by congestions on her chest and suffered from breathlessness after any exertion; when she was tired the coordination of her movements deteriorated sharply; she was embarrassed by difficulty in controlling her bladder and by a growth of hair on her chin. The doctors she went to could do little to help her about any of these ailments and discomforts. She could not endure at all the heat of the Israeli summers, though Benjamin had put air-conditioning into the bedroom and living room of their house, after their first summer there. During the *khamsims*, in particular, she felt that she was suffocating, drowning in the thick fluids of her chest. So every summer she left the country, and spent some months either with Bertie and Rachel or with Joel and Pamela – usually flying to and fro, but sometimes travelling by boat.

During her absences Benjamin was well cared for: after many trials they had found a servant, a Roumanian woman, who came in every day, and who was 'almost as good as Annie'. Benjamin himself kept on the whole in good health, though he had been warned against too much excitement or exertion of any kind, because of the condition of his arteries. But he worked in the little orchard he had planted on his plot of ground, and went often into Tel Aviv on business. He dabbled in the Tel Aviv stock exchange; he was part owner, with a group of South Africans, of an orange-grove near Pardess Hanna and sometimes travelled out to see it; he had put some money in a plastics factory in which he hoped David might one day be persuaded to take an interest. He also travelled to and from South Africa, though much less regularly than Sarah. His finances stood the strain of these expenditures very well; not only because he had invested his money successfully both before and after settling in Israel, but because Bertie in the meantime had prospered; and Bertie had always been most conscientious in using the opportunities that came his way not merely on his own behalf, but in his father-in-law's interests too.

As a result of diligence, determination and some good luck, Bertie now merchanted industrial ores on a fairly big scale from South Africa and the Rhodesias to Europe and Japan; he had acquired shares in the operations of many of his suppliers; he had invested in real estate. He, too, travelled frequently – he had been once to Japan, several times to England and the continent, and he went regularly on business to the Rhodesias and East Africa. He had done particularly well for himself and his father-in-law in buying heavily in gold-mining shares just after the country-wide strikes, riots and shootings of 1960, when prices were at their lowest and there was a panic flight of capital out of South Africa. He had been convinced that the revolution which people all over the world were expecting would not take place. Two years later the stock exchanges of London, New York, Paris and Johannesburg agreed with him, and the prices of gold-mining shares had risen dramatically – in spite of sporadic, ineffective outbreaks of sabotage in a few of the country's biggest cities. With the cash he realized as a result of this successful calculation of the chances, Bertie bought a big house in Saxonwold, complete with enormous garden, swimming pool and tennis court.

About the time that he and Rachel moved into the house, Adela Klein, who had never married, was sentenced together with seven others, to four years' imprisonment for belonging to 'a group conspiring to bring about the violent overthrow of the government of the Republic'. She was defended at her trial by Advocate Dora Katzeff (née Magid), who was winning a formidable reputation for herself not just as that relative rarity, a woman barrister, but also as one who was ready to take on briefs for political prisoners – which many other members of the Johannesburg Bar were more and more avoiding. The most damning evidence against Adela and the others in her group was given by Ntuli, whom, it came out at the trial, had been in the pay of the Special Branch since his first arrest six years before.

Rachel cried when she saw in the paper the photograph of the seven in the dock, raising their arms in a clenched fist salute as sentence was passed. Adela's face was clearly recognizable: drawn, haggard and open-mouthed. But Bertie remained stony. The members of the resistance movement, he said, had been irresponsible as much towards themselves as towards the people they were supposed to be leading. How did people like Adela imagine that without outside help on a vast scale they could run a revolution, with their duplicating machines and their home-made bombs, against the undivided, ruthless power of a modern state; a state whose army and police were efficient and fully equipped, and which could never, because of the colour-line, be white-anted or corrupted from within? Only when South Africa had hostile black states on its border, he said, would white hegemony come under any real threat; and even then it would take decades, perhaps, for the threat to become effective.

Yet, having spoken in this way, and having jeered down Rachel's disagreements with him, Bertie later promised her that they would clear out of the country, soon, within a couple of years; conditions were intolerable. Every list of banned or arrested people included names of acquaintances; the boats going to England continually carried away friends of theirs; every time one went out into the streets one was confronted again with the insanity and injustice of the system upon which the country was founded. Annie had twice reported that she had been questioned by what she assumed to be Special Branch men about Rachel's activities.

Rachel did not believe Bertie when he spoke of leaving. He had been saying it at intervals ever since she had married him; and the result was that they now had a new house and that he was more deeply involved in his expanding business than ever before. For herself, she did what she could: the work she had made particularly her own was in connection with the African children's feeding scheme. Three times a week she drove out to Alexandra Township, and together with other white women from the city and black women from the township, saw to it that hundreds of children got a meal of soup and thick slices of bread and peanut-butter. There were children, she knew from speaking to people at the university's medical centre in the township, who were quite literally kept alive by these meals. On most other days of the week she spent some time organizing and collecting money, by letters, phone-calls and visits, so that the work could go on. If she was sneered at by Bertie in his bad moods as a Lady Bountiful, this seemed a small price to pay for the sense she had of carrying out a self-evidently useful task. She had remained firm in her decision not to take part in political activity of any kind – she had herself and the children to think of, she said, quite apart from the fact that both the means and ends of all political action still seemed to her utterly implausible and unpredictable. It amused her that even such work as she was doing was enough to bring her to the attention of the Special Branch. What minds they must have! But the evidence of what minds they had was visible everywhere in the country; never before, now that all opposition to the government appeared to be effectively throttled, had it seemed so constricted, so isolated, so *boring* a place to live in. The irony was that at the same time it was prospering in an unprecedented way. Money-making had altogether replaced politics as the major topic of everyone's conversation.

Bertie and Rachel's youngest child, and second daughter, Helena, was the beauty of the family; but Mark, who had grown into a bespectacled little schoolboy, was still Rachel's secret favourite, the one she watched most closely over and responded to most intensely. She was extravagantly proud of the success he was having at school. Both she and Bertie knew that had it not been for the children their marriage would have broken up on more than one occasion; however, Rachel now believed that they had at last settled down together, at a distance that was amicable ordinarily, and that disappeared at once when they had anything to do for the children. Bertie had become more considerate, less resentful towards her, for which she was grateful.

Sometimes she despised herself for feeling gratitude for so little; at other times she reminded herself that several of her contemporaries had suffered much worse things than she had in her marriage. Apart from the few, like Adela, who had been imprisoned, or had had their husbands imprisoned, there had been some sensational divorces, one suicide, a couple of tragic accidents, and many who had simply aged with a startling rapidity, becoming fat, lined, middle-aged, and completely boring in no time at all. Whereas she had at least managed to keep her figure, and, she hoped, some of her liveliness too. She suspected that Bertie was occasionally unfaithful to her on his business trips; but she made a point of not enquiring too closely of him what he did while he was away from her. And he offered no information on his own account – though there were times, in his bewilderment at some of the scrapes he got himself into, when he was tempted to; indeed, he sometimes found himself positively wanting to ask her for her advice.

For his infidelities were far more extensive than Rachel, even in her most dejected and suspicious moments, ever imagined. Other women had become for Bertie a more passionate enthusiasm than card-playing or bookbinding had ever been. He restrained himself when he was in Johannesburg; but on his trips he hunted women with a zeal that was both cold and inflamed, self-regarding and self-destructive. Every aspect of the pursuit was irresistible to him: the initial speculation, the talk, the silences, the glances given and received, the tension before the first embrace and the tension of a different kind after it, the assignations, the tremors, the clothes, the absence of clothes, the sighs and groans he heard, the tears he dried, the expressions of lust, tenderness, hunger, gratitude or despair on faces that had been unknown to him a few hours or a few days before, the rooms and flats he saw at unlikely times, the danger. Sometimes he marvelled at his luck; sometimes he promised himself, after harrowing scenes or on receiving alarming letters, that he would never go in for it again; always he did. So far his luck had held. Always he remained, at the same time, a hard and ambitious business man, a devoted father, a considerate husband. In fact, he was far more considerate towards Rachel now than he had ever been before his first adventures as an amorist. It was from the time that he had ceased being faithful to her that Rachel believed they had at last settled down together.

2

While she was staying with Rachel and Bertie, Sarah woke early one morning, before dawn, with a severe headache and a feeling of numbness in her left arm and leg; at the same time she felt a sensation of burning or excitement in those limbs. She had no recollection of anything having happened to her in the night: no dreams, no blows falling on her, no starts or shudders running through her. She lay still, hoping that the pain in her head would pass. She thought of getting up to take an aspirin, but the effort seemed to her much too great to make, though the bathroom was just next door.

When she opened her eyes again the headache was gone. So was the tingling numbness in her left side. She felt warm and rested. Pale, lemon-coloured sunlight lay just within her open window, spilling over the sill on to an oblong of the floor; in her myopic sight the branches of a bare tree in the garden were confused with the bars of the burglar-proofing. But beyond those streaks of darkness she could see a space of winter-blue sky. The air was cool in the room, and she knew without moving from her bed what it would be like outside: calm, glittering, windless, the sky enlarged by its own single blueness, the sun diminished, an odour in every bit of shade. Winter had always been her favourite season in Johannesburg; it was in the winter, especially, that the altitude of the city, thrust six thousand feet up on the high ridge of the Witwatersrand, became more than a figure, more than an abstraction; it was a quality of the air, thin and pure, which she breathed in and felt directly against her skin.

The house was quiet. The older children must have already left for school; Bertie for his office. It was time to get up.

She tried to do so. Seconds or minutes of horror passed, her heart plunging within her, unuttered cries crowding thickly in her throat, before she was collected enough to prove to herself that she was able to move. She lifted her hand and passed it in front of her face, she straightened her legs cautiously. She made another effort and this time she managed to get out of bed. But her left arm and leg obeyed sluggishly, awkwardly, remotely; she knew their heaviness or inertness to be something altogether different from the kind of clumsiness which in the past had so often dismayed and irritated her. Tremblingly, she dragged herself into the bathroom. At the sight of her face in the mirror she began to cry: she saw an old, fat, frightened woman with unkempt hair, crying.

The slight stroke Sarah had suffered left no outward sign, after she had spent a week in bed, other than that she now dragged her left foot slightly when she walked. But inwardly her deterioration was more pronounced. Her memory, which had always been quick and strong, began to fail her – not in any way that was noticeable to anyone but herself and those who knew her closely, but quite markedly, all the same. She forgot what she had written to whom in her letters, she could not remember the names of the characters in the novels that she read, and so stopped reading them altogether, she muddled the dates of recent public events, she began to call Sharon 'Rachel'. She repeated herself; again and again, and always with the same earnestness as if the subject hadn't come up before, she spoke especially of how sorry she was that David wasn't yet married. It was no life, a bachelor's, she said, least of all when it was spent travelling around so much in those Afro-Asian countries, whose new names she also invariably forgot.

Together with this went a decline of another kind: she became emotionally craven in her dealings with people, she treated everyone as she had once treated only her brother, Samuel. He, poor man, had died four years previously, after an operation for the relatively obscure abdominal condition of pancreatitis; but Rachel was often reminded of him, when she saw her mother smiling eagerly at jokes which did not amuse her, agreeing with the views of visitors whom Rachel knew she would have dismissed in silence just a little while before, when she saw her flattering Bertie anxiously, or even little Mark. She copied people, quite unconsciously, in trivial ways. When Sharon had Marmite on her bread, Sarah asked for Marmite, too; when Bertie spoke dismissively of some public figure, Sarah might repeat his words verbatim a few days later. She developed a sad, empty mania about her mail: she began to wait for the postman in the mornings long before he could possibly be expected to arrive, she even used to stand on the pavement, looking down the wide, empty, tree-lined suburban road, watching for him. Afterwards, when Rachel thought of that time of her mother's life, the image which came most often into her mind was that of Sarah standing at the gate, waiting for a message which no postman could ever bring. The memory made Rachel sadder and more bitter with regret than almost any other in her life; but at the time she frequently felt, within her pity, an unreasonable exaggerated vexation.

'He won't be here for *hours*, mom.' Struggling to hide her irritation, she would go between the winter-brown lawns towards Sarah, who stood at the end of the garden path.

'Sometimes he comes early,' Sarah would answer apologetically, her hand on the gate.

Rachel would say, 'Come in for tea,' or 'Come and see what Helena's doing,' or 'Do you think you could address some envelopes for me?' and Sarah always agreed willingly. But not much later she would go falteringly down the path again, look in the letter-box, and, if there was nothing in it, remain standing there. When the postman went past and brought nothing, she began at once to wait for the next day's delivery.

Once at the dinner table Rachel flew at her angrily over some foolish, repetitive remark she had made. Sarah was silent, her fingers busy on the table; then she said, 'You must be more patient with me, Rachel. I'm doing my best.' She added thoughtfully, her head lifted, her brow exposed, her gentle brown eyes troubled and remote, 'I'm better when I'm on my own.'

Her life had become a waiting: strangely familiar, barren, all-absorbing. When she was with others she fretted and

533

demeaned herself, afraid that she would be despised, disregarded, cut off from them, forgotten; she attached herself to any event, no matter how trivial, which she knew to be forthcoming. Weeks before Mark's birthday she began asking Rachel if she had started her preparations for his party; she asked Bertie again and again if he had confirmed the booking for her return flight to Israel; when she went out with them in the evenings she would be dressed hours before they were ready to leave. But when she was alone, the tension of her expectancy was sometimes much calmer, wider, and bleaker; her impatience was allayed by her certainty that what she was waiting for would come. She did not ever speak of it, or name it to herself, or try to envisage it, but at such moments she felt herself wholly ready for it.

3

Sarah stayed longer in Johannesburg than she had originally planned to, and when she left it was in company with Bertie, who flew with her as far as Rome, and then put her on the plane to Tel Aviv. He went on to Brussels. In May of the following year, earlier than usual, she set out once more, for England this time, though Benjamin had his doubts whether it was wise for her to do so.

However, Joel and Pamela thought she looked better than they had expected her to, after the letters they had had about her from South Africa and Israel. She was frailer than she had been, and they noticed at once the way she dragged her left leg. But she spoke firmly, she was delighted to see them and their little boy, Asher, and she liked the tall Victorian semi-detached house in Highgate they had moved into since her last visit to London. The stairs were a problem for her, but she managed to get up and down them slowly, one step at a time, her hand always on the banister.

Pamela was pregnant again, four months gone. She had had a miscarriage before the birth of Asher, and Joel was anxious that she shouldn't take on too much extra work because of Sarah's arrival. So they had arranged for a daily woman to come in. But so far as the visit was a burden at all to Pamela, it was mostly because of the disagreeable fact that Asher did not like his grandmother, and showed it openly in spite of Pamela's reproofs. In her weakness and self-doubt Sarah was deeply hurt by this: she was incapable of realizing that she could far more easily win over the little boy by ignoring him and his whims than by trying to curry favour with him.

Asher was a quick, skinny, tense child, precocious for his age; he had a large head, bright eyes, and hair as thick and black as Pamela's. When he cried or frowned or laughed the wrinkles of his forehead always ran around, never through, a wide space of skin between his eyebrows, giving him the appearance of always being inwardly attentive, unrelaxed. He was learning to read, he drew well for his age, and was a great maker of abstract patterns not only with crayons on pieces of paper, but with his toys, his blocks, his books, or with things which he took out of the kitchen cupboard and which Pamela might later find ascending the stairs in order of size. He was affectionate and responsive in his ways, but since leaving his babyhood behind him he had become physically standoffish; he did not enjoy being cuddled or handled by anyone. One of the things he did not like about his grandmother was that she always wanted to stroke his arms, to feel the silky lobes of his ears between her fingers, or to have him sit on her lap.

But he had other reasons for not liking her: he thought her face strange and ugly, with its complicated wrinkles, the glasses she wore, her untidy hair; he noticed that she did not speak as his parents did; he was put off by the clumsiness and hesitancy of some of her movements. And he noticed, too, that though Sarah was so much older than his parents, she was dependent on them. This made him uneasy; it also roused in him the assertive and experimental desire to try out, through Sarah, the effect of his own power over all these grown-ups, in whose power he knew himself to be.

One night in his bed he asked Pamela how old people had to be before they died.

'Very old,' Pamela said.

'As old as Sarah?'

'Older,' Pamela answered, as calmly as she could, speaking out of the tangle of emotions that the child had tugged at. He looked very small against the white sheets and pillow of the big bed they had recently bought for him. She had drawn the curtains and the room was in shadow.

He put his thumb in his mouth, yielding himself to all the familiar pleasures and insecurities of bedtime. Pamela leaned over him and kissed him on the forehead; she inhaled the scent of his warmth and of the soap she had just washed him with. His hair was still a little damp from his bath. Though she had not intended to, Pamela said, still stooped over him, 'You must be kind to Sarah. She isn't staying with us for long, and she likes you very much. So I don't want you to speak nastily to her.'

His eyes moved alertly, suspiciously, in their clear whites; he took his thumb out of his mouth, then put it back again, saying nothing. At that moment, with darkness approaching, he wanted to be friendly with Sarah, he wanted to be friendly with the whole world; that he had ever appeared to want anything else was inconceivable to him. Pamela's gentle rebuke had the effect of making him hurry towards his sleep as quickly as he could, without even taking his usual precaution of singing and humming for a few minutes as an incantation against the darkness and differentness of the night-time world.

4

Joel was working as the assistant to the American director of a new institute, which was backed by American funds; most of the money came from the foundation established by Lily Davidson's department-store family. The institute was intended to encourage and carry out research into modern Jewish history; the plans were also to encourage general research into the nature and development of modern racialism and totalitarianism. Several private libraries had been amalgamated; premises had been acquired off Knightsbridge; the first research students had been appointed; some ambitious projects for publication and conference-holding had been approved. Professor Davidson was one of the trustees of the institute; and he had made the suggestion to Joel, who had been lecturing at a teacher-training college in Battersea, that he apply for the job. So far, Joel was happy with the change. He got on harmoniously with his boss, Oscar Traub; he was drawing a much better salary than before; it was possible that the institute would do useful work.

As in his job, so too in his marriage, he felt himself to be luckier in many ways than he deserved. For if there was gone from his relationship with Pamela the fierce, insecure, almost wrathful need to assert, that *only* he, *only* she had ever experienced what they shared, and if they now saw themselves as a couple like most others, living through the unpredictable, recurring cycles of marriage – cycles of calm, of argument, of passion, of indifference, of animated conversation and unnoticed silence – such a development was hardly to be mourned over. They were not poorer than they had been, nor were they less grateful to one another. And they hadn't had the delight and anxiety of Asher, then, or the thought of the new baby coming.

So there he was. What more could he want?

To that question, Joel knew, with a self-distaste that was sometimes amused and more often just tired, there could be one of two responses: an inchoate babble of demands, pleas, complaints, accusations and self-accusations; or a stony silence. He did not know which was better; but he knew both to be unsatisfactory. More and more frequently, however, he had felt that if only he had the strength of mind and will to persist with the one or the other – the babble or the silence – he might be able to find a better answer to the question than any he had yet known. But perhaps that was just another delusion. He felt something of the same kind, too, when he was as near to peace as he ever came – when he was playing with Asher, or lying untroubled in bed with Pamela, or absorbed in his work at his desk, or working in the garden at home, or strolling across the Heath or through Highgate Wood on a Sunday morning: that if only he had the courage of his own happiness, if only he could welcome without guilt or fear his own undoubted, abundant good fortune, he would never need to ask such a question of himself.

But how could it be done? How could he throw off the habit of speculation and worry, of using the present to nag himself about the past and the future, of feeling a welter of angers and bewilderments that life would be what it was – so inconclusive, so muddled, so wide in range, so limited in certitude, so sensitive to pain and so indifferent to it, so utterly lacking in meanings, intellectual assuagements, moral commensurations? How could he, on another level, learn the trick of not feeling guilty towards the luckless and suffering whose lives crossed his own – let alone towards such groups as the Africans in South Africa, out of whose labour and deprivation had come the down-payment Benjamin had given him for his house; or the massacred Jews of Europe, whose records his institute was now trying to keep? How could he, especially in his responsibility for Asher's quick smallness and frailty, forget that the world contained all its ordinary, ancient menaces, and an unimaginably grotesque, huge new one as well?

If only! No other phrase in the language was so utterly useless.

His own life, his own actions, still seemed to him haphazard and disconnected, entirely accidental. The likely future of the human world filled him with dread; the blankness and business of the natural world appalled him as often as it delighted him; he was as far as ever from knowing with any certainty what he was living for.

But things, he repeated often to himself, reprovingly, truthfully, had worked out well for him.

5

At night there were falls of rain; in the mornings the sun shone out of a clear, washed sky; by afternoon the clouds would be gathering again. The season filled out and filled up, day by day, spreading and penetrating; not the smallest garden or open place of the high, cluttered suburb was excluded from it. The weight of the leaves on the trees, the prodigality of the pink and white blossom already fallen and lying in the drifts in the gutters, the sudden intensities of light at unexpected hours, the resonance of birdsong, the confusion of scents that hung over certain streets – all seemed parts of a single resurgence, giving and taking equally from it. Though the winter had been long and the early spring disappointing, everyone had the appearance of being surprised by the swiftness with which the summer had come again, the lavish openness of its skies, and the thick concealments of its foliage.

Sarah's winter in Israel had been a mild one, but she enjoyed the length of the evenings and the earliness of the dawns; she delighted in the unfamiliar intricacies of green that filled the garden. Expeditions tired her, so she went out seldom. But she met Joel and Pamela's friends, when they visited the house, and was struck again by how many of them were South Africans. 'You've got a *landsleit verein* of your own,' she told Joel. 'Like the Jews in South Africa in the early days.' She spoke to Pamela of her early years in South Africa, and more often still of her girlhood in Lithuania, which she had never before been in the habit of doing; she described the school she had attended, or her father's moods, or an argument he had had with her mother when he had found a copy of Renan's *Life of Jesus* in the house, or her mother's guilt after his death, and how she had returned thereafter to the most rigid orthodoxy. Pamela was fascinated equally by the remoteness of that life in Marniyus and by the familiarity of so many of the emotions and situations Sarah described. She asked all sorts of detailed questions, some of which Sarah could not answer: had their house been built of brick or wood? Who had owned it? Had it had a garden? What was it lit by? What kind of shops were there in Marniyus? How many other Jewish girls had there been in her high school? Had they been kindly treated?

Pamela also bought a Russian primer, and began going through it with Sarah. But she was as little assiduous a pupil as Sarah was a teacher, and by the end of June they had hardly got any further than the letters of the alphabet.

A particularly frequent visitor to the house at this time was Ivor Glickman. His parents had hastily shipped him off to England a year before, following his quiet announcement that he would rather go to jail as a conscientious political objector than be called up into the South African army, when he finished school. He was now doing his A-levels in physics, maths and chemistry at a cram-school in the West End, and hoped to get a place in a university when he completed them. He lived nearby, and often did baby-sitting for his cousins.

He kept Sarah company when Joel and Pamela went out on their own in the evenings, for, over her protests, they had decided she was not strong enough to be left alone with Asher.

So Ivor was with her one night, while Joel and Pamela were at dinner with the Traubs, when Sarah collapsed. She had gone to bed early; Ivor, sitting downstairs, heard her some time later call out strangely. When he opened the door of her bedroom he found her half on the floor, her legs still on the bed, her nightgown up to her thighs. 'Sarah!' he shouted, lifting her on to the bed. The blue colour receded from her face; it became utterly pale, the edges of her lips the whitest of all. The noise of her breathing filled the room, a hoarse, hurried pant, interrupted by irregular, listening pauses. To the terrified young man standing over her it seemed that Sarah herself, comatose on the bed, was listening to them, too.

He ran downstairs and phoned for an ambulance; then, with trembling hands, dialled Traub's number. The voice that answered him told him that Joel and Pamela had left for home just a few minutes before.

They arrived as the ambulance men were carrying Sarah down the stairs on a stretcher. They had seen the lighted ambulance at the gate, and rushed distraught into the house. There was no need for Ivor to speak; he stood with his hands lifted helplessly behind the stretcher. Joel leaned over it, in the hall. Sarah's eyes were wide open, bright and brown, filled with a mortally hurt, striving intelligence. She recognized him; she knew the hurt she had suffered; he was sure of it. Her glance rested on him, a black, quivering point of comprehension, surrounded by lambent, living colour. Then she was carried out of the house.

6

Sarah was aware that she had been brought into a hospital; there was a vision in her mind, a sense in her body, of being carried interminably, high off the ground, smoothly, down long, greenish silent corridors. She wondered how the hospital could be so big that she never came to her room or ward; then the forward gliding motion would halt, and she would know that she was in a bed, quite still, and that someone – Joel or Benjamin, she wasn't sure who – was sitting at her side. She wanted to tell him that she wasn't in pain and she wasn't afraid; but before she could speak or move he would be gone and she would again be gliding along, prone, on a flat surface, through those endless, soundless, unpeopled corridors. It seemed to her altogether out of proportion, to have such a huge hospital and to be made to travel such distances through it, when she needed so little space and had so little time. Still she went forward, on and on, soothed by the motion and yet made impatient by it. Would they never be satisfied? Would she never arrive?

She died, unconscious, in the morning, while Joel was not there; he had gone home to have some breakfast and to see how Pamela was. They had told him at the hospital that no change could be expected for the next few hours, and then they phoned him at the house with the news. 'But you told me nothing would happen,' he shouted childishly at the woman on the other side of the line; then apologized to her. 'I'm sorry. I'm sorry.'

He put the phone down. Two sobs shook him and he struck the wall with the side of his clenched fist. When that racked, dark moment was over, he knew that she was gone from him. Now he had to do what had to be done. Pamela was standing in the hall; she had sent Asher out of the house to play with a neighbour's child. She was in tears, and the sight of her face almost unmanned him. He walked through the kitchen into the garden. The flowers, the lawn, the leaves of the trees glistened with moisture; the sun shone between smouldering clouds; the open windows of the backs of the houses looked out upon their gardens.

7

'As for man, his days are as grass; as the flower of the field so he flourisheth. For the wind passeth over it, and it is gone; and the place thereof shall know it no more. But the loving kindness of the Lord is from everlasting to everlasting unto them that fear Him, and His righteousness unto their children's children.'

Because he was the elder son, Joel dug the first spadeful of wet clay out of the mound to the side of the oblong grave, and let it fall. The noise it made when it struck the coffin was almost embarrassingly loud, reverberating as if it had fallen on to something hollow. Then David came forward, followed one by one by the other men who had come to the funeral – Jonathan, Ivor, Peter Dewes, Oscar Traub, three or four others. There were no women at the graveside.

The rabbi – a youngish, fair-bearded man, wearing a four-pointed velvet hat, a long black robe, and a collar with white crossing tapes, rather like a barrister's – intoned another prayer. The group began walking towards the little prayer-house. Behind them they heard the gravediggers continue the work they had begun. The rabbi washed his hands in the tiny ceremonial fountain with Hebrew lettering above it, and re-entered the bare prayer-house. A further prayer was said there, the rabbi enunciating the Hebrew words with a sharp, hissing precision. Joel and David responded with the Kaddish, both using the Sephardi pronunciation they had learned in Israel. *Yitgadel v'yitkadash, shmai rabah* ... The service was over.

They dispersed to their cars. Tears were running down David's cheeks, though he made no sound – he was not even breathing deeply – and he walked with a decisive step, his thin shoulders slightly hunched. He slammed the door of the car behind him; then wiped his face with his hand and looked out of the window, waiting for the others to come. Through the heavy air they could hear the shovelling going on, a hundred yards away, among the ordered gravestones and markers.

The cemetery was hidden by hedges, set among fields, approached through a narrow, secretive lane; driving to it Joel had been surprised by how rural the scene was, like a fragment of another, forgotten England, with tall elms bulging out at corners where the lane turned, and hedges opening at wooden-barred gates. But the traffic roared on the Watford By-pass, not five minutes away, and they were soon back on it; among the dazing miles of sprawl that led towards London, or were London, or were something to which no name could be given. Ivor was at the wheel; the car was his, and he drove fast; Joel sat beside him in the front and David in the back. All of them were relieved that the ceremony was over; they felt an especial relief, perhaps, because they knew that Sarah had set not the slightest store by the rites and prayers they had gone through. But Benjamin, whose doctor in Israel had advised him not to make the trip to London for the funeral, had insisted on an orthodox service and David had wanted one too.

That his contrary, self-assertive, irresponsible kid brother had become a sombre balding man, with a lined brow and an uneasy eye – eccentric, self-contained, religious-minded, and apparently set on remaining a bachelor – always seemed to Joel against the order of things. A few days after the funeral, when the two brothers said goodbye to one another, they both yearned for the time when their separations had always been brief, their differences and decisions never final, always able to be reversed or forgotten. In the shock of grief their emotions were what they had been then: as open, as easily roused and communicated, felt with as little reserve or shame. But nothing else was the same. Those days were gone.

'This is the last call for British Overseas Airways flight to Rome, Lydda, and Teheran. Will all passengers pass at once through the south exit doors,' repeated the magnified yet hushed female voice over the public address system.

Joel and David put their arms around one another, their cheeks met roughly, they stood apart with bright, full eyes.

'You'll tell Dad we want him to come and stay with us.'

'Ja.' David nodded. 'He won't though. So long, Joel.'

With a strange absent-mindedness, gently, his glance averted, he touched Joel on the cheek, before he turned and joined the throng going slowly through the open glass doors. He was taller than most of the people in the group. Joel saw him showing his bus-ticket to the girl who stood at the door; he exchanged a word with her, bending his head forward, encumbered by the bag and raincoat he was carrying. The angle of his neck moved Joel painfully. Then he looked back, lifted a hand, and began to climb the steps into the bus.

8

In the street outside the terminal Joel remembered walking there with his mother, and telling her of his affair with Pamela. Now she was gone, no longer interested in his success or failure, or Pamela's; and he was forever diminished as a result. From other deaths that had touched him closely – Professor Viljoen's, of cancer; Harry, his friend from the kibbutz, drowned in an accident off Caesaria – he knew that all that particular irreplaceable portion of the living self which is turned to one person, and to one person only, for response, for dialogue, for recognition, is itself silenced and destroyed by their going. So much of the living must always die with the dead.

It was a fairly stiff walk to his office, but he decided not to go by bus; he wanted time to recover from his parting with David. He thought of David travelling towards the airport, and he hoped that his plane would arrive safely at its destination, and that he would find Benjamin well on his arrival. According to David, Benjamin had taken the news of Sarah's death more calmly than might have been expected. In his restless, mordant manner, David had added that he suspected that Benjamin was even a little gratified to know that he had survived her, though he was more than ten years older than her. 'He's getting pretty old,' David had said, in palliation of the harshness of his remark. 'This last year, I thought he'd aged a lot.'

What was to happen to him? Would he stay in Israel? Even David was seldom there, nowadays; for the last several years he had been moving from one Afro-Asian country to another, on technical aid missions for the Israeli government. Fortunately, he'd been in Israel on leave, in the house, when Joel had telephoned with the news of Sarah's death, and there were still a few weeks of his leave to run out before he would go back to Uganda. And then?

Joel was almost certain that if Benjamin did choose to live with one of his children, it would be with Rachel, not himself. Only since the birth of Asher – or, to be more precise, since the circumcision of Asher, which had been carried out by their doctor in a quasi-ritualistic manner – had he finally accepted Pamela as a daughter-in-law. Only then had he for the first time offered them financial help, which they had used in buying the house. From Pamela's mother they hadn't had a penny; she had been furious about the divorce from Malcolm, and it had turned out that her husband, Mr Truter, the retired bank manager with the honest, hangdog countenance, was a confirmed anti-Semite. In her letters to Pamela, Mrs Truter never failed to ask maliciously, when the occasion presented itself, whether she had read this or that of Malcolm's, or had heard the latest news of his spectacular political career.

It had caused a great stir in South Africa when Malcolm Begbie had announced his support for the government; he had been the first prominent English-speaking intellectual to do so, though a few others had since followed his example; there was talk that he would go into the cabinet, after the next election. He was a great embarrassment to the reviewers in the London weekend papers, who could never discuss his work without making uneasy, inaccurate references to Malraux and Roy Campbell.

Irritably, Joel turned his mind from that preoccupation, that source of insecurity. But he noted how easily he had fallen into it. Life, as they said, went on. It did indeed, he thought; in all its tediums, habits, pleasures, irritations, self-importances. So that occasionally one roused oneself to say, 'Is that all? Is this life? What's all the fuss about? What does it matter?' And there were the other moments when one felt it was too much to bear, it couldn't be that something so painful, so complicated, so important, so far-reaching, could be just for creatures like human beings to carry unaided. But from where could aid come?

Walking through Kensington, his eyes flickering on and off a hundred things – buildings, girls' legs, traffic lights, trees, cars, clouds in the sky – his body adjusting itself to the movements of other pedestrians, his feet falling firmly on the pavement, Joel was filled with a quiet, private fear which he could confess to no one, not even to Pamela, perhaps to Pamela least of all: that his mother's death might lead him into one of those nervous crises or near-prostrations that had afflicted him in the past. He had had one, lasting many months, two years after his marriage. He knew as little as ever why they came, how he emerged from them, what to do while he was within them. But he did know the form they took: the draining-away from within himself of all spontaneity of response and interest, the growth within him of a sense that his entire life was an imitation of life, a bad counterfeit, and not the thing itself, an obsessive brooding over particular random defeats or frustrations, an aimless thrashing about in speculation and a despair which were dignified more than they deserved by being called metaphysical or philosophical. The most debilitating and frightening aspect of the condition was that it seemed to be merely an exaggeration of what, on reflection, he ordinarily felt about himself; when he was within it, it seemed to him that he had never been out of it, not once in his life. Perhaps if he had the courage to persist in that state, too, to welcome it, to be grateful for it, he would be better off. But this seemed to him unlikely. He had found no alternative to trying to keep sane.

9

'He's been impossible today,' Pamela complained, pushing back her hair with her hand, when she met him in the hall. 'Listen! I've tried to get him down and he just carries on –'

Joel hung up his raincoat, put down his briefcase, and listened. The noise from upstairs sounded as though Asher was simply throwing his toys against the wall. However, when Joel came into the room he found him on his knees, in his blue and white spotted pyjamas, building a small tower on the floor with his wooden blocks.

'Look, daddy,' he said. He took his heaviest lorry, aimed it at the structure from a few paces away, and sent it skidding across the floor. The blocks fell with a great crash, and Asher laughed, looking up for approval.

Joel laughed too. 'Marvellous! Do it once more, and then jump into bed. Has mummy read your story to you?'

He lifted his head, as if surprised that Joel did not know, and said gravely, 'Two stories.'

'Two stories! And you're still not in bed? Come on, come on.' He picked up the little boy, he felt him struggling and kicking in his arms, his bones as frail as a bird's, his skin all smoothness and warmth. In Joel's eyes his laughing, wriggling son, simply shone – shone in so many ways – with the gleam of his hair, with the flash of his green-brown eyes, the white of his tiny teeth, the suffused glow of his skin.

'But you said I can do it once more!'

Joel threw him on his bed, on his back, and his whole body bounced; arching himself back, Asher tried to bounce again, delighted with the sensation. He did not succeed and was at once off the bed, with a single flail of his bare feet.

'You said I can do it again.'

'All right, just once.'

In the end Asher built his tower and destroyed it twice, while Joel sat on the bed and watched him. Then he asked for another story; when this was refused he said he wanted a drink of water.

'Go and get it yourself.'

He scampered out of the room, and Joel closed his eyes, lying back on the bed; he heard as if from a distance, in his fatigue, the sound of water from the bathroom, running on and on. He seemed to doze; he was not aware that the water had been turned off until Asher said from the door, 'Now I want to do a wee.'

'Well, do a wee. I'm not stopping you.'

Again Asher ran out of the room. His wee was not an impressive or convincing affair; a long urging silence was followed by the tinkle of what sounded like a half-dozen drops into the lavatory bowl.

'And now?' Joel asked him when he came into the room. 'Any more excuses?'

Asher wasn't sure what the word meant, but he thought one up, nevertheless. 'We must tidy up the blocks.'

It took only a few seconds to tidy the bricks away, and Asher surrendered; he raised his face perfunctorily for a kiss and climbed between his sheets. Joel tucked him in and kissed him again. 'Good night, love.' Asher was singing before he was out of the room.

He and Pamela ate their meal in silence, both of them tired and preoccupied with their own thoughts. Afterwards Joel washed up. When he came into the living room he found her lying full-length on the couch, in a special posture which he knew to be 'relaxed': it came out of a book on childbirth which she was studying. But he did not tease her or speak to her; he took up a book and began to read.

Later, she talked about what she and Asher had done during the day, and he told her about his day – about saying goodbye to David, about what had happened in the office. He thought of telling her something of what he had felt while walking from the terminal; but was relieved that he did not have to.

He went back to his book and Pamela went back to her relaxation. She relaxed so successfully that she fell asleep on the couch. She dreamed she was back in South Africa, in Cape Town, on the beach, with the sun shining strongly. The scene was vividly before her, in all its colour and sound; then, without knowing how the transition had taken place, she was swimming, carried immense distances by breakers which lifted her again and again, and sent her plunging towards gleaming, safe shallows. The freedom she had in the water with her own body, its lightness and ease of movement, enraptured her; she did not know why until she woke to find herself on the couch, still burdened with the child she was carrying.

10

Three weeks before the date the doctor had given her, Pamela was admitted to the maternity home. She was taken upstairs in a lift, and Joel was put in a waiting room. Some minutes later a nurse told him he could go up and say goodbye to her. 'She's going to have a busy night tonight,' the nurse said, nodding her head in a proprietorial fashion.

Pamela was on a high bed; she was wearing a short, white nightgown. Her face was smooth, lustrous with excitement and apprehension. She leaned her head against his chest, and he put his arm round her. Though he did not intend to do it, his hand went under the nightgown and ran up her naked back. He felt a pang of desire for her; in such a place, at such a time, it seemed utterly inappropriate, almost indecent.

'Am I going to be all right?'

'Of course. Don't worry, sweetheart.'

He was sent downstairs again, to the waiting room. He felt far more nervous than he had before the birth of Asher, for he knew now what he hadn't known then: how much the baby would mean to him, what a life of its own it would have. He held a magazine in his hand, and read bits of it; most of the time he just stared at the wall in front of him. He heard a baby crying in the distance, at the end of some corridor, crying without pause for minutes on end, and he wondered how they could let a baby into a place like this, where peace was essential. It was only when the crying stopped that he realized how stupid his irritation was. It was a maternity home, of course babies cried in it.

At five in the morning Pamela gave birth to a girl. She was named after her grandmother, Sarah.

DAN JACOBSON

THE CONFESSIONS OF JOSEF BAISZ

Josef Baisz is as remarkable a creation as the imaginary country, Sarmeda, in which he lives. Throughout his career – whether as soldier, scholar, husband, murderer or kidnapper – he is driven by the overwhelming urge to subvert and destroy. A man of peculiar genius, this desire spurs him on to 'greater' things until he finally arrives at the inevitable and yet crushingly unexpected denouement of the tale which he himself narrates.

THE EVIDENCE OF LOVE

Kenneth Makeer – intelligent, South African and black – travels to London to study law where he meets a fellow South African – a white girl – whom he eventually marries. Yet mixed marriages are outlawed in the Union, and so when they return home they come face to face with racial intolerance and hatred at its most brutal.

This is a passionate, harrowing and dramatic story which hurtles towards its ugly and untimely conclusion.

'It is scrupulously well written. It is very much the sort of novel that counts' *Guardian*

'An admirable writer has written another admirable book' *Spectator*

DAN JACOBSON

HER STORY

Celia Dinan died some two hundred years ago – back in the twenty-first century. As her life is rediscovered it becomes apparent that she is the author of a powerful and passionate tale – a tale which only she could have written but which 'everywoman' will painfully acknowledge as her own.

THE PRICE OF DIAMONDS

Lyndhurst, South Africa, is a declining diamond-mining town, much like Kimberley, where the author of the novel grew up. As long-term business partners and friends, Mr Fink and Mr Gottlieb find themselves tempted away from the straight and narrow towards the devious ways of trading illicit diamonds. In this compassionate and humorous novel, Jacobson reveals the serious themes hidden beneath the comic life of his characters.

DAN JACOBSON

THE WONDER-WORKER

As events switch between London and Switzerland, Jacobson introduces us to a host of vivid and extraordinary characters. Most notable amongst these is London-born Timothy Fogel, a child with the wilful belief that he has been endowed with special powers. As events unfold it becomes apparent that this belief has cataclysmic implications for all involved. *The Wonder-Worker* is a remarkable and evocative novel about obsession, passion and the extraordinary power of the human imagination.

THE TRAP AND A DANCE IN THE SUN

The Trap and *A Dance in the Sun* bring together Jacobson's initial two novels – stories of racial confrontation and social injustice on the South African veld. In *The Trap*, relations between the white farmers and their black workers are brought on to a sinister and harrowing conclusion whilst *A Dance in the Sun* sees two young innocent bystanders becoming embroiled in a long-standing family saga. These stories have retained their freshness and their power to move the reader.

'This author is stylish, he tells everything in simple words, but his undertones are subtle…it is quite masterly' *Observer*

OTHER TITLES BY DAN JACOBSON AVAILABLE DIRECT
FROM HOUSE OF STRATUS

Quantity	£	$(US)	$(CAN)	€
☐ THE CONFESSIONS OF JOSEF BAISZ	7.99	12.99	19.95	13.00
☐ THE EVIDENCE OF LOVE	7.99	12.99	19.95	13.00
☐ HER STORY	7.99	12.99	19.95	13.00
☐ INKLINGS: SELECTED STORIES	7.99	12.99	19.95	13.00
☐ THE PRICE OF DIAMONDS	7.99	12.99	19.95	13.00
☐ THE RAPE OF TAMAR	7.99	12.99	19.95	13.00
☐ THE STORY OF THE STORIES	7.99	12.99	19.95	13.00
☐ THE TRAP AND A DANCE IN THE SUN	7.99	12.99	19.95	13.00
☐ THE WONDER-WORKER	7.99	12.99	19.95	13.00

ALL HOUSE OF STRATUS BOOKS ARE AVAILABLE FROM GOOD BOOKSHOPS OR
DIRECT FROM THE PUBLISHER:

Internet: **www.houseofstratus.com** including author interviews, reviews, features.

Email: **sales@houseofstratus.com** please quote author, title, and credit card details.

Hotline: UK ONLY: 0800 169 1780, please quote author, title and credit card details.
INTERNATIONAL: **+44 (0) 20 7494 6400**, please quote author, title, and credit card details.

Send to: **House of Stratus Sales Department**
24c Old Burlington Street
London
W1X 1RL
UK

Please allow for postage costs charged per order plus an amount per book as set out in the tables below:

	£(Sterling)	$(US)	$(CAN)	€(Euros)
Cost per order				
UK	2.00	3.00	4.50	3.30
Europe	3.00	4.50	6.75	5.00
North America	3.00	4.50	6.75	5.00
Rest of World	3.00	4.50	6.75	5.00
Additional cost per book				
UK	0.50	0.75	1.15	0.85
Europe	1.00	1.50	2.30	1.70
North America	2.00	3.00	4.60	3.40
Rest of World	2.50	3.75	5.75	4.25

PLEASE SEND CHEQUE, POSTAL ORDER (STERLING ONLY), EUROCHEQUE, OR INTERNATIONAL MONEY ORDER (PLEASE CIRCLE METHOD OF PAYMENT YOU WISH TO USE)
MAKE PAYABLE TO: STRATUS HOLDINGS plc

Cost of book(s): —————————— Example: 3 x books at £6.99 each: £20.97

Cost of order: —————————— Example: £2.00 (Delivery to UK address)

Additional cost per book: —————— Example: 3 x £0.50: £1.50

Order total including postage: ———— Example: £24.47

Please tick currency you wish to use and add total amount of order:

☐ £ (Sterling)   ☐ $ (US)   ☐ $ (CAN)   ☐ € (EUROS)

VISA, MASTERCARD, SWITCH, AMEX, SOLO, JCB:

☐ ☐

Issue number (Switch only):

☐ ☐ ☐

Start Date: **Expiry Date:**

☐ ☐ / ☐ ☐   ☐ ☐ / ☐ ☐

Signature: _____

NAME: _____

ADDRESS: _____

_____

POSTCODE: _____

Please allow 28 days for delivery.

Prices subject to change without notice.
Please tick box if you do not wish to receive any additional information. ☐

House of Stratus publishes many other titles in this genre; please check our website (**www.houseofstratus.com**) for more details.